GIVER OF ROSES

THE GUARDIANS OF GADIEL

KATHLEEN MORGAN

 Revell

Published by Fleming H. Revell
a division of Baker Publishing Group
P.O. Box 6287, Grand Rapids, MI 49516-6287

Printed in the United States of America

Library of Congress Cataloging-in-Publication Data
Morgan, Kathleen.
    Giver of roses / Kathleen Morgan.
        p. cm.—(The guardians of Gadiel ; bk 1)
    ISBN 0-8007-3094-1 (pbk.)
    1. Princes—Fiction. 2. Quests (Expeditions)—Fiction. I. Title. II.
        Series: Morgan, Kathleen. Guardians of Gadiel ; bk. 1.
PS3613.O745G585 2005
813'.6—dc22   2005007727

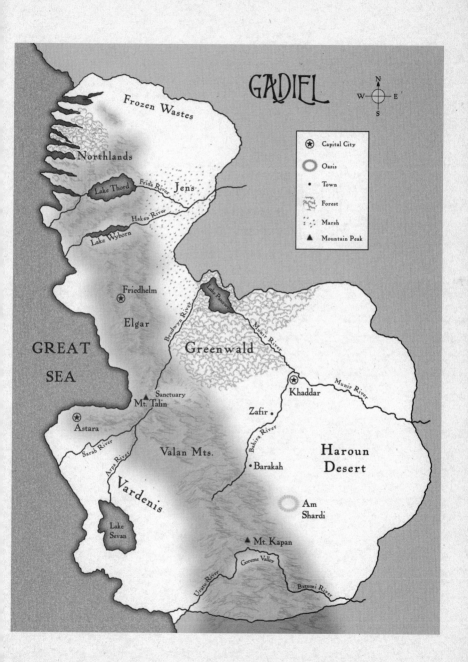

I will lead the blind on their journey;
    by paths unknown I will guide them.
I will turn darkness into light.

Isaiah 42:16, New American Bible

Fortress of Astara, Land of Gadiel, Year of the Ancients 952

A frigid wind blew down from the heavens, impaling the bleak winter's day with piercing needles of ice. The sun veiled its rays behind a hazy pall, muting the land in flat, forbidding light. Frost coated the withered brown grasses and skeletal trees, and billowed thickly from the mouths of friend and foe alike.

Danae tugged the thick, dark gray cloak tightly to her, tucked back a recalcitrant lock of pale yellow hair, and hunkered yet further into the hood's relative warmth. Still, as her gaze encompassed the army slowly massing on the plains just below Astara's colossal gates, a sudden, premonitory chill no clothing could contain coursed through her body. Yet how was this day any different from the long months and years of her captivity in Astara? Why would this moment always stand apart from any other she had spent gazing down on the army of her own people, praying for deliverance?

She glanced along the line of tuniced and gowned Astarians crowding the length of the rough, tan-mottled agarat stone battlements, her gaze finally alighting on the somber faces of the royal family Karayan. Horror widened the elegant, silver-haired Queen Takouhi's eyes. Worry darkened the ailing King Haig's face. Fear tightened Prince Hovan's eternally petulant mouth.

It was the stoic resolve stiffening Crown Prince Vartan's shoulders and lifting his strong, proud chin, however, that filled Danae with the greatest foreboding. Though she knew not from whence the presentiment came, somehow, some way, this day his destiny teetered on the sheerest of precipices. She knew, and it tore at her heart.

Amid a deafening blast of trumpets, four battle-clad horsemen rode to the front of the army and drew up before Astara's gates. The two outside riders bore bright red and gold banners on tall, spear-tipped poles. As the wind snapped the silken cloth to and fro, even from this height Danae could make out the emblazoned gold helmet with its horsehair crest—the symbol of the hereditary rulers of Hylas. The banners of her country, yet banners that filled her with dread.

She shook her head fiercely, as if the act in itself could disperse the crazed tumult of emotions churning within. This was madness. Slowly but surely, her people were winning the battle against Astara, in a siege that had now lasted three long, excruciating years.

It was past time the royal Gadielean city yield. It was past time the Hylean king's wife be surrendered, whether she wished it so or not. Calandra did not belong here with the Gadielean king's troublesome younger son, nor was she deserving of the painful price the city must pay for her presence. Yet as dearly as Danae desired the vain, selfish Queen Calandra to submit to her husband's lawful authority, she feared, oh, how she feared, the price might now come too dear.

Far, far too dear if Prince Vartan lost his life in the doing.

"Hail, King Haig," a voice bellowed suddenly from below.

Danae's gaze narrowed. That voice. She knew that voice . . . Her breath escaped in a horrified gasp. It was Ladon. In spite of the years—and probably *because* of long-suppressed memories—a confused mix of emotions rippled through her.

King Haig shot his eldest son a questioning glance. Danae saw Vartan pause to sweep his wine red cloak edged in gold back from his shoulders, then mouth Ladon's name. His father nodded and stepped forward.

"Aye, what do you wish?" he shouted back.

"I bring you a proposition. A proposition to end the war."

Beneath the horsehair-crested bronze helmet with its ornately scrolled cheek plates and nose-guard, Danae saw Ladon's mouth lift in a feral smile. She looked back to where Vartan stood, off and slightly behind his father's right. A bleak ray of sudden sunlight glinted on shoulder-length, chestnut brown hair and smoothly shaven cheeks, catching the subtle jump of muscle in his tautly clenched jaw.

Danae's heart went out to him. Vartan was no fool. Three years of thwarting King Feodras's commanding general and battle champion had surely taught him much about Ladon's brutally treacherous ways. Nothing good would come of this proposal.

"Aye, and that proposition is?" King Haig roared back, his haggard features reddening with the unaccustomed effort. "Spit it out, man, before I lose what little patience I have with you!"

Instead of angering the Hylean warrior, his enemy's goading appeared only to please Ladon the more. "We weary of this war," he cried. "But honor must be salvaged, yours no less than ours. To that purpose, on the morrow at midday, send down your greatest warrior. Send him to meet me in a fight to the death. If *he* wins, Feodras gives his word he'll withdraw and take his army back to Hylas. But if *I* win"—Ladon's smile grew all the wider—"Astara must surrender."

King Haig leaned forward and clenched the stone wall until his knuckles whitened. Beneath his crown of costly jewels and hammered gold, his thinning gray hair fluttered dispiritedly in the wind. "S-surrender?" he all but choked out the word. "And what honor is in that? Tell your king—"

"Feodras gives his word Astara will not be sacked, nor will its citizens be harmed," Ladon cried. "All he desires is Calandra and the satisfaction of knowing he is victor. To gain those, he gives his word, a word he'll honor until his dying breath." With a vicious jerk, the Hylean reined in his nervously prancing horse. "You've two hours to make your decision. Two hours, King Haig, and then the offer is no more."

As if to add a final emphasis to his words, Ladon signaled his mount forward. Once free of the confinement of the other horses, he sharply kneed the animal so that it reared high, pawing the air. Then, with a burst of maniacal laughter, he pivoted his horse and galloped away.

For several tension-laden minutes, the Astarian king regarded the four retreating horsemen. Finally he turned, meeting his eldest son's gaze

Danae could only guess what emotions arced between them. Vartan was Astara's greatest warrior, and Ladon knew it. Vartan, at thirty-two a man in his prime, was graced with keen intelligence and battle-honed strategic abilities. He had always been the one sure obstacle to the Hyleans' overwhelming forces. Without Vartan, Astara was surely doomed.

Yet even as she watched the two men, Danae knew what the answer would be. For the sake of his people, Vartan Karayan would risk his life. To risk was to retain some vestige of hope for a successful outcome. But there was no hope, none whatsoever, in a battle to the death with Ladon.

Years ago, it was said the Hylean champion had traded his limited span of years for immortality. It was said he had given his soul over to Phaon, the Dark Lord. Danae knew the rumors were true.

Vartan hadn't a chance. Ladon was now invincible.

Ladon's offer couldn't have come at a worse time, Vartan thought as he followed his father and the rest of the royal entourage back into the palace. They moved down the long, polished marmora stone corridors to one of the private reception rooms. Earlier this very day, he had inspected the subterranean caverns that held Astara's food stores. Thanks to a mysterious leak from the city's main well—a leak no one had noticed until now—most of the remaining food was ruined.

There were barely a week's rations left. After that, they had less than a month before starvation and disease set in. Whether or not his father accepted Feodras's proposition, Astara couldn't hold out much longer.

But could Feodras be trusted to keep his word? Vartan knew Ladon could not. There was something crazed, indeed almost fanatical, about that warrior's hatred for Astara—and especially for him. This wasn't the first time, after all, the Hylean had challenged him to battle. Before, though, Vartan hadn't seen any need to sacrifice himself in a foolhardy, and most likely fatal, display of masculine prowess—especially not to please the likes of Ladon.

The Hylean champion's reputation had preceded him from far across the Great Sea. Not only had the man never been defeated in battle, but he had never once—*ever*—ostensibly suffered wounding of any kind. Though Vartan didn't believe in the God of the Ancients, much less in an evil counterpart, there was still something sinister and otherworldly about Ladon . . .

Astara's royals entered the reception room, its high ceiling and walls covered in vibrantly painted scenes of the valiant deeds of past Gadielean kings. They immediately strode to the black marmora stone hearth in the center of the room to warm themselves. Servants offered them cups of bracing, spiced hot salma, then exited, shutting the huge, intricately carved turkawood doors behind them. Vartan turned to his father.

"The only question that remains is not whether we will accept Feodras's offer—we haven't any choice. The question is, once Astara surrenders, can Feodras be counted on to honor his word?"

"And *I* say it isn't a matter of options or lack thereof, but a matter of pride," King Haig stoutly replied. Cup in hand, he gingerly lowered himself to sit on the wide, stone bench encircling the fire. "I'll not dishonor House Karayan by sacrificing you in some fool's quest." He sighed and shook his head. "If Ladon were a mortal man, I would send you out and gladly. You're the best of us, my son, and few could defeat you. But Ladon . . ."

A bleak look clouded his pale blue eyes. "Perhaps we should just offer an outright surrender. At least then you'd live past the morrow. Or, better still, you might try one last time to rally the Diya al Din tribes to us. Or even the Dwarves of Elgar. They, at least, were once our loyal liege men."

"And why not the Dragonmaids of Mount Talin as well?" Hovan offered with a smirk. The sandy-haired prince paused to empty the contents of his cup, then struck an exaggerated, considering pose. "But who *could* we send to ferret out their secret portal? Vartan is certainly the most pure in heart of us, but there's that minor matter that he *has* tasted the pleasures of the flesh, at least a time or two. Still, perhaps just this once, considering our dire straits, those men-hating serpent riders might make an exception."

Vartan sent his brother a scalding look. The sneer on Hovan's face faded as he turned pallid.

"They won't come," Vartan growled. "We've already tried that and were rebuffed. And neither will the Greenwald Elves, given their king's view of me after I nearly eloped with his favorite child and married her over his strenuous objections . . ." His voice trailed off as he thought of his ailing wife, Aelwyd. By sheer will Vartan forced himself to return to the considerations at hand. "Neither will the Northern Rune Lords, who never even joined the first alliance, aid us. *Nothing* binds Gadiel's people anymore. Nothing has for hundreds of years, not since the time of the Ancients. And we don't have the luxury of hundreds of years to mend the wounds caused by the treachery, deceit, and greed—on *all* sides. Not now, not with the Hylean army at our gates and our people on the brink of starvation!

"As for an outright surrender, that won't save me in any case," he added, turning back to his father. "One way or another, Ladon will see me dead. Indeed, it's to Feodras's advantage as well. With you ailing, Father, I'm now the threat and will remain so for as long as I live."

"But Feodras said no citizen would be harmed!"

Vartan gave a disparaging snort. "Aye, I may not be *harmed*, but I'd wager I also won't long remain in Astara, or even Gadiel for that matter. My wasting away in some Hylean dungeon still ultimately serves both Feodras's and Ladon's purposes."

His father's extended silence was confirmation he suspected the same.

"Where Ladon is concerned," Vartan finally continued, "whether the tales are true or not, if we don't surrender I'll have to meet him sooner or later. I far prefer it while I'm strong, rather than when half-dead from hunger or sickness. The morrow might well be the only chance, if there indeed *is* any chance, I'll ever have to defeat him."

He leaned down and clasped his father by the shoulder. "It'll take a miracle, I know, but I *must* try. Give me your leave, Majesty. Please."

"Nay." King Haig's eyes filled with tears. "Not you, Vartan. Not you!"

"Then who, Father? Would you instead shame us by sending out an inferior warrior?" Hovan demanded, sidling closer. "We'd be the laughingstock of the Hylean army, we would. Indeed not only the laughingstock, but we'd risk delivering an insult that might compel Feodras permanently to rescind his offer. Are you willing to risk all of Astara for the sake of one man's life? Even if," he added with a derisive curl of his lip, "that one man *is* your most beloved child?"

When did we cease to be brothers and become so at odds? Vartan wondered, gazing into eyes now blazing with malevolent antagonism. When had the little brother six years his junior, who had once hung on his every word and imitated his every move, changed into such a spiteful, selfish man?

Had it happened in that year Hovan had lived in Feodras's court, sent to learn the ways of diplomacy to prepare him for a future role in service to Astara? Or had it instead been slow and insidious throughout their youth, as Hovan inevitably discovered he would never, no matter how hard he tried, gain the father's acclaim he so avidly sought? Leastwise, not the kind of acclaim as a warrior that had always come so easily for his older brother.

The old question rose once more in Vartan's mind. Must he own some of the blame for the man Hovan had become? Had he somehow failed him, in not being more of a brother? But what more could he have done? He loved Hovan, as did their father. What else *could* they have done to show that love?

"Hovan's right, Father," Vartan replied, heartsick that now, in what might well be the last hours he would spend with his brother, there still seemed no way to quench the hatred Hovan clutched so mightily to him. "If I must be sacrificed for Astara's sake, Hovan and Zagiri will still remain." He smiled in sudden, sad remembrance. "And Korien, too. There'll always be your grandson to remind you of me."

"Far better," his sire muttered, "that *you* live to be a father to your son. A son needs his father. And Aelwyd . . ." He sighed. "Aelwyd will always need you."

Frustration filled Vartan. Did his father think him so self-absorbed that a hero's death was all that really mattered? He loved his son with all his heart. Korien was his pride and joy. And Aelwyd . . . though she was no longer the vibrant, exciting woman he had married, she wasn't to blame. Perhaps it *was* his own arrogance that had ultimately brought them to this sad place in their bond union. She was his wife. He would always honor her as such.

"I don't want to die, Father. I love my family, my life. If there were any other way . . ."

Vartan paused, his glance momentarily ensnared as the door opened. Aelwyd walked in, garbed in a shimmering, soft green gown with long sleeves. Danae followed, carrying a chubby, two-year-old Korien in her arms.

The look on Aelwyd's beauteous face warned him of what was to come. She knew; she had heard. Vartan squared his shoulders and turned to face her.

13

"What do you mean to do?" his ebony-haired, Elfin wife demanded in a low voice, drawing up before him. "The news must be all over the city by now, yet *I* had to hear from a servant that that cursed Hylean warrior means to kill you on the morrow. A servant, Vartan!"

For a fleeting instant, Vartan's gaze found Danae's over his wife's shoulder. At the question burning in his eyes, her lips tightened and she gave a small shake of her head. He should've known. Danae was no gossipmonger. Some other servant had run to Aelwyd with the news.

"There wasn't time, my love." He forced what he hoped was a conciliatory smile. "We've but two hours to come to a decision. A decision that must be made as prudently and dispassionately as possible."

"In other words," Aelwyd all but hissed, her voice rising now on a thread of hysteria, "a decision made without any thought given for your responsibilities to your wife and son. How can you be so selfish? So—so puffed up in your misguided sense of self-importance that you, once again, fail to consider anyone but yourself? But why should this surprise me, any more than all the other insensitive hurts you've inflicted on me? You're a hard-hearted, arrogant man, Vartan Karayan!"

With that, Aelwyd clasped her arms about herself and began to weep, loudly and piteously. Korien, his blue eyes wide, whimpered and squirmed in Danae's arms, reaching out to his mother. Vartan clamped down hard on his impulse to turn his wife around and march her from the room. As embarrassing as it was to expose their marital problems before the others, it wasn't as if his family wasn't already aware of them. Aelwyd's erratic behavior and unpredictable mood swings had been rapidly worsening ever since their son's birth.

He heard Hovan cough behind his hand in a failed attempt to stifle a laugh. Rage seared through him. How dare his brother gloat after his own thoughtlessness had brought Astara to the brink of disaster? True, Vartan and Aelwyd had defied the strictures against Elf and human unions—strictures Vartan now realized might well have been sound—but at least *they* were lawfully wed. At least Vartan hadn't stolen another man's wife, the Queen of Hylas no less, whom Hovan now lived with in flagrant adultery!

But even that didn't matter anymore. Once their father had decided to shield his youngest son and Queen Calandra from King Feodras's wrath, there was no turning back. All that was left for Vartan was to serve his king and people, and to do so the best, the most honorable, way he knew how.

Vartan took Aelwyd in his arms. "Hush, sweet one," he whispered into the fragrant mass of her hair. "I love you and Korien. Never would I willingly choose to leave either of you. But, if I must, I'll die to protect you. You know that."

"Nay!" she wailed. "There must be some other way. There must!"

"If there is, we'll find it, my love." Gently, he pushed her from him. "You must leave us now to do just that." Vartan looked to Danae. She stepped forward. "You must go with Danae," he said, glancing back to his wife. "Will you do that?"

Aelwyd gazed up at him through her tears and, for an instant, Vartan thought she'd leave quietly. Then her jaw hardened, and she savagely shook her head.

"Nay. I won't go unless you come with me. Come with me, Vartan. Please!"

Renewed frustration filled him. "Aelwyd, you know I can't. I told you—"

She reared back and slapped him in the face. "Selfish, arrogant beast!" she screamed, pounding now at his head and

body. "How *dare* you deny me? I won't have it, I say! I won't
. . . have it . . ."

With that, Aelwyd swooned. Only Vartan's swift response
in catching and swinging her up into his arms prevented
her from falling to the floor. The imprint of his wife's hand
still stinging his cheek, he hefted her slight form close, then
turned to his father.

Where he expected pity he found only concern.

"Is she all right, my son?"

"I think so," Vartan ground out between clenched teeth.
"I need to take her back to our quarters, though."

"And what of Feodras's offer? Time grows short."

A heavy weight pressed down on Vartan, and he fought
hard against a sudden swell of despair. "Do nothing without
first gaining Feodras's word—*from his own lips*—that he'll
spare Astara and all its citizens. And if you obtain that word,
then there's nothing left but to accept his offer. Whatever you
decide, Father, I will do."

Tear-bright eyes met his. "I know that, my son. I know."

It was but an hour until the evening meal when Danae
finally found a few blessed minutes of solitude. She hurried to
the private inner courtyard of Vartan and Aelwyd's quarters.
There, even in the chill of winter, a green and tan striated
fountain shaped like one of Gadiel's many palmlike desert trees
flowed, filling the air with the soothing sound of water.

She took a seat near the small iron brazier filled with fire-
hot coals, pulling her cloak to cover her simple woolen gown.
The brazier's heat soon warmed and calmed her. If she closed
her eyes, blocked out the unsettling events of the day, Danae
could almost imagine life went on as it always had since she

first came to Astara and was taken into the Crown Prince's household.

The youngest child of one of Feodras's cavalry generals, Danae was possessed of many talents—among them the skilled use of the curved Hylean lyra and the gift of a hauntingly lovely voice. She had grown up in frequent contact with the royal court. In time, she had caught the eye of the king's second wife, a young, exceptionally beautiful woman from the neighboring district of Pyramus. Calandra had eventually offered Danae a position as one of her lady's maids, and for a long while the two girls—Calandra at the time having barely left girlhood herself—were inseparable. Then one day, a handsome young Gadielean prince named Hovan Karayan arrived in Feodras's court for an extended stay.

Danae had watched them fall in love. With what she now knew had been misplaced loyalty, she held her tongue, never revealing Calandra's infidelity to her husband. Danae had refused, however, to run away with Calandra and her lover when Hovan's time at court came to an end. Unfortunately, Calandra was even more determined *not* to be parted from her friend and favorite lady's maid. By the time Danae awoke from the sleeping potion Hovan had slipped into her food, they were far out on the Great Sea, sailing for Gadiel.

She sighed, leaned forward, and extended her hands to warm them over the glowing coals. As ashamed as she was to admit it, the betrayal still festered in her heart. Their relationship had irrevocably changed. She would never again serve Calandra.

Calandra's tearful pleas soon turned to threats. Threats progressed to beatings until, one day, Vartan ventured upon Hovan preparing to punish Danae yet again.

The two brothers nearly came to blows over her, before Hovan at last agreed to Vartan's offer to buy the recalcitrant seventeen-year-old Hylean girl. And though Aelwyd was initially less than pleased with the purchase, she, too, soon formed a fast friendship with Danae. A friendship that endured, despite the Elfin woman's gradual but apparently inexorable descent into madness.

Aelwyd's illness notwithstanding, Danae had eventually found peace and contentment in the Karayan household. She had nursed her friend through a difficult first pregnancy, stood by her at Korien's birth, and had become all but a second mother to the beautiful baby who had now grown into an energetic toddler. She had also, over the years of frequent contact with Vartan Karayan, come to know, respect, and finally fall in love with him.

"He fills your thoughts more than ever, doesn't he?" a voice softly intruded on Danae's pensive musings. "But indeed, he fills all our thoughts, today, this most tragic of days."

Hot blood flooding her cheeks, Danae jerked around to find Vartan's younger sister, Zagiri, standing beside the fountain. The water's soft music, she realized, must have muted the sound of the other woman's approach. Danae rose to her feet.

"I-I don't know what you're talking about," she stammered out a response she instantly knew sounded silly and false. Still, it took a moment under Zagiri's steady, compassionate gaze before she finally relented. "Well, aye, I suppose I *am* thinking of Vartan. It's just so cruel, so unfair . . ."

Her eyes began to sting, and she flushed all the more. "I'm sorry," she mumbled, glancing down to hide the tears. "It's just that . . . just that he's always been so good to me . . ."

"I know. I understand . . . more than you might realize."

Slender and of medium height like Danae, thirty-year-old Zagiri had a pleasant face, smooth, pink cheeks, and a gentle mouth. She wore her wavy, dark brown hair cut short and was always garbed, despite her regal status, in a rather shapeless, hooded, long brown robe. Considered cursed with a strange sort of madness—Zagiri mouthed prophecies that made little sense—the middle child of the royal siblings had always treated Danae kindly, in time even becoming her spiritual mentor.

She gestured to the bench Danae had just vacated. "Let's sit. We've things to speak of. Important things, such as how you alone can now aid my brother."

Danae all but fell back onto the bench. "Aid Vartan? How?"

Zagiri walked over and sat beside her. "How else," she asked, her voice low and melodious, "but to teach him of Athan and His precious Son, Eisa? Then, though Vartan may die, he will live."

Of course, Danae thought. *To accept the All-Knowing, the Creator, into one's heart was to gain immortality in the Afterlife. And, according to Zagiri, Vartan was not and never had been one of the Faithful.*

"I would do that, and gladly," she said, "but what could I say, as unschooled as I still am in the ways of Athan, when all your efforts have failed? Especially now, when there's so little time left?"

"We're all instruments in Athan's hands. Some He uses for one task, and some are meant for others. You're called to aid my brother in the hard times to come. I must mouth prophecies no one of House Karayan or of the city of Astara believes."

"Well, I believe them!"

Zagiri smiled. "But then, you aren't of House Karayan or of Astara, are you?"

Danae grinned. "Nay, I'm not."

19

"Yet, since you do believe, I've one last prophecy to share with you." She paused, closed her eyes for a moment, then turned the full force of her striking sea blue gaze—eyes Danae had long ago noted were the same shade as her older brother's—on her. "It's not of my making, mind you, but it's past time you know of whom this Prophecy speaks."

"And what exactly is this prophecy?"

"Listen closely, dear friend," Zagiri said, drawing even nearer and dropping her voice. "I dare not utter it too loudly in these troubled times, for fear some unholy creature might overhear and seek to put an end to it before it can be fulfilled."

"Is that possible?" Danae asked, frowning in puzzlement. "To prevent some divinely inspired, future event?"

"Unfortunately, aye, if the instruments are unwilling or choose the wrong path." She smiled sadly. "It's the one variable in the Divine plan: our right—one of Athan's greatest and most loving gifts—to refuse Him."

Zagiri took Danae's hand. "Now, listen . . . and hear with the ears of your heart." She intoned:

> Desperate times,
> Death and destruction.
> The Guardian returns,
> Blind to his destiny.
>
> Evil breaks free,
> A land lost in shadows.
> The Guardian returns,
> From ruin to rebirth.
>
> All praise to the Son
> Whose marks he now carries.
> The Guardian returns,
> His hands filled with roses.

"It comes from the *Song of the Ancients*," Vartan's sister explained after a brief pause, "this Prophecy of prophecies."

Along with *The Covenant of Athan*, the *Song of the Ancients* was one of the Faithfuls' two most sacred books. Danae's mouth quirked. "It must be well into that holy tome then, for I've yet to study it. But what do those verses mean? What are the marks this Guardian carries? And what does this person hope to do with but a handful of roses?"

"I've yet to discern the true significance of the marks," Zagiri replied, "though I have my suspicions. The Guardian, however, is meant to save Gadiel. And the blue rose has always been the sacred flower of the land, symbolic of truth, unity, and a pure, loving heart. Those who go in peace must always carry blue roses. But over the centuries, as the Old Alliance fell by the wayside and distrust and feuding grew more and more prevalent in the land, so the blue rose of Gadiel began to disappear. Now, there are few to be found anywhere."

Danae had seen the stylized blue flower encircled by a golden crown emblazoned on the white silk banners flying from various positions around the city, but had never thought to ask about its significance. Now Danae knew, understood. It was the flag of Gadiel, and the royal city of Astara had the singular honor, above all cities, to display it. There was, though, yet one unanswered question.

"Why do you tell me this? Why now, when most likely I'll rejoin my father and my people on the morrow? What will it matter, when I'll soon put Astara and Gadiel far behind me and return to my former life?"

"Will you, Danae? Return to your former life, I mean?" Zagiri averted her gaze, a faraway look in her eyes. "What if Athan asks you to do differently? Will you, too, refuse Him?"

"After all you've taught me of Athan, and how I've come to love Him and His Son, you know I couldn't." Even the consideration made her heart ache. "But what could He possibly want from me, leastwise in regards to Astara and Gadiel? I'm no heroine, and certainly not the one of whom the Prophecy speaks."

A sudden thought assailed Danae, and with it came a rising presentiment. "Whom *does* the Prophecy speak of, Zagiri? The one who brings the roses, who saves the land?"

A soft, enigmatic smile touched the other woman's lips. "The giver of roses."

"The giver of roses?"

"Aye. Vartan, of course. Didn't you know? In the ancient tongue, his name means 'giver of roses.'"

2

That night Ladon clasped a finely wrought, golden goblet between his hands, admiring the interplay of sparkling light and crimson shadow as he swirled the contents to and fro. *An exceptional, well-aged brew,* he thought, *with hints of turkawood and spice, overlaid by a rich, fruity bouquet. But then, over the years, life in Feodras's court couldn't help but refine my already inbred, patrician tastes. The blood of kings, after all, runs in my veins.*

One step at a time, though, he reminded himself with a smile. He had glimpsed his true destiny the moment he had set foot on Gadiel's soil. This land was meant for him. And Astara was the portal to the rest of Gadiel. The portal as well, someday, to Hylas itself when he would finally possess sufficient power and prestige to return there and claim the throne.

He had known Vartan, that ever-cautious, shrewdly gifted prince, would eventually accept his challenge. All it required was the proper information and timing. And, thanks to Phaon's most generous loan of a cadre of demons and other Nether Realm denizens, he finally had the information he needed.

Prince Vartan, fool that he was in denying the existence of otherworldly beings, had been heedless of the lesser demon that, from the shadows, constantly stalked him. The Fiend had earlier today followed Vartan down into the depths of the city as the prince performed his quarterly review of the food stores. Food stores that had inexorably been dropping, even before a cleverly executed and heretofore undetected leak in the city's main well fouled nearly all the remaining rations.

The hideous, winged spy had wasted no time returning with the news: Vartan now knew Astara was in dire straits. And Ladon, ever one to seize any advantage offered him, had wasted no time presenting, yet again, Feodras's proposal. A proposal that, at long last, had been accepted.

"Destroy Vartan Karayan and exterminate the male line," Phaon, his overlord, had demanded. *"Serve me well, and this land is yours."*

Ladon lifted the cup to his lips and imbibed a long, satisfying draught. Aye, he'd serve Phaon well. And, when the time came, if Feodras couldn't be persuaded to break his word to the Karayans . . . well, his refusal only hastened the inevitable.

High in the palace's upper tiers, Vartan felt stifled by the heat of the circular hearth fire in their quarter's gathering room. He moved outside, where the evening air seemed to open its arms in a cool, welcoming embrace. Save for the bits of twinkling stars overhead and the muted, red glow of thousands of enemy campfires in the distance, a deep blackness shrouded the land. Pausing outside his door, Vartan inhaled deeply, willing his anger to ease, the chaotic tumult of emotions to settle.

It was, after all, a night like so many others. Yet it was also a night that stood apart, a night that relentlessly mocked him. Mocked him and all he had done, and not done, to lead his land and city to this final, grievous end. No matter how hard he tried to deny it, with every breath he took, with every beat of his heart, the hours ticked by on what was most likely the last night of his life.

Vartan walked for a time along the upper parapets, passing the occasional guard who nodded a greeting. Apparently noting the prince's frowning countenance and purposeful stride, each man left him to his own thoughts.

It was well they did. He was in the foulest of moods. What could anyone say, save to skirt the issue altogether or, worse still, awkwardly offer a pitying farewell?

Vartan's mouth quirked wryly. Well, he supposed there *was* another option. Each could echo Aelwyd's continuing sentiments and berate him for being a glory-hungry, obstinate, and selfish fool.

With a weary sigh, he paused at the covered, colonnaded porch that always afforded an impressive view of the city and surrounding countryside, all the way out to the Great Sea. Perhaps he *was* a fool, urging his father to accept Feodras's offer to allow the Hylean and Gadielean champions to determine the final outcome of this interminably disastrous war.

But what other choice was left them? They were surrounded now on three sides by Hylean forces and their brutish, half-human allies, their backs cut into a steeply impregnable mountain, their food supplies all but exhausted. It was but a matter of time before riots and looting broke out as the Astarians, in their desperation, scavenged for even the tiniest morsels. As keeper of the city and captain of the guard, Vartan would then be forced to call out his soldiers to regain control in any way they could.

Stiff-armed, he gripped the balustrade, his fingers curling around the cold, smooth stone. Aelwyd was right. He *was* a fool. Still, in face of the rapidly dwindling options, he far preferred being the fool to watching the citizens of Astara turn on each other. Watch them like wild animals caught in a trap, gnaw off their own legs before the Hylean army next took its turn.

Nay, he wasn't going out to meet the reputably invincible Ladon for the glory. There seemed scant glory in almost certain suicide. Despite the hope he had offered his father earlier, Vartan no more believed in miracles than in the divine beings who worked them.

On the contrary. He was facing Ladon out of sheer cowardice and pride. He hadn't the heart to endure Astara's final, and undeniably imminent, death throes. In that, he *was* proud, selfishly so.

When he had come to maturity as Gadiel's crown prince, his father, increasingly debilitated by lung sickness, had gradually relinquished more and more command to him. Since then, it had been *his* able leadership, *his* battle prowess, and *his* wise decisions that had brought Astara to its greatest military might and prosperity. And it wasn't vainglory prompting such an admission. He had always viewed his own accomplishments with a ruthlessly honest, even cynical, eye. But Vartan, in the service of his people, also wasn't ashamed to exploit every one of his talents.

In the end, everything—*everything*—he had ever done had been for the betterment of Astara and its citizens. Indeed, he had hoped one day to extend his influence to the entire realm. Hoped to rebuild the Old Alliance.

It hadn't been an impossible dream. Far from it. Thinking back, Vartan didn't even need all the fingers of one hand to count the times he had failed. His plans had always been crowned with success. But now . . . now this one failure would blot out all the good he had ever done, forever ending his dreams. His name, in the years to come, would be uttered in tones of bitterness and contempt. This one failure could be the end of them all.

His shoulders sagged. Vartan sucked in a sharp, unsteady breath. How could it have come to this? Where had he gone wrong?

He had argued with his father until he was hoarse, trying to convince him to send Calandra back. But either his father had evolved into some hopeless, if ill-advised, romantic, or he had been misled by a secret guilt over having failed Hovan. One way or another, it didn't matter. For once, King Haig had turned a deaf ear to his eldest son.

Perhaps Vartan's efforts would have been better served appealing instead to Hovan. Problem was, his brother had long ago ceased to listen to him. If only . . . if only he had been a better mentor to Hovan. If only he had exerted a greater influence and control over him.

But he hadn't, indeed, couldn't. For all his drive to do the best for his people, Vartan lacked the heart for ruthless tyranny, for brutality and devious politics. But Hovan, the pampered yet still endlessly grasping youngest, had no such lack. By whatever means were at his disposal, Hovan always attained what he desired. Calandra, another man's wife and queen, wasn't the first such prize, nor had she been the last. In his apparently endless quest to fill that strange, insatiable hole in his heart, Hovan couldn't seem to help himself.

If only Hovan had found a way to live his life with some semblance of honor and integrity . . . Vartan sighed again and shook his head. There was nothing to be done for it now. Astara's hope now lay in King Feodras's hands.

It seems, Vartan thought with the blackest humor, *that I'm the final stumbling block to everything.* At his death, the Hyleans would march into Astara, most likely loot a bit to reward the army, then march out. Calandra would be restored to her husband's forgiving arms. The Hyleans and their allies would depart from Gadiel's shores, and all would return to life as it had once been. All save he, who would be dead, no further threat to anyone. No threat as the future strong and able Gadielean king who might take it into his head someday to seek revenge.

All so simple, Vartan thought, *yet all* too *simple.* Something lay behind this sad turn of events, something deeper, more complex—even sinister. He knew it; he felt it down to the marrow of his bones. The answers, however, were shielded from him.

In time, he knew he could've sorted through the mystery and arrived at some plan to fight back. He had always been able to surmount any obstacle, any threat. But time was no longer his friend.

There seemed nothing left for him to do but die.

Danae couldn't sleep. Perhaps it was her unrelenting worry over Vartan and what the morrow might bring. Perhaps it was but the lingering effects of her talk with Zagiri. Or perhaps it was the emotional and physical toll the day had taken on her, driving her past the point of exhaustion to a bowstring-taut tension. Aelwyd's hysterics had gone on and on, until Danae was beside herself trying to find some way to soothe the distraught woman while at the same time protecting young Korien from seeing his mother in such an agitated state.

But mother and child had been put to bed hours ago, and Danae's sleep still wouldn't come. Her thoughts, no matter how fiercely she tried to squelch them, returned time and again to Vartan. What was he doing, thinking, this night?

She prayed he had finally taken his rest. He would need all his faculties and full strength about him on the morrow. The consideration of him lying awake, dwelling endlessly on the battle to come, was heart wrenching. He didn't deserve to suffer—not tonight *or* on the morrow.

Athan, Eternal One, Lord of all, she thought, lifting a quick, fervent prayer heavenward, g*ive him peace. Give him the strength to overcome the evil that surrounds and protects Ladon. Guide his arm and let his sword strike true. He is, after all, a good man.*

He was also, Danae knew, likely the only one who possessed the warrior's prowess to best Ladon in a fair fight. The Hylean warrior, even before he had made a pact with Phaon, had been a formidable opponent. Vartan Karayan, however, had always been his match. But now . . . now with a protective aura of evil about Ladon, only Athan-imbued powers could defeat him.

But Vartan wasn't a believer. At best, he paid a respectful, if disinterested, lip service to Astara's current pantheon of false gods. Because of that, on the morrow he'd go into battle woefully vulnerable.

Tears welled and trickled down Danae's cheeks. *He can't help it, Eternal One. He doesn't yet know You, and there's no time left to convince him.*

Teach him of Athan and His precious Son, Eisa. Then, though Vartan may die, he'll live . . .

As if Athan Himself had plucked them from the air and placed them in Danae's mind, Zagiri's words returned with all the physical immediacy of her actual presence: *"Teach him of Athan . . ."* Danae blinked hard in the darkened room, trying to make out if her friend really *was* there. She wasn't.

Danae shoved up in bed. Myriad excuses whirled through her head. What if Vartan was already abed, Aelwyd in his arms? How could she speak to him, much less dare intrude on husband and wife in their bedchamber? And even if she *should* find him elsewhere, what could she say that would make him listen to her? On this night of all nights, he surely had matters of far more pressing import—leastwise to himself—on his mind.

But how could she not at least try? The morrow would be too late, and she'd live with the consequences of the deed undone for the rest of her days. Regrets for Vartan's sake. Regrets for her failure to obey her beloved Creator.

She dressed, ran the cochashell comb Aelwyd had given her for her last birthing day through her hair, then slipped from her tiny room. Passing down the corridor to the nearest outside door, Danae quickly made her way along the parapet walkway. Though she knew not why, something drew her in that direction. She only hoped it was Athan leading her to Vartan. If not, she'd be forced to knock on the prince's bedchamber door and fabricate some excuse to speak privately with him.

Blessedly, she found Vartan standing in the colonnaded portico, staring out toward the sea. For an instant Danae's courage failed her. He looked so dejected, his arms stiff, his shoulders slumped, as he gripped the stone railing. What could she possibly say, what comfort could she offer, that would make any difference?

"M'lord?" Before she lost her nerve, Danae stepped forward, closing the distance between them.

Vartan whirled around, his eyes wide with surprise. "D-Danae," he said, his voice rough, unsteady. "I didn't hear you . . ." He gave a harsh laugh. "Already my warrior's skills begin to desert me. At this rate, by dawn's light I'll be a quivering, terror-stricken mass of flesh and bone."

"Nay. Nay, m'lord!" She rushed to his side. "Never will you be anything less than the magnificent man and warrior you've always been. I just startled you, that's all. You were so deep in thought . . ."

He smiled and, reaching out, touched her cheek. "Ah, my sweet little Danae. Your confidence in me has always outstripped the reality of the man I am. Still, tonight it comforts me." His hand fell back to his side. "But why are you about so late? Is there something wrong? Has someone sent you to fetch me?"

She shook her head. "Nay, m'lord. Not tonight. I . . . I couldn't sleep and was drawn to seek this place, that's all." She gestured about her, hating herself for the half lie. "The view . . . it always fills me with awe—and peace."

"Aye." Vartan turned back to stare out, once more, over the darkened land. "I imagine it does, looking down upon the armies of your people, counting the days until Astara falls and you'll finally be free. Well, that day may well be upon you, lady. On the morrow, you might well be reunited with your countrymen."

"I'd never wish such a thing, m'lord," Danae whispered, "if the price was your life. My freedom's not worth that."

A low chuckle rose from beside her. "That's kind of you to say. But then, you're one of the kindest people, servant though you are, I've ever known. Your presence has never failed to soothe me." He turned to her. "Why is that? What is it about you that has such an effect on others? On me?"

Warmth flooded her cheeks. "I . . . I've no special gifts, m'lord. And I doubt I've such an effect on most people. I surely wasn't of comfort to your wife this day."

"Ah, aye. Aelwyd." Vartan sighed. "She's terrified. Her safe, circumscribed little world is crumbling around her, indeed has been for the past two years. She hasn't the strength anymore to find her way through it all. She's never been very strong. I realize that now. I don't know what she'll do after I . . ."

31

After I'm gone? Silently, Danae finished the sentence for him. Her heart twisted. She wanted to cry out for him not to think such a thing. He couldn't die. He just couldn't!

But she knew as well as he the odds were against him. She wasn't about to pretend or play a game that was, in the end, unkind and dishonest.

"Aelwyd adores Korien," Danae said instead. "He'll always be a comfort to her. And she'll have the presence of your family to uphold her. She'll get through this. She's a Karayan now."

"Aye, she is. Still, if things go badly on the morrow . . ." He paused to inhale, then exhale a deep breath. "I know you'll be eager to reunite with your people. But would you . . . could you . . . first see to their safety? It's important I know they'll be safe from whatever . . . whatever might happen once the Hylean army enters Astara."

"My father is an officer—one of Feodras's generals." She had never told him this before, fearing he might find some way to use the information. But suddenly it no longer mattered. "I'll enlist his aid in their protection."

Vartan's lips lifted in a brief, sad smile. "Thank you, Danae."

She wanted to say she'd do that and more for him, indeed, *anything* he wanted, but feared how her words would sound—and what she might do if he asked. He needed love—comforting—and Danae knew now no solace would be forthcoming from Aelwyd. The only love and comfort she could offer, though, would be her presence if he wished it. Her presence and the knowledge of Athan.

"The night grows cold," she said, taking in his long, loose crimson shirt, black woolen hose, and tall, soft tur-hide boots. "If you mean to stay here a time, I could fetch you your cloak."

He glanced down at himself, then shook his head. "My thanks, but I don't need it. Before the sun returns, I want to experience every sensation possible, live as much of what remains of my life as I can. And that includes enduring this night's winter cold."

"Would you prefer to do it alone, m'lord?"

"Why?" Vartan shot her a wry glance. "Are you offering to stay with me?"

"If it pleases you, aye, m'lord."

He turned to face her then. "And if it pleased me, as well, to spend this night in your arms, what would you say to that?"

She could hardly breathe. He had moved so close now that the heat from his big, powerful body set her blood afire. She closed her eyes, clenched her hands into fists. *Help me, Athan! Help me keep You ever before me!*

"I'd say, m'lord," Danae replied at last, opening her eyes to meet his searching gaze, "that you've a wife and you'd never do such a dishonorable thing. Especially tonight, of all nights."

"And *I'd* say, save in your mind, I'm not feeling especially honorable tonight. Especially when I look into those big, soft brown eyes of yours." Once again Vartan touched her cheek, then, after what seemed the most achingly tender moment of Danae's life, let his hand fall away. "But if you choose to stay, you're safe with me, as safe as you've always been. I'll leave at least one soul behind, I vow, who still thinks well of me."

"You'd leave many behind, m'lord. Never doubt that." She hesitated, wondering how to broach what she knew she must tell him of Athan. It was his only chance—whether of body or of soul—to save himself on the morrow. But how? How?

Just begin, Child of Mine, came a voice in her mind. *For his sake. You've little time left.*

A chill breeze rushed across the parapet just then. Danae shivered. She gestured to a long, stone bench standing about ten feet behind them. "Could we sit, then? It'll be more comfortable and better protected from the wind."

"As you wish, lady."

In silence they walked to the bench and sat, Vartan taking great care to keep a proper distance between them. Danae smiled. He had always been a man of his word. Astara would suffer a great loss in losing him.

The realization brought freshened tears. Savagely, Danae blinked them back. Vartan didn't need her pity or futile weeping. He needed Truth.

"You found me once at prayer," she forced herself to begin. "Though you warned me it was an act frowned on by the King, unless it was in reverence to the sanctioned gods, you didn't betray me to your father. That was merciful of you."

"In case you didn't ascertain it at the time, I'm hardly a religious man." He gave an amused snort. "Indeed, I suspect my father isn't, either. How could he be, with a daughter who so openly worships one god instead of many?"

"Then how do *you* find peace in life? What gives you hope and purpose?"

He shrugged. "I find peace in the knowledge that I've tried always to do my best, to live my life with honor. Indeed, even on the morrow I'll find honor in dying for my family and people. And as for hope and purpose? Astara's future and the continuation of the Karayan line, of course, give me my hope and sense of purpose. What else is there?"

"There's Something, Someone, outside ourselves," Danae said softly. "There's Athan."

Vartan chuckled. "I see Zagiri has been at it again. But I ask, what's the difference between one god or many? Either way, I don't believe in any of them."

"Do you believe there's Light and Darkness in this world?"

"I believe men can be good or evil and, many times, a combination of both. I don't believe, however, that Light and Darkness originate from some source or beings outside us."

"It's said Ladon's extraordinary strength and invulnerability arise from the Dark One. That he made a pact with Phaon."

He gave a sharp laugh. "Well, I've already told you. I don't believe in any of those myths."

Frustration filled Danae. She knew she was going about this awkwardly. If only she had the eloquence to speak of her heart's truest love!

"Then why are you so convinced you won't survive your battle with Ladon? Is his strength and prowess so much more than yours, if it stems only from himself?"

"What do *you* think?" Vartan's response escaped as a low growl. "No one has ever defeated or even wounded him, no matter if he fought one man or twenty. I'm not fool enough to imagine I can do better!"

"Did you know even his own countrymen fear him?"

"Not enough to banish him from their midst!"

"Nay, they use Ladon. Of that there's no doubt." Almost unconsciously, Danae rubbed the spot on her right forearm that bore a reddish-purple mark. "It might well be my people's undoing. Heed my words. When this war is over, Feodras won't easily be rid of Ladon. These days, Ladon serves a far more powerful and demanding master."

She turned to Vartan and grasped his arm. "That's why I speak to you this night of Athan. Only Athan can defeat the powers of Phaon. And only those who follow Athan can hope to overcome those who've yielded their souls to the Dark Lord."

"Do you now think me so desperate I'll stoop to grop-ing after some imaginary god to vanquish another imaginary god?" He shook her hand away. "I'm sorry if this offends you, Danae, but the only god I'll ever worship is my own strength and intelligence, my honor. Those things are tangible. Those are things I can take and mold, can control. If nothing else, I've always been a practical man. I don't chase after unattain-able dreams and illusions. I take what I have and do the best I can with it."

"And that's enough for you? Can you say you've never once wondered if there wasn't more?"

She was losing this battle, but didn't know what else to do. Zagiri should be here, not her. Growth in Athan's way took time. It took openness to mystery. It required faith. But, most of all, it took an honesty to admit there was more to life than the physical, material world, and the courage to risk all in order to gain it.

He looked away. "Nay, it's not always enough. But then, I've never expected life to be more than it is. And life, for the most part, has been very good to me."

"So life is your god, is it, Vartan? Along with your great strength, intelligence, and honor?" She shook her head. "Yet what if you were to lose your strength and become as a help-less babe? What good then would your precious intelligence be? Where would you find your honor?"

"I'll never let that happen. I'd die first."

Suddenly, Danae felt cold, as if some hand had brushed its icy fingers down her spine. She shuddered and wrapped her arms about her. It was almost as if . . . as if he had just prophesied—accepted even—his own death.

"I don't want you to die, Vartan." Her words came out softly, full of a deep, sad yearning. "But you will, if you give up hope. Phaon is at his strongest in the absence of hope."

He released a long, slow breath and leaned forward to cradle his head in his hands. "I know you mean well, Danae, but there's no honor in now asking for help from a god whom I struggle yet to believe in. Not when I've turned my back on him all my life. How can I expect any fealty, when I've never once offered it?"

"Athan loves you, Vartan. He knows you're a good man. He understands. Just please, I beg you. Don't give up hope!"

"Then be my h-hope, Danae," he said, his voice breaking, "for I fear my strength has all but left me. I'm afraid. I don't know which way to turn."

"I'll be your hope and gladly." Danae scooted close and wrapped her arm about Vartan's shoulder. He stiffened momentarily then, with a groan, laid his head on her shoulder.

"Promise me one thing," she whispered into his thick, dark hair.

"What's that?"

"On the morrow . . . if things do come to appear their bleakest, lift your thoughts, Vartan, if only for the briefest of moments. Lift your thoughts to Athan and ask Him to help you. Do it for Astara, for your family, if you can't do it for yourself."

"Danae—"

"It's such a little thing, Vartan," she said. "And if there's no Athan, then it won't matter, will it?"

He didn't respond for a time, until Danae feared he never would. Then Vartan sighed.

"If things come to their bleakest—and I've the wherewithal to remember—I'll try. But not for my sake. Never, ever, just for mine."

Midday came far, far too swiftly for Vartan's taste. Everything seemed heightened and so exquisitely precious—he was loath for any second to pass, knowing each experience might be his last. The feel of the warm water coursing across his skin as he bathed that morn, the silken brush of his dark blue shirt as he slid it over his head and down his chest, the rich, warm flavor of the honey-sweetened, spiced salma Danae served him in the inner courtyard.

They said little, he but thanking her for the hot drink and she smiling wanly and nodding, the splashing, gurgling fountain filling the silence between them. After stacking fresh faggots in the brazier and lighting them, for the day was as bleary and cold as the one preceding it, she left him to his thoughts. A short while later, however, as if knowing he'd wish it so, Danae brought Korien out to him.

Vartan held his son close for as long as the little boy would allow it, then set him down and watched him play. It was the only time that his eyes burned with unshed tears. They'd had so little time together, he and his son. Two years weren't nearly enough, yet for them, it must suffice for a lifetime.

Danae reentered the courtyard just then, Korien's breakfast on a small, inlaid wooden tray. She walked over and laid the tray on the bench beside Vartan.

"Would you like to see to his meal, or would you rather I help him?" she asked, meeting his gaze.

He considered that for a moment, and decided he'd enjoy watching the two of them together. "I think Korien would do better if you assisted him." He smiled. "I don't spend enough time around him to truly know his likes and dislikes. In that, at the very least, Aelwyd was right."

"The past three years haven't been easy on either you or Aelwyd, nor have they permitted you much time together." Danae paused to cut a wedge of tangy tur cheese into several bite-sized pieces. "I've watched you many a time with Korien, though, and you're a good father. Never doubt that."

Gratitude filled him for her kindhearted statement. She called his son over and began to offer him the cheese along with a chunk of freshly baked, brown bread. In the past year or so, busy though he'd been, he had noticed Danae blossoming into a beautiful young woman. Her hair, the color of ripening grain, was shiny with health and fell in sinuous waves to the middle of her back. Her skin was smooth, with the faintest wash of color shading her high cheekbones. And her eyes, framed by long, dark lashes, were a deep, gentle brown.

If the truth be told, though, it was her slender young body that had finally snagged his admiring attention. Last night wasn't the first time his mouth had gone dry looking at her, especially when she had innocently offered to stay with him. Some man, some day, would count himself a king in taking sweet Danae to wife.

But not him. Never him. He remained true to Aelwyd, though for some time now he had greatly feared she would never again be a loving wife, much less recover from her madness. *Not that,* he thought with a surge of black humor, *I'll have much longer to honor those vows. This very day, Ladon will likely make Aelwyd a widow.*

"Have you had a chance yet this morn to look in on my wife?" he asked, banishing his unpleasant thoughts. Time enough for those when the time came. All that mattered now was his family and clasping to him every precious moment he could with them.

Danae didn't immediately answer, instead occupying herself with offering Korien a cup of milk. Finally, she lifted her gaze. In it, Vartan saw sadness—and regret.

"She refuses to leave her room, m'lord, as long as you're here."

Somehow, though Danae's gently couched admission didn't surprise him, the realization he might never have a chance to say even a few, parting words to Aelwyd twisted his heart cruelly. "And is she playing yet another game in which I must grovel for her forgiveness, or do you think she truly *is* at the limits of her endurance? I want very badly to say farewell, to hold her once more in my arms, but I also don't wish to cause her additional harm." He grimaced. "Leastwise, no more harm than I've already caused."

"Aelwyd seems so distraught, I fear she's on the brink of making herself physically ill." Danae hesitated, chewed on her lower lip. "Perhaps later, before you leave to fight . . ."

"Aye, perhaps later then." Vartan's glance turned once more to his son. Korien had finished what he wanted of his breakfast and had resumed his play, pulling a carved wooden horse on wheels across the stone floor. Love and a soul-searing anguish flooded Vartan.

Ah, Korien, my son. May you never doubt that I loved you. And someday, when you're old enough to understand what I did this day, may you be proud of me.

Vartan shoved to his feet. "I still need to meet with my parents, say my farewells. Then I must garb myself for battle. If Aelwyd asks, I'll return thereafter. If she wishes to see me . . ."

Danae stood. "Aye, m'lord. I'll tell her."

Something arced between them in that final, poignant moment. Something akin to joy swelled in him. *She understands,* he thought. *She understands why I must do this and she accepts, even respects me for it.*

A sense of deep kinship with this young woman filled him. *At another time and place,* Vartan thought, *we might have become friends. In another life, we could have become even more.*

It wasn't enough, but it had to be. He had never been a man to bemoan his fate or weep over what might have been. Far better to seize something he *could* do, even if that something had finally come to this moment, this day, and what he'd soon face down on the battlefield.

Vartan smiled. "Thank you, Danae. Thank you for everything."

He turned, strode over to where Korien sat playing with his horse, and knelt to pull his son into his arms once more. For a long, inexpressibly tender moment, Vartan hugged him tightly. Then, with a kiss to his forehead, he released Korien. Without a backward glance, he walked from the courtyard and out of his quarters.

With an unnerving finality, Astara's thick bronze gates slammed shut behind Vartan. He glanced over his shoulder, swamped by an impulse to turn his warhorse back to those gates and pound on them, begging them to reopen. Never had he known such terror. The realization shamed him.

But only for an instant. He swallowed hard, squared his shoulders, and forced himself once again to face the armed warrior awaiting him. It was far, far too late to change his mind now. The entire Hylean army spread out before him. At his back, the people of Astara watched from the walls. Whatever fate lay in store, the time had come to face it.

He urged his mount forward, drawing up when only a few yards separated him from Ladon. As if lit from within by some unnatural source, his enemy's eyes glowed brightly. His thin sliver of a mouth lifted in a mockery of a smile.

"So, we meet at last on the field of battle," the Hylean champion said. "I began to despair you'd ever crawl out of that safe, snug fortress of yours. And you wouldn't have today, either, would you, if you'd had any other choice?"

If he meant to demoralize him before they even crossed swords, Ladon might as well have spared himself the effort. Vartan was too experienced in the ways of battle to let some opening taunts unman him. "And do you mean to bore me to death, then?" he snarled back. "After leading me to imagine your physical prowess, not your tongue, was your greatest weapon?"

The Hylean's gaze narrowed to murderous slits, then he laughed. "Well said, Prince of Astara. Have your moment of bravado. There'll be few enough left you." In a blur of motion Ladon's hand moved to his sword hilt and curled around it. With a sibilant hiss, the weapon slid free of its sheath.

Instantly, Vartan gripped his own sword. Before it was half drawn from its scabbard, however, Ladon attacked. Vartan barely managed to wheel his horse sideways and lift his shield to defend himself. His opponent's surprising strength and momentum in bringing his sword down on the shield almost unseated him.

His horse staggered, lost its balance, went to its knees. Only his riding skill and strong legs kept Vartan on the animal's back. Ladon, however, didn't pause in his hacking onslaught. All Vartan could do was hunker down behind his shield and endure blow after blow until, finally, an opportunity offered itself.

He flung his shield up to meet yet another sword strike in midair, halting its downward arc for just an instant. An instant long enough to lean around and thrust his own blade into a vulnerable gap in the Hylean's cuirass.

The sword plunged deep into Ladon's left side, high in his chest wall. He cried out, but whether in rage or pain or surprise, Vartan couldn't be sure. And then, in the next instant, Vartan had his answer. He pulled the blade free. It was clean.

His heart sank. His worst nightmare had come true. Ladon *was* invincible.

Then there wasn't time to consider anything but the battle before him. His opponent attacked yet again. It was all Vartan could do to parry the almost superhuman blows. Parry, defend, and back away, over and over and over.

Minutes seemed like hours. Sweat—despite the frigid day—poured down his face, into his eyes. He gulped in air, his breath soon coming in tortured gasps. His sword arm ached from the endless times he met and deflected Ladon's attacks. His fingers, curled about his shield's handgrip, grew numb from the incessant, forceful bashings.

And still the onslaught never wavered. Vartan had never seen a man with such stamina. There was no chance—none whatsoever—to recover enough to form his own offense. There was nothing—absolutely nothing—to do but endure the shame of being so quickly, so easily bested.

It wasn't long before his warhorse, forced constantly to back away, stumbled. Once more the animal went down. This time, Vartan's strength was no longer sufficient to maintain his seat. He tumbled backward, out of his saddle.

His shield struck him full in the face, stunning him. His sword sailed from his gauntleted hand, landing several feet from where he fell.

As Vartan's horse struggled to regain its footing, with a bestial growl, Ladon drove his sword into its neck. The unfortunate animal shrieked in pain and sank back to the ground, barely missing Vartan, who had just climbed to his feet. In horror he watched his horse thrash about, grunting pitifully as its lifeblood gushed from the cruel hole. Then his horse went still.

With a savage battle cry Ladon instantly drove his own mount toward Vartan. Vartan leaped aside, but the animal's shoulder struck him a glancing blow, sending him flying. As he shoved painfully back to his knees, the Hylean wheeled his horse around and charged yet again.

Frantically, Vartan looked about for his sword. It lay too far away to reach in time. But, by some good fortune, his shield was only an arm's length away.

He grabbed for it, rolled over onto his back, and at the last second flipped its razor-sharp, pointed bottom upward. It was too late for Ladon to halt or even turn his horse away. The animal plowed over Vartan, the shield point ripping a long, deep gash from chest to belly.

Even as its forward momentum carried it over and away from Vartan, the horse screamed and fell. The Hylean warrior was flung from his saddle. Vartan seized his chance. Climbing to his feet, he ran for his sword, retrieved it, and raced back to where Ladon, even then, was staggering to his feet.

Vartan slashed down hard on Ladon's right shoulder, cutting through steel- and leather-jointed pauldrons, attempting to sever the arm from his body. He sliced through muscle and sinew, the momentum of his stroke carrying his sword downward until its tip embedded a few inches in the frozen ground. Yet, when he wrenched the blade free and stumbled backward, Ladon's right arm was still attached.

Worse still, he was even then using that very arm to thrust his sword straight at Vartan. Vartan leaped aside, but it was too late to avoid the oncoming weapon. Sharp steel sliced into his left upper arm. Pain rocketed through him as the sword tip glanced off bone, then plunged through his flesh to the opposite side.

Before he could even suck in a sharp breath, Ladon withdrew the weapon and thrust at him again. This time, Vartan managed to deflect the sword point aimed at the vulnerable spot just above his steel breastplate. The Hylean, however, recovered immediately and slashed downward.

Despite the wrist-to-knee mail hauberk Vartan wore beneath his dark brown padded tunic and steel breastplate, Ladon's blade drove into his upper thigh. The pain was excruciating. Myriad lights danced before Vartan's eyes. For a long, agonizing moment, he thought he might pass out.

As it was, the pain and the sword's downward momentum sent him back to his knees. Before he could recover, Ladon kicked out at his right hand, sending Vartan's sword flying. Next, flipping his weapon in the air, the Hylean grasped the blade with both hands and swung it up, then angled downward. The thick, heavy hilt struck Vartan in the side of his head. Only the leather padding within his steel helmet prevented Ladon from smashing his skull. Nonetheless, it dazed him.

He plummeted forward. His head hit the frozen ground hard, bounced back up, then hit hard again. Everything went black, though from some distant place, Vartan could still hear.

High overhead, in the direction of what he knew must be Astara's walls, he heard cries of dismay, women screaming, men shouting out their despair. He groaned, rolled over, and blinked hard. The blackness held.

Reaching up, Vartan wrenched off his helmet, swiping at the blood he could now feel flowing down his face and into his eyes. Then, from the darkness, freshened pain ripped through him. Something sharp—Ladon's sword—drove through the narrow opening between his breast- and backplate on his right side. The blade's tip plunged through flesh, then metal, pinning him to the ground.

Gasping, gulping for air, Vartan clutched blindly at the weapon now impaling him to the earth. Even as he grappled with it, thrashing wildly for the momentum he needed to rip free, he heard footsteps moving away. Then through the fire in his side, the blood pounding in his head, and the almost deafening clamor that was now part anguished shouts mixed with shrill keening, the footsteps returned.

A booted foot kicked his remaining good arm away from the sword at his side, slamming it outstretched on the ground. Vartan squinted up through the blood and blackness, struggling to see. If it was the last thing he ever did, he wanted—oh, how he wanted!—to look his enemy in the eye. But even that most insignificant of victories wasn't to be his.

Twice more sharp metal drove into him, first through his right wrist, and soon thereafter, through his useless left. He hissed, grinding his teeth to keep from screaming. Tears burned his eyes, as much from the shame and utter, pride-crushing impotence as from the pain.

It was over, then. There was nothing—absolutely nothing—more he could do. Not skewered to the ground like some piece of meat.

"You disappoint me, Karayan," Ladon's voice, thick with contempt, came out of the darkness. "I'd hoped for at least an hour or two of entertainment before I killed you. But now, to exact the full measure of torment, I'm forced instead to leave you writhing on the ground. For a time longer, at least, the sight will provide me with a bit more pleasure."

It was getting hard to hear. The roar overhead kept fading in and out, as did Ladon's voice. He sucked in deep, groaning gulps of air.

"But perhaps that's for the best," his enemy added, chuckling. "This way you'll bleed to death if the cold doesn't take you first, but before either kills you, you'll live to hear us ride past your broken body and enter Astara. We won't, however, take the city quite as peacefully as Feodras promised."

"Feodras gave his word," Vartan moaned, his worst fears stabbing through him to mingle with his bodily torment. "He . . . gave his word!"

"And he kept it, too," the ruthless voice said, "just as he promised, until his dying breath. But his word's no more. I killed him in his tent just before I rode out to meet you. The army's now mine to order as I please."

"Nay!" Vartan cried. "You've your victory over me. Suffice it to take Calandra and leave Astara in peace. I beg . . . I beg you, Ladon!"

"*Beg* now, is it?" Once again, the Hylean chuckled, the sound hollow, pitiless. "If it wasn't more expedient to kill you and be done with it, your begging *would* be a most pleasing consideration—you groveling before me, with my army and your people looking on. Aye, the thought of you crawling to me and kissing my boots is *most* pleasing indeed."

Ladon moved closer, apparently squatting beside him, for Vartan's hair was suddenly ensnared and his head wrenched back. "But then, there are other pleasures equally enjoyable. Such as what I plan to do to your family when I enter Astara. Since you won't be there to see it happen, I'll tell you about it instead."

His fingers tightened until Vartan thought Ladon might rip the hair from his head. "First, though I've not decided yet precisely how I'll do it, I'm going to kill your son. We can't be leaving any spawn of yours alive, can we, to cause future problems? And then, I think I'll take your wife as my personal slave. I hear she's quite lovely, and I've never had an Elfin woman before. I'll also kill your father, and perhaps your mother, too. Hovan will be saved for later, of course, after he's been made to pay for all the inconvenience he's caused me."

"N-nay," Vartan whispered hoarsely, tears now clogging his throat and coursing down his cheeks. This couldn't be happening. Feodras had given his word. But Feodras was now dead. "Mercy, Ladon. Have mercy on them . . ."

"Mercy?" Ladon roared with laughter. "But I thought you knew. I serve Phaon, and there's no mercy in *that* lord's heart. Only death for all who dare stand against him. For you and all your family, Vartan Karayan. For all of Gadiel!"

With that Ladon released him and, in a squeak of leather and clink of metal, rose. "My horse—to me!" he called out, apparently signaling to one of his men. "We've a city to sack and more Karayans to kill. No man, though, will touch this warrior or put an end to his suffering before its time, or he'll answer to me. The Crown Prince's sword and armor are also mine. As are," he added cryptically, "his heart and soul."

"Curse you, Ladon!" Vartan roared, all but strangling on his bitter despair. He twisted and writhed on the ground, attempting to break free of the blades pinning him there. The metal only bit the deeper, cruelly tearing at his flesh until he couldn't endure any more. Oblivion encroached, and he had to stop, gasping in agony.

And then horses—thousands strong—moved forward and, at what seemed the very last second, parted around his ruined body. On and on they came, followed by thousands more foot soldiers. Many of them, Vartan could tell by their characteristic stench and thudding footsteps, were big, dim-witted Gadielean Daegols. He heard Astara's bronze gates scrape open and cried out for them to halt, for them to close. His voice, however, was drowned in the rhythmic, relentless reverberation of the army marching past him.

Desolation engulfed Vartan. He had failed . . . failed to protect Astara. Failed to protect his family. All was now tragedy, death, and destruction.

"Lift your thoughts, Vartan," a soft, sweet voice rose suddenly from the depths of his anguished heart, mingling with the now receding stamp of marching feet. *"Lift your thoughts to Athan and ask Him to help you. Do it for Astara, for your family, if you can't do it for yourself . . ."*

Danae . . . How was it possible? he thought, even as the edges of his consciousness frayed and his mind grew fuzzy and slow. How was it possible that now, in the darkest moment of his life, he remembered her and the words she had spoken just last night, a night that now seemed an eternity ago? And what had he said in reply?

A long moment passed as Vartan struggled to find the words dancing out there, tantalizing him just beyond his reach. Ah . . . aye . . . something about if things came to their bleakest and he had the wherewithal to remember, he would call on Athan for aid.

For the sake of his family, his people, it had seemed as nothing to swallow his pride and all but grovel before a man he despised. For the sake of his family, his people, he would grovel just as gladly before this mythical Athan. He had, after all, nothing left to lose.

"Please," he croaked, fighting with all his might against the onrushing blackness. "Please, Athan. If you truly *are* there . . . if you truly *do* love me as Danae says you do . . . spare my family. Spare my people. Please . . ."

~ ~

As she watched what Vartan and many others on both sides would consider a humiliating defeat, all Danae could see was a brave man taking on an impossible task for the love of his people. A man not afraid to lay down his life for his beliefs or for others.

More than anything Danae had ever wanted, she wanted to be down there on the battlefield with Vartan. Not because she would have been any help, but because she felt so strongly aligned with him and what he was attempting to do in spite of the overwhelming odds against him. He must feel alone down there, but he wasn't. Her heart was with him, even as she stood high above, gripping this wall.

And then nothing mattered anymore. Vartan fell, impaled on Ladon's sword, and next run through with his own sword, and then with Ladon's dagger as well. Tears welled in Danae's eyes, trickled down her cheeks. She had feared it would come to this, even as she had hoped—oh, how she had hoped—that it wouldn't!

"Athan's will be done," she whispered brokenly, even as around her the citizens of Astara screamed out their anguish. At that moment, it was a cry of pain for their hero and Crown Prince. But soon, all too soon, their thoughts would turn to their own welfare. With Vartan's defeat, Astara would soon fall.

Her heart one huge, gaping wound, she looked to where King Haig stood, his face ashen, tears streaming down. Beside him, Vartan's mother and sister clung to each other, weeping. Hovan, however, was nowhere to be seen. And Aelwyd . . . Danae doubted the distraught woman could have pulled herself from her bed if she had wanted to.

A hush fell over the crowd. As one, their gazes riveted below. Ladon, now remounted on a fresh horse, pointed his sword at Astara's gates. King Haig squared his shoulders, then turned to one of his retainers. The man immediately hurried down the parapet walk. Five minutes later, the city gates began to open.

The Hylean army surged forward. For a few panic-stricken minutes, Danae feared they'd trample Vartan, all but spread-eagled before them on the ground. Then, as they reached him, the cavalry, and after them the foot soldiers, parted.

Danae didn't remain long on the wall. Vartan's passing she would mourn in her own time and way, but for now she must turn her thoughts and actions to the living, to her promise that she'd see to the welfare of Vartan's wife and son. It was the last thing she could do for him, to honor him.

Her father would surely be in the forefront of the Hylean army as it entered Astara. The sooner she found him, the better able she'd be to enlist his aid in protecting Korien and Aelwyd.

She reached one of the stone stairways leading down to the road just inside the city's main gate. Below her, a somber-faced crowd blocked the lower steps. Frustration filled Danae. Short of climbing over them, there seemed no means to get close enough to catch her father's attention as he rode by. *If* he were even still alive, she suddenly realized. It *had* been three years, and the dangers of laying siege to a fortress the

51

size of Astara were enormous. What if he were dead? What would she do?

And then Danae saw him riding a few rows behind Ladon. He was dressed in the traditional crested helmet, cuirass, and battle armor, but as befitted his rank, his was far more embellished, glinting with gold and silver. He looked strong and proud, and her heart did a little flip-flop.

"Let me pass," she cried, pushing her way through the others as best she could. "Father! Father! It's Danae!"

At first he seemed not to notice amid the din of hoofbeats and marching soldiers that swallowed all other sounds. But then she saw him pause and glance around as if he had heard her. She redoubled her efforts, jumping up and down, waving her arms over her head.

Finally, from among the milling bodies and strange faces peering down at him, she saw his eyes widen. A joyous smile wreathed his weathered, battle-hardened features. "Danae!" he cried, urging his horse around the others riding by, moving steadily toward her. "Danae!"

With that the people stepped aside, allowing her to descend the stairs. Her father leaned down as she reached him, slipped an arm about her waist, and effortlessly lifted her to sit before him.

"Ah, sweet daughter!" He wrapped his arms around her and bent to kiss her on the cheek. "Are you well? Did these people treat you kindly?"

She returned his hug, then gazed up at his beloved face. How she had missed this good, loving man! If only the price once again to be with him hadn't been so dear . . .

"Aye, Father," Danae replied. "I was well treated. Prince Vartan took me into his home. In time, I became almost like one of his family."

"And how so, Daughter? Did he force you to warm his bed?"

She knew that concern, as well as concern for her safety and welfare, must have preyed heavily on him these past three years. And if she had remained in Calandra's service, knowing what she now knew of Prince Hovan, Danae suspected that such a fate would indeed have been hers. But not with Vartan. Never with him.

"Nay, Father." Remembering the man who lay there, dying or perhaps already dead outside the city, a bittersweet sadness filled her. She sighed and laid her head on her sire's chest. "Prince Vartan is—*was*—an honorable man."

"If he was so kind," he muttered, even as he kneed his horse to pick up its pace and rejoin the rest of the army, "why didn't he set you free long ago? Your people, after all, awaited you just outside his city's gates."

She had wondered that herself for a time, until it no longer mattered. Perhaps Vartan had seen the calming influence she had on Aelwyd, who even then was a few months into her pregnancy and beginning to evidence signs of her mental instability. His first concern, of course, had to be for his wife and unborn child.

Or perhaps Danae's urge to leave Astara had died, bit by bit, as her admiration and then love for Vartan had grown. For a long while now, Danae had come to live each day just for the precious moments in which she could see or be near him. And the times he noticed her and shared even a few kind words with her—for he truly *had* always treated her kindly—had been the best part of each day. Aye, she loved him, as a woman loved a man, even as she accepted that she would never be that kind of woman to him. She loved him because she couldn't help but love him, and was content.

Or perhaps, just perhaps, her acceptance of her time in Astara was Athan's work instead. Before she had come to the royal city, Danae had never known of the All-Merciful, Eternal One. Perhaps it was Athan who, in the end, had called her to this place in order to find Him. Whatever the reason, Danae knew her stay in Astara had been a life-changing event. Difficult but life-changing, and she was glad for it.

"It doesn't matter anymore," she said, as the memory of Vartan's request to see to his family's welfare once more filled her mind. "What does matter is we assure the safety of Prince Vartan's wife and son. Will King Feodras truly keep his word that no harm will come to any of Astara's citizens?"

Her father grimaced. "Aye, he would *if* he lived. But just before Ladon rode out to face Prince Karayan, one of the royal retainers found the king dead in his tent."

"How?" she whispered, a terrible premonition flooding her. "How did he die?"

"No one knows. There was no mark of any kind on him, no wound. Rumor has it, though, that Ladon was one of the last to see him."

Ladon. It seemed his hand was on everything of late, and none of it boded well for House Karayan.

"I promised Prince Vartan I'd see to the safety of his wife and son, Father." She looked up at him. "Will you help me in that?"

He wouldn't meet her gaze. "If Ladon means to take his revenge on them, there is nothing anyone can do to stop him. They most assuredly are doomed."

Frustration—and a rising sense of unease—filled her. "If everyone gives up before they even try, then of course no one will *ever* stop Ladon! He'll have won without ever lifting a finger."

"Nay, Danae. You don't understand. You haven't seen what I've seen these three years . . ." He swallowed hard, a haunted expression creeping into his eyes. "Stay clear of him, Daughter. Obey me in this. All I want is to finish this sad, misbegotten quest and return home, never to soldier again. And isn't that what you want, as well? To return to the green hills of Icelos and live again in peace and simplicity?

Icelos . . . home . . . It seemed like another lifetime now. And why not? Vartan was gone. Her duties to his family would soon be at an end. In but a short while more, there'd be nothing left for her here.

But first she must fulfill her promise. It was the last thing she could do for the brave man who had touched her life in so many ways. Because she was a woman and must stay behind when warriors rode out to fight, didn't mean she failed to put as high a price on honor as they did.

"Aye, Father," Danae replied. "I want to go home." *But only,* she added silently, *after I've seen to Aelwyd and Korien's well-being.*

Ladon had killed enough today. It was past time he be stopped. The dilemma was, if a man the likes of Vartan Karayan had failed in the attempt to stop him, what could *she* possibly do?

ꙮ ꙮ

They found the Hylean champion high up on the city's parapet walkway. In his hands he held a squirming, screaming child. For an instant frozen in time, Danae stood rooted to the spot, horror sucking the strength from her limbs and the breath from her lungs. Then blessed air surged in.

"Nay!" she cried, finally finding her voice. She rushed forward, aware of nothing save that Ladon had Korien and she must rescue the little boy. Rushed forward, past soldiers and palace servants clustered in miserable little groups, only to have her arm jerked back, almost dragging her off balance.

"I told you to stay clear of him, Daughter!" her father said, pulling her close to whisper harshly in her ear. "The child is doomed. You'll only seal your own fate if you try to interfere."

"Then so be it," she whispered back, turning to him. "But I'll not stand by and watch—"

Before she could utter another word, her father tugged her even farther away, encircling her body with one arm, while with the other he clamped a hand over her mouth.

"I haven't found you again to lose you over the likes of some ill-fated Astarians," he snarled. He paused to glance over his shoulder. "Rope! I need rope and a cloth to gag her if she refuses to obey," he called softly to a soldier standing nearby. "Fetch them for me!"

At his words, all the fight drained from Danae. Her father was still a powerful man, his muscles honed by years of battle and living in the saddle. There was no hope of escaping him. Even if she did, she knew he'd but catch her, then bind and gag her. Yet to stand helplessly by and not lift a finger to save Korien . . .

Tears once more filled her eyes, but this time they were tears of shame and frustration. Danae gripped her sire's hand and wrenched it from her mouth. "Father, please! I promised . . . I have to try."

"Karayan was wrong to ask such a thing of you. Selfish and wrong. But then, what did he care? Your life was a fair enough trade for that of his family."

"N-nay," she said on a sob. "It wasn't like that. *He* wasn't like th-that."

"Well, it doesn't matter anymore how he was or wasn't," her father growled, his voice gone ruthless and hard. "He's dead, and I mean for you to survive the day. So obey me in this, Daughter. Obey me, or I'll have you taken away."

Leave or stay. Neither choice was acceptable. *Oh, Vartan . . . Vartan . . . I'm sorry. So sorry . . .*

And then the time for decisions was past. A dark, shuttered expression on his face, Ladon turned slowly, held Korien out by one of his little arms, and dangled him over the parapet wall. Aelwyd, standing but a few feet away in the grip of a Hylean soldier, shrieked and, hands extended, strained to reach her child.

In that moment, when time seemed sickeningly to slow, Vartan's father strode forward to confront the Hylean champion. "Have mercy on the child," he said. "He is innocent. If you must punish someone, punish me. I am to blame, not the child."

"Aye, that you are, old man." With his free hand, Ladon reached out, grasped King Haig by the neck, and squeezed hard. Haig's eyes bulged. As the air was inexorably choked from him, he grabbed at his enemy's hand, fighting to free himself. It was to no avail.

Queen Takouhi screamed and ran toward the two men, but she was immediately caught by another soldier and pulled back. Tears streaming from her eyes, she watched helplessly as her husband turned red, then purple, and was slowly strangled. Finally, when Haig slumped limply in Ladon's powerful grasp, the Hylean warrior released him. The old man plummeted to the stone floor and lay there, unmoving.

Takouhi somehow managed to break free. She dashed to her husband and gathered him in her arms. Rocking him to and fro, the old woman looked heavenward and began the ritual keening for the dead.

As the eerie, wordless sounds filled the air, everyone present, Ladon included, watched as if mesmerized. Then, with an amused shake of his head, the Hylean turned once more to dangle Korien over the parapet wall. An expression of pure malevolence spread across his face, and with a simple opening of his hand, he released the sobbing child.

Aelwyd screeched. With what must have been a superhuman surge of strength, she broke loose from the man holding her. Arms outstretched, she raced toward her child. Her forward momentum was so great, however, that she didn't stop when she reached the parapet wall.

Whether by accident or intent, Aelwyd sailed over the wall and downward, all the while screaming Korien's name. Screaming and screaming until, finally, she screamed no more. Takouhi ceased her keening. Not a soul moved.

Ladon stood there for a long, tension-laden moment, impassively gazing at the ground below. Then, a smirk on his lips, he turned. "Well, save for the conveniently unavailable Prince Hovan, I think the male line of House Karayan is now quite extinct. Time to enjoy the fruits of our labors, wouldn't you say?"

With that he strode off, followed by all his men save one. After a few seconds more, Danae's father released her.

She whirled around, fury blazing in her eyes. "Are you happy now?" she demanded hoarsely. "Are you satisfied?"

"Nay, I'm neither happy *nor* satisfied," he said through gritted teeth, his face gone pale. "But there was nothing any of us could do. *Nothing*. You have to believe me, Daughter. There is nothing *anyone* can do against Ladon."

"Perhaps not." She swallowed hard against the lump forming in her throat. "But better to have tried, to have defied him and died like Prince Vartan, than to stand here like cowards. And that's what all of us are, Father. Cowards."

"But cowards who live to see another day." He reached for her, but she backed away. Pain twisted his face. "Come,

Daughter. Soon you'll forget all this. Once we're back home in Icelos, you'll forget."

"Nay, I won't." Shaking her head, Danaë continued to back away. "I won't, for I won't be returning with you to Hylas."

"Where will you go then, if not home?" He gave a sharp laugh and gestured about him. "There's nothing for you here. Indeed, once we leave these shores, these people may well turn on you in revenge. You won't be safe here, Daughter."

And what did personal safety matter at a time like this? When she had failed Vartan?

An intense weariness flooded Danaë, leaving her drained . . . hopeless . . . defeated. He was right. There was nowhere for her to go, no sanctuary where she'd ever find release from the memory of this day's terrible events. Yet Danaë also knew she couldn't return to Hylas, much less ever call herself a Hylean again.

On this most wretched of days, her life had once more spun on its axis and irretrievably changed. What direction she must next take she didn't know. That was in Athan's hands. Athan who, for some unfathomable reason, had permitted this tragedy to unfold . . .

With a strangled sob, Danaë sank to her knees and buried her face in her hands. Her father was right. There was nothing more she could do here. Nothing.

4

Something—some sound or perhaps just the day's events still preying on her mind—woke Danae that night from a deep, dreamless slumber. She had taken to her room early, as much from emotional as from physical exhaustion, though sleep hadn't come quickly enough to provide the surcease she so desperately sought. Part of it, she knew, was the pandemonium down in the city below the palace, the din of looting, the clamor of terrified people, the noise of wood splintering and objects shattering. Occasionally as the wind shifted, Danae also caught the acrid scent of smoke.

She knew she was safe enough up here in the palace. Ladon and his officers, after all, had wasted no time seizing it as their headquarters. Safe enough, at least, as long as that Hylean warrior was kept occupied with other activities. Perhaps safe enough forever. Ladon now had his pick of all the women in Astara—women who included the newly widowed Calandra. In spite of her father's worries to the contrary, likely that brutish warrior had no further interest in some callow girl. Danae could only count that a blessing.

As she lay there in the darkness, she was nonetheless glad she had locked her bedchamber door. Though once again under her father's protection, the world as she had known it—

The sound came again. This time, Danae recognized it as a light tapping on the wooden shutters of the room's only window. She rose, wrapped a handwoven woolen blanket about her, and crept to where the heavy draperies held out the winter cold. Parting them, Danae leaned close to the shutters.

"Who is it?" she called out softly.

"Hurry, Danae. Let me in," came a low but distinctly feminine voice. "It's Zagiri."

Quivering with excitement, Danae shoved the draperies aside and unlatched the shutters. Zagiri scrambled inside.

"What are you doing here?" Danae demanded as soon as the shutters were once again locked and the draperies drawn. "When I didn't see you up on the city wall, I hoped you'd found some way to escape. If Ladon discovers you're still in Astara . . ."

"All the more reason we flee this place as soon as possible." Vartan's sister hesitated, then hugged Danae tightly. "I heard . . . heard what happened to Father, Aelwyd, and Korien. Oh, Danae, how could even a man like Ladon so callously kill that little boy?"

Danae wrapped her arms about Zagiri. "Because Korien was Vartan's son, and for some reason, Ladon has always hated Vartan." She swallowed hard, dreading the next bit of news she must deliver. "Your mother's dead, too. Afterward, on the way to the dungeons, she managed to grab one of the soldier's daggers and stab herself. She bled to death right there in the palace's entry hall."

Zagiri inhaled a shaky breath. "Aye, I'd heard that, too. Poor mother . . ." For a long moment, she looked away and didn't speak. Then she turned back, hastily swiping away her tears. "Yet one m-more reason to leave A-Astara," she said, her voice still unsteady. "No family is left to keep me here—to keep *us* here."

"What of Hovan?"

"Hovan?" She gave a snort of disgust. "He never even waited to see how Vartan fared. I don't know where he slunk off to, but I'd wager he found some way to escape Astara. Otherwise, Ladon would've found him by now."

"Aye, you're most likely right."

"Pack up your things, but take only what you absolutely need, and we'll be off." Zagiri released Danae and stepped back. "I've a pony cart waiting down by that old gate near the granary, and after we retrieve Vartan, we've a long night's travel ahead."

Retrieve Vartan? Danae's heart skipped a beat. "But Vartan's dead, Zagiri. *If* he's even still out there on the plains. By now, Ladon may well have sent someone to bring in his body."

"Oh, he's still out there." The other woman smiled grimly. "I overheard some soldiers talking about it. Seems Ladon plans to leave my brother impaled on the ground for all to see, until he finally becomes carrion for the scavengers. Even in death, Ladon intends to dishonor Vartan."

"But if we take Vartan," Danae said, warming to the idea, "we'll have thwarted at least some of Ladon's plans. Then we can bury Vartan where Ladon will never find him. Until the day Astara is won back from that soulless brute. Until the day Vartan can be returned for the hero's burial he deserves."

"Precisely." His sister looked Danae in the eye. "So, are you with me, sweet friend? Will you answer Athan's call?"

Is this *the direction my life must next take?* Danae wondered. *Is* this, then, *Athan's will?*

"I have one last prophecy to share with you . . ." Unbidden, Zagiri's words filtered into her mind. *"What if Athan asks you to do differently . . . Will you, too, refuse Him?"*

Nay, she would never refuse Athan, but Vartan was dead. There now wasn't any possibility he had ever been the fabled Guardian spoken of in the Prophecy. And, despite Zagiri's earlier assurances to the contrary, Danae hadn't been able to aid him, not even in turning him to Athan.

Yet Zagiri had also taught her there were times when blind faith was all Athan required, and one had but to allow Him to lead wherever He wished. Times to set out blindly, trustingly, into the darkness.

She dragged in a deep breath. "So do you think Athan's calling me to join you?"

"I don't think, Danae. I know."

"Then so be it. There's nothing left for me here anymore, either."

☙ ❧

It didn't take Danae long to pack the few things worth taking. A few changes of clothes, the cochashell comb Aelwyd had given her, and her mother's cherished necklace—a costly midnight blue zagat stone surrounded by equally valuable but smaller, dark red biries—were gathered in a small bundle. In addition, she took only her lyra in a separate cloth bag. In the ongoing chaos of looting and pillaging, it was a surprisingly easy thing to cross through the city to the granary gate where an elderly man awaited them.

He promptly led out a big, dappled gray pony hitched to a long wooden cart. In it were a bed of straw and several blankets and large, thick furs.

"Take care, m'lady," he said as he helped Zagiri up onto the seat. "Not all of Ladon's army are safely inside the city walls, you know."

"It'll be all right, Mesrob." Zagiri turned in the seat to glance back at Danae, who had thrown in her bundle and lyra and climbed into the back of the wagon. "Athan's with us."

"Glad to hear He's looking out for someone, then," the old man muttered as he slid the bolt on the small door in the city's wall. "He's certainly been no friend this day to Astara *or* the rest of your family."

"So it would seem, but in time, who knows?" She slapped the reins over the pony's back, and the animal started forward. "Have faith, old friend. Someday, Astara will be ours again."

With that, they departed the city. The night was bitterly cold. With the clouds all but occluding the moon, it was as black as the depths of some bottomless pit. Danae shivered and pulled one of the furs up over her. They'd be fortunate indeed if they managed to find Vartan in this darkness.

Surprisingly though, Zagiri headed straight for him. The moon peeked fleetingly around a cloud, and silver light glinted off the blades of the two swords and dagger still pinning Vartan to the ground. He lay there unmoving, covered in blood, his eyes closed, his face relaxed now in peace.

Tears stung Danae's eyes. For a moment she couldn't move. It had been hard enough to watch his brutal defeat from the city walls. It was quite another thing to be so close now that only a few steps separated them. She feared if she touched him, after all that had transpired today, she'd finally shatter into a million tiny pieces.

Zagiri wrapped the reins around the wagon's brake arm and climbed down. "Come, Danae. We daren't linger here overlong. I fear it'll be hard enough freeing those blades, much less carrying Vartan to the cart."

Her friend's words jolted Danae into action. She flung aside the fur, grabbed up a blanket, and scooted from the

64

cart. Steeling herself not to think about what she was doing or who the man was lying there, Danae gripped the blade imbedded in Vartan's left wrist and worked to pull it free. Then she turned to his right wrist. Once the tips were liberated of their earthly sheaths, they came out easily. Zagiri had more difficulty extracting the sword in Vartan's side, and it eventually took their combined effort to do so.

"Remove his cuirass," the older woman then said, tossing both swords into the cart. "And his pauldrons, vambraces, and greaves. He'll be heavy enough with that chain mail still on, but we can't spare the time to get that off him as well."

As Danae kneeled to unbuckle the armor and Zagiri backed the cart as close to where her brother lay as she could, the clouds once more swept over the moon. In nearly total darkness, they rolled Vartan onto the blanket and dragged him to the back of the cart. It took them several attempts, and just as many halts to catch their breath, before they finally muscled him up into the little wagon.

"Cover him," Zagiri tossed over her shoulder as she headed back to where Vartan's armor lay. "If we happen on some Hyleans, I don't want them to see him."

As if we could hide a man as big as Vartan Karayan for long, Danae thought, but chose not to mention that. She tossed several blankets over him, then the furs. By then Zagiri was loading what remained of Vartan's body armor, as well as his shield, sword, and helmet, into the back corner of the cart.

"Why must we take all of that along?" Danae asked. "He won't be needing it anymore."

"Perhaps not, but it was Vartan's. Not to mention," she added as she climbed back up on the pony cart seat, "I don't want Ladon or his filthy minions getting their hands on it. It's the royal armor and shouldn't fall into enemy hands."

As her friend unwound the reins from the brake arm, Danae hurriedly climbed into the cart. With Vartan and all his armor in the back, there wasn't much room left. She found herself sitting far too close to him.

"Zagiri, perhaps I should ride up front with you," she said. "The armor—"

"Stay with him, Danae. Hold him," Zagiri's plea rose from the darkness. Then she clucked to the pony, and he set out briskly. "Pray for him. Pray to Athan with all your heart."

Confusion—and no small amount of revulsion—filled her. Hold a dead man, though that man was once someone she had loved? "It's too late to pray for Vartan," she said by way of protest. "He's gone, Zagiri. Gone."

"We can't know that. My brother was a powerful man. There may yet be a tiny spark of life left in him. And, until that spark dies, we can yet pray for Vartan, for his soul. Won't you do that one last thing for him, Danae?"

If she truly thought there might be life left in Vartan, Danae would've done that and gladly. But he was so limp, so cold. She jerked back her hand from where she had momentarily touched the side of his face. Her gut churned, and she had to swallow hard against the bile that rose in her throat. She couldn't do it. She just couldn't!

"Hold him. Pray for him. Pray to Athan with all your heart."

The cart swayed with a hypnotic cadence. The night wind whistled and careened around her. And then the clouds parted once more, and a brief flash of moonlight bathed the winter-stripped land.

She saw Vartan, saw his bruised, blood-streaked face, his strong mouth, his handsome visage, striking even in death. An aching tenderness, a bittersweet longing, filled her. Had it

66

been just last night they had sat together on that porch high up in the city, and she had clasped him to her in comfort? In the depths of her anguish for his pain, she had never been so happy, holding him for an all too brief, glorious time in her arms.

Danae had never thought to hold him again, yet the opportunity was once more, for one last time, hers. It wasn't enough, would never be, but she'd seize it nonetheless. She had thought there was nothing more she could do for Vartan, but she had been wrong. There was yet one thing more.

Lifting the furs and blankets, Danae crept up next to him. With a sigh, she cradled his poor, battered body close to hers, shut her eyes, and began to pray.

Dawn brought Danae back to a disorienting wakefulness. A rhythmic swaying combined with a disconcerting thudding beneath her ear left her confused, then frightened. Where was she? What had happened to bring her to this unfamiliar place?

Then remembrance returned of Zagiri's nocturnal visit, their escape from Astara, and their rescue of Vartan. Vartan, the fallen hero, whom she now lay beside, her head on his chest. A chest that rose and fell and, she suddenly realized, contained a beating heart.

A beating heart!

But it couldn't be! Her own pulse accelerating, Danae levered herself to one elbow and flipped back the blankets and furs. She stared down at Vartan. His features were still relaxed in that serene look she had taken for death, but his color had returned, and his skin, when she hesitantly touched it, was warm.

Her glance lowered to his chest. It moved now with slow, even breaths. Once more, she pressed her ear to his heart and was rewarded with a strong, powerful beat.

"Z-Zagiri . . ." Danae could barely choke out the word. "Vartan . . . Vartan's alive!"

Her friend wheeled about on the cart seat and stared down at her. "What are you talking about?" Her gaze dropped, took in her brother, and gradually her expression of surprise transformed into one of joy. "Athan be praised! He has answered our prayers, Danae. He has saved Vartan. Saved him to fulfill the Prophecy!"

Danae was tempted to object that Vartan's life was of more import than the fulfillment of some dubious prophecy, but she decided against it. After what Zagiri had so recently endured—her home overtaken and almost her entire family slaughtered—Danae supposed she couldn't fault her for clinging to the hope of Karayan retribution and a return to power.

"Aye, Athan be praised," she murmured in reply. Then she suddenly gasped as she noticed the blood coating the hand with which she had clung to Vartan in her sleep. The blood was fresh and still wet.

"He's bleeding, Zagiri!"

"See where it's coming from!" his sister cried. She surveyed the road ahead and signaled the pony to a fast trot. "We're not far from the friend I'm hoping will take us in. See if you can staunch the flow!"

Danae leaned over Vartan and found blood oozing from his right side at the site of one of the sword thrusts. He also lay in a puddle of blood. She bit her lip, thinking hard and fast. The wound would likely need cautery to stop the bleeding, but for that they needed a fire and iron.

She looked around her. A good-sized river about five miles south of them ran down from the mountains, meandering through tall, spreading turkawood trees lining its banks. To her left rose steep-sided cliffs that offered no haven for a pony and cart. To her right, lush, fertile plains descended gradually to the distant sea. In summer they obviously were a sprawl of hayfields and pastures for the bovine, meat-producing ashta-raks. There were few places to hide on either side, if and when Ladon discovered Vartan's disappearance and sent out riders to track them.

They needed to put as much distance as possible between themselves and Astara, and as quickly as possible. Unless there was no other option, they didn't dare stop. In the meanwhile, if it were possible, she must find a way to keep Vartan from bleeding to death.

Grabbing the cloth bundle she had stuffed her belongings into last night, Danae pulled out a clean undershift. She tore it into several large pieces and then, folding one piece into a fist-sized pad, she pushed it through the slash in Vartan's chain mail and pressed the cloth against his wound. Crimson fluid soon stained the bandage, and Danae was forced to place another piece over it. She pressed against the wound as hard as she could and was finally rewarded with a slowing, then cessation, of the bleeding.

"Having any success?" Zagiri inquired, keeping her gaze riveted straight ahead.

"Aye, I think so." With one hand, Danae loosened the belt about Vartan's waist and shoved it up a few inches to hold the pads in place. She refastened it only snugly enough to maintain a constant pressure. She then proceeded to examine Vartan's other wounds.

His thigh wound was long but only an inch or so deep, and it appeared to have clotted. She covered it with another piece of her undershift, tucking the edges inside the slash in his woolen hose. His wrist and left upper arm wounds also oozed, but a snug wrapping several times around each of them seemed to halt the bleeding. The rest of his body bore an assortment of minor cuts that required no immediate care.

"How much farther until we reach your friend?" Danae asked as she drew the blankets and furs back up around Vartan. Though the sun was rising over the mountains and promised a far more pleasant day than the past few, it was still quite cold. The sooner they got Vartan out of the weather, the better.

"Voshie lives about three miles past the Sarab River. There's a ferry. It's the only way across or, leastwise, the only way across for a pony cart. You know how to swim, don't you?"

Danae rolled her eyes. "I was hoping to ride the ferry. Or am I supposed to dive in and pull us across?"

"Nay." Her friend laughed. "I was just asking in case of an emergency. There should be a ferryman to pole us to the other side."

"That's encouraging." Danae paused to lift the coverings and check Vartan's side. There was no further sign of bleeding. "So, how do you know this Voshie, considering she lives a good distance from Astara?" she asked as she once again tucked the coverings around Vartan.

"Voshie's a widow whose two sons are now grown and live elsewhere, with families of their own. I met her through her sister, Amma Serpuhi. She's a holy woman, an *amma* whom I spent some time with about five years ago. Serpuhi lives in the wilds of a high mountain valley nearly fifty miles from the village where Voshie resides. I initially planned for us to go all the way to Serpuhi's, but now for Vartan's sake I think we had best stop a while at Voshie's."

An *amma* . . . Danae had heard of these special women. They were spiritual mentors seasoned in the ascetical way, led by Athan to live in solitude. This was the first time, however, Zagiri had even made mention of having experienced such a life herself.

"It must have been hard," Danae said, "to live in such peace and seclusion—I mean— and then return to life at Court."

"Aye, it was." Zagiri shot a quick glance at Danae, then her brother. "It near to ripped out my heart to leave Amma Serpuhi, but Athan wished it. For me, my place of service was to Astara and, it now seems, to my brother."

"Do you think he'll live?" Tenderly Danae brushed Vartan's cheek, shadowed now with a day's growth of prickly beard. "Already, it seems a miracle he has even survived, but that wound in his side is grievous. And I fear Ladon will soon come after us."

"Aye, it *is* a miracle. And most likely we'll need a few more miracles if Vartan is to live to fulfill the Prophecy. But then, that's in Athan's hands. All we can do is try our best to discern His will and obey."

Danae had thought she accepted Vartan's death as Athan's will. But now, with Vartan back among the living, Danae didn't know how she'd fare if she lost him again. If that *were* Athan's will, could she accept it once more with grace and love? She wasn't so sure that she could.

For the time being, such a consideration existed only in the realm of possibilities. The odds were certainly against him, but all they could do was deal with the here and now. That was task enough for anyone.

Danae looked ahead to where the turkawood trees drew ever nearer. *One step at a time, Eternal One,* she thought. *The rest is in Your hands. Only help me always to know and do Your will. Even if, in the doing, You must once more take Vartan from me.*

71

"By the everlasting fires!" Ladon roared that morning, pacing back and forth in the palace's high-ceilinged, gaudily painted reception room. "Who *dared* touch the prince? I want the person responsible brought back alive, do you hear me? Alive!"

To a man, the group of officers standing before him visibly quailed. Satisfaction filled Ladon. They'd waste no time in ferreting out the presumptuous fool who had taken Karayan's body. And body it surely was by now, after lying out there all night in the bitter cold.

Still, he needed proof. Phaon wouldn't settle for anything less than the Astarian prince's moldering corpse. Ladon had enough explaining to do already about how and why Prince Hovan had slipped through his net. Though his officers assured him Hovan was still most certainly somewhere inside the city, that no one could've possibly escaped, Ladon wasn't convinced. It almost seemed as if something—or Someone—conspired to thwart him.

Well, he *still* had accomplished a good amount of work. King Haig was dead, as were the Crown Prince and his squalling spawn. Only Hovan still lived in defiance of the Dark Lord's command. And it wasn't as if that sniveling adulterer, after all, was of any real concern. Vartan had been the only true threat.

Ladon turned to eye his officers for a sharp, assessing moment. They'd not fail him. They'd not dare. Still, they were only human.

Best he boost his chances of finding Vartan Karayan before someone had opportunity to bury his body, hiding it forever from demonic eyes. Best he send out a cadre of Fiends and Yigols.

One way or another, he'd soon have a body to bring to Phaon. It was only a matter of time.

As they neared a tiny, thatch-roofed, peat-stacked cottage that lay on the farthest outskirts of a small village, Danae could see dark storm clouds building in the distance behind them. Even here, the wind had already picked up in intensity, dashing wildly about to buffet the cart and set the barren tree limbs to rattling. The temperature was also dropping rapidly. Snow—and lots of it—would likely soon be in the offing.

Danae tucked the furs more snugly about Vartan. He slept peacefully on, whether from exhaustion or unconsciousness she had yet to ascertain, but either way he didn't suffer. She only hoped he'd not waken until after they had seen to his injuries, especially if the wounds still required cautery.

Zagiri reined in the pony about ten feet from the cottage and turned to Danae. "Give me a moment while I speak with Voshie. Though I don't doubt she'll take us in, in fairness I must warn her of the grave danger of doing so."

"For myself, I ask nothing," Danae said. "But if we don't get Vartan out of this storm and care for his wounds . . ."

An anguished look in her eyes, Zagiri nodded and climbed down from the cart. "I know. He's Astara's—and Gadiel's—only hope, after all. Not to mention," she added with a wan smile, "he's my big brother."

"My prayers go with you, Zagiri."

Zagiri nodded and headed toward the cottage's front door. Before she could even lift her hand to knock, the door opened and a plump, gray-haired woman stepped out. She immediately hugged Zagiri, and for a long moment, the two women stood there together. Then Zagiri released her and stepped back.

As she talked, the other woman listened intently, nodding a few times, and finally glanced in the wagon's direction. As she caught Danae's eye, Danae managed a smile. *Please Athan,* she prayed. *Let her take us in. Please.*

Then the woman said a few more words to Zagiri and went inside, shutting the door. Danae's heart sank.

Vartan's sister hurried over. "Voshie wants us to take the cart around to the back door. It's more secluded there, and no one will see us bring Vartan in that way. And, as Voshie said, the fewer folk who know of our presence here, the better."

Relief flooded Danae. *Thank you, Athan!* She grinned. "Aye, the better for all of us, I'd say."

Just then Vartan stirred, and a low moan escaped him. Danae looked to Zagiri. "He may be beginning to waken. We must hurry."

His sister climbed up into the cart and took her seat. "Aye." She signaled the pony forward.

As they reached the back of the cottage and halted, the first big, fat snowflakes began to fall. Danae glanced up into a sky that had turned dark and ominous. They hadn't arrived any too soon.

But that, she was beginning to realize, seemed to be Athan's way. He provided just what they needed, just when they needed it.

5

Through a haze of pain and a throbbing headache, Vartan came slowly back to consciousness. For a brief, horrible moment, he thought he must have died and passed through to an afterlife he had never believed in—going straight to a place of torment. What had Zagiri called it—the Abyss? The Nether Realm?

It was most definitely a place of suffering, if the way his body felt was any indication. And, he added, blinking his eyes, it was black. Black as the darkest night, black as the heart of the man who had put him here.

He tried to push himself up, but excruciating pain stabbed through his side. He sucked in a sharp breath, fell back. Then, gritting his teeth, he tried again—just as unsuccessfully.

"By the stone of Calidor!" he groaned, cursing his weakness.

"Oh!"

Vartan froze. He heard movement nearby. Someone else was here with him in the darkness. Slowly, he turned his head in the direction of the voice.

"Who . . . who are you?" He sounded rusty, his throat raw and dry. "And why is everything . . . everything so black?"

"V-Vartan?"

The voice—definitely a feminine one—moved nearer. She smelled of fresh hay and clover. And it almost sounded . . . sounded like—

"Danae?"

"Aye, Vartan. It's Danae."

Confusion filled him. Why would a girl as sweet and kind as Danae have joined him in the Nether Realm? It made no sense.

She came close and, as if she might be sweeping her hand in front of his face, he felt air move. For some reason, it irritated him.

"What are you doing?" When no reply was forthcoming, he ground his teeth. "Danae? Are you there?"

"Aye, Vartan. I'm here. Can't you see me?"

Her question caught him up short. Well, of course he couldn't see her! Surely they were in some dungeon, or a deep, subterranean cavern, or—

"Can *you* see *me*?"

"It's morning, Vartan. Of course I can see you."

Suddenly, he was aware of other sounds. A fire—peat by the scent of it—crackling somewhere, perhaps in another room. A ruminant, horned tur bleating indignantly, then the murmur of another feminine voice, from her tone, gently reproving. The creak of wagon wheels moving away far in the distance.

He swallowed hard, his thoughts racing back to the day of the battle. Ladon . . . striking him hard with his sword hilt . . . His head hitting the ground with a stunning intensity, then bouncing up to hit it hard again . . . Everything had gone black after that, though he had still remained conscious. Conscious enough to hear Astara's gates open, Ladon's army march past him.

Conscious enough to recall the Hylean's threat to kill—

Terror exploded within him. "My family!" he cried hoarsely. "Korien, Aelwyd! My parents, brother, and sister! How did they fare, Danae? Where are they?"

"No one knows what became of Hovan. And Zagiri, why, she's just outside, helping our friend Voshie milk the turs."

"And the others? What of the rest of my family?"

She laid a hand on his arm. "Rest, Vartan. Time enough to speak of all that, once you've regained your strength."

"Nay!" He twisted his arm to grab her wrist. "Tell me now, Danae. *Now!*"

"Pl-please, Vartan."

He thought he heard a catch in her voice. His grip tightened. "Tell me, Danae, and be done with it," he said, even as he fought the tendrils of dread wrapping themselves about his heart. "It won't get better with the waiting. Tell me, please."

"I-I failed you," she whispered. "I couldn't protect them, and Ladon killed your father, then dr-dropped Korien from the city walls. Aelwyd tried to save Korien, falling to her death after him. And your mother"—she choked back a sob—"in her despair, your mother killed herself."

With each word that slipped from Danae's lips, Vartan felt as if he were being stabbed anew. He released her arm. Ignoring the pain, he rolled away, drawing up his legs. It was too much. He clutched his arms about himself. Too much.

Nearly all his family was dead. He, though, had somehow survived, only to become a helpless, impotently blind man. And Astara . . . he well knew what had become of Astara.

He had indeed arrived in the Nether Realm, and he hadn't even had to die to get there. Phaon, the Dark Lord, hadn't been the one to bring him to this, though. It had been Athan. Athan . . . the God he had called upon in his last moments of consciousness. Athan, curse Him. Ah, curse Him!

"Vartan?"

Danae's soft voice pierced the smothering fog of his anguish. An irrational rage filled him. For a few seconds, he battled with his need to strike out, if only verbally, at her. Finally, however, reason returned. It wasn't her fault.

"What do you want, Danae?"

"Would you like me to stay with you? Or to fetch Zagiri?"

And what good would that do? he wanted to shout at her. But it wasn't her fault. *It wasn't her fault!*

"Nay. Just leave me. I need some time alone."

"But Vartan—"

"Please, Danae! Pl-please . . ."

As the tears rolled down his cheeks and sobs began to wrack his body, she rose and ran from the room. And, in the blackness that was now his life, Vartan wept until he could weep no more.

❧ ❧

He must have finally cried himself into exhaustion, Danae realized, tiptoeing back into Vartan's room an hour later. He lay there, his back to her and arms clasped before him, his breath now slow and steady with the rhythm of sleep.

Tears filled her eyes. It was all so unfair. By some miracle he had returned to life, only to be crippled in one of the worst ways imaginable. Or, leastwise, one of the worst ways *he* could ever imagine. Vartan had always been a man of action. Blinded, he'd never be so again.

She desperately wanted to go to him, take him in her arms, and exchange his heart of pain for one of peace. But nothing could do that, nothing save time and Athan's healing.

A hand settled on her shoulder. "Come," Zagiri whispered. "Let him be for now."

Danae sighed, then turned from him. She followed her friend into the main living area. Fresh snowflakes dusting her hair, Voshie sat warming herself on one of the two benches placed near the fire. At Danae's entry, she glanced up and smiled.

"How fares the young prince?"

"Physically, he seems on the mend. But his heart . . ." Fresh tears swelled, and with an angry motion, Danae swept them away. "I fear . . . I fear that even if his wounds don't kill him, the loss of his family will. Especially . . . especially the loss of his little s-son!"

"Now, now, sweet one." Zagiri wrapped an arm about her shoulders and led her to the other bench placed before the fire. "Sit."

Guiding her movements, Zagiri pressed her onto the bench, then took a seat beside her. Sobbing uncontrollably, Danae crept close, burying her face on the other woman's chest. For a time Zagiri said nothing, only holding Danae tightly to her.

Finally, though, as Danae came to an end of her weeping, Vartan's sister began to stroke her hair. "We've all suffered grievously in the past days. *All* our lives have changed forever. But you and I have gone on, and so, in time, will my brother."

Danae lifted her head. "How can you be so certain? He's at the limits of his strength, holding on now by sheer courage alone. And you weren't there to see the look on his face when I told him about K-Korien."

"Nay, I wasn't, and I'm glad of it, too." A fierce determination blazed in Zagiri's eyes. "We both have our work cut out for us. You're to be the comforter, the one Vartan can turn to and find solace for his ravaged heart. And I must be the

79

little burr beneath his saddle, pricking and prodding at him to live to fight another day."

She paused, a speculative light in her eyes. "I'm thinking, though, when it comes to getting him to eat and caring for his wounds—which both need to be done soon, by the way—it's best you approach him. In his current state of mind, he'll flat out refuse me. He's thinking, I'm sure, to simply starve himself to death, if his wounds don't fester so that infection kills him first. You on the other hand . . . suffice it to say my brother has a soft spot in his heart for you. As much as he may wish to die, he'll not so easily deny anything you ask of him."

Though she wasn't as certain as Zagiri seemed to be that Vartan would listen to her any more than he would his sister, for the first time since she had discovered he still lived, Danae felt hope stir in her breast. "Truly, Zagiri? Do you think it possible that, between the two of us, we can turn Vartan around?"

"He has a tender heart, but he's strong in every way that matters. And, with Athan's help, he'll rise from this even stronger than before. He must, after all, or he'll never vanquish Ladon and drive the evil from the land."

For some reason, Zagiri's words failed to comfort Danae. In fact, she was sick to death of hearing her harp on that cursed Prophecy. She reared back, glaring at the other woman.

"And do you know how tired I am of hearing that? With all that's been heaped on Vartan of late, why do you persist in mouthing further plans for him, and all he still has to do to . . . to save the land and confront Ladon yet again? Hasn't he suffered enough? Hasn't he *done* enough? Or won't you be satisfied until Vartan's finally and truly dead?"

Instead of a return flare of anger, or even one of pained surprise, Zagiri gazed back at her with compassion and understanding. It only made Danae the madder.

"He's your brother, Zagiri!" she cried, scooting away from her. "Can't you, for just one moment, have some pity on him? Allow him a time to grieve and heal before you begin pushing him down that supposedly preordained path you've determined he must tread?"

"The path was never preordained by me, Danae," her friend replied softly, "but by Athan. As are all our paths."

"A-aye, but *we* know and love Athan. Vartan doesn't. After what has happened, I wonder now if he ever will. Just give him some time, Zagiri. That's all I ask. He doesn't need that cursed prophecy, or Athan, shoved down his throat right now."

"As if any of us can force another to come to Athan. Faith is a gift, Danae. A gift from Athan to His children. You know that."

She hung her head. "Aye, I know. I just don't want us to add to Vartan's suffering, that's all."

"And we won't." Zagiri reached out to take Danae's hand. "But Vartan also needs hope, something to cling to until he's ready to learn more. We must never fail to offer him hope."

Hope . . . Danae's lips lifted in a weak smile. What had Vartan said that night, high up on that porch overlooking the land? *"Astara's future and the continuation of the Karayan line . . . give me my hope . . . What else is there?"*

He had told her he was a practical man, that he didn't chase after unattainable dreams and illusions. He just took what he had and did the best he could with it.

But he, just as she had warned, had now lost his strength and had become, with his blindness, as a helpless babe. All his former attributes were now as nothing.

Hope . . . Aye, no man—or woman—could long live without it. But Vartan had also vowed he'd never let himself become as a helpless babe. For a man such as he, that was surely to lose all hope. And he had told her he would die rather than let that happen.

❧ ❧

He could hear the women talking in the other room. Though their voices were low, Vartan couldn't help but overhear snatches of their conversation. Enough, at least, to realize they were talking about him.

Most likely, especially knowing his sister, they were plotting how to cheer him up. He sighed. In most cases, family and friends were a blessing. In this case, he just wished they'd leave him alone. He didn't want to be cheered up. He just wanted to die and be done with it.

It was only a matter of time until Ladon and his minions caught up with them. Danae, Zagiri, and even this kind woman who had taken them in would then pay dearly. Far better that he died and relieved them of that danger. Once he was gone, Danae and Zagiri could move on. Once he was gone, hopefully Ladon would finally be satisfied.

Didn't the women realize he was no good to anyone anymore? That he was nothing but a useless weight about their necks, a burden that would only drag them down to their destruction? He had failed enough people already. He didn't want their deaths on his conscience as well.

If only he could just go to sleep and never wake up. If only some dagger was near at hand. But even if it were, he couldn't see to find it. Vartan dragged in a deep, despairing breath. He was condemned to a living death, and helpless to do anything about it.

"Oh . . . good. You're awake."

82

Wonderful, Vartan thought. *I've fallen so low that I can't even tell when someone has crept up on me.*

"So, Danae," he snarled. "Have you taken to spying on me now?"

She sucked in an indignant breath. "I was doing no such thing! Your wounds need care, and I just thought to see if you'd yet awakened."

"Well, I'm awake and my wounds don't need care. So you can just leave me alone."

Danae paused, and Vartan could almost hear the wheels spinning in her head. "Go, Danae," he ground out, purposely making his voice sound harsh and unfriendly. "I meant what I said. I don't want you to take care of my wounds, not now, and not ever."

Instead of being intimidated as he had hoped, she strode over to stand beside him.

"And why's that? Do you doubt my abilities to properly care for you? Because if you do, you've no cause for fear. Growing up as I did without a mother, I cut my teeth nursing many a warrior in my father's army. I know what I'm doing, Vartan Karayan."

He could just imagine her standing there before him, her hands fisted on her hips, glaring down at him in righteous indignation. He wouldn't win this battle, no matter how hard he tried. He hadn't the strength, at any rate, for a prolonged debate.

"Fine," he muttered. "Do what you want. I don't care."

"Then, until you do care," she said, her voice gentling, "I'll do the caring for the both of us. Just give me a moment. I need to fetch the supplies."

Aye, do that, Danae, Vartan thought sourly as he heard her hurry from the room. *Just have a care for your heart. I'm not worth your time or effort. I'm not worth saving, and the sooner you admit that, the better it'll be for you.*

Unbidden, memories of Korien, of Aelwyd of the midnight hair and equally black temperament, flooded him. Of his father and his sweet, gentle mother. At least they had all died quickly. His fate, however, might not be so swift or merciful.

If only, oh, if only, he could simply will himself to die!

"Take it away, Danae. I'm not hungry."

Later that evening, Vartan found himself yet again fighting back angry words. He knew Danae wanted only to help him. Still, as he lay there propped up on several pillows, he was just as determined as she. He had no appetite and saw no reason to continue to support a body that was now all but useless. Setting his lips in a tight line, he stared up at her with sightless resolve.

She expelled what he knew must be an exasperated breath. "You need to eat to regain your strength, not to mention to help your wounds heal. And it's only a bit of broth, Vartan. It'll taste good."

"I told you, Danae. I don't want anything to eat."

"Well, they say you can always tell when a man's starting to feel better," his sister's voice rose suddenly to Danae's right. "That's when they turn stubborn and ungrateful."

Vartan glared at where he imagined Zagiri to be. "I'm not ungrateful. Can't either of you women get it into your heads that I just want to be left alone?"

"Left alone to do what, Brother? Curl up into a little ball and die? I'd have thought better than that of you, Vartan Karayan. You'd never have allowed any of us to do such a thing."

Though he was loath to speak harshly to Danae, Vartan had no qualms about telling his sister exactly what he thought. "Danae?"

"Aye, Vartan?"

"Would you be so kind as to leave Zagiri and me alone? And close the door behind you, if you would?"

"Er, there's no door to this room, Vartan."

He clenched his teeth and drew in a sharp breath. "Then would you just leave us alone, please?"

"You must be very angry," Zagiri said when it was evident Danae had finally departed. "You always did become exceedingly polite and precise when you were mad."

"I don't need you lecturing me, Zagiri, especially not in front of others." He tried to sit up even farther, but pressing down on his wounded wrists sent spikes of pain up his arms, so he gave up the attempt. Besides, if the truth were told, his whole body felt weak and flaccid.

"Well, then, don't refuse to cooperate when others are trying to help you." She pulled over a chair and sat. "We didn't drag you back from death's door, you know, to let you now finish what Ladon began. Not to mention risking our lives and Voshie's as well, in the doing."

"You should've left me there," he muttered, averting his gaze. "I'm of no use to anyone, not anymore."

"Why? Because you're blind?"

"Why else?" Leave it to Zagiri to be painfully blunt.

"And is that the true sum of you, then? Your eyes?"

"No one will follow a blind man," Vartan growled. "A blind man makes for a pretty pathetic warrior."

"Athan makes all things possible, Brother." Zagiri's voice lowered, went softer. "And already His hand is on your life. You're the first man who has ever survived a battle with Ladon. You've escaped his clutches, and now, after what Ladon did to you, you've become even more the man described in the Prophecy."

"Don't speak to me of that cursed Prophecy!" he cried. "It isn't about me!"

"Once, you believed it was."

"Aye, when we were still children. But as I came into manhood and realized there was no Athan, much less His so-called murdered Son, I saw the Prophecy for what it was—just part of some pointless, pathetic fairy tales."

"Yet, more and more you personify that hero. Perhaps it was a fear of the Prophecy's terrible purchase price that turned you from it—and Athan—as much as your purported lack of belief in His existence. It would frighten any man, Vartan. But only the true hero—the Guardian—would embrace it nonetheless."

"And do *what*, Zagiri?"

"I don't know, Brother. That has yet to be revealed." By the rustle of her robe, he knew she had leaned forward. "But think on this: The Prophecy speaks of the Guardian returning in desperate times, when evil roams freely over the land—the Land of Gadiel. And if such desperate times aren't upon us now, with the fall of Astara and with Ladon in power, I don't know how it could get much worse. Think on that, Brother. Think on that and then tell me you'd rather lie there and die. You, who are our last and greatest hope."

She rose to her feet. "I'll have Danae keep the broth warm, in case you somehow manage to find your appetite." Without another word, his sister left the room.

Vartan lay there for a long while, frustrated and seething, one instant battling his despair, the other, flailing out against the tiny ember of hope his sister's words had fanned back to life. He didn't believe—or want to believe—in some higher being who ruled his life. He had always been fiercely proud of his independence. He was no pawn to be toyed with, then callously cast aside, ever reliant on some god's mercurial whims.

Always before, he had controlled his own fate, made his own decisions, be they wise or foolish. But they were *his* decisions, *his* choices, *his* life. And he had always, always known who and what he was. To now give his life and will over to the control of some mysterious being would be the end of him, leastwise of the man he had always known himself to be. All Vartan could be sure of was he'd no longer be Vartan. And that certainty did indeed terrify him.

Still, he ached to avenge his family. Never to see that bright-eyed little boy of his again or watch him grow into the man he deserved to become . . . Vartan closed his eyes against their sudden sting. And his mother and father . . . and Aelwyd. Ladon must be punished. He must!

But how? *How?*

The chance he'd ever again regain his sight, much less the ability to wield a sword against Ladon, was so close to non-existent that even to hope was ludicrous. Still, there was the remote possibility someone else would rise to take vengeance on Ladon. As hard as it would be to cede that privilege to another, there would still be some victory in living to witness it.

But only if he lived.

Vartan dragged in a resolute breath. He needed time to heal. His survival so far had been nearly a miracle. Perhaps the eventual return of his sight might be one, too. All he could do was live one day at a time, until his new path in life became clear. Though he refused to believe in Athan or the Prophecy, he did believe in fate.

"Danae? Are you there?" he called out, gritting his teeth against the stabbing pain that any effort elicited.

Before he could gather breath to call out again, she was at the doorway. "Aye, Vartan? What do you need?"

"A bowl of that broth, if you will. My appetite has returned."

◒ ◓

In the next several days, as a fierce snowstorm blew across the entire region of Vardenis, Vartan grew steadily stronger. He soon progressed from sitting up in bed to short stays in a chair, then to taking brief walks about the cottage. Every new endeavor, however, reminded him not only of the terrible insults his body had suffered, but of his utter dependence on others for almost everything he did.

His inability to see, with the resultant need to be led around, was the greatest humiliation he had ever endured. He hated having to ask for assistance, having to be directed how and where to take nearly every step. He, who had not long ago commanded others, was now forced meekly to obey.

Though Vartan ate what was placed before him, permitted his wounds to be cared for without protest, and moved about only under guidance, he still fought a bitter battle with his despair. He spoke only when spoken to, preferring the company of his own dark thoughts. Zagiri finally threw up her hands and most times left him alone. Danae, however, seemed incapable of giving up on him.

He both hated and cherished her for it.

Sometime in the wee hours of the seventh morn, as he lay in bed thinking of her, Vartan gradually became aware that the winds had died. The storm was passing at last. Would that the storms of his own life come so swiftly to an end. But that, most likely, was not to be. His wounds were healing; his strength was returning. Indeed, he wondered wryly, what else *could* he do, with such determined nurses as Danae and his sister?

"Ah, good. You're awake."

"Zagiri!" Vartan expelled an exasperated breath. "Will you please stop sneaking up on me?"

"One would think your hearing would've started to improve by now. That's what happens with the blind, isn't it? The other senses are supposed to sharpen?"

He bit back a sarcastic comment about her lack of tact, deciding the effort would be wasted. "Aye, I suppose they are—over time. I've been blind barely a week now, you know. But you'll be the first one I'll inform, once my hearing improves."

"Well, you'll have to work on that while we're on the road. We're leaving here. Now."

"What?" Awkwardly, Vartan shoved up in bed. "Why?"

"For one thing, the storm has passed, and it's already beginning to warm. Though it's yet a few hours until dawn, once the sun's out the snow will melt. We need to make as much time as we can, while our tracks will disappear with the melting snow. Once the ground clears, they'll become engraved in the mud for all to see. And, for another"—her voice took on an odd tone—"some of Ladon's underlings are on their way."

"How do you know this?" Though he had feared the time would come when the Hyleans would begin to scour the land for him, Vartan had attempted to put it from his mind. "Surely even his scouts couldn't have made it this far. The storm has only just ended."

"I had a dream," his sister said. "A voice told me we *must* leave. That to tarry here a moment longer would be to put your life in jeopardy."

"Oh, is that all? Another dream?"

"Aye, another dream. A dream I intend to take very seriously."

"Fine. It matters not to me whether I go or stay. You'll soon discover, however, what a burden it'll be for two women to drag along a man who can be of absolutely no help to them."

"Oh, Vartan!" Zagiri sighed. "Just try and not go out of your way *purposely* to make things any more difficult, will you? The rest, we're already prepared to handle."

Remorse filled him. "I'm sorry. I didn't mean it that way. I suppose I was just feeling sorry for myself again."

She walked over and laid a hand on his shoulder. "I know it's hard for you. You've always been the one to take care of everyone else. But there's nothing wrong with allowing others to care for you when you need it. You only honor Danae and me, you know, by entrusting us with the task. By trusting us to protect you."

He closed his eyes. "I *do* trust you and Danae. I just don't want to be the cause of your deaths."

"There you go again, Brother, feeling sorry for yourself and taking the burden of the entire world back onto your shoulders." She knelt and clasped his face between her two hands. "So I'll say this once, and never forget it. You didn't cause anyone's death. Instead, you did your utmost to try to prevent them. But you were betrayed. Ladon lied. Feodras failed you. And, as great a man as you are, Vartan, you're only a man. Whether you want to accept it or not, this time you're going to need divine help to overcome and triumph."

He managed a lopsided grin. "You were doing well until you mentioned the divine help."

Zagiri chuckled and released his face. "Well, then, we're making progress, aren't we? Who would've thought you'd ever accept being told you were just a man?"

"Failure, where one has never failed, can change a lot of things."

"Aye," she said, her tone sobering. "Just remember, Brother. Out of seeming failure can come great victory, and out of death, new life."

"Another one of your religious proverbs?"

"And why not? It's past time you began to listen—and learn."

6

"If you imagine I'm *ever* going to wed that preening, bloated toad, you're as big a fool as our father when he thought, in the first place, to name you my matchmaker!"

Schooling his rising exasperation behind a mask of wounded incredulity, Ra'id Abd Al'Alim calmly stared back at the young woman who so defiantly challenged him. "Now Sharifah, calling Musa Ben Ja'far a bloated toad isn't only unkind, but also a gross exaggeration. He's just a bit short and plump, that's all."

She gave a snort of disgust. "Easy for you to say, Brother. But then, you'd not be the one he takes to his bed!"

"Nay, thank the Blessed Waters for that. Still, it'd be a very comfortable bed," Ra'id said, grinning in an attempt to charm his sister toward his view of things. "Musa is one of the wealthiest Desert warlords among all the Diya al Din tribes, after all. And he's taken quite a fancy to you."

"Aye, as have all the other potential husbands you've tried to foist on me these past two years." Sharifah tossed her shoulder-length mane of jet-black hair. "One just wonders if their fondness isn't based primarily on my value as Prince Kamal's only daughter, than on any of my personal attributes."

Ra'id laughed. Striding over to an etched bronze tray set upon crisscrossed, carved rafawood legs, he took up a delicately curved silver flask by its handle. "Care for some wine?" he asked, lifting the container high.

Full, rose pink lips twisted in a mockery of a smile. "Trying to get me drunk so I'll sign Musa's marriage contract? If so, I must be winning this battle."

"Your singular determination to refuse each and every man I bring to you is beginning to wear thin, Sister dear." Ra'id grimaced and set the flask back on the tray. If he was to win this battle, he needed all his wits about him too. "You know your duty. Sooner or later, you're going to have to do it."

"Aye, as are you, Brother. You are, after all, Father's heir. But I don't see you rushing to stand beneath the marriage canopy and speak any bond vows."

Sharifah strolled to a low couch filled with vibrantly colored pillows and sat, lounging back only after taking great care to spread her fine, crimson silk gown about her. Her damask overrobe, threaded with gold and black, matched the sheen of her hair. With her honey-colored eyes, a pert, pretty nose, delicately oval face, and lithe and sensuous figure, even Ra'id wasn't blind to the effect his sister had on men. She was fast acquiring a reputation, though, that was seriously diminishing the pool of suitors eligible to ask for her hand.

"First things first," he finally replied. "Before I wed, Father wants his daughter safely in a husband's care, and that's how it must be."

"Well, then you may never wed, Brother dear, for I've yet to find any Desert lord worthy of my hand. And I refuse to bind myself for life to anyone I don't respect or love."

"Love?" Ra'id choked back a laugh. "And since when have *you* gone all soft and romantic? You, who'd just as soon slit a man's throat as kiss him?"

She shot him a disgruntled look. "I only slit the throats of our enemies." At her brother's sudden arch of an ebony brow, she quickly amended that. "Well, I suppose there were a *few* ill-chosen suitors whom I did cut up a bit. But only because they presumed liberties I hadn't allowed them."

"Sharifah—"

"I deserve the same right as you to choose my bond mate!" she cried, sitting up. "I deserve the same right to be happy. Are you determined to deny me that, Ra'id?"

"I'd never deny you your chance at happiness. That isn't my intent." He sighed. "Still, this matter must be settled, and soon. Father grows impatient with the both of us."

"So, he's back to questioning your fitness to rule, is he?" Sympathy gleamed in her striking eyes. "I'm sorry, Brother. I wouldn't add to the conflict between you if I could avoid it. Truly, I wouldn't. But I must also follow—"

A servant flung open the door to the sitting room. "M'lord. M'lady. The Hakeem requests your immediate presence."

Sharifah looked to Ra'id, who even then was heading her way. In a swish of silk and damask, she rose from the couch. Ra'id joined her, holding out his arm. She took it, and they walked from the room, heading down the covered outside corridor that spanned all four sides of a large, inner courtyard garden.

Their father, the Hakeem, awaited them in the library. As soon as the thick doors had closed and they were alone, he strode toward them, holding out a small roll of parchment. From its size and appearance, Ra'id could tell the missive had been sent from one of their spies via a trained messenger hawk.

"It's over then," Prince Kamal said. "Astara has fallen. The Usurper and his sons are either dead or missing. The Crown Prince's wife and young son have also been murdered, and the Usurper's queen has taken her own life." He smiled. "It seems, in one fell swoop, the Karayan line has been all but eliminated."

"Al'Alim be praised," Ra'id said, using the Desert term for the Omniscient, All-Knowing Creator. "At long last, our house will regain its rightful place as ruler of Astara and Gadiel."

"We may first have to wrest it from the Hyleans," his father muttered. "And rumor has it their champion is a formidable warrior."

"Then perhaps it's time to gather all the warlords and prepare for battle. The sooner we attack, the better our chances."

"Aye." The Hakeem nodded. "I appoint you my emissary. Set out on the morrow. You have, after all, twelve tribes and twelve warlords to win over, which, in itself, will be the greatest test yet of your future fitness to rule. And, as you say, the sooner we attack, the better."

They were well into the foothills of the Valan Mountains before the sun edged past the tallest peaks of the coastal range. There were, according to Zagiri, two more ranges—the middle and tallest range, known as the Spine of Athan, and the easternmost range—the Ibn Khaldun or Son of the Eternal. Since this furthermost range of mountains was on the Desert side and was considered Diya al Din territory, it had long been spoken of in their language. It was also, Zagiri informed her, named in Desert tongue for Eisa.

As the morning drew on and the sun shone full and strong, even the rising altitude and once again dropping temperatures did little to dampen Danae's spirits. The storm had left a sparkling blanket of white all about them, setting off the dense, drooping branches of the evergreen bedrosian trees and deep gray rocks and crags to perfection. The air was cool, crisp, and clean. Vartan was alive; they were safe, and hope for the future swelled in her breast. Surely Athan, whose mighty hand had created this beautiful day and stunning wilderness of stone, would ever be at their side.

She glanced over her shoulder to where Vartan sat in the back of the cart. Besides his armor, which Voshie had promised to hide in some nearby cave, they had left behind most of his old clothes. His battle tunic had been irreparable at any rate, and wearing it would have set him apart and drawn undue attention, so Voshie had altered some of her late husband's garments to fit Vartan. He now wore a long-sleeved tunic of coarse, dark green wool over his black, patched woolen hose and tur-hide boots. A nondescript gray-brown, hooded cloak completed his dress.

An errant breeze ruffled his dark hair, blowing a lock briefly across his beard-shadowed face, but he seemed not to notice. As if deep in thought, his gaze was fixed somewhere off in the distance, a distance he could no longer see.

Danae's heart swelled with longing. He was so heartbreakingly beautiful, she thought, admiring the strong clean line of his jaw, the proud lift of his well-formed head, his unmistakable aura of virility. Even blind, Vartan was more man than most of his sighted brothers. Or leastwise, she reflected with a wry smile, he seemed so to her.

She must content herself, however, with remaining near and aiding him in whatever way he might need. Though Vartan was now a widower and a prince without a kingdom, he was and would always be far above her in breeding and position. There was no hope of there ever being anything more between them. Still, there were times, like just now, when the sight of him filled her with such love, such yearning . . .

"Is he doing all right?"

Danae whirled around. "What?"

"You seemed to be staring at my brother for an inordinate amount of time," Zagiri said, "and I began to wonder if there wasn't something wrong with him."

Warmth flooded Danae's cheeks. She straightened on the seat to stare directly ahead. "There's nothing wrong with him. Nothing at all."

"Nay, I suppose not, in your eyes." The other woman chuckled. "In his sister's view, however . . ."

"You never said where we were headed," Danae muttered, deciding it was past time to change the subject. "Are we simply trying to put as much distance between us and Ladon as fast as possible, or do you have a specific destination in mind?"

"Both, actually." Zagiri pointed toward the north and east. "About three days' journey in that direction is the Goreme Valley. My friend, Amma Serpuhi, lives in the rocky cliffs there, in a cell hollowed out from the mountainside. That's where we're going."

"She lives in the side of a mountain? How . . . how primitive. And she lives alone, didn't you say?"

"Aye. Serpuhi lives alone but within a day's journey of other *ammas* and *abbas*. The Goreme's a narrow but very long valley, and is the perfect place to go alone to seek Athan."

"And why are we heading there, rather than trying to find sanctuary with some of Vartan's allies? If Ladon finds us in that valley, there'll be little chance of escape."

Zagiri shot her an amused glance. "Well, for one thing, the Karayans *have* no allies. The other peoples of Gadiel made that quite clear when they refused to come to our aid against Feodras and his army. And, for another, the Goreme Valley is a holy place, one of the few left in Gadiel, and just as famous as Sevan House on Mount Talin. *Such* a holy place that no evil or evildoers dare enter."

Danae frowned. "I've heard of Mount Talin—that's where the Dragonmaids are said to live with their dragons—but I've never heard of Sevan House."

"Blessed Metsamor, one of the most holy of men and instrumental in propagating the Faith in Gadiel, founded Sevan House more than seven hundred and fifty years ago. It was a place where holy women joined together in vowed community for prayer and works of peace. Then the dark times came, when first heresy, then schism, and finally a resurgence of the old pagan religions began to undermine the Faith. Outright attacks followed, and the holy houses, as beacons of Eisa's hope and love, were some of the first places destroyed. Yet Sevan House still remains, despite the loss of all the other houses that sprang from its pious example."

"Because it was a holy place? And what did you mean when you said no evil or evildoers dare enter a holy place?"

Fleetingly, Zagiri glanced at her. "Aye, because it was such a holy place. Though in time the sisterhood died off when no further candidates were permitted to join, it's still and always will be a holy place. Athan was so pleased with the lives of the women of Sevan House that He blessed the spot for all time. Blessed it so that even Phaon and his evil minions—be they human or inhuman—simply cannot enter."

"How sad the work of those holy women died out with them," Danae murmured. "Perhaps someday, though, new holy women will be permitted to worship in Sevan House."

"Aye, but for the time being, any who now wish to consecrate themselves to Athan must either defy the law and take to the hermetical life or become a Dragonmaid."

"A Dragonmaid?" Her interest piqued, Danae turned to Vartan's sister.

Zagiri grinned. "Didn't you know? The Dragonmaids are a loose form of a holy sisterhood. And it's said a sacred portal—

invisible save to the Dragonmaids and their dragons—actually lies somewhere in the vicinity of Sevan House. They come and go through it to their secret lair, which Serpuhi once told me is called Sanctuary. It's also said only the pure of heart can ever use that portal. Hence the Dragonmaids have lived in peace and safety all these many hundreds of years. Evil can't enter to threaten them there either."

"If that sacred—and secret—portal is in a holy spot," Danae said, "it sounds like an even safer place to take Vartan than the Goreme Valley."

"Oh, aye, and wouldn't that be a thought?" His sister laughed. "First and foremost, they don't take kindly to men in their midst. The Dragonmaids are all vowed virgins, bound to their dragons for life. The presence of males would only . . . only contaminate the purity of their existence. Even if we *were* able to get Vartan through their portal—which we can't—it wouldn't go well for him there."

"So they hate men, do they?"

"Nay, I wouldn't say they hate men. They just find them a nuisance and a decided distraction to the practice of their own form of spiritual life. So they don't allow them, which keeps it all very nice and simple."

"But they serve Athan?"

"That's what I've always heard. I've never met a Dragonmaid or been through their portal, after all."

"I think I'd like to someday." Danae chewed on her lower lip, then nodded. "Aye, I'd like to meet a Dragonmaid and see her dragon. I've always thought dragons were very beautiful and special creatures."

Zagiri laughed. "Well, have a care for that curiosity of yours. Dragons have sharp teeth, long claws, and breathe fire at the most inopportune times. Nor do they like strangers, be they male *or* female."

"Then I suppose I'll have to content myself with admiring them from afar."

"Aye, that you will, my friend, epsecially since we're not heading anywhere near the vicinity of Mount Talin on this particular trip."

Just before sunset, in the deep folds of a protruding cliff, they made camp high up on the lofty heights of some nameless peak. Though Voshie had provided ample rations for the three-day journey and no cooking fire was needed, the bone-numbing cold that slowly encroached with the retreating sun all but demanded a warming fire. After unpacking the cart, getting Vartan settled, and gathering bits of dead wood dropped from the bedrosian trees, they soon had a brisk fire burning.

Zagiri then excused herself to find a private meditation spot somewhere outside. Danae chose to stay with Vartan. She hung a small iron pot over the fire to boil water for salma, then took out her lyra to play for a while. The bronze strings felt good, familiar, beneath her fingers. The sweet sounds soothed her and, after a time, she even began to sing.

All the while, Vartan said nothing, only sat there staring stonily ahead. When steam began to waft from the heating water, Danae put away her lyra.

"You've been extremely quiet today," she ventured as she spooned some of the spiced salma powder into two cups.

Vartan's lips quirked, but he didn't look her way. "Aye. My thoughts were occupied with considering my options, what few I have left at any rate."

"What sort of options?"

"Now, don't get all tense and anxious," he replied, turning toward her. "For the time being at least, I've set aside further thoughts of suicide. I was but considering what useful—and honorable—ways I could still continue to be of service to Gadiel."

"Oh, I see." Danae couldn't help the relief that flooded her voice. "And did you come up with any ideas?"

He sighed and shook his head. "Nay, I did not. Every way I turned, I hit an impregnable wall. Blind, I'm unable to fight, so any hope of returning to Vardenis and rallying my remaining people is out of the question. Loyal though they might be, how could I lead them? And, though the other peoples of Gadiel have strong leaders of their own, they'll never join with me to regain the royal city of Astara and drive Ladon and his forces from the land."

"What happened, Vartan, to create such a tragic severing of the peoples of Gadiel?"

"It goes back a long while." He paused to rub his unshaven jaw. "Do I look any different with this beard growing in? Enough to disguise who I really am?"

"Well, not yet." Danae cocked her head, examining him. "Perhaps in time, though, when your hair and beard get longer. And then if we added an eye patch to lend you a more rakish, piratical look . . ."

Vartan chuckled. "Why not two eye patches, one for each eye? Since I can't see anyway."

There was pain beneath his attempt at humor, but at least he seemed slowly to be coming to some kind of acceptance of his blindness. She was glad for that.

"That's a thought to consider. In the meantime, though," she said, directing the conversation back to his options, "would you mind telling me what caused the terrible divisions between your people?"

"You ask a difficult thing. Karayans were, after all, responsible for a lot of the hard feelings and distrust."

"Oh, I didn't know. I beg pardon for—"

He held up a hand. "I'll tell you, Danae. It's common enough knowledge, after all." Vartan paused, dragged in a long, deep breath, then began. "May as well begin with the easiest tale to tell. The break with the Elves of Greenwald was my fault. Myrddin, High King of the Elves, was a good friend. I destroyed our friendship, however, when I fell in love with his daughter Aelwyd. As kindly as he could, Myrddin took me aside and warned me of the grave danger to an Elf woman who wed a human man. He explained why there was such a firm proscription against such unions, and why he, too, must forbid us marrying.

"In those days, though, there was such fire between Aelwyd and me. A fire neither of us could—or wanted to—resist. And I, in my youthful arrogance, imagined we'd be the exception."

Danae couldn't help a wistful smile. "But don't all lovers imagine their love can surmount every obstacle?"

"Most likely, but we were wrong, and Aelwyd paid the price for my proud, selfish nature." Vartan swallowed hard. "You saw how it was. Though never my intent, I all but destroyed the woman I loved."

What could she say to ease the anguish burning now in his sightless eyes? Vartan hadn't meant to harm Aelwyd, but just loving her had done that for him. Yet if the same decision had been hers, would she have forfeited the few glorious years he and Aelwyd had had, before the Elf woman had become pregnant with his child and set the whole, tragic sequence of her decline into motion?

"It was her choice as well as yours," Danae finally replied. "And Aelwyd thought you worth the risk."

"Aye, I suppose she did, at least in the beginning. *I*, though, should've made the right decision for the both of us. *I* should've heeded Myrddin's warning and walked away."

Danae sighed. "You're quick to take the responsibility of the world on your shoulders."

"Aye, perhaps so. In the end, though, I *was* the reason the Elves turned against the Karayans." His lips lifted in a mocking smile. "So you see, when it comes to women, Hovan isn't the only fool."

She bit her tongue rather than utter the unkind opinion she had of Vartan's brother. And Vartan was wrong to compare his own tragic marriage with the damage that Hovan had wrought. But Danae also knew it was useless to point that out just now. Vartan was still deep in mourning.

"That explains the rift with the Elves," she said instead, as she added a couple spoonfuls of rich kelavi clover honey to the cups. "What of the other peoples?"

He shrugged. "The Dwarves have always been a greedy, suspicious lot. Though they were once our most loyal liege men, it didn't take much to set them against us. The falling-out happened a few hundred years ago and involved mineral rights in one of the mountains in the Spine of Athan. We came out as the victors of that altercation, but that was the end of our alliance with the Dwarves.

"The Rune Lords of the North have never been in the Alliance, though we were, for a time, supposedly friends. I'm not certain what happened with them. That split occurred even farther back, perhaps four or five hundred years ago. And the Diya al Din . . ."

Vartan's mouth tightened. "They didn't take kindly to the Karayans seizing the throne of Astara and the kingship of Gadiel from them. When King Tiridates II, King Hakob's son, died without legitimate male heirs, a dispute over the crown arose between his two daughters. One had wed into the Al'Alim royal family of the Diya al Din, and one had wed a highly placed Karayan noble. The Karayans prevailed in that altercation as well, and that was the end of any friendship with the Desert tribes."

"So, now that it's evident why you can't expect any support from allies," Danae said, pouring steaming water into the two cups and stirring them, "and why you've seemingly hit an impregnable wall, what are you planning to do next? Since I've never known you to be a hesitant or indecisive man."

Vartan gave a harsh laugh. "Well, *this* time you will. As hard as it is to admit, I honestly don't know what to do."

Danae took his hand, placed a cup of salma in it, and watched as he took a careful sip of the hot beverage. "Has it ever entered your mind," she then asked, "that perhaps, just perhaps, the reason you're running into walls is because all the options you've heretofore considered are no longer the right ones for you?" She knew she was treading once more in dangerous waters, but Vartan had to begin to face Athan and His plan for him. "That perhaps you need to look elsewhere, or at least view things from a different perspective?"

He scowled over the top of his cup. "And would that place and perspective perhaps have something to do with that god of yours? It won't ever happen, Danae! Not ever!"

"But why, Vartan?" She set aside her own cup and scooted over until she could lay a hand on his arm. "Why are you so adamantly against turning to Athan? You weren't even this vehement the night before the battle, when I asked you to call on Him for help."

"Because I *did* call on him, and he *didn't* listen!" Vartan turned a pain-ravaged face to her. "After Ladon had impaled me on the ground, he told me what he planned to do to my family. And as Astara's gates opened and the Hylean army marched around me, I thought of what you'd said about asking your god for help. I groveled before him, *begging* him to spare my family and my people, Danae! Just that, and nothing more. And he did nothing, absolutely nothing!"

"He spared your life."

"But I didn't ask him for that!" Vartan set his own cup aside. "Is that the trick, then? Ask him for what you *don't* want, and then you'll get it?"

His confusion and anguish seared right through her. What could she say, when *she* didn't even understand why Athan sometimes did what He did? That was so much a matter of faith, and Vartan was nowhere near ready to hear that.

She took his hand, squeezed it gently. "I don't know why He did what He did, Vartan. Better, I think, to ask not why Athan didn't answer your prayers and give you what you wanted, but rather why He left you alive. What does He still want of you, and how can you best serve Him? *That*, you can do something about. The rest is in Athan's hands."

He muttered something foul and furious beneath his breath. "I don't care what your Athan wants, *if* he even truly exists!" he finally ground out. "Besides, I'm no more use to him blind and in exile than I am to anyone else."

"And why is that? Because you can't settle for doing anything less than what's grand and glorious? As you've always done before?"

She could feel Vartan tense, the muscles and sinews in his arm shorten and bunch. She knew she had struck a sensitive spot with her question, perhaps even reopened a barely healed wound. Danae loathed goading him further, even as she suddenly realized the small opening might be the pathway into his heart. Sometimes, after all, suffering was the surest road to Athan.

"The path to Athan isn't for the proud," she said softly. "Only the humble of heart can find their way—and only after they recognize and accept their utter dependency on Him. It's what Eisa taught during His time on this earth, Vartan. That without Him and His Father, Athan, we can do nothing."

"I'm not very good at playing weak and helpless, Danae."

"Oh, but this isn't weak and helpless at all!" Excitement filled her, and she lifted a quick, fervent prayer for the right words. "It's the hardest thing you'll ever do in your life. It demands all the strength and courage you possess. But the reward, to draw ever closer to the source of all Goodness and Love and be transformed into the person you were always created to be . . ." she said, a fierce joy flooding her, "well, in the end, it's the most grand and glorious quest of all. In the end, it's the only honor and purpose in life that truly matters."

She didn't want to answer Ladon's summons, but knew she must. Phaon was now her liege lord and, for as long as Ladon had need of her, Phaon had bound her and her sorceress powers to the Hylean warrior. Still, as Ankine drew up before Ladon's bedchamber door that night, it was all she could do to choke back her hatred and revulsion. Phaon had commanded her to aid the Hylean in the takeover of Gadiel. So far, all Ladon had used her for was to warm his bed.

For a fleeting instant, Ankine wondered if Phaon realized how miserably Ladon squandered her true talents, then thought the better of questioning it. Phaon hated her for what she had once been, for *Whose* she had once been. Further pain and degradation only bound her to him the more.

Her knock was answered with a harshly impatient "Enter!" She grasped the handle engraved with intricately carved roses, pushed it down, and opened the door. Instead of awaiting her in bed, for a change the big, blond Hylean was sprawled in a chair before the hearth fire. His feet were bare, but he was clad in black hose and an open, black silk shirt. He swirled a golden cup of some liquid in his hand.

His cold, dark gaze met hers, sending a chill streaking down into the core of her being. She steeled herself for what was to come, closed the door, and strode forward. He'd not see her disgust or fear, or any reaction whatsoever. He never had. He never would. She had little left to be proud of, but she would always have that.

"Come closer, my flame-haired beauty," Ladon said, his voice rough with desire. "I've great need of you this night."

"Aye, m'lord," Ankine murmured as she drew up before him. "How may I serve you?"

His gaze raked her from head to toe. He licked his lips, then sighed. "You tempt me, you do, but this night I've more need of your sorceress powers than of your body. You're to find me a man—a man who was mine, then was taken from me. I want you to return him to me."

Her relief almost made her dizzy. Fetch a man? Nothing could be simpler.

"Who is this man, m'lord? And where can I find him?"

"His name's Vartan Karayan." Ladon's face contorted with a sudden, surprising fury. "And as to where to find him, why, that's your task, of course."

Vartan Karayan had been the crown prince of Astara. Though Ankine had never met the man, she knew now why Ladon wanted him. Someone had stolen his body right out from beneath the Hylean's nose, and Ladon didn't like that.

She almost smiled in satisfaction, but didn't dare. Not while Ladon still had dominion over her. But someday . . . someday she'd repay him for his brutality. In the blink of an eye, she'd shrivel the man to a pile of ash. Indeed, she counted on Phaon giving her leave to do so, when her liege lord was finally done with him.

In the meanwhile, she was still Ladon's to command. "As you wish, m'lord." Ankine bowed and turned to go.

"Wait. There's more."

She halted, swung back to him. "Aye, m'lord?"

"I sent some of Phaon's demons to sniff out what had become of Karayan," he said, his glance straying to the leaping tongues of flame in the hearth. "They discovered he lives and is under the protection of his holy witch of a sister. Hence, I must now send *you* to fetch him."

None of the demons, be they lesser or greater, could get near a holy *amma* or *abba*, Ankine well knew. And though Zagiri Karayan was only a second-degree *amma* and had yet to reach the third and highest level of enlightenment and spiritual union with Athan, she was advanced enough to thwart most demons. Indeed, her powers were likely now the equal of Ankine's own.

"It'll still be difficult, m'lord," Ankine said. "She'll fight to the death to protect her brother."

"Then take Karayan when his sister's not close by." Ladon swiveled his gaze back to her. The threat burning there was warning enough of the consequences of failure. "Phaon gave you to me because of your purported cleverness. Use that ring. It should even the playing field a bit."

"To do that, I need some idea where to begin, m'lord."

He gave a low, hoarse laugh. "Last seen, they were in the Valan Mountains, traveling northeast. You'd better hurry. I'd wager they're headed for the Goreme Valley."

Alarm shuddered through her. The Goreme Valley? By the everlasting fires, not there! Anywhere but there!

"Then I beg leave immediately to depart," she replied with as much outward calm as she could muster. "As you say, I must hurry."

His glance dropped to the contents of his cup. He swirled it around and around until Ankine thought she'd scream. Then, with a dismissing wave, Ladon motioned her away.

Any other time, Ankine would've counted herself fortunate to escape the Hylean's presence with her body unsullied and her dignity still intact. This time, however, Ladon had forfeited bestowing one humiliation to heap yet another upon her—one that tore at her heart more cruelly than a physical violation ever could.

It had been four years now since she last had contact with any *amma*, Ankine thought as she hastily departed the chamber. Four years, yet in many ways it seemed like yesterday. Four years of anguished regret and unrequited yearning.

Aye, she must indeed make haste. She must use the ring to open the portal, find Vartan Karayan, and be done with the whole sad, sordid affair. Find and take him before he entered the Goreme Valley and was forever beyond her reach.

Failure was unthinkable. Ankine didn't even want to consider what would become of her if she failed.

7

The second day's journey, which took them to the edge of the Spine of Athan, was relatively uneventful. A distant flight of dragons heading southwest filled Danae with such excitement and delight that Vartan couldn't help smiling. But then, he had to admit he also found great fascination with dragons. Not that he would ever willingly get within a mile or even two of one. Tales were the dragons were fiercely protective of their riders and would just as soon flame any foolhardy intruders to cinders as look at them.

Still, he had always admired them from a distance for the beautiful, mysterious creatures they were. Creatures whose origins and true purpose were lost in the mists of time. As King of Astara and hopefully, someday, even King of Gadiel, Vartan had intended eventually to delve into the issue of the dragons and their riders. Indeed, someday, he had dreamt of forging an alliance with them. There was so much, after all, from which both sides could benefit.

But that dream had died along with all his others. Now he must find new dreams, new goals for his life. Vartan sighed. His greatest fear was that the scope of his glorious aspirations had shrunk permanently into a tiny, severely circumscribed arena of sightless limitations.

The low murmur of the women's voices behind him, rising from the driving seat, was punctuated just then by Danae's sudden laugh. The sound was throaty and full, as if it had risen from deep within her being. It was the voice of a woman, not a girl. Like a plucked string of her lyra, the sound vibrated through him.

How was it possible, after all he had endured and lost of late, that his body could so easily stir to just the sound of Danae's voice? He didn't feel like much of a man anymore. He'd never again be able to support or protect a family—not even if fate forced him hereafter down the path of a simple commoner. He'd never be worthy of *any* woman, ever again.

Yet how he hungered for even the briefest touch of Danae's hand! How his heart quickened when she was near. Perhaps it was nothing more than his need for her soothing presence, for the sense, however fleeting it was, that he was safe, cared for, cherished.

It was likely to be expected. He was, for all his humiliating limitations, still a normal man with normal needs. And it had been months now—*many* months—since Aelwyd had last shared his bed.

That unrequited yearning was part of the reason he had propositioned Danae the night before his battle with Ladon. She was so beautiful, so warm and caring, and he had been hungry for the comfort he knew she could give. Shameful as his behavior had been, he had wanted, just once more before he died, to know the pleasures of a woman's body.

Vartan was glad Danae had refused him. If they had lain together, it would've been harder now to keep his distance from her. And now, more than ever, he must do just that.

Danae deserved better than the man he had become. If it was the last thing he ever did, Vartan intended to set her free of whatever misguided loyalty still tied her to him. Set her free to find her happiness—as far away from him and the dangers that would surely dog him to his dying day as possible.

❧ ❧

Sharifah watched her brother give final instructions to the servants preparing for the journey to come. She choked back a savage swell of envy. Ra'id would likely be gone from Khaddar for months. Garnering the support of twelve disparate and extremely stubborn, self-interested Desert tribes was a monumental undertaking. Few common causes had ever brought them all together at one time. She wondered if the crown of Gadiel would be enough to do so now.

Still, at least Ra'id would be free of the stifling constrictions of city life and the even more restrictive control of their father. That alone was incentive enough to send him—or anyone—headlong into a seemingly impossible quest. If only there were a way to convince her father and brother to allow *her* to ride along . . .

Stepping back out of the Desert sun—uncomfortably warm at midday even in winter—Sharifah retreated into the cool, concealing shadows of the covered porch. She didn't want her brother to know she was here until she was ready to approach him. Didn't want him to catch her watching him. He was possessed of a quick, keen intelligence and could, if she wasn't careful to hide them, read her innermost thoughts.

Her gaze softened with affection. From time to time as he spoke with the servants, her brother distractedly shoved the sleeves of his robe up past his elbows, only to have them, each time he gestured, tumble back to his wrists. He was dressed in a long, loose traditional *thobe*, the lightweight gray wool his only concession to the cooler winter temperatures. His black hair fell gently to the base of his neck, and his strong blade of a nose and high cheekbones were stunning in profile. He seemed the epitome of the proud, virile Desert lord. His demeanor, however, whether he spoke with noble or commoner, was, as always, intent but kind.

Nay, in the end, Ra'id wouldn't be the problem. She had always been able, sooner or later, to play on his soft heart. Soft, at any rate, when it came to his little sister. Their father, however, was another story. What ploy could she come up with to win him over?

As if summoned by her thoughts, the Hakeem, his endless entourage of fawning advisors following closely on his heels, hurried just then into the courtyard. With long, sure strides, Ra'id immediately headed over to join him. After rendering his sire the bow the Hakeem's regal position demanded, Ra'id straightened and, beckoned by his father, drew close.

For a time the two men talked, their heads inclined in deep conversation. Observing Ra'id once more, Sharifah couldn't help but wish she could find a bond mate even half as wonderful as her brother. Surely, when Al'Alim had created Ra'id, He hadn't fashioned only one man like him in all of Gadiel. But if there *were* another man of her brother's ilk out there, he had yet to cross her path. It seemed the only option left Sharifah was to go out and find him herself.

Find him herself . . .

A glimmer of an idea flashed through her mind. It might be the perfect solution for both of her most pressing problems. She took a step forward, intending to broach the subject with her father and brother, then thought better of it. Prince Kamal generally looked askance at any of her ideas. Best to approach Ra'id first, gain his support, then maneuver *him* to approach their sire.

At long last, Sharifah's patience was rewarded. In a flurry of regal robes, the Hakeem departed, his obsequious bevy of counselors once again close on his heels. Ra'id turned back to his servants.

She lost not a moment joining him.

"I want you to find Jamal," he was saying to one of the young stable boys. "Tell him to meet me here"—he shot Sharifah a questioning glance, then looked back at the boy—"in fifteen minutes. Can you do that, lad?"

The boy nodded eagerly, then wheeled about and scurried off.

"You just missed Father," he next said, his glance moving back to his sister. "Unless, of course, that was an intentional omission on your part."

Her mouth twisted wryly. "Whatever would lead you to imagine that, Brother dear?" She grasped his arm, unable to contain her excitement an instant longer. "I have an idea. An idea that might ease some of the burden I've placed on your shoulders of late."

He arched a dark brow. "Indeed? And what burden would that be?"

"Why, the burden of playing my matchmaker, of course."

"So, you've decided on the bloated toad after all?"

Sharifah gave a low, mocking laugh. "Hardly. I *have* come to the conclusion, though, that I need to play a more active role in discovering my future bond mate." At the look now darkening her brother's expression, she hurried on. "With your approval, of course. Which is exactly why we need to do this together. Which is exactly why this mission to the tribes is the perfect opportunity."

"What?"

"Now listen to my plan, Ra'id, before you automatically discount it out of hand." She leaned close. "Think about it. It'll be a wonderful adventure; it'll get me out of this dreary city and away from father's equally dreary and incessant nagging. And I'll be able to see, firsthand, every eligible man in the entire Desert. Surely with twelve tribes to choose from, I'll find at least one suitable man to take as bond mate."

"One could but hope," he muttered. "This isn't, however, a bond mate hunting expedition. I have serious—and extremely difficult—work to do. Work, you know as well as I, at which I dare not fail. I don't need—"

"Aye, you *do* need me." Immediately, Sharifah cut him off before he could talk himself out of accepting her proposal. "First, any one of the Desert warlords would dearly love to wed one of their sons to the Hakeem's daughter. That, in itself, is a priceless incentive to dangle over their heads to get them to join us. You don't have to make any binding promises, mind you, just imply the possibility. And I'll play my role to the hilt, pretending to be quite taken with each and every young lordling presented me."

Ra'id eyed her with sudden interest. "Aye, go on."

"Secondly, I can be an extra set of eyes and ears for you," she added, her excitement growing. He was beginning to take the bait. Oh, thanks be to Al' Alim! "You know I possess a decided talent for picking up all sorts of useful information, information that'll aid you in your negotiations. If for nothing else, you should take me along for that alone."

"You're indeed a clever woman, Sharifah. I've always valued your insights."

Her brother chewed on the inside of his cheek, a trait he had carried over from childhood. It boded well for her. It meant he was giving her plan serious, *very* serious, thought.

She watched and waited in silence, knowing that saying too much was just as bad as saying too little. Her brother had to digest the information so as to make it his own. Once he claimed ownership, however, he'd commit wholeheartedly.

Even more important, he'd convince their father it had been his own idea from the start.

Such was the way of the Desert. Women were responsible for most of the really excellent ideas, but the men always had to be skillfully manipulated to take all the credit. She didn't like it, never had, but it was the way it was, and she had learned to use the system with consummate mastery. Someday, though . . .

"I like it." With a resolute nod, Ra'id apparently found favor with the plan. "I like it a lot." He paused, the vestiges of a smile lifting his lips. "I also think this proposal is best presented to our father by me. What do *you* think, Sister?"

She smiled. As well as she knew her brother, he also knew her.

"I think," she said, lowering her glance, "it's best you talk to Father. He always likes your ideas far better than mine."

A finger crooked beneath her chin, and he lifted her gaze back to his. "Aye, and frequently they are to *his* detriment and *my* advantage. Never cease to be my advisor, Sharifah, even when the day finally comes that I rule as Hakeem. I value your insights far more than any of those men Father calls his counselors."

Gratitude filled her. Like Ra'id, she received little approbation from their sire. Prince Kamal's way was to motivate by constant criticism and, sometimes, even by threats. Perhaps it was why she and Ra'id were so close, so supportive of each other.

"And *I* value your confidence in me, Brother," she replied. "I won't fail you."

His smile widened, and his dark brown eyes lit with compelling warmth. "I know, Sharifah. I know."

That night, she watched him from the shadows. Watched as some pale-haired young woman helped him into the cave, led him to a spot out of the chilling wind, then left him to return to the cart outside. There wasn't much time. She had to act—and act now—or risk losing the last opportunity she might have.

Ankine glanced to the hazy ring of light glowing a few feet from her. The opening was adequate to walk Karayan through, and once they stepped past the portal, no one could enter after them. No one could call them back. Not even Zagiri.

Once more, she looked to the cave's opening. The two women were well out of sight. She inhaled a steadying breath and strode quickly over to where the prince sat. Kneeling, she laid a hand on his shoulder and began quickly to weave the charm spell.

He jerked when she touched him. "D-Danae?"

Ankine modulated her voice to sound like the young woman. "Aye, Vartan. It's Danae. I've something to show you. Will you come with me?"

"What is it?" He frowned up at her in puzzlement.

She thought fast. "I've found a tunnel off the back of this cave. I think we should explore it."

"And what good would my opinion be? I can't see anything."

"Aye, but you *can* navigate the darkness better than I. Besides, I'll feel safer with you along."

Vartan smiled. "So, it's the pleasure of my company you're really wanting then, is it?"

Enough of this teasing banter, Ankine thought. *It's time to move.* She tugged on his arm.

"Aye. Will you come?"

He climbed to his feet. "If it pleases you, of course. I could use some exercise, what with sitting in that cart all day."

"Come then. Let's go."

Her arm tucked in his, Ankine began to lead Vartan across the cave in the direction of the portal. *Only a few more yards,* she thought, her heartbeat quickening in anticipation. Only a few more yards, and she'd have him.

"Vartan?" A voice sounded behind them. "Vartan, where are you going?"

He froze, jerked his head around. "Danae?"

Ankine intensified her charm spell and inexorably drew him forward.

"What are you doing?" Danae cried, moving toward them. "Who are you?"

"Come! Now!" Ankine shoved him toward the portal.

"Zagiri!" the young woman screamed behind her. "Zagiri! Hurry! Help!"

A hand grabbed Ankine's arm. With a low curse, she marshaled her powers and flung Danae away, sending her flying backward. She heard her hit the floor—hard.

"Stay! I command you!"

Ankine wheeled around. There in the cave's mouth stood Zagiri. Her eyes blazed with a fiery light, and her hand was lifted toward her brother. As her gaze settled on Ankine, she paled.

"You!"

In a flutter of long, black cape, Ankine looked back to the portal. Vartan had halted.

"Come back now, Brother," she heard Zagiri say, the low, melodic tone of command vibrating in her voice. "Come back to me."

Immediately, Vartan obeyed. Ankine ground her teeth in frustration. She had two choices. She could command him to turn back to the portal while she simultaneously held off Zagiri, but in the effort her control over the portal would fade. Chances were the portal would close before she could get both

Karayan and herself through it. And if it closed prematurely and left her on this side . . .

Panic seized her. They were too close to the Goreme Valley. If Zagiri somehow bested her and forced her to go with them to the valley . . . It was too terrifying even to imagine!

To distract her, Ankine sent a quelling blast of power in Zagiri's direction, then turned and flung herself around and past the oncoming prince. Flung herself through the portal, closing it instantly behind her.

There'd be other opportunities to seize Vartan Karayan, she told herself. Surely he couldn't remain forever in the Goreme. Once he again stepped foot outside its holy protection, she'd be there, waiting for him.

In the meanwhile, all she had to do was convince Ladon that it was only a matter of time until she could strike anew. In the meanwhile, all she had to do was survive.

❧ ❧

"Who was that, Zagiri?" Danae asked, staring at the spot where the glimmering portal had once been. She climbed back to her feet and shot the other woman a quizzical glance.

Zagiri stood there, her face white, her expression strained. "A woman I once knew, a student of Amma Serpuhi. Her name is Ankine. Ankine Yerevan."

"She doesn't seem to be a friend of your *amma's* anymore," Vartan growled, finally speaking up. "She bespelled me. But perhaps you also acquired such powers in those years you spent with that *amma* of yours. When you commanded me to halt, I immediately did so."

"What Ankine wrought on you was evil, Brother," his sister muttered tautly. "You didn't really want to go with her. I but used and strengthened that desire for your good."

119

"Perhaps. It felt all the same to me, though. Like I was being pulled to and fro between two wills stronger than my own."

There was anger beneath Vartan's calm words. Zagiri didn't look all that happy either. Danae decided the best course was to divert the direction of the conversation.

"What happened, Zagiri," she asked, "to turn this Ankine to evil? For evil it was, wasn't it, her intentions for Vartan this night?"

"Aye." Her friend sighed. "I'd wager she was sent by Ladon." She looked to Danae. "I first met her eight years ago, when I came to study with Serpuhi. Ankine was already her student, and had been since she was a wee babe. Serpuhi found her abandoned one day at the edge of the Goreme Valley. Some families do that, dedicating one of their children to the service of Athan."

"An ancient, barbaric custom," Vartan ground out. "Father tried to outlaw that practice."

"As did his father and grandfather before him," Zagiri offered dryly. "Yet, like the Faith they also tried so hard to eradicate, pockets of believers steadfastly remained."

Her brother gave a snort, but said nothing more.

Once again, Danae attempted to move the tale along. "So Ankine was raised and taught by Amma Serpuhi. What happened then to turn her to evil?"

"Ankine was one of the brightest, most talented of Serpuhi's students. Even I could see that. For all her youth, she progressed rapidly in her spiritual formation. Indeed, I never saw anyone so afire with the love of Athan and Eisa. Yet I also saw a strong will and fierce pride in her accomplishments. Serpuhi struggled mightily to bend those to Athan's service. In the end, though, Phaon found some way into Ankine's heart."

As if in sad remembrance, Zagiri sighed. "At least, that's what Serpuhi wrote me in a letter four years ago. That Ankine had turned from Athan and rejected His Love, putting her own pride above His Wisdom and Goodness. She refused to listen to Serpuhi, refused to humble herself and ask forgiveness, so convinced was she that she was in the right. And that, when Ankine was finally banished from the Goreme Valley, she took with her the ring entrusted to Amma Serpuhi, the Ring of Blessed Metsamor, given to him by Athan."

"The Ring of Blessed Metsamor?" Vartan frowned. "What was so special about a ring?"

"Athan originally intended it to be used in visiting the sacred places, of which Blessed Metsamor had many due to the proliferation of the holy houses in those days. The ring, when removed, can be expanded to a circular portal large enough for a few people to walk through. The ring bearer chooses the destination. The portal opens to that spot and the ring bearer walks through to the intended location. It works the same on the other side. From whence you came, to there you return."

"And you're guessing the other side tonight was somewhere near Ladon?"

Zagiri nodded. "Where else would she be taking you? Though Ankine's now in thrall to Phaon, it seems likely the Dark Lord has loaned her to Ladon. There can be no other explanation."

He expelled a frustrated breath. "Then no matter where I go, no matter how far I get from him, I'll never escape Ladon." Vartan looked her way. "I warned you, Sister. It won't end until he sees me dead, and any near me may well suffer the same fate!"

"We'll be safe once we enter the Goreme Valley. Have no fear of that."

"So that's to be my fate, then?" He clenched his hands at his side. "To hide away in some desolate valley for the rest of my life? A fine prospect, to be sure!"

"I'm no soothsayer!" Zagiri snapped, evidently at the end of her patience. "I can't see into the future. All I know is Athan wants us to go to the Goreme and Serpuhi. After that, we'll see."

Danae glanced from brother to sister. What a hot-headed pair they could be.

"Nothing's served bemoaning the circumstances that brought us all to this pass," she said. "Let's finish unpacking the cart, get a fire going, and have our supper. Things will seem a lot brighter then."

Vartan's lips twitched. "Ever the peacemaker and bearer of hope, aren't you, Danae? Well, it really doesn't matter anyway. Athan has spoken, Zagiri has obeyed, and I don't have any choice in the matter. Whether I like it or not, we're going to the Goreme Valley."

"Vartan!" his sister cried in exasperation. Then she inhaled a steadying breath. "Fine. Let's make a fire. If you would, Danae, gather some wood. Vartan and I can finish unloading the cart."

Danae nodded. "Aye. Best you stay close to him. I'd be of no help if *she* should return."

"I don't think she will. The creation of the portal, even with the aid of the ring, drains a great amount of power. Even," she added with a grim smile, "from one as talented as Ankine."

8

"We're entering the Goreme Valley, Vartan."

Wrenched from his intermittent dozing by the announcement, he shoved to his elbows in the back of the straw-padded cart as it began its downward descent. "Indeed? And pray, what do you see, Danae? Is it truly as bleak and desolate as the tales would have it be?"

She laughed. "Nay, on the contrary. It looks quite pleasant, even for winter. There's a small, ice-clogged river running through the middle of the valley floor—which is quite broad and flat—and several stands of bare-limbed trees lining its banks for as far down the Goreme as I can see. The river takes several twists and turns, but they're long and gentle. I imagine in the summer grass grows well, and perhaps even some food crops."

"Aye," Zagiri chimed in just then. "Farther down the valley, some of the *abbas* grow several kinds of grain. Amma Serpuhi has an outdoor stone quern that she uses to grind certain grains into flour. For her effort, she receives a share of the flour. Another *amma* raises mouflons. Once a year, all the *ammas* and *abbas* gather to help shear them and clean the wool. Some weave the wool into blankets and robes. Each of them keeps a milch tur and has his or her own vegetable garden. And there's always fresh fish to be caught in the river."

"Sounds like a pretty self-sufficient band of hermits," Vartan muttered. "No wonder no one ever sees them."

"They come to the Goreme to find peace and solitude, Brother. To seek closer union with Athan and Eisa."

Vartan's lips drew into a tight line, but he restrained himself from offering his thoughts about those who ran away from their obligations. "So I've heard," he answered instead. "And this Amma Serpuhi's mountain dwelling. How much farther until we reach it? Riding in this cart is becoming tedious."

Zagiri chuckled. "Aye, it is, but especially for you without even the consolation of the scenery to distract you. But take heart. We're almost there. Serpuhi's cell is the first one we'll encounter once we reach the valley floor—which, by the way, will be very soon now."

Irritation filled him. Was his sister never to spare him one moment to forget his blindness?

"Good," he forced out the word in an unnaturally bright tone. "I look forward to meeting this mythical holy woman of yours."

His sister dragged in a deep, exasperated breath. "Since she's not mythical but a flesh-and-blood woman, that's but one more fairy tale you'll have to accept as fact, won't you?"

"One among many, if you've anything to say about it, eh, Zagiri?"

Behind him, Danae giggled.

Vartan arched a brow, but didn't bother to turn. He'd see nothing at any rate.

"And what's so amusing, Danae?" he flung instead over his shoulder.

"Oh, nothing but listening to you two peck at each other all the time. Have you and Zagiri always been so at odds?"

He chuckled, the tension draining from him in one refreshing rush. "Aye, pretty much so, now that I think on it. But it's not meant in a mean-spirited way. It's more a battle of wills and intellect, isn't it, Sister?"

As the cart's downward angle suddenly changed to a level plane, Zagiri gave a disgruntled snort. "Most times anyway. You *do* have your aggravating moments, Brother."

"Me?" Vartan pretended affronted disbelief. "And exactly when would those moments be? When I best you in some way, perhaps?"

"To be sure." The cart drew to a halt as she reined in the pony. "Now, as much as I dearly enjoy trading barbs with you, we're here. I need to climb the trail up to Serpuhi's cell and explain why we've arrived."

"If she's such a highly placed holy woman, won't she already know that?"

The cart swayed slightly as his sister climbed down. She walked to the back of the cart, close to the side where he was now sitting. "Aye, she most likely will. But if she doesn't, you'll at least spare *her* your sarcastic comments, won't you, Brother?"

"I've never been given to rudeness, and well you know it."

"Except with me, of course."

He laughed. "Of course."

She turned and, from the sound, began to walk away.

"Zagiri?"

His sister halted. "Aye, Vartan?"

"Have I ever thanked you for all you've done in getting me as far as this?"

"Nay, but it doesn't matter. You know that."

"Well, it matters to me, Sister. Thank you. Thank you for everything."

125

A short, sharp laugh escaped her. "Perhaps you shouldn't thank me so prematurely, Brother. You have yet to experience Amma Serpuhi."

He frowned and said nothing more. Zagiri's footsteps soon faded from hearing. Pillowing his head beneath his arms, Vartan laid back down. Zagiri's parting jibe had surely been more of her teasing, but he thought he had also heard a note of promise in it. The realization filled him with unease.

"I don't think she meant that as a threat, Vartan," Danae's sweet voice suddenly pierced his morose musings. "It's just that she looks up to Amma Serpuhi and all she represents. Serpuhi was her teacher."

"Aye, I know." He sighed. "I'm sorry if I seem ill-tempered of late. You must think me an ungrateful boor."

"Zagiri and I understand what you're going through, Vartan. Your whole life, as you once knew it, is dying before your very eyes, and you're struggling to find a new one in its ruins."

For some reason, her words plucked at Vartan's memory. Why did they sound so . . . so familiar? Then, unbidden and most certainly unwelcome, lines of the Prophecy wafted past. *". . . blind to his destiny . . . from ruin to rebirth . . ."*

The recollection offered no comfort. On the contrary, it filled him with anger. It wasn't, however, Danae's fault, and likely not even what she was referring to. She was just trying to ease his shame over his foul moods and unfair treatment of them.

"Tell me what's going on," he said, hoping a change of subject would dispel the growing disquiet that so darkened his spirit these days. "What this Amma Serpuhi looks like, her reaction to Zagiri, and anything else you think interesting."

He could hear her half turn on the seat.

"Zagiri's walking up a narrow dirt path to a small, cavelike opening in the mountainside. And at the base of the path—actually about twenty feet from the base—is a large stone quern with a long pole protruding from its center. Likely it's used to push the two big round stones around on themselves to grind the grain."

When she paused, Vartan said, "Go on."

"The mountainside around and above the cell is very steep. It would be hard to climb it if the need ever arose," she continued. "The whole valley, as far as I can see, looks that way. The only way in or out, at least at this end, seems to be the road we took."

"Easily defended then, but once an enemy breached the road defenses, perhaps a trap."

"Aye, but only if the tales about no evil trespassing here are untrue. Oh!" Danae exclaimed, "Zagiri's at the mouth of the cave now, and a woman has come out to meet her."

"Tell me about her, please."

"She's a small woman, just a little taller than Zagiri's shoulder. Her hair, which she wears short like your sister, is white, and she looks rather old. She's wearing the same rough, brown hooded robe as Zagiri. I can't see her eye color from here, but she appears very kind." Danae paused. "She's nodding and smiling at Zagiri, and now she's looking in our direction. Oh, she's so beautiful, Vartan! There's such a look of peace and joy about her."

He had heard enough. If the truth were told, the last thing he wanted to hear was a description of the consummate holy woman. He didn't want her to be special at all. If she was, he might be forced to face exactly what he dreaded—the truth about their imaginary Athan. The reality of His existence. And the terrifying words of that cursed Prophecy.

"They're motioning to us, Vartan," Danae's voice, excited now, pierced the gloomy turn his thoughts had taken. "They want us to come up."

Confronted with the moment he had been dreading ever since they had left Voshie's house, Vartan suddenly wasn't all that eager to meet this fabled holy woman. He didn't need her or her god crammed down his throat, though he knew that was—indeed had always been—part of the plan in coming here. He sighed. Well, the time had come to set them *all* straight. It was best to come to an immediate, unmistakable understanding and be done with it.

Setting his resolve firmly in place, Vartan scooted to the back of the cart and waited for Danae to come around. After sliding off the end, he allowed her to take his arm and guide him over to and up the steep little path to the *amma's* cave.

"Vartan," Zagiri then said, rendering him, he realized, first privilege in the introductions as the new king of Astara, "this is my teacher and beloved friend, Amma Serpuhi. Serpuhi, this is my brother, Vartan Karayan, and our friend, Danae."

"Welcome, my lord. Welcome, Danae," he heard the holy woman say, her voice soft, calm, and with such well-modulated tones Vartan felt a passing curiosity as to the source of her familial bloodlines. "I've been expecting you and am honored to offer you the hospitality of my simple home."

So, she has been expecting us, has she? Vartan thought. But then, who could refute that claim, one way or another, now that they were here? If nothing else, this Amma Serpuhi was a clever woman, and quick-witted enough to seize every advantage presented her.

He held out his hand in the direction of her voice. "Thank you, m'lady. Your kind hospitality is most appreciated, and won't be presumed upon any longer than absolutely necessary," Vartan replied, responding in *his* most regal of tones. Best way to keep her at bay might well be to play the kind but aloof king. Not that, he added as a wry aside, he really *was* king of anything anymore. Still, the charade had its uses.

"You may stay for as long as Athan wishes." She then took his hand.

For a fleeting instant, Vartan thought he felt a warm tingling pass from her hand to his, traveling up his wrist to his forearm before it seemed to pause and immediately dissipate. It happened so quickly that he couldn't be sure if the odd sensation was real or if, because he had half-expected something bizarre from her, his imagination had played tricks on him.

"Unless, of course, *you* decide otherwise," she next said, giving his hand a final, firm squeeze and releasing it. "You're always free to remain or go, at your desire. In the meantime, you are most certainly welcome."

So, she had taken his challenge and accepted it. A grudging respect flared in Vartan. His little ploy to intimidate her and set the tone of their future interactions had failed. For all her purported holiness, this woman was indeed a force to be reckoned with.

"And will you still offer me the shelter of your home and the sanctuary of this valley, m'lady," he asked, deciding there was no further point in subtleties, "once I apprise you of my feelings—or lack thereof—for your purported god?"

"Vartan!" his sister exclaimed on a sharp intake of breath. "There's no need to insult—"

"It's quite all right, Zagiri." Ever so gently, Amma Serpuhi cut her off. "Your brother's entitled to his beliefs or"—a faint note of humor filled her voice—"lack thereof. Pray, don't trouble yourself, m'lord," she continued, next directing her words to Vartan. "I've always known your feelings. Indeed, even as you drew near the valley, I felt your rising apprehension in regard to our first encounter. Be at peace. There are no stipulations to my welcome. None whatsoever. I serve all equally. Indeed, I can do no less and call myself Athan's beloved."

He smiled. "Good. I meant no insult, but neither did I want there to be any misunderstanding."

"And there is none, m'lord. None."

Silence settled over the gathering. "Come," Amma Serpuhi finally said. "I've prepared extra food for the supper meal in anticipation of your arrival. Take your ease while I see to your pony. Then, after we eat, we can all help unload the cart."

"I'll help you with the pony, Serpuhi," Zagiri piped up. "He's a good animal, but he does have his little quirks. In the meanwhile, Danae can assist Vartan into the cave. Can't you, Danae?"

"Oh . . . aye," Danae replied, taking him by the arm. "Won't you come with me, Vartan?"

He felt like all the women were suddenly talking around him and, as always, it abraded his pride. Still, he gritted his teeth and nodded, obediently following Danae's lead. As hard as it was to endure, Vartan knew he had no other choice. None, at any rate, that wouldn't make him look the fool. But how it grated. How it shamed him!

"Duck your head," Danae said by way of caution after a few steps forward. "The cave's opening is small. In fact, bend over and put your hand on your head so you'll truly see what it takes to come and go through this entrance. You might well be surprised how low it is."

He was indeed surprised, finding he almost had to bend double to enter without banging his head. But then according to Danae, the *amma* was a small woman. And the smaller the opening to the outside, the less wind, snow, and cold air would penetrate in winter.

Despite the chill of the day, it was amazingly snug and warm inside, especially after Danae led him sharply left and down a short tunnel to the main chamber. "Tell me," he said as they finally halted, "what does the dwelling place of a holy woman look like?"

"You needn't be so unkind about it." Though gently couched, there was reproof in her voice. "Amma Serpuhi has treated you with the utmost respect. You owe her the same, at the very least."

Once more, shame swept through Vartan. What was the matter with him? He didn't even recognize himself anymore.

"You're right. I do owe her that." He paused, dragged in a breath. "Just describe the place so if I need to move about on my own, I won't trip over something and fall headlong into the fire."

"That shouldn't be a problem. It's pretty spare." Danae once again took his hand and led him around to the right. "The room's a large circle, with a stone-lined hearth in the center, about ten feet from the side wall." She lifted his hand and pressed it to a rough rock wall. "Can you tell by the sound of the fire approximately how far it is from here?"

"Aye. And also by the heat and smell of it."

"Good. You're using your other senses better and better with each passing day."

Vartan smiled. In her own way, Danae was trying her best to give him a feel for his surroundings. In the doing, he knew she hoped to foster his independence, even if in a very limited and safe environment. But then, she had always been so in tune with him, knew him better than most of his family did. Knew him better than Aelwyd ever had.

"Tell me more about this room," he said, skittering immediately away from the warm swell of affection those realizations stirred. His true emotions for Danae must remain tightly locked away in the deepest recesses of his heart. He had made his decision, and for her sake, must keep to it.

"Let's see. There's a small pallet on the floor," she said as she led him around it, "a rough-hewn, wooden bench here"—his right shin bumped against a low, hard object—"and some shelves here that hold several cups and bowls, a pitcher, and an iron cook pot. And that," Danae said, drawing him to a halt as they completed the circle, "is apparently the extent of a holy woman's dwelling place."

"She obviously, then, isn't a hoarder of material goods."

"Nay, it wouldn't appear so." Once again Danae let go of his hand. "Why are you so opposed to speaking with her about Athan? Are you afraid Serpuhi, in spite of yourself, will convince you of His existence?"

Vartan reached up and scratched his jaw, a jaw, he noted, that was fast becoming covered in soft beard. "Perhaps. I don't know. I'm not myself anymore, and I don't like—nay, I *hate*—what I've become. It's all I can do just to get up and face another day, and now you and Zagiri bring me to a woman who, from all I've heard of her, desires to change me even more. Why *wouldn't* I be wary of her?"

"She can't force you to change, Vartan," Danae said softly. "And she wouldn't, even if she could."

"How do you know that?" he cried. "You've only just met her!"

"Because she believes what I believe, and we believe you must come to Athan of your own free will, or not at all. Athan's a God of love, a benevolent Father. He's not and never will be a slave master. And Eisa . . ." She sighed, and the sound was full of such deep affection that Vartan felt a momentary stab of jealousy. "Eisa's Athan in human form and loved us all so much He sacrificed Himself to save us. He, who was without taint of evil, died for us, who are so full of taint and

132

the tendency toward evil. Can you imagine such love, Vartan? Can you?"

"Nay, I can't, and don't necessarily want to, either." Why was it that, even with Danae, when talk swung around to this Athan of theirs, he began to feel uncomfortable? Was it an unwillingness to hurt them with cruel words, or more an irritation that they wouldn't listen and respect his right to believe what he wished? Or perhaps the unsettled feelings sprang from some other source entirely? But if so, what *was* that source?

Danae expelled an exasperated breath. "Do you know how frustrating you can be? Why, you're the most stubborn man I've ever met!"

"And, of course, there's not the slightest bit of stubbornness in these repeated attempts of yours to bring me to Athan, is there?"

For a long moment, Danae said nothing. Then she sighed. "Fine. Your point's taken. I only want the best for you, Vartan. That's all."

"Then respect my wishes in this." He reached out and found her hand, lifting it to his lips for a brief, forbidden kiss. "What I need most from you right now is your friendship and support, not ill feelings between us. Can you do that for me, Danae?"

"Aye. Still, I won't lie to placate you, or hold back the truth when it needs to be spoken."

He chuckled. "You're becoming quite the little rebel, aren't you? I'm beginning to think I never really knew the true Danae, back in Astara."

"And does it displease you?"

Vartan cocked his head, considering that for a moment. "Nay, I suppose not. It'll take some getting used to, though."

"We're both changing, aren't we?" The statement came out on a breathless whisper. "But then, after what has happened, how could we not?"

At her words, painful longings and anguished regrets assailed him once more. *Ah, Korien . . . Aelwyd . . . Mother and Father . . .*

With a savage effort, Vartan gathered the memories and shoved them back into that secret chamber of his tightly guarded heart. He wasn't strong enough yet to allow them to batter at him for long. He wondered if he ever would be.

Releasing Danae's hand, Vartan pulled his own back to hang at his side. "Aye," he said, his voice husky with the effort it took to keep it from quavering. "How could we not?"

❧ ❧

That night, but one slumber more before Ra'id and Sharifah were to depart, they were summoned once again to meet with their father. This time, however, it wasn't a private audience. As they entered through the gilded, red rafawood doors of the throne room, Prince Kamal awaited them beneath a silken canopy shot with Desert colors—emerald green for the large, fan-shaped fronds of the rafa tree, sapphire blue for the sky, and silver for the countless stars of the night. Lined on either side of the Hakeem were his equally countless number of counselors.

Ra'id shot his sister a quick glance. "Something's afoot," he muttered through lips that barely moved. "A change of plans, most likely."

"Just as long as Father isn't regretting his decision to allow me to accompany you," Sharifah whispered back. "I can bear almost anything else, if you can."

"We'll see. You never know, though, with Father."

Then they came within earshot of the throne and the Hakeem's loyal sycophants, and had to fall silent. Ra'id, followed by Sharifah, rendered the Hakeem the required obeisance, then straightened.

"We've come as you commanded, Majesty. How may we serve you?" Ra'id then asked, meeting his sire's piercing gaze.

"Is all in readiness for tomorrow's journey?" Prince Kamal leaned forward.

Ra'id nodded. "Aye, it is."

"There has been a slight change in plans. Nothing, though, that should preclude your planned departure."

Here it comes, Ra'id thought, feeling the tension rise. No matter how hard he tried, it seemed his father would never be satisfied with anything he did. He was only surprised it had taken this long—until the very night before they left—for the meddling to begin.

He bowed once more. "It will be as you command, Majesty. Only tell me what more I need do."

"Oh, there's nothing more for *you* to do," the Hakeem said. "Farid and Malik will see to their own arrangements. I have decided they'll accompany you. Their maturity and political acumen are well suited to temper your youth and inexperience."

They would also, Ra'id well knew, be given implicit leave to countermand any decision he made. He choked down a bitter swell of anger. No doubt they would also periodically apprise their prince of any inappropriate actions Ra'id might take. In other words, Farid Ben Wasem and Malik Abd al Rashid were being sent along to spy, not to mention keep a tight rein, on him.

The anger quickly dissolved into pain. Would he never, then, win his father's trust and respect? He had long ago relinquished the hope of ever having his love. But what would it finally take? Winning him the crown of Gadiel?

The loss of that crown was a festering wound in the hearts of the Diya al Din, a wound passed down from generation to generation of the Hakeem's heirs. Some rulers dealt with it better than others, but Prince Kamal wasn't one of them. Why he chose to take out his frustration on his children, however, was a mystery to Ra'id.

Sharifah moved close, surreptitiously seeking his hand in the adjoining folds of their robes, and gave it a comforting squeeze.

"You've no comment, my son? Am I to take that as a sign of your displeasure?"

His father's voice, edged with a barely veiled challenge, jerked Ra'id back from his impotent musings. He forced a smile.

"Nay, Majesty. I was but considering all the ways Malik and Farid would be useful to me on this quest. I thank you for your generosity in sparing two of your most valued advisors."

The Hakeem smiled, though the act passed no further than his lips. "See that you *do* use them well, my son, and my sacrifice will be your gain." His gaze next turned to Sharifah. "They can be of service to you, as well, my daughter, aiding you in your choice of a husband. A choice I expect to be forthcoming by the end of this undertaking."

Beside him, Ra'id heard Sharifah inhale a sharp breath. He now returned her favor, giving her hand a warning squeeze.

A strained smile on her face, his sister nodded her assent. "As you wish, Majesty."

Their father reclined in his chair. "Good, good. But one thing more. Only an hour ago, I received another message from our spy. There has been an unusual amount of activity around Astara and its environs of late. Armed parties riding about and alarming reports of sightings of undead creatures." He shuddered. "Creatures such as demons to be more concise."

"Searching for something, are they?" Ra'id asked.

"Or someone." Once more, the Hakeem leaned forward. "It's rumored that Vartan Karayan's body was stolen right out from beneath this Ladon's nose. Some rumors even hint that Karayan lives, and the search for him is the reason for all the activity coming now from Astara."

"Likely rumors are all they are, Majesty. A defeated people are prone to invent all sorts of tales in order to bolster their flagging hopes."

"Aye, that's quite possible," his father replied. "Still, as you travel the Desert, stay alert to any unusual events or strangers. If the Hyleans have failed to eliminate the Usurper's heir, then we must finish the task for them."

His mouth tightened in grim resolve. "One way or another, all trace of Vartan Karayan *must* be wiped from the face of Gadiel. I'll not be cheated of what should always have been mine. One way or another, the crown must finally return to its rightful owners!"

9

As if his forthright pronouncements on the day of their arrival
had set the parameters for all concerned, no further discussion
of Athan was forced on Vartan. True, Serpuhi continued to
lead prayers and study the holy books with Zagiri and Danae
before going off on her own each day for several hours of private contemplation. However, no invitations to join in were
ever made to Vartan. And for his part, he either endured in
respectful silence or, if the weather permitted, made his way
outside to sit.

The weeks passed in what Danae would have called a stale-
mate—except there were times when she'd steal a surreptitious
glance at Vartan and get the sense he was listening despite
his elaborate pretense to appear bored and disinterested. She
never mentioned her suspicions, however. Not to Serpuhi or
Zagiri, and especially not to Vartan.

He'd speak when he was ready, the old woman had told
her. He'd ask when he couldn't bear any more unanswered
questions, and cry out his need when his heart ached with
the unrequited yearnings. But not a moment before, Serpuhi
cautioned, and not because of anything they could say to
hasten him along.

So the weeks passed, and one day flowed into another. Danae's knowledge of the Faith grew, filling her with joy and wisdom. She discovered how Athan-permeated each and every breath and beat of her heart was. She lived for the moment, intensely, richly, and so overwhelmed with love that, sometimes, it almost bordered on agony. But oh, what precious, heart-searing, sweet agony!

Spring came, gilding the valley in fresh, new life. Trees budded; lush, rich grass forced its way past the winter-killed turf. Myriad flowers, in a dazzling array of hues from alabaster to buttery yellow to amethyst and vermillion, appeared. The wind blew warm and gentle, like a lover's caress. The air filled with delicate perfume, and birds sang.

Yet Vartan, still entrapped in a dark, introspective world increasingly of his own making, seemed not to notice. He kept to himself, spoke rarely unless first spoken to, until it seemed to Danae as if he were once more sinking deeper and deeper into despair. He took to grinding the grain that was delivered weekly, then rationed out as flour to the valley's solitary inhabitants. Serpuhi refused to allow him to work on the holy day of rest, but the rest of the week it pained Danae to watch him down there like some beast of burden, pushing that long pole around and around for hours. Though Vartan claimed it did him good, both mentally and physically, to contribute something of value, all Danae could think about was how far he had fallen, that this was now all he could offer anyone. She sensed the same thoughts had crossed his mind, which only made her heart ache the more for him.

"It's the hardest thing I've ever had to watch," Zagiri said of a sudden one late spring day as she stared down at her brother from the cave entrance, where all three women were weaving dried river reeds and grasses into baskets. She glanced at Serpuhi, who sat on her right. "If you'd known Vartan before

. . . oh, but he was such a proud, magnificent prince and warrior! And a good one, too, Serpuhi. True, he was pleased with his abilities, which were many, but he never flaunted them or used them to cause hurt. He was just grateful for what he'd been given, and he always tried to use his talents for the welfare of all."

"I never doubted your brother was a good man." The old woman paused to draw the beginning of a new, russet-colored length of reed into the coil of pale brown grass and hide its end between the coils. "But his pride has also been an obstacle to the opening of his heart to Athan. Until a man such as he is brought low . . . well, I fear he'll never listen closely enough to hear anything."

"And what more does Vartan need to endure, to bring him low enough?" Danae cried.

She knew there was anger in her voice. She knew that when it came to Vartan, she struggled—and struggled mightily at times—in the acceptance of Athan's will. "He lost his home, his kingdom, his family. His blindness has broken him until he's nearly a helpless cripple. He has lost all his hope, relinquished all his dreams. What more does Athan require of him?"

"Nothing more, child." Serpuhi looked up, a sad smile on her lips. "But Vartan's will is as strong as his pride. And he fights—oh, how he fights!—against Athan."

"If only he wasn't blind," Danae whispered, glancing down to hide the tears. "He can do nothing in his blindness. It robs him of his future and that, I think, pains him most of all."

"Aye, it would anyone."

"Why won't you take it from him then, Serpuhi?" Zagiri asked of a sudden. "I've always wondered why you haven't healed him of his blindness."

140

Surprise—followed swiftly by a wild rush of excitement—shot through Danae. She jerked up her head to stare at Amma Serpuhi.

"You . . . you can heal . . . heal even blindness?"

"She can heal far more than that," Vartan's sister said. "Once, I even saw her bring someone back from the dead."

In her studies of the Faith, though Danae had heard tales of earlier holy men and women who could do such things, they had almost exclusively been the feats of those who had walked with Eisa in the ancient times. A gift of Athan, to be sure, but one rarely granted since then. But if Serpuhi had been honored thusly . . .

"You can heal Vartan?" she asked on a breathless whisper. "You can cure him of his blindness? Then why haven't you?"

The old woman calmly returned her gaze. "Because it's not Athan's will that I do so. I tried, that first day, when I touched him. Perhaps it was presumption on my part, imagining his healing would open his eyes back not only to the world, but to Athan's love. Or perhaps I was in too much of a hurry and failed to consider Athan's true intent in allowing Vartan to be blinded."

Her mouth tightened in self-deprecation. "I meant well, but I was mistaken. It's not my decision, nor within my power, to heal the prince. It's Athan's, and His alone."

Zagiri and Danae's glances met. In Zagiri's eyes, despair flattened the color to a dull gray green. Danae choked back her own disappointment. She had never even considered that Serpuhi had such powers, and now to have that exhilarating swell of hope so cruelly dashed . . .

"At least Vartan never knew." Struck by a sudden thought, she swung around to Zagiri. "You never told him of the possibility, did you? Oh, say you didn't, Zagiri!"

"Nay, I never did," her friend murmured. "I wouldn't do that to him, or to Serpuhi. But I hoped. I hoped . . ."

Almost as if drawn to the object of their conversation, three pairs of eyes turned to gaze down at the tall, dark-haired man doggedly pushing the stone quern around and around. Compassion filled Danae. *Oh, Vartan,* she thought, *if I could, I'd give you my sight. But I can't. I can't.*

"We must be strong in this," Serpuhi said, almost as if she had read Danae's mind. "We must be strong for Vartan and allow him to run his own course in his own time. He can come to Athan no other way, not and find Him as He must be found. If you love Vartan, Danae, let him do it as He wills. And if you love Athan, trust Him. He won't easily give up on the prince. He loves him, you know, as much as He loves any one of us."

So Serpuhi had ascertained her true feelings for Vartan! And that, after all her efforts to hide it, imagining she had managed to bury her love so well. *But then, even Zagiri knows,* Danae realized belatedly, meeting her friend's perceptive gaze. How they must pity her for her foolish, futile hopes, for her arrogance in daring to dream of a man who could never be hers.

Mortification filled her. She looked down, unable to bear gazing at either of them. She loved Vartan, loved him as she had never loved any other, and there was no shame in that. But it had been *her* secret, precious and unsullied. Exposed now to the glaring light of day, Danae saw how it must appear to others. She felt so foolish. So prideful and callow and foolish.

Yet she couldn't help loving him, and she would never apologize for it—not to Zagiri and Serpuhi, not to anyone. To deny her love for Vartan would be to deny herself, and she would never do that. Never.

With a superhuman effort, Danae glanced up, first meeting Zagiri's, then Serpuhi's gaze. "It'll be as you ask," she said, her voice strained. "I trust in Athan and His love for Vartan. For Athan—and for Vartan—I'll be strong. I'll not interfere."

After midday prayers three days later, she found Vartan, as was his usual habit, sitting alone on the rocky cliff outside the cave. It was another pleasantly cool spring day, though far off in the distance, thick white clouds were beginning to mass into possible thunderheads. Far enough away, however, that Danae intended no change in her plans.

"Our supply of smoked fish is running low," she said by way of announcement as she plopped down beside Vartan, "and Amma Serpuhi says it's time for the fish to be awake and swimming the river again. Would you like to go fishing?"

He gave a derisive snort. "And what purpose would I serve? As bait, perhaps?"

"Nay, as a fisherman, of course," she replied, determined not to let his lack of enthusiasm dampen her spirits *or* her resolve to involve him in yet something else he could do to feel useful. "You *do* still have use of your hands, don't you, as well as feeling enough in them to tell when a fish is tugging at the end of a line?"

"Aye," he admitted rather grudgingly. "I can't see to cast properly, though."

"That's but a minor problem. I can cast the line for you, then hand over the pole. We can catch twice as many fish that way, too. I'd really enjoy the pleasure of your company."

She pushed to a squat and grasped his arm. "Will you come help me? We've four mouths to feed, you know."

He shot her a sightless look, but the corners of his mouth tugged upward now. "If I can truly be of use, of course I'll help. You know I've never been the sort who likes others to wait on him."

"Exactly." She pulled on his arm. "Come along. I've got one pole already that Serpuhi uses, and a knife, extra line, and hooks to make us another pole once we're at the river."

Vartan climbed to his feet. "Want me to carry anything?"

"Just this basket to hold the fish." Danae slipped a deep, lidded basket with a long carrying strap over his head to hang across his chest. Then she took him by the elbow. "Ready?"

He nodded. "What choice have I? You evidently had all this predetermined for me even before you asked."

Danae laughed. "You know me too well."

"Exactly," he said with a smile.

It took the good part of a half hour to reach the river, given the slow pace they had to keep to prevent Vartan from stumbling on the uneven terrain. They passed several beehive-shaped stone huts along the way, huts which Zagiri had several weeks ago explained had been cells for Serpuhi's students. She even pointed out the one she had used. Large enough for a cot, small circular hearth, a stool, and a shelf or two, the little dwelling looked snug and cozy.

Danae was tempted to ask Amma Serpuhi, now that warmer weather would soon be upon them, if they could move into three of the huts to ease the crowded living conditions in Serpuhi's cell. Though the old woman had never once uttered a complaint or even intimated she wished it otherwise, Danae knew she must secretly long for her solitude. And with four huts, all of which were in reasonably good repair and within easy walking distance of each other, she, Zagiri, and Vartan could each have one of their own.

She smiled to herself. It was indeed an excellent idea, and one she decided she would broach just as soon as they returned from their fishing expedition.

It didn't take long to find a reasonably long, straight branch to use as the second fishing pole. After getting Vartan settled on the riverbank with a line and baited hook in the water, Danae set to work trimming the branch and adding her own line and hook. Then, after casting into the briskly flowing water, she took a seat on the boulder next to Vartan.

For a time, they sat in companionable silence. Like one who never seemed to tire of gazing at her beloved, Danae's glance kept straying to Vartan. In the past months, his beard and mustache had come in fully, and his hair had grown past his shoulders. He looked a far different—almost barbaric—but equally attractive man. Working outside at the quern had not only added color to his skin, but, along with the simple but healthy meals of late, had restored much of his earlier muscle and bulk. Save for the blank stare and his inability to move about as independently as a sighted person, Vartan now appeared fully recovered.

Fully recovered at least physically, Danae was quick to amend that observation. He still carried deep, unhealed wounds on his heart and likely would for a long time to come.

"You're staring at me," he said unexpectedly. "Why? Am I drooling or growing a huge wart in the middle of my forehead?"

Danae laughed, the morose mood her thoughts had stirred immediately evaporating. "Nay, though there *is* a spot on your left cheek that I'm keeping a close eye on."

He chuckled. "It's hard to be gloomy around you for long. Indeed, I don't know how I would've survived thus far without you."

She could feel the blood flush her face. "I didn't do all that much—"

"Say thank you, Danae. Accept the compliment, for it's meant from the bottom of my heart and with the deepest gratitude."

"Thank you, Vartan," she whispered, feeling even more embarrassed.

"Now, why were you staring at me?"

"How do you know I was staring?" She was prevaricating, but no appropriate excuse, save the truth, came readily to mind.

He smiled. "Oh, just little things. The way your breathing changes. And you stop moving. And the air as it passes you feels different, like you've changed the position of your head."

"That's amazing, you know. How sensitive your perceptions have become. I wish I noticed things like that."

"And *I* wish I could see again. Not just so I could do the things I used to do, but because I hunger for all the beauty in the world, beauty I've always taken for granted. I miss the sight of the sunrise and sunset. I miss the deep azure of the sky, set off by those big, white clouds. And I miss those beautiful brown eyes of yours. I could lose myself in them, I could."

Danae blushed again but, blessedly, didn't have to reply as a fish suddenly struck on Vartan's line. He noticed it before she could even open her mouth to tell him, and he jerked upward hard, setting the hook. A long, plump fish followed, shining sleek and wet in the sunlight.

"Oh, Vartan!" Danae cried as she captured the flopping fish, deftly removed the hook, and placed it in the loosely woven basket that now hung partially suspended in the water. "You've got a real knack for this. Have you fished much before?"

"Only a time or two as a lad." His mouth lifted slightly. "A crown prince of Astara, even when young, has scant opportunity for such simple if pleasant endeavors. Still, I enjoyed the few times I was able to sneak off with old Mesrob. Did you ever chance to meet him? He worked in Astara's granary, and we'd make our escapes through the old granary gate. We had our share of fun, we did."

"Aye, as a matter of fact, I have met him," she replied, remembering that night they rescued Vartan. "And now you've all the time in the world to fish," she said, then stopped short, realizing how he might take her words. "I'm sorry, Vartan. I didn't mean—"

Just then, a fish swallowed her hook. Danae was too occupied with bringing in her catch to notice how Vartan had taken her well-meant but tactless comment. At last though, when her fish was safely tucked away with its fellow captive, she turned back to him.

"Vartan—"

"Bait my hook, will you?" he asked. "The weather's starting to change. We need to catch at least a few more fish if we can."

She looked to the west, where she had earlier seen the thunderheads forming. They were now huge and gray, and had moved a lot closer. A storm seemed definitely in the offing.

Danae quickly baited both their hooks, cast his line back into the river, and then her own. Luckily, two fish soon snapped up their hooks. Once more, now keeping a close eye on the rapidly worsening weather, she baited and cast the lines.

Thunder rumbled in the distance. Lightning flashed. She glanced uneasily at Vartan.

"This had better be our last catch. We don't need to get caught out in the open in the middle of a thunderstorm."

He shrugged. "At least if we were hit by lightning, the fish would already be cooked for supper."

"Aye, but so would we."

The sound of thunder moved closer. The wind began to pick up, streaming down from the heavens now with a definite chill. Danae's line dove beneath the water just then. It was a large fish and a fighter, and took her the good part of ten minutes finally to bring it in. By then, the ominously gray clouds had nearly reached the valley.

"Vartan, let's get back to the cave." Danae dropped the last fish into the basket, then pulled it from the river. "This storm isn't going to wait much longer."

He sighed, retrieved his line, and pushed to his feet. "You're probably right. I don't like the feel of that wind. I also don't like the sound of the thunder."

Just then, bright light flashed high on the mountainside. A deafening crack of thunder almost immediately followed. Danae jumped and momentarily clutched Vartan's arm before releasing it. This was ridiculous, she scolded herself. Vartan depended on her. She couldn't let herself fall to pieces over a bit of loud noise.

"Here," she said, slipping the basket strap over his head and grabbing his pole, "take the fish and let's go!"

They set out at a fast walk, Danae leading, Vartan following, his hand on her shoulder. For a short while the storm seemed to abate, though the wind picked up in intensity. Then rain began to fall in fat, gentle drops that rapidly increased in speed and size until it was raining hard. Lightning came again, spewing from the clouds now roiling over the valley, followed by earsplitting rolls of thunder.

It was too late to turn back to the river and the questionable shelter of the trees. "Let's try to reach the huts," she cried above the ever-worsening din. "It'll be safer inside one of them than at the river."

His head lowered against the now sleeting rain, Vartan nodded and forged on. The ground became slick, forcing

Danae to slow their pace or risk having Vartan trip and fall. Again lightning struck the mountainside, this time just above Serpuhi's cave.

The thunderclap was so loud Danae stopped to cover her ears. In that moment, the air around her seemed suddenly alive. Her skin tingled. She felt the hair lift from her head.

She had experienced that sensation once before in an open field. She knew what it meant.

"Get down!" Danae screamed. When Vartan hesitated, she shoved him sideways with all her might.

He lost his balance on the wet grass and fell. Then something slammed into her, enveloping her in a blinding blast of heat and light, sucking the air from her lungs.

It was the last thing she remembered.

Gasping for breath, Vartan climbed to his knees. His ears rang, and the air was thick with the smell of sulfur. For a long moment he crouched there, his head almost touching the ground, the rain drenching him.

Then the growl of thunder, blessedly moving away from them now, reminded him of their continued danger out here on the valley floor. He groped around and his hand touched an arm.

"D-Danae?"

She didn't answer. He crawled over, reached out to find and touch her face.

"Danae?"

Still no answer or movement. Terror gripped him. Vartan scooted nearer until his knees touched her side. Sliding his hands beneath her, he pulled Danae close and staggered to his feet. She was a light enough burden, easily carried, but he suddenly realized he didn't know which way to go.

"Zagiri! Serpuhi!" he shouted. "Help me!"

He heard a voice, then another, from some direction off to his right. He began walking toward them. There was no time to spare, if what he feared had actually happened. If Danae had been struck by lightning . . .

Then Zagiri was there. "What happened?" She paused, apparently looking at Danae. "By the blood of the ancients! She looks . . . she looks . . ."

"Don't say it," Vartan snarled, quickening his stride. "She's not. I'd know it, and she's not!"

His sister's hand settled on his arm. "Then come. We daren't waste any time. The huts are only ten feet to your left. Let's take her inside one so I can have a closer look at her."

He followed Zagiri because he had no other choice. Relinquishing Danae to his sister's care, however, was one of the most difficult things he had ever done. Her examination was apparently brief, for he soon heard her lean back.

"How is she?"

"She doesn't look good, Vartan. She has a terrible, pasty gray color, and she's barely breathing. What happened?"

"I think lightning struck her."

"Oh, nay." Zagiri dragged in a shuddering breath. "Nay!"

He heard Serpuhi's approach before she even neared the beehive cell's front door. Though Vartan didn't know why, relief flooded him. If anyone could help Danae, he was suddenly filled with a certitude that Serpuhi could.

"How is she?" the older woman asked as she knelt beside Vartan and Zagiri.

"See for yourself," Vartan heard his sister say. He ground his teeth, knowing full well Zagiri hedged out of fear of his reaction.

He reached out, found the *amma's* hand. "Help her, please." The full impact of what had happened to them suddenly

150

struck him. Despite his best efforts to control it, his voice quavered. "Don't let her d-die."

She covered his hand with her other one. "It's in Athan's hands now. Danae's barely with us. You know that, don't you?"

Hot tears stung his eyes. "Help her. Zagiri said you're a holy woman. Ask your Athan to spare her life."

"And do you think then, Athan would turn away if *you* asked Him yourself?"

Anger swamped Vartan, churning up to fill his mouth with the bitter taste of gall. "What makes *you* think I haven't asked help of Him before?" he all but snarled. "Because I have, and it didn't do me any good. He did worse than ignore me. He did the opposite of what I asked."

"He didn't ignore you, Vartan," Serpuhi softly corrected him. "He heard you. He just didn't give you what you wanted. He gave you something else."

"Then how can I dare ask Him for Danae's life?" He lowered his head, almost drowning in his sense of futility and frustration. "I don't know Him. I'll ask the wrong thing again and . . . and lose Danae."

"But do you *want* to know Him? Do you?"

What a time to be asking such a question, Vartan thought, his anger swelling anew. Danae barely clung to life. Why was it all suddenly about him?

"Eisa loved us all so much that He sacrificed Himself to save us. Can you imagine such love, Vartan? Can you?"

As if she were speaking the words even now, he heard Danae's sweet voice, a voice filled with conviction and love. He had felt, even then, her words tugging at his heart, filling him with a longing to know, to experience what she seemed to have in her relationship with this God and His murdered Son. But instead, he had shoved the feelings aside, convinced

151

they were nothing more than weakness and cowardice seeking a way—some chink—into his beleaguered heart. Yet now . . . once again . . . he teetered on the brink of disaster and had nowhere else to turn.

Nowhere . . . and no right to ask, either.

"It doesn't matter," Serpuhi whispered, leaning close. "*He* doesn't care. He has never cared who has the right and who doesn't, for *none* of us are worthy, Vartan. *None.* All He asks is that you come to Him with an open heart. Can you do that?"

"A-aye," he groaned, reaching out with his other hand to find and take Danae's hand. "Aye, if He truly *is* who you and Zagiri and Danae say He is. Who *wouldn't* want to know Him?"

"Who wouldn't, indeed?"

Serpuhi pulled her hands away. In the next instant, Vartan sensed she was laying them on Danae. For long, tension-fraught seconds, all was silent. Then a warm tingling began to flow from Danae's hand to his—the same strange sensation he had felt the first time he had taken Amma Serpuhi's hand.

Vartan jerked away, knowing the feeling now for what it truly was. Power of some sort flowing out of the old woman. The knowledge filled him with fear. How could he be certain, even now, if it was for good or for evil? He couldn't, but he hoped . . . Oh, how he hoped!

Sucking in a deep, steadying breath, Vartan once more groped for Danae's hand. The warm tingling came again, but went no farther than his hand. If there was evil in this power, then he would endure it with Danae. And if it were for the good, then he'd welcome it instead.

Terrified as he was of it, of this Athan who hovered now at the edge of his tightly guarded boundaries, Vartan knew he'd gladly face it all, if only it would bring back Danae. He'd face that, and so much more, for her. Sweet little Danae, the woman whose confidence in him had always outstripped the reality of the man he was.

And then, almost at the same instant the unnerving tingling in his hand ceased, Danae stirred, groaned. His heart swelling with a joyous relief, Vartan leaned close.

"Danae?" His eyes burned with tears. "Danae?"

"A-aye, Vartan? What happened? Where am I?"

"You're safe, sweet lady. Safe among friends. Safe," he added, moisture streaming unashamedly now down his face, "where you've been all along. Safe in Athan's love."

10

The group of Hylean officers, down in number by half now, milled about in anxious, restless groups, awaiting the arrival of their new king. Watching them from the secret peephole in the tapestry on the wall opposite the Astarian throne, Ladon smiled grimly. Let them stew a bit. It only enhanced the fun once he began to play them one against the other. And play them he would, for they were all, to a man, incompetent imbeciles.

As incompetent as Danae's now dead father, who could offer no acceptable explanation for her strange disappearance.

His gaze moved to the two slender figures chained, one on each side, to the base of the massive, carved turkawood throne chair. His lips curled in satisfaction. Proud Calandra and tormented Ankine. Both beautiful and eminently desirable women in their own right. Both in thrall now to him, to serve his every need, obey his slightest command.

Calandra had only imagined she was escaping misery when she fled her aged, impotent husband to run away with that upstart prince. But Hovan Karayan had now deserted her, and the silvery blond–haired woman was now his. He enjoyed "punishing" her on a regular basis for her selfish folly. And, because she feared him so, Ladon thought he might find great pleasure in her for a long time to come. He very much, after all, liked the taste and scent of terror.

Ankine, however, was an entirely different matter. If she feared him, she kept it well hidden. Indeed, she kept every emotion tightly guarded from him. Still, Ladon guessed that her feelings for him ran more the way of hatred and loathing. She only thought she came to him as a frigid bedmate, not realizing there were times when her animosity practically seethed from her.

And, after terror, Ladon adored hatred and disgust most of all.

He fed on strong emotions, the more destructive the better. They seeped into him, permeating to his very blood vessels, where the invigorating effects coursed through his entire body. They were a drug, stimulating, exhilarating, life-sustaining. And, like a drug, they were addicting. He required more and more, stronger and stronger, until now he sought to elicit such intense emotions at every turn.

A tremor of anticipation ran through him. He'd feed richly this day. First on the terror of his officers, when he ordered them to begin a systematic sweep down the coast of Vardenis, from sea to the mountain foothills, rooting out any pockets of resistance and bringing all inhabitants under Hylean dominion. The terror would come when he gave them but a week to accomplish what would normally take months. The price for failure—which he fully expected to exact—would be the execution of yet another officer, drawn by lot.

He had an overabundance of officers anyway. This was but one amusing method to pare away the less useful of them. They were, after all, to a man more highborn then he. From childhood onward, he had seen that knowledge glimmering in their eyes and heard it in their voices whenever they thought he couldn't overhear. Even now they secretly disdained him, the discarded by-blow of an illicit union, though half of that union *had* been a king.

But no matter. Hatred, terror, loathing—he welcomed it all. He was in no danger from anyone. Phaon had seen to that.

Ladon's glance moved from Calandra to Ankine and back again. Which one should he take to his bed this eve? His gaze alighted on the flame-haired sorceress. Aye, Ankine. He had yet to complete the elaborate torment he had devised for her after she had failed to bring back Vartan Karayan.

As she had claimed, there would be other chances. A man like Karayan wouldn't long hide behind the skirts of women in some holy valley. He'd make his break sooner or later.

There'd be traps aplenty waiting for him. It was, after all, but a matter of time, and Ladon had planned for every eventuality. Ankine, in the meanwhile, must be thoroughly and most forcefully convinced she dare not fail again. And her ongoing education this eve, he thought, licking his lips in anticipation, would be sweetly satisfying indeed.

Save for two small, healed burns—one on the back of her upper left shoulder and one on the front of her midchest—her singed clothes, and some ringing in her ears, Danae didn't look as if she had almost died from a lightning strike. Still, though Serpuhi assured him she'd fully recover, Vartan refused to leave Danae's side that night, or the next day, as she dozed fitfully off and on. By the morning of the third day, however, Serpuhi was forced to drag him outside so Zagiri could help Danae bathe and wash her hair.

They sat there for a time, out on the overlook of what Serpuhi had informed him was now a lush, green valley. Though Vartan had all but made a pact to begin learning of Athan and the Faith if Danae's life was spared, Serpuhi hadn't once brought up the subject again. She truly meant to let him initiate the process, or not, Vartan realized, a new, heightened respect for her filling him. Was she but a supremely clever strategist, he wondered, or just honoring his free will?

Either way, *his* code of honor demanded he hold to his part of the bargain. And, if the truth were told, if this enigmatic Athan really was a loving, benevolent God, then he *did* want to know of Him. One way or another, there was nothing lost in a bit of instruction and prayer. In the learning, he'd either be led deeper or find it just didn't suit him. All he had to do, as Serpuhi had said, was keep an open heart.

"Will you teach me of Athan?" Vartan finally blurted, turning to her. "I still don't understand all that happened when you brought Danae back, but I felt a power in you . . . a power unlike any I've ever felt before. And I'd like . . . like to understand . . . to know more about its source."

"Yet the knowing frightens you, doesn't it? You wonder still if this power comes from good or evil."

"Aye, of course I do. If there's a good, a holy God, then there's likely an evil one, too. And evil can masquerade as good."

"But does Good ever masquerade as evil?"

He shrugged. "It wouldn't seem so."

"What do you seek, my son? What do you hope to find, in learning of Athan?"

"Answers," Vartan was quick to reply. "Answers to why all this happened to me and what I must now do. If there's some purpose to be found in this tragedy, I need help discovering it. I've tried and tried, but . . ." He expelled an exasperated breath, leaned over, and scrubbed at his face with both hands. "Truly, Serpuhi, I don't know what I really want or need anymore."

"Athan may never heal you of your blindness. You do realize that, don't you? Just because He healed Danae doesn't mean He has the same plan for you."

"Danae's life is worth more then my sight. And indeed, what good *is* my sight if, in the seeing, I still don't understand, still don't comprehend life's true meaning and purpose?" He lifted his head and stared straight ahead. "Danae once accused me of making my strength, intelligence, and sense of honor my god. She also warned me of the consequences of doing so. I refused to pay her much heed then, thinking in my arrogance that such a thing would never happen to me. But it did, Serpuhi, as it eventually does for us all. It just happened to me sooner than I anticipated."

"Aye, it happens to us all," she said. "But there's nothing easy about a life lived in the service of Athan, either. In the beginning there are a great many battles and a good deal of suffering, and only afterward comes the true joy. It's like those who wish to light a fire: At first the smoke comes, and they choke and cry. But so it must be. We kindle the divine fire in ourselves through tears and hard work."

"I'm not afraid of tears and hardship." Vartan smiled grimly. "As long as I know the prize is worth winning, I'll do whatever it takes."

"Sometimes, in the journey, you'll not even be certain of that."

He turned to her. "You're a most confusing woman. Before, it seemed all you wanted was to win me over to Athan, and now . . . now you're doing everything in your power to discourage me from even beginning."

Serpuhi chuckled softly. "Nay, not discourage, only caution and, in the cautioning, provide strength and consolation for the road ahead. If you're forewarned of the trials to come—trials all who seek Athan endure—you'll more easily recognize them and not let them defeat you. Remember always that the Evil One wants nothing more than for you to give up, to fail. He wants Gadiel for his own."

"Well, I'm certainly no threat to that particular goal." Vartan gave a harsh laugh. "I can't walk more than a few feet without tripping and falling on my face. My people are scattered and demoralized. Indeed, if I hadn't found sanctuary here, by now I'd likely be back in Ladon's hands, if not dead, then hanging in a cage from Astara's walls."

"Yet you remain a threat, and a potent one, my son. Athan has always been Gadiel's only true hope. No man can go against Phaon alone and prevail. Yet a man who trusts in Athan is a man like no other. Athan is his shield, his fortress, his strength."

"Aye," he ground out, his frustration growing apace with his confusion. "And how am I to do this? Where do I begin?"

She touched his hand. "You must begin at the beginning. You must learn of Athan and His son, Eisa. You must learn of Their abundant love. You must begin by studying the ancient, holy books."

"Then let's begin." A fierce resolve filled him. "The longer it takes, the longer my land's held in thrall to Ladon and his overlord. There's not a moment to waste."

"Aye, there's not a moment to waste," Serpuhi replied, amusement in her voice. "And you, my son, have a *very* lot to learn."

☙ ❧

Though blessed with a quick mind and an exceptional memory, Vartan's instruction nonetheless went slowly. Before, he had always worked best with things he could see and hold. He demanded proof, believing only what he thought held some reasonable semblance of logic. Yet, he found to his frustration that many of the tenets of the Faith were based precisely on that—faith.

"Trust when all seems impossible," Serpuhi said to him one fine, early summer's day. "Faith isn't found in the wisdom of men, but in the power of Athan."

"But I've a mind," Vartan muttered, "and in my mind so much of this doesn't make sense. You're asking me to believe Eisa died on a tree and then brought Himself back to life?"

"He was Athan's Son and God in His own right. Yet you saw how I, a mere mortal, brought Danae back from the brink of death. How can you not believe Eisa was able to do what I did?"

"It's simple, really." He expelled an exasperated breath. "I was there when you healed Danae. I felt the power flow through you to her. But this Eisa . . ." He shook his head. "I wasn't there to see or experience Him. His followers could've made it all up."

"So, are you saying you believe in Athan now, but not Eisa?"

Vartan shook his head. "I don't know. Aye . . . nay . . . perhaps."

"Give it time. Be patient with yourself. Be patient and know that if you continue to seek Him, you'll surely find Him."

"I'm trying, Serpuhi. This is all just so different from how I used to do things."

"Aye, and that's because, like the rest of us, you learned to do things the wrong way. Transformation takes time, time and a lot of hard work. It also demands all the courage you possess." She laughed. "And, at first, you breathe a lot of smoke, too."

He couldn't help but laugh in turn. The more he got to know Amma Serpuhi, the more Vartan marveled at the woman. He had never known anyone who possessed such wisdom or such joy. And her patience with him was phenomenal.

Vartan knew he tried her. A part of him still stubbornly resisted, even as another part fought to keep an open mind and heart. Unfortunately, he admitted, the stubborn part was so aligned with his pride as to be inseparable. His pride, he had never before realized, was so ingrained that it pervaded him, heart and mind. It was the source of his unwillingness to change, and he found its eradication a battle he was ill-prepared to fight.

With Serpuhi's gentle guidance, he was, though, slowly becoming aware of pride's surprising limitations. Becoming aware of the prison his life had become, even before he had lost his sight. The realization both chastened and exhilarated him. The first step toward freedom, after all, was to know you were a prisoner.

"Aye, I'm in the midst of heavy smoke right now," Vartan said with a chuckle. "Indeed, by the time I finally find my way through it, I'll be as browned and tasty as one of your smoked fish."

"It's good to see you can still keep a sense of humor and a healthy perspective about it all." She gave his hand a quick squeeze, then released it. "Now, it seems we're to have a visitor. Here comes Zagiri, and by the look on her face, she has something to say."

"Does she now? It's about time. She has all but avoided us for the past day or so. I imagine it's something I inadvertently said to offend her. That's usually what it is."

"Nay . . ." The *amma's* voice faded for a long moment. "I don't think so. This is something else altogether."

From the ever louder sound of her sandaled footsteps, Vartan could tell his sister was drawing near. He straightened,

161

looked up, and smiled in welcome. Zagiri, however, forestalled the usual greetings and came right to the point.

"I had a dream the night before last," she said as she sank to the ground before them. "It was from Athan. In it, He told me two things. First, He said it was time for Vartan to leave the Goreme."

He could feel the tension begin to knot his shoulders. "Indeed? Where then are we next to go, and why?"

"Athan didn't say why, save that time grows short and your destiny calls," Zagiri replied. "A destiny that now calls you to the Desert."

"*What?*" His tone a sharp mix of shock and outrage, Vartan nearly shouted the word. "*The Desert?* Save for Ladon waiting in Astara, the Desert's the last place I need to go. The Diya al Din want my head as much as Ladon does. Indeed, what with our long-standing enmity, they likely want it even more!"

"I didn't make the request, Brother," she ground out. "I only bear the message."

He didn't know what to say. Finally, Vartan turned to Serpuhi.

"And what do you think, Amma Serpuhi? Does this tale of Zagiri's make any sense to you?"

"Zagiri knows when a dream's just a dream and when it's a special vision sent by Athan. Though the message is indeed unfathomable, I've also found that Athan frequently communicates that way. What matters in the end isn't whether we understand it or not, but that we obey. In time, if we do so, Athan's intent usually becomes clear. And, even if it never does, it doesn't matter."

"Well, it matters to me!" He could barely keep the angry frustration from his voice. "I'm not ready to go. We've only just begun my instruction, Serpuhi. I haven't learned enough.

I'm not strong enough. And I don't yet know what Athan wants from me."

"Aye, but you do, my Son. He wants for you to obey Him and go to the Desert. It's just that simple."

"So, is this some sort of test then?" Vartan's hands clenched at his sides. "If so, I don't find it amusing. I'm not some puppet to be sent hither and yon, leastwise not without some reasonable explanation."

"And that's your pride speaking," Serpuhi said softly, then sighed. "I'll admit I, too, wanted more time with you. You've come such a long way, yet still have a long way to go. But apparently Athan intends for you to have other teachers. Or even just Him alone."

Sweat trickled down his spine, but it wasn't from the warmth of the day. It was from fear, stark fear. To go back out into that unfriendly, dangerous world when he had finally begun to feel comfortable here . . . He wasn't ready. Wasn't prepared. He didn't feel encompassed in Athan's protective love yet. But then, perhaps this Athan's love was as unfriendly and dangerous as the world He created.

Bitterness filled him. "Am I being cast out, then? Is that it?"

Serpuhi sucked in an anguished breath. "Oh, nay! I know what you face outside the Goreme. I'd never force you to go. The choice is yours, Vartan."

Aye, he thought, and what good would it do to hide here, if he didn't continue to build his relationship with Athan? A relationship that would now go nowhere, if he turned his back on this call. And it wasn't as if Zagiri would make this up. She knew as well as he the possible consequences for him if he left the valley. Nay, she truly believed this was Athan's command, or she never would have revealed it in the first place.

"That's right, isn't it?" His thoughts an agonized tumult, he leaned down to rest his face in his hands. "Athan always allows us our free will. But what good will it do me if I don't heed His call?"

"In the end, it'll do you nothing that's worthwhile and good," Serpuhi replied. "But many men don't care. All that matters is they've lived their lives their own way, securely tucked away in their own comfortable, if self-deceptive, illusions." She laid a hand on his shoulder. "I never said this journey would be safe or easy, did I?"

"Nay." With a quirk of his lips, Vartan finally glanced up. "You never did. Well, leastwise I'll have Zagiri with me, and her protection as a holy woman."

"There was one more thing Athan told me, Brother."

He turned to her. "Aye, and what was that?"

"I won't be journeying to the Desert with you and Danae. Athan told me I must, instead, leave you, go to Sevan House, and 'prepare the way.'"

"Prepare the way for whom or what?" Once more, Vartan could feel the anger build. "Are you certain He meant that, Zagiri? Danae and I'll be helpless against Ankine, or whatever other evil creatures Ladon is sure to send against us." He shook his head with a savage vehemence. "If that's the way it is, I'll go out alone. I won't allow Danae to risk herself. Not for me."

Zagiri expelled an exasperated breath. "Don't be a fool. Danae's more than just a companion on the journey. She's your eyes. Without her, you won't need to waste time worrying about evil creatures. You'll surely fall off some cliff long before you encounter any of them."

"Well, if my destiny is to die, I suppose I'll die, won't I?" he snarled. "But I *won't* allow Danae to die with me. Athan will just have to lead me Himself."

"Vartan! How dare you put conditions on—"

"Enough, you two," Serpuhi said, laughing. "In the end, it's not Vartan's decision anyway, whether Danae goes or stays. It's hers. Fetch her if you will, Zagiri. I see her coming back from where the milch tur is pastured. Bring her here, and we'll soon have this whole matter settled."

He knew what Serpuhi and Zagiri hoped for. That Danae would agree to accompany him. Yet, though Vartan knew his own plan was so foolhardy as to be suicidal, he didn't want Danae involved in this mess. Let her refuse. *Please*, he thought, lifting a quick, fervent prayer. *Make her see the futility of continuing to join her fate to mine.*

Still, even as he awaited her return and considered every possible argument to sway her, Vartan knew all his schemes were doomed to failure. Danae would no more desert him than he'd desert her. In some curious way they were bound to each other, their lives and fates entwined. When it had become so, he didn't know. Perhaps it happened that night on the porch. Perhaps it occurred some time before or after that.

It didn't matter, not now. His sister, whatever the reason for her calling, *was* deserting him. And that left only Danae to carry on, joined to a helpless, ill-fated man until a horrible death finally found them.

No time was lost preparing for the journey. Zagiri had stressed that Athan said time was of the essence. Plans were made for them to set off that very night. If anyone or anything was spying on the road out of the valley, they'd not so easily notice the little group in the darkness. Zagiri would remain with Danae and Vartan for a time, until the mountain roads diverged, one leading northeast toward the barren Ibn

Khaldun range that ran to the Desert, and the other leading directly north toward Mount Talin and the now deserted Sevan House.

As twilight descended over the Goreme Valley, Zagiri found Danae. "Will you come with me, walk with me?" she asked the younger woman.

Danae nodded. Fastening the last leather tie on the pack she was to carry, she rose to her feet. They had decided not to use the pony cart this time, fearing it would not only attract too much unwanted attention, but also be difficult to maneuver in the increasingly inhospitable terrain of the Ibn Khaldun. Instead, both Vartan and Danae would carry tall, stout walking sticks and packs. Hopefully their supply of food and water would get them through the mountains to Am Shardi, the first oasis said to lie just at the eastern edge where mountains met Desert.

After that, they hadn't planned for their next route. Athan had only said Vartan was called to the Desert. The rest was in His hands.

Danae followed Zagiri down the valley past the beehive huts, until they came to the river. Her friend chose a fallen turkawood tree trunk for them to sit upon. For a while, they watched the trees swaying in the warm, gentle breeze and listened to the rushing water.

Finally, however, Zagiri cleared her throat. "Though he hasn't said it, I know Vartan's very angry with me." She sighed and looked down. "He thinks I'm deserting him."

"At times, Athan asks hard things of us." Danae reached over and took her hand. "It's hard enough even for me to accept. Vartan still needs you, Zagiri. How can Athan ask such a thing, at such a time?"

"I don't know. But He has. It's up to you now."

166

"Me?" Danae gave an unsteady little laugh. "And what can I do, save to lead him where he cannot see to go? I'm so afraid, Zagiri! Afraid I'll fail him—that he'll die because of me."

"And he fears the same for you. But you're both in Athan's hands now, and I don't think *He'll* fail either of you." She gave Danae's hand a little squeeze. "You've always been meant, you know, to be together."

"Then it's not over?" Danae asked. "That day in Astara, you told me I was to help Vartan by teaching him of Athan and Eisa, and that I was Athan's instrument to aid Vartan in the hard times to come. But Vartan now knows of the Eternal One and has accepted Him. And he's come safely through some very hard times."

"So you've been wondering if your task is fulfilled? Is that it?"

"I'm not saying I *want* it to be finished. Far from it. I was just wondering . . . wondering if Athan had told you anything more? About our future, I mean?"

Her friend looked away for a time, then sighed and turned back to her. "Nay, He hasn't. Or, leastwise, not anything more than that it's imperative you both continue to serve Gadiel through Him, and that no matter what comes in the days and weeks ahead, your life and Vartan's are inextricably bound, and always will be."

Danae smiled. It was all she had ever wanted—to remain close to Vartan. And ever since Zagiri had revealed the Prophecy to her, she had known Vartan was called to serve Gadiel. So it made sense, Athan's plan. In continuing to aid Vartan, she, too, was serving Gadiel. Lives being bound, however, didn't necessarily mean they would ever become man and wife.

"I'll miss you." She lifted Zagiri's hand to press it against her cheek, then released it. "What will I do without you, without your wise counsel?"

"We'll meet again, all of us. I just know it."

"Truly?"

"Truly." Her friend grasped Danae's face, leaned over, and kissed her on the forehead. Then she released her.

"Always live with a sense that you can be more than you ever thought you could be, for you've yet to tap your deepest potential. And never fear the Desert, be it the one of sand or the one where Athan may call you to purify your heart and intentions one day. Instead, face and befriend it, for true freedom comes with detachment from the things of this world. Always gaze inward and reflect on Athan's holy words. Never fear being vulnerable. Never fear risking everything to be deeply changed and transformed."

"I won't, Zagiri," she breathed, taking the cherished words and tucking them deep within her heart, even as she wondered over things said that had never even been hinted at before. "And know that I'll do everything in my power to help Vartan, and I'll stay with him for as long as he needs me."

"He'll need you forever. Didn't I already tell you that?"

Danae smiled sadly. "Aye, you did. Still, I'll never stand in the way of his happiness."

"You *are* his happiness. Don't you know that?"

She blushed and averted her gaze. "Nay, I don't, but it doesn't matter. It's enough that *I* love him."

"Then let that suffice for now." Zagiri climbed to her feet. "Come, it's time we had our supper and a short nap. Our departure draws near."

"Aye, so it does."

Danae stood. Together, they walked back in the soft summer darkness.

11

Serpuhi's parting gift to them was a thick, nearly impenetrable fog, which, she told them, would shield their departure as they passed by Ladon's soldiers encamped not far from the entrance to the valley. Follow the light, she said, and it will lead you safely through the darkness.

Still, there were times when Vartan wondered if they'd make it through the gauntlet of sleeping soldiers. They passed so closely he could hear their soft snores and the rustle of their movements as they turned, drew a blanket up more snugly about their shoulders, or scratched some offending body part in their slumber. But for once, thanks to the fog, his enemies were as blind as he.

In time, they moved beyond the encampment, and silence enveloped them once more. The light, which Danae finally informed him was actually a soft glow, never faded, leading them onward through the night. Eventually the fog Vartan felt as a cool dampness on his skin dissipated, and he knew they were once again exposed for any and all to see.

They walked for what seemed endless, mind- and body-numbing hours, traveling a mountain path sometimes barely wide enough save to go single file. The path was bordered on one side by a steep, rock-sided wall and, on the other, by a cliff that dropped off precipitously into nothingness. They spoke rarely, fearing their voices might give them away. In the long, dark silence, Vartan's emotions swung chaotically from sadness to concern over what lay ahead, to a wavering sense of peace and acceptance that seemed to come and go with each passing breeze.

His thoughts turned to Amma Serpuhi's parting words. "Don't fall into the trap of trusting in yourself to become your own guide, your own god," she had said. "Be willing to listen for the voice of Athan in your life. And remember: The person who prays for the presence of Athan is already in His presence. Though the times to come will be hard, will test you body and soul, never forget you are called to turn away from evil and do good. Let peace always be your quest and aim. Peace of heart and peace with all men."

Peace of heart . . . peace with all men . . .

Vartan smiled at the irony of Serpuhi's words. Had she meant something deeper than what appeared on the surface, when she had spoken of peace with all men? Did she truly comprehend the depth of the enmity between the Karayans and the Diya al Din? That peace was the last thing either side would ever seek? Yet how could Gadiel hope to prevail against Ladon and his Hylean army, if all the peoples didn't set aside their differences and join together as one?

Well, he thought, *this is definitely one dilemma only Athan could resolve.* It was surely beyond his feeble human abilities. He would be willing, though, to serve as Athan's herald and call them all together. *Not that Athan had yet to request that,* Vartan added wryly. Indeed, at present, he had no idea what Athan *did* want of him. There was likely a lot more listening in store, before *that* ever happened.

Zagiri left them sometime in the wee hours of the night. After tendering her tear-choked farewells, she hastened away, not wishing to prolong the leave-taking. In the end, Vartan relented and pulled her into a smothering hug.

"Have a care, Sister," he whispered. "And don't forget me in your prayers. I'll be needing them, you know."

"As if I could ever forget a big, conceited lout like you," she said, sniffling. Zagiri then extricated herself from his grasp and stepped back. "Now, get on with you. You've yet a lot of mountain to cover before dawn."

He had dearly wished for his sight to return, if only to see his sister one last time, but that was not to be. Vartan nodded and turned to follow Danae. *Take care of Zagiri,* he thought, lifting a quick prayer. *She's all I have left of my family. Take care of her and, if it's Your will, let us meet again.*

About sunrise, Danae called a halt to their journey. "It'll soon be daylight. It might be wiser to take shelter until dark."

"Aye. Once Ladon's minions discover we've slipped past them, they'll be hot on our trail. And, considering I can't move very fast without my vision . . ."

Her hand settled on his arm. "There's a cave about five minutes' walk down this path. We could see if it suits."

"Lead on, then." He smiled. "I'm yours to command."

The cave was indeed most adequate for their needs. It was deep, according to Danae, and high-ceilinged enough that Vartan wouldn't have to worry about banging his head. It also provided a good vantage to watch for any approach from several angles. She soon had the bedrolls unpacked and a cold supper ready.

"Feels strange," Vartan said as he chewed a piece of bread and cheese and swallowed it, "eating supper in the morn."

"Aye. I suppose it's but one of many things we'll have to readjust to in the days to come. I'm particularly concerned about the Desert. What with summer upon us, and from what I've heard of the heat . . ."

He paused to take a swig of water from the leather water pouch. "You speak as if you've never been in a desert. Are there no deserts in Hylas?"

"Nay." Danae laughed. "Hylas is mainly a mountainous country, with some areas of lush, verdant pastureland, surrounded on three sides by the Great Sea. And even its many isles are little more than rugged lava rock that, over time, have become populated with all manner of plant and animal life carried on the fresh ocean breezes. It's quite a lovely land, it is."

There was something akin to sad yearning in her voice. "You sound as if you miss your home." He set aside his bread and cheese. "After Astara fell, why didn't you return to Hylas with your father?"

"I no longer felt any kinship with my people, not after watching your family destroyed. My people just stood there and didn't offer one protest." Danae sighed. "There was more, too. Though I didn't understand at the time why, or from whence the certainty came, I also felt I was meant to remain in Gadiel. And it didn't take long for the reason to become clear."

When she didn't explain further, Vartan leaned toward her. "And that reason was?"

"You. Athan meant for me to help you."

He reared back, not knowing what to say. A part of him was glad she had chosen to stay because of him. Yet another part was just as reluctant to accept her selfless sacrifice.

"I can offer you no guarantee of anything, Danae," Vartan finally said. "No guarantee except that of hardship, suffering, and perhaps even death if you continue to stay and help me. You know that, don't you?"

"Aye, I do. I'm not afraid."

"Well, *I* am!" He lowered his head and rubbed his face

172

with both hands. "I need you, need your help, and we both know it. But it doesn't make it any easier, aware as I am of the danger you're constantly in because of me. Aware, as well, I'd be helpless to protect you. It eats at me day and night."

"The choice is mine, Vartan. It's not your responsibility—my safety, I mean."

"It has always been before." He gave a harsh laugh. "Do you imagine it's so easy for that to change, just because I'm blind? I've lost my sight, Danae, not my feelings or my sense of duty and protectiveness toward you."

"I didn't mean to disparage you or your honor." Her voice dropped to a whisper. "But I do have some say in the matter, too, don't I? Or is it to be like it was before? You the lord and master, and I the obedient servant? I only wonder if you'd feel the same if I were a man?"

Frustration filled him. "Nay, I didn't mean it that way. I just meant . . . Vartan paused. She was right. Once again, his pride had stepped to the forefront. What mattered was that *he* remain in control, be the protector, the lord over all. He meant well but, in the doing, he also robbed others of the opportunity to excel, to contribute something of their own that was equally worthwhile. And that, at the very least, was selfish and arrogant.

Vartan expelled a despairing breath. *Ah, Athan,* he thought, *Serpuhi was right. I have so very far to go, so much yet to learn.*

"Forgive me, sweet lady," he said. "You do indeed have some say in the matter. It's your right to choose how and what you must do. Though I doubt I'll ever cease to worry about you, I'll try harder to be more gracious in accepting your brave offer and your loyalty to me. As I would do if you were a man."

173

"Thank you for that."

He wanted to say more, to tell Danae why his feelings for her intensified his fear of losing her, but didn't. It would serve no purpose, save to complicate things even more. Right now, the last thing either of them needed was more complications.

"There's the matter of what we should do once we enter the Desert," Vartan said instead. "I fear some untruths might have to be told. I hate to ask you to lie, but—"

"It could well mean your life if we don't," Danae was quick to interject. "I know that."

"Still, I hate to ask you to do it. I hate to do it myself . . ." He sighed. "Well, there's nothing to be done for it, I suppose. It would be extremely unwise for you to call me by my given name. The Diya al Din are suspicious enough, and word may have reached them by now that I'm still alive."

"Do you have another name in mind, then?"

"Aye. Call me Ara. Ara Kocharian." He smiled in remembrance. "As a child, my nickname was Ara, which is the name of a legendary Gadielean warrior. Even then I lived to play heroic warriors, so my mother named me for the famous Ara."

"And the Kocharian? Another legendary hero as well?"

Vartan shook his head. "Nay, just the family name of some distant relative, far removed. The mention of it shouldn't provoke any questions with the Diya al Din. It's actually quite common."

Danae giggled. "Then Ara Kocharian it is."

He scratched his chin, thinking. "One thing more. The Diya al Din have strict rules about women. They aren't permitted to travel unchaperoned, unless they're traveling with their husband or relatives."

"I suppose I could be your sister."

"You could, save that as an unwed woman you'd be fair game for any Desert warrior who took a fancy to you. As your brother, I'd be hard-pressed to turn down *all* offers for your hand. When it comes to women, after all, the Desert men are renowned for their fierce pride and prickly egos."

"What are you suggesting then?"

"Isn't it obvious?" He couldn't help it. Her apparent lack of enthusiasm to play the part of his wife grated on his own masculine ego. "For your safety, I think it best you pretend to be my bride."

"Oh. And what exactly would that entail?"

"Nothing *too* onerous, I vow," he muttered in rising irritation. Why was she being so halfhearted about this? "We might have to occasionally share a kiss or some other innocent sign of marital affection. You might also be required to defer to me as your husband—the Diya al Din are quite keen on a woman's proper role. And, at the worst, we might—on hopefully extremely rare occasions—have to sleep in the same bedchamber."

"But *not* in the same bed."

"Nay, not in the same bed." Vartan lifted his head heavenward and rolled his eyes. "I'm not suggesting anything immoral, Danae. I'd never treat you in such a manner."

"You offered to bed me that night in Astara."

He had been afraid that little slip of the tongue might come back to haunt him. "You're a very desirable woman, Danae. And that night, I wasn't myself. Surely you must have guessed, even then, that Aelwyd and I had slept apart for a long while? I was lonely, convinced I'd probably be dead on the morrow, and you were so sweet and warm and caring. Will you hold that against me for the rest of our lives?"

"Nay." She sighed. "I beg pardon. It was unkind and unfair of me to bring that up."

"It must have disturbed you deeply. I've never known you to hold grudges."

"It wasn't a grudge!" she cried, scrambling to her feet. "It was . . . it was . . . Oh, never mind. Just never mind!"

With that, Danae strode from the cave. Completely baffled at her response to what he had thought was his mildly put, conciliatory reply, Vartan rose and made his halting way toward the cave entrance. At the sound of her sobs, however, he drew up a few feet inside the entrance.

It tore at his heart to hear her weeping, somehow knowing it was because of him. Was it the result of his self-serving proposition that night in Astara? Had it truly offended her that deeply? Or was it because she now feared any situation portraying them as husband and wife would, ultimately, lead to the same unpleasant possibilities? Likely exhaustion and the stress of the past weeks had also contributed to her overwrought state, as well.

Vartan squared his shoulders and tentatively made his way toward Danae. She must have finally heard his approach, because she ceased weeping.

"Vartan!" she cried. "What are you doing out here? The ledge and trail leading up to it are very narrow. If you'd taken a wrong step, or lost your balance—"

"Well, I didn't, though it surely would've simplified your life if I had," he growled, suddenly not certain what to say to her. "And I came out because I heard you crying. I don't know exactly what I did to cause it—being the tactless brute that I am, there are so many possibilities—but I'm sorry. I'd never purposely hurt you. Please believe that."

"I-I know," she said, hiccupping softly. "And you aren't a tactless brute." She stood, reached out, and touched his arm. "Now, come back to the cave. It isn't safe for you out here."

A surge of irrational fury flashed through him. Vartan grabbed for her hand and pulled her hard up against him.

"And *I* say, don't treat me like some helpless, ignorant child! Though I may not be the man for you, I still have my pride. Tell me the truth. *Always* tell me the truth. And if posing as husband and wife is so distasteful, then we can be brother and sister. It's just that you're a beautiful woman, Danae, and that blond hair of yours will be highly prized by many Desert men. I humbly beg pardon, but I only thought to protect you."

Her fingers entwined in his coarse linen shirt. Her breaths came in short, shallow gasps. Then, with a soft little sigh, she leaned against him, her head finding a resting place on his chest.

"Hold me, Vartan," she whispered. "It's not your fault. It's me. And I'm just so tired . . ."

He didn't need to be asked twice. With a groan, he pulled her the more tightly to him, wrapping his arms about her and resting his cheek on the top of her head. She smelled of wild herb grass and flowers, and her woman's curves fit so perfectly against his body. A savage yearning swelled within, and it was all Vartan could do to contain the impulse to take her sweet face in his hands and kiss her.

But he didn't. Just being close to Danae shredded his honor into thin, insubstantial bits, but what little he could seize he clung to with all his might. Not for his sake, but for hers. For her and the precious loyalty and kindness she had always shown him.

"Be my sister then," he said into the soft, fragrant tumble of her hair. "It's up to you, sweet lady. And be assured, on my word of honor, I will never, *ever*, treat you disgracefully."

"I know that," her voice rose from his chest. "And I've never doubted it." She hesitated, then sighed. "Perhaps it's best I do as you suggest, and pretend to be your wife. I wouldn't wish to cause you more hardship or worry."

Vartan inhaled deeply, savagely quashing the renewed swell of yearning her words stirred. She was not for him. He had nothing anymore to offer her. Nothing.

"It's no hardship, sweet lady," he said, holding her close for a few more forbidden seconds. "And the worry is a precious burden. As precious as you are to me."

Not long after they set out that night, Danae began to hear strange scuttling noises. At first she attributed the intermittent sounds to falling rocks, some bouncing down from high above, others stirred by their passing. After a time, though, the noises gained a certain uneven rhythm of their own. She and Vartan were being followed.

Vartan apparently drew the same conclusion at the same time. He moved close enough to lean forward and whisper in her ear.

"We've company."

She nodded and kept walking. "I noticed. Any idea who or what?"

"From their surefootedness, something that likes to prowl about at night," he replied. "I'd wager they're Pedars. They're a bit too quick and nimble to be Daegols. A meager blessing, to be sure, but it's something."

"How so?"

"Pedars are smaller, about the size of a child. If it comes to it, we might be able to hold them off for a time. They fight dirty, though, and they're very sneaky, with excellent hearing and sharp, pointed teeth. One thing for sure, we mustn't allow them to get ahead of us. They can hide by turning to stone. Then, once their enemy has passed them, they re-form back into themselves and take their opponents by surprise. Oh, and they use short, razor-sharp swords and daggers and are quite adept at skewering people with them."

"How comforting," Danae lamented, tamping down her rising apprehension. "Any suggestions on what we should do?"

"None, save keep ahead of them and hope they don't catch up to us before sunrise. They aren't overly fond of daylight. It quickly crisps their skin and blinds them."

"Night or day, I don't think I'd like to meet any Pedars. Can you walk faster if you take a tight hold on my arm?"

"There's little other choice. I'll just have to."

For several hours they managed to stay ahead of their pursuers. Inexorably, however, the little goblinlike beasts slowly narrowed the distance, until Danae could clearly hear their soft, snorting grunts and scrabbling sounds. Occasionally, when the breeze shifted, she also caught scent of a foul, fetid odor. Likely Pedars weren't overly fond of bathing, either, she thought.

"There may come a time when I drop back," Vartan said just then. "If so, immediately throw down your pack and run. I should be able to hold them off until you get safely away."

"Nay." Vehemently, Danae shook her head. "I won't leave you to fight them alone. We've both got stout walking sticks and daggers. We'll meet them side by side."

"And should we both die, then? Or what if I somehow survived and you didn't? I'm just as dead, alone in these mountains. Be sensible, Danae. Do what I ask."

"Together we've a chance to defeat them, Vartan." She blinked hard against the sudden swell of tears. "I'll never forgive myself if I don't at least give you that chance."

"Danae—"

"I'm staying, Vartan, and there's nothing you can do to change that!" *And please, Athan,* she prayed, *please help us.*

He expelled a ragged breath. "You're right, of course. I can't make you do anything. But if we manage to survive this, I vow I'll—"

"What's that?" Far up on the trail now winding ever higher, Danae thought she saw an unusual glow. "That light up ahead?"

"Funny thing, that," he growled. "I don't happen to see any light."

Excitement filled her. Ignoring his sarcastic comment, she tugged on Vartan's arm. "Can you run? I think . . . I think it's a man holding a torch."

"Unlikely. It's probably just the moonlight glinting off some polished facet of stone, Danae. There's little chance—"

"Aye, it *is* a man!" she cried, quickening her pace even more. "And he's beckoning to us. Hurry, Vartan. Hurry!"

Almost dragging him along, Danae climbed the path that became increasingly steeper. Vartan was wrong. The man wasn't an illusion. He was real and dressed in the rough brown robe of a holy *abba*.

A wild hope flared. Perhaps this man might be able to help them escape the Pedars!

She could hear the little beasts drawing ever nearer. Danae didn't dare turn around for fear the Pedars would be upon them. She looked up the trail to where the older man—now, in the flickering torchlight, she could tell he was at least middle-aged—stood calmly awaiting them. And still the Pedars came on, until she could almost feel them.

"Athan, help us," she gritted between panting breaths. "Help us!"

"Aye, help us," Vartan added his own plea, "for this woman's bound and determined to get us both killed."

Perhaps it was the exhilaration of sanctuary awaiting at the end of the trail. Or perhaps she was getting so starved for air that the gravity of their situation no longer mattered, but Vartan's sardonic comment struck her as amusing. She laughed and, in surprising response, the man up ahead laughed, too.

The sound of his mirth took wing, soaring across to the opposite cliffs, echoing back and forth across the narrow river gorge below until the air reverberated with the deep, rich sound. And at the first peel of his laughter, the Pedars shrieked in terror. Danae glanced over her shoulder just in time to see the hirsute band of ugly little beasts slam to a halt, then all but climb over each other in their haste to turn and scramble back down the trail.

Then there was no time for further gawking. Vartan, unaware of her sudden slowing, slammed into her. If not for his quick response in grabbing her, Danae might have tumbled backward off the trail.

"By all that's holy," he cried, pulling her close, "why didn't you warn me you were going to stop?"

"I didn't know . . . until I looked back and saw the Pedars turn and run for their lives." She leaned into the solid circle of his arms. "We're safe, Vartan. They've gone."

"It was that man's laughter that frightened them away, wasn't it?" He scowled. "It nearly deafened me. What manner of man is he, anyway?"

"He looks like an *abba* from the Goreme." Danae reached back and took one of Vartan's hands. "Come. Let's go meet him."

He resisted the tug on his hand. "What he may appear and what he truly is can be two different things. The man might just as easily be a demon in disguise."

"Perhaps, but I don't think so. And one way or another, we'll face that problem if and when it truly becomes one."

"I don't know about you," he muttered as he finally allowed himself to be led forward once more, "but I'm not so certain I'm up to confronting any demons just yet."

"Neither am I," Danae said. "But hush now. We're almost there."

The man smiled benevolently down at them. "Welcome," he said when Danae finally drew to a halt with Vartan at her side. "I've been awaiting you, and am quite pleased you managed to make it here ahead of those Pedars."

"If it hadn't been for you, we wouldn't have."

She stared at him with unabashed interest. *He doesn't look very demonic,* Danae thought. On closer inspection, he appeared to be in his fifties, smooth shaven with long, graying hair that fell to his shoulders. His eyes were dark—it was difficult to tell their exact color in the torchlight—and kind. Deep furrows crinkled at their corners. The kind of furrows that came from a lot of smiling.

"My name's Danae, and this is . . ." She hesitated, the use of Vartan's nickname still slipping most awkwardly off her tongue. "This is—"

"I know who he is," the man said. "Welcome, Vartan Karayan." He held out his hand.

Danae guided Vartan's hand to meet and grasp the man's.

"And you," Vartan lost no time in demanding. "Who are you called?"

"I go by many names," their new host said with a chuckle. "Best, though, to just call me Garabed. Abba Garabed."

Though Vartan shook his hand, Danae could tell he wasn't yet willing to lower his guard.

"And how did you know to expect us?" he asked. "And me, most specifically?"

Garabed smiled. "How else? Athan told me you were coming. Now, let us be on our way. The Pedars will eventually rediscover their courage and try again."

When he turned and began to walk away, Vartan called out. "Wait. Where would you be taking us?"

"You are called to the Desert." He gestured toward a dark opening in the mountain behind him, an opening Danae hadn't noticed until now. "This tunnel will lead you safely there."

"And will you accompany us to the Desert, then?"

Abba Garabed shook his head. "Nay. This particular journey is yours and Danae's alone. Another time, perhaps."

Danae moved to Vartan's side and took his arm. "Come. Let's go."

He refused to budge. "And how do we know this man isn't leading us into a trap, or into one of those tunnels in the Valans that are said to have no end? I need more reason than his claim Athan told him of us, to believe him. Phaon's minions could just as easily say the same thing."

Danae hesitated. Vartan spoke true. How *could* they really know the truth about Abba Garabed?

She looked to the older man. In his dark eyes burned the knowledge of her doubts. There was no anger, though, no recrimination or even affront. There was only compassion—and love.

"We know because I can look into his eyes," Danae said. "I can see the man he is, and I trust him. And because you cannot see, *you* must trust *me*. Will you, Vartan?"

For a moment, Vartan didn't reply. Then he expelled a long, slow breath. "Aye, I trust you. Always and forever."

Danae tugged on his arm. "Then come. Let's go."

This time, Vartan followed. As they drew up to the *abba*, Garabed handed her his torch.

183

"The journey through the mountains to the Desert is long," he said. "This torch will burn for you, though, until you reach the end. Trust in that—and Athan—when the doubts assail you."

She accepted the flaming brand, her fingers clenching about it. "My thanks for everything. How can we ever repay you?"

"No need, my child." Garabed smiled. "I was sent to aid you. Likely you've not seen the last of me."

"Then I look forward to the next time."

He nodded. "Aye, until the next time."

With that, Danae moved past him, Vartan following, into the mouth of a cave as black as a moonless night. A chill breeze, rank with the scent of old, musty air, struck her in the face. She shivered, and for an instant her steps faltered. But only for an instant.

Their destiny awaited them somewhere at the end of this tunnel. There was no turning back. Athan called, and they must answer. And, like this tunnel, which they must trust would lead them safely to daylight, so they must trust that the future, which unfurled just as dark and obscure as this tunnel, would lead to an equally good end.

12

In the tunnel's black, silent void seconds blended seamlessly into minutes, and minutes into hours, until Danae finally lost track of the time. Had the day come and gone? Was it once more night outside this massive mound of endless stone?

The cold damp seeped into her bones until her limbs turned stiff and aching. The stillness became so heavy and encompassing she began to feel as if she were entombed. *Which we, in a sense, indeed are,* she thought, before hastily quashing that image and the terror it so readily stirred.

Doubts assailed her in the hours they walked along in the black corridor of stone, their only light the torch Garabed had given them. Though, true to his word, the flaming brand burned ever brightly, Danae began to wonder if she could depend on it any more than she could the man himself. What if it had all been a trick? What if Garabed had schemed with the Pedars to appear their savior, while all along intending to send them into the mountain, never to be seen again?

Many were the times she considered turning around and heading back to the tunnel's entrance. If Garabed's intent had been evil, there was yet hope he might've already departed with the Pedars, thinking they'd never retrace their steps. The way back, after all, was a fixed number of steps, while the way forward was unknown and potentially infinite.

Still, something held Danae to her course. Was it but her pride, refusing to be humbled in the confession that she had been wrong? Yet what value was her pride when it might be the death of Vartan? Nothing was worth that.

Every time she opened her mouth to utter the admission, however, the memory of the moment she had looked deep into the *abba's* eyes held her tongue at bay. The surety she had felt rushed back to engulf her in renewed confidence. Garabed was a good man, a holy man. Athan had sent him to them. To doubt the *abba* now was to doubt Athan.

And so, for a time more, Danae would journey onward, fighting her doubts and fears, laying them at Athan's feet. Somehow, even if the purpose for sending them into this living death had been for evil, she trusted Athan would turn it to good. He had said, after all, that Vartan's destiny lay in the Desert, and they had yet to reach it.

"Do you think we might stop for a time?" Vartan's voice rose just then from behind her. "We haven't eaten since this morning, and I'm hungry. We both, I imagine, could also use a few hours' rest."

Remorse flooded her. She had been so intent on getting them through the mountain as quickly as possible, she hadn't stopped except to swallow a few gulps of water.

"Aye, of course." Danae halted, lifted the torch high, and glanced around. The passage was narrow right here, but up ahead it widened a bit. "Let's walk on to where there's more room for us to stretch out. I'm hungry and tired, too."

They quickly consumed the remaining bread and cheese, then untied the blankets fastened to the bottom of their packs and spread them out. One final time, Danae checked to make certain the torch was securely shoved into a crevice on the wall, then, tucking her cloak more snugly about her, she lay down on her blanket. It didn't take long, though, before the stone-cold surroundings and dampness seeped through to start her to shivering.

"May I make a suggestion?"

Danae turned over to face Vartan, who lay a few feet from her. "Aye? And what might that suggestion be?"

"It's horrendously cold in here. Would you be willing to double up on the blankets beneath us, sleep close to one another, and use both cloaks to cover us? I fear it's the only solution to prevent us both from freezing to death while we sleep."

Danae knew it was a wise plan, but still . . . "Aye," she said at last, accepting there was indeed little other choice. "At a time like this, it does seem the best thing to do."

"The lesser of two evils, so to speak," he said with a touch of humor in his voice.

She chuckled. "Aye, but remember one thing. Though we may be pretending to be husband and wife, we're really more like brother and sister."

"I could hardly forget, could I, with all your gentle reminders?"

"Nay, I suppose not." Danae climbed to her feet. "Now, pray get up so we can combine our blankets."

He immediately did so, and they were soon ensconced close together. For a time Danae lay there, too acutely aware of Vartan's body behind her for any hope of sleep. She could tell he lay there equally wide awake.

She knew she could trust him. That had never been the issue. It was her own traitorous body and emotions she didn't trust. She wanted him, as a woman wanted a man. What would he do if she turned, took his face in her hands, and kissed him? Would he kiss her in turn, then pull her yet closer, joining their bodies in a far more intimate union?

There was no doubt Vartan desired her. He had admitted it to her on several occasions. Though he was an honorable man, Danae felt certain he'd not refuse her if she offered. And, oh, how she wanted him, wanted to give herself to him!

But it would also be wrong. They weren't and never would be husband and wife, and to share a carnal knowledge of each other's bodies in any other way was forbidden, an offense to Athan. Even worse, it might destroy the fragile link Vartan was finally beginning to build with the Eternal One. And, without Athan, he could never discover or achieve his true destiny. The destiny that, in the end, offered him the greatest surety for happiness.

Her own desires weren't what mattered. What mattered was Athan and Vartan. What mattered was the destiny calling Vartan, a destiny that held no place for her as his lover. So Danae comforted herself with the solace that she was his friend, and that, if only in the purest of ways, she could spend a few hours resting beside him. It wasn't enough, but it was all she could ever have. She forced herself to find some peace with that.

After a time, his warmth began to penetrate her chilled, aching muscles and she finally relaxed. His slow, rhythmic breathing soothed her, as did the satisfying awareness of his presence. Danae began to doze, in her drowsiness unwittingly pressing yet closer to him.

A hiss of breath between clenched teeth jerked her back awake. "What is it?" she asked, gone suddenly tense and wary. "Did you hear something?"

"Nay," Vartan ground out hoarsely. "It's all right, Danae. Just go back to sleep."

"But there must be something—"

"Please, Danae. Just . . . just lie still and go back to sleep!"

There was something strained in his voice, but what caused it she couldn't ascertain. She lay there for a time, tense and listening, but after a while, languor filled her anew and she again relaxed against him.

Sometime later, Danae awoke. Vartan snored softly behind her. She made a move to sit and found he had wrapped his arms about her, effectively pinning her close to him. He was warm, and in his embrace her muscles and bones no longer ached. She wanted to lie here like this forever.

But it was past time they rise and continue their journey. Her glance lifted to the torch. Its light had imperceptibly changed, burned a little less brightly. Though it amazingly had burned so far, Danae knew now it had a predetermined life.

"Vartan?"

He didn't answer, only muttered something unintelligible in his sleep and snuggled the closer. Danae squirmed in his arms.

"Vartan, wake up. We must be going."

His breathing changed. He dragged in a breath.

"Aye . . ." His voice was husky with sleep. "I'm awake."

"Well, let me go then," she said, pressing against the circle of his arms. "You're holding me so tightly I can scarcely breathe."

It was a slight exaggeration, but it had the desired effect. Vartan released her and scooted back.

"I beg pardon. I didn't mean anything by it."

"I know." Danae shoved to her elbows, then sat up. "We were both just so cold. But we did survive, didn't we? We didn't freeze to death."

"How long do you think we slept?" He didn't move, just lay there still flat on his back.

189

She shook her head. "I don't know. A few hours, or maybe a lot longer. One way or another, I feel rested. How about you?"

"I'm fine." At last, Vartan pushed to a sitting position. "Shall we pack and head out?"

"Aye. It's best we do." Her glance strayed to the torch. She considered telling him its light was waning, then thought better of it. No sense adding to his worry. She could at least spare him that.

Leastwise until the torch finally died.

Vartan wasn't aware the torch had gone out until Danae told him. He had guessed something was amiss when she drew to an abrupt halt, but momentarily he hoped she had at last seen the opening at the other end of the tunnel. Still, her somber admission didn't surprise him. In truth, quite some time ago he had begun to have serious doubts they would ever emerge alive from this subterranean corridor of stone.

Still, though he heard the underlying fear and despair in her voice, he refused to allow her to lose hope. While there was still breath in his body, Vartan would protect Danae as best as he could.

"I suppose you and I are now on an equal basis," he said. "Both being unable to see anything, I mean."

"Aye, but that only makes things worse, not better!"

"On the contrary." He reached out and found her hand, giving it what he hoped was a reassuring squeeze. "For one thing, we still have our other senses and can feel our way forward by listening and running our hands along the walls. And for another thing, I'm finally more qualified to lead the way than you are."

Surprisingly, she laughed. "Aye, I suppose you are, aren't you? And that pleases you immensely, too."

Vartan stepped past her, tugging on her hand as he did. "Aye, it does. Now, come along. Time is precious. We've got to be close to the end of this mountain. Abba Garabed *did* say the torch would last just long enough to get us to the end, didn't he?"

A bit more animation now brightened her voice. "Aye, he did. Indeed, perhaps the opening's just around the next bend or two."

He actually did very well traveling the tunnel blindly, only running into a wall once as it took a sudden turn to the left. His bruised forehead and shin were quickly forgotten, however, as they rounded the corner and a gust of fresh, warm air hit him squarely in the face.

"Light!" Danae cried at that same moment. "I can see daylight!" She twisted her hand in his to grab him by the wrist, scooted by, and pulled him forward. "Oh, hurry, Vartan. It's over. We're through the mountain!"

He knew the moment they stepped from the tunnel. The hard rock floor changed to soft, yielding sand. The hot Desert sun slammed into him with the force of a great, raging hearth fire.

"Oh, how lovely!" Danae exclaimed beside him. "I never imagined . . ."

"You're surely not talking about the Desert, are you?" Vartan couldn't hide the amazement in his voice. He had always hated the Desert and everything about it.

"Why, of course I am. It's so big and open, and the sand shimmers like diamonds in the sun. And the sky—I've never seen such a cloudless, intense shade of blue."

"The reason it's cloudless is because the sun and sand suck all the moisture from the sky. This is a parched, barren land where few things grow and water is scarce. You can easily die out here, if not from the heat then from the savage desert creatures that prowl about. And not all of those creatures, by the way, are wild animals. Some of them are human."

"Like the Diya al Din?" she asked, her excited, happy tone now gone solemn and downcast.

Vartan truly hated to frighten or discourage her, but she needed to gain a healthy respect for the Desert as quickly as possible, or risk endangering them both. "Aye, most certainly like the Diya al Din. They're divided into many tribes. Some of those tribes would as soon kill you and then ask questions, if they so much as caught you drinking from their wells. The law of the Desert's a harsh, unforgiving law. It breeds harsh, unforgiving people."

"Then what are we to do, Vartan? We can't hide from them forever, not in these wide open spaces."

He sighed. "We do the best we can, Danae. The rest, I suppose we put in Athan's hands. There's little other choice, if you continue to cast your fate with a blind man. It's not as if I can do much to protect us."

"Don't say that!" She moved close and took his hand, lifting it to her lips for a brief, tender kiss. "There's no other man I'd ever wish to be with, no man I'd ever feel safer with."

Gratitude filled him, though Vartan knew the truth was far different from the way she viewed it. Danae didn't realize how close he had come to trying to make love to her last night as they had lain close to avoid the cold. Especially when she had so innocently snuggled yet nearer to him, arousing his passion. For an instant or two, he had thought he'd go mad with the effort it took not to react to her, take her, turn her over onto her back, and cover her sweet lips—and her equally sweet body—with his.

And the only reason she still felt safe with him was because, save for their brief encounter with the Pedars, they had yet to confront any real threat. But when they finally did . . . well, all her naïve illusions would be shattered once and for all.

"I thank you for your confidence in me," he mumbled, not knowing what else to say. "Now, can you tell me what time of day it is?"

Danae went silent for a moment. "Aye," she then said. "It's late afternoon. Why do you ask?"

"Because we need to get our bearings before we set out for the nearest oasis, which, unless we're much farther north thanks to that tunnel, would still be Am Shardi. The night sky will help us do that."

"So we stay here tonight, is that it?"

"Aye." Though the Desert cooled considerably after dark, the realization that there'd be no need to endure another night with the temptation of Danae in his arms filled Vartan with relief. *Thank you for that, Athan,* he thought. *You apparently know me well enough to know, leastwise when it comes to Danae, I'm not that strong.*

"I think I should tell you I'm not well versed on navigation by the stars," Danae interrupted his thoughts.

"But I am, and I'll teach you. Once you can recognize a few key constellations, the rest is easy. And, one good thing about the Desert."

"What's that?" she asked with sudden interest.

"The night sky's so black, and the stars so near and bright, you feel like you can almost touch them. It won't be hard to learn the stars. Not hard at all."

Just before dawn, they left the relative haven of the mountains, traveling north and slightly east into the Desert. As the sun rose, the sands absorbed the heat and radiated it upward. The air grew still. It wasn't long before Vartan felt as if he were being cooked alive.

Drawing their cloaks close and their hoods up to protect them from the burning rays didn't improve things. Desert garb, though just as enveloping, was woven of a light, airy fabric. It was also white to reflect the heat, whereas their black, woolen cloaks absorbed it.

Still, there was nothing to be done for it. It was either sweat or burn.

"How do you feel about the Desert now?" he asked as they trudged through the deep sand. "Still find it beautiful?"

"I'm sure it's quite lovely in the winter," Danae replied, leading him along. "And the sunrises and sunsets are gorgeous."

"You're determined to find something good in everything, aren't you?"

"That's because there's something good in just about everything, Vartan."

He frowned. "You said you knew Ladon. What could've ever possibly been good in him?"

"He wasn't always so single-mindedly cruel," she said softly. "I knew him growing up. He was only six years older than me. His mother died when he was but a babe, and his father . . ." She paused. "His father was King Feodras, but since Ladon's mother wasn't Feodras's wife, Ladon could never be officially claimed as his son. The Queen, however, still chose to view Ladon, who quickly grew to a strong, handsome young warrior, as a potential threat to her own sons. She did all in her power to humiliate and break him, encouraging the rest of the Court to do the same. In the attempt, all she managed to do was make Ladon even more determined to prevail. Prevail at all costs."

194

"It's still no reason to give over your life and soul to Phaon. No victory's worth such a price."

"Nay, it isn't," she said. "I think, though, Ladon never saw any other path. One who lives without hope—or love—doesn't feel he has many options."

For some reason, Danae's words reminded Vartan of his brother. Was that what had happened to Hovan? Though he had been surrounded by a loving family, had Hovan failed to see or appreciate it? Had he, too, lost hope, imagining his options dwindling until all he saw left to do was seize whatever he could, no matter the cost? Even if the cost was the annihilation of his home and family?

After all that had happened, Vartan now understood what the loss of hope, the dwindling of options, could do to a man. It shriveled the soul, scoured away the honor, and stoked the fires of anger and despair. Yet, in the end, *he* hadn't chosen death and destruction, chosen Phaon.

It wasn't solely the result of his own strength, however, that had turned the tide for him. It was the love of his sister, of Danae, and of all the people who had helped save his life and care for him. It was also the sweet, healing balm of Athan's love, a love Vartan had only recently come to know.

Was that the difference then? Even in his darkest times, he had been surrounded by love and had the wherewithal to recognize and accept it, while apparently neither Hovan nor Ladon ever had. It was terrifying to imagine the gaping chasm the absence of love, or the inability to accept it, had seared through to their hearts.

But at least Hovan was dead and no longer able to harm anyone. Ladon, however, was very much alive and bent not only on Vartan's destruction, but likely on further unholy acts in Phaon's service. Acts Vartan feared might well continue to involve Gadiel. Acts that, in the absence of love or compassion, were sure to wreak pain and terror wherever Ladon went.

"Ladon may not feel he has many options," Vartan said at long last. "That makes him a very dangerous man. And we won't be free from that danger until he's dead."

"Aye, I know that." She sighed. "If only there were some way to make him see, to turn him from Phaon . . ."

"Don't even consider it, Danae!" At her wistful tone, fear swamped him. He knew her well enough to guess what she was thinking. "It would be fatal to get near enough to the man even to try."

"I won't. I'd be afraid he'd find some way to extract your whereabouts from me, and I'd never forgive myself . . ." She gave a self-disparaging little laugh. "I'm no fool. I'd never endanger you to try to save him."

"It's not me I'm worried about, sweet lady. It's you."

Danae chuckled. "Then we're both quite safe, aren't we, one looking out for the other?"

They walked along in silence for a while. Vartan could feel the sun peeking in under his hood, and he tugged it yet farther down. Not that it mattered, but by now he imagined it covered over half his face. Sweat beaded and poured down his forehead and cheeks. His clothes, beneath the cloak, stuck to him damply. His throat felt parched, but he dared not squander what remained of their precious water. By his calculations, they were at least another three or four hours from the oasis.

For once, he was almost thankful for his blindness. The Desert sun, of itself, was painfully intense. When it shone down on the taupe-colored sand, however, it reflected up in millions of tiny, bright lights. Sooner or later, a man was forced repeatedly to close his eyes to prevent them from being burned away. Of course, just as soon as a person did that, he managed to stumble over some rock or prickly desert plant that happened to jump in the way.

And the shimmering heat, rising from the land, sucked the moisture, then the life from a man until there seemed nothing left but a dry, empty husk. The tongue withered, cleaving to the roof of the mouth. Sweat rolled from the body faster than it could ever hope to be replaced, even if there *had* been enough water to spare. And all a man ever saw, no matter where he looked, were mirages and endless, killing sand.

Vartan hated bringing Danae into this. He'd have far preferred she keep her naïve little illusions about the Desert. It was enough that he, as a young warrior in training, had been required to survive out here for two weeks on his own. The experience had been invaluable, but had reinforced his decidedly poor opinion of the Desert. It was indeed an uncivilized, savage land peopled by equally uncivilized, savage people.

But there was nothing to be done for it now. They were here, and here they must remain until Athan told them otherwise. Problem was, Vartan wondered if he'd recognize Athan's voice if he heard it. Up until now, everyone else had done the hearing and then conveyed the message. Now the people around him had dwindled to just Danae.

He grinned to himself. There didn't seem a whole lot of messengers left. Sooner or later, it seemed Athan might be forced to speak directly with him.

"Vartan!" Danae's excited voice pierced his thoughts. "I . . . I think I see an oasis! I see green—tall, green-fronded trees, and grass, and . . . and . . ." Her voice faded.

"Aye?" He didn't like the sudden change in her tone. "What else do you see?"

"There are people there, A-Ara," she replied, finally bringing herself to use his nickname. "A large number of people."

He choked back a frustrated curse. He wasn't ready to deal with Diya al Din of any kind, even if they *were* just one of the simpler nomadic tribes. *If* that's who they were.

"What else do you see?" Vartan asked, pulling her to a halt. "Is there any design on their tents, or some banner to identify what tribe they are?"

"Why would it matter?"

"Oh, it matters," he muttered. "They all have their special customs, and the more I know, the better our chances of convincing them to allow us to share the oasis."

"The tents are shaded by the trees, so I can't tell if they've any design or not." Danae went silent for several seconds. "There's a banner, though. It's hard to make out—oh, there, a breeze has caught it and I can see the cloth!"

"Describe it to me." He couldn't contain the sharp edge of urgency in his voice.

"It's made of silk, in colors of green, blue, and silver." She paused. "I can see no emblem or design on it, though."

"By the sword of Calidor!" Vartan's gut knotted in despair. "It doesn't have an emblem or design," he whispered, "because it doesn't need any. Those are Desert colors, and only one family has the right to carry them."

"Do you know now how to approach them to gain their hospitality?"

"They're hospitable enough to any they call friend. If they learn who I really am, however, there'll be no hospitality for me. Indeed, my life will be forfeit."

"Why?" She gripped his arm, her fingers digging into his flesh. "Who *are* these people?"

"The Abd Al' Alim, the royal family of the Diya al Din. And that banner is the Hakeem's, their ruler." He gave a low, harsh laugh. "So much for my destiny awaiting me in the Desert."

"You can't know that! There's always hope."

"Nay, not anymore," Vartan said. "It can't get much worse than this, Danae. We dare not turn back or we'll die in the Desert. Yet if we go forward, we'll just as surely die!"

13

"Ra'id, I think you should come out and see this."

At the sound of his sister's voice, taut with an urgent excitement, Ra'id looked up from the bit of parchment he was writing on. "What is it, Sharifah? I'm rather busy just now, scribing Father yet another of the endless reports he keeps demanding. Can't it wait?"

"Nay, it most certainly can't." She shot him an irritated glance. "We've got two unexpected visitors—a man and a woman—and they're not of the Desert. If you tarry even an instant longer, they'll be dead at Malik and Farid's hands. Even now, they've got swords at their necks."

Choking back a savage curse, Ra'id slammed down his quill pen, jumped up, and stormed from the huge, tur-skin tent. "Where? Where are they?" he demanded as soon as his sister caught up to him.

"There, down by the edge of the oasis." She pointed in a southerly direction. "If you bend your head a bit, you'll see the crowd forming through the trees."

Once again Ra'id strode out, his long legs soon carrying him to and through the crowd. Just as Sharifah had claimed, two fair-skinned people, one a bearded, dark-haired man and the other a pretty, blond-haired woman, knelt with hands tied before his father's two pompous and overbearing spies. The man looked to be a bit older than Ra'id, likely in his early thirties. The woman—as she suddenly lifted her head, Ra'id realized she wasn't just pretty, but stunningly beautiful—appeared young, probably in her twenties.

"And is this how we show Desert hospitality to strangers?" he asked, drawing up behind Malik and Farid. "The Hakeem won't be pleased to hear of your unkind behavior."

The two men, swords now lowered, wheeled around to confront Ra'id. "Y-your father," Farid stuttered in his indignation, "enjoined us to see to your own and your sister's protection. And these two brigands were trying to sneak into camp, no doubt to assassinate you, m'lord."

"Indeed?" Ra'id arched a brow and fisted his hands on his hips. "I'll admit the woman's comely enough and might have, at my express invitation, made it into my tent. I'm certain there are at least ten or twenty of my warriors, though, who would've cut this man to shreds before he came so near as fifty yards from me."

"Aye," a deep, unfamiliar voice rose from behind Kamal's two toadies. "Especially since my blindness would've immeasurably slowed my taking them all on, *if* I even knew how to fight."

Ra'id stepped forward, shoved Malik and Farid aside, and came to stand before the kneeling man. He was dressed in the coarsely woven tunic and breeches of the typical Nonbeliever, his beard thick and unkempt, his hair long and wild. He was also quite filthy.

"So you're blind, are you?" Wrinkling his nose in distaste, Ra'id leaned down and waved a hand before the man's eyes. There was no response.

"So it seems," the dark-haired stranger replied.

"What's your name and where are you from?"

"I'm called Ara Kocharian. I'm a trader, and I and my wife, Danae"—he paused to indicate with his head the woman beside him—"are recent refugees from the royal city of Astara. You *have* heard Astara has finally fallen to Ladon and his Hylean army, haven't you?"

"Last time I looked, we *were* still part of Gadiel," Ra'id said silkily, not at all pleased with this commoner's bold demeanor, "and frequently apprised as to what goes on in the rest of the land. So, aye, I'm well aware of what happened to Astara. Good riddance, I say, to the Usurper and his brood."

Though he carefully watched this Ara Kocharian for any kind of reaction to his well-chosen words, Ra'id saw none. Either the man held himself under the strictest control, or he truly was just a commoner and didn't care who ruled, just as long as he was left alone. Still, there was something about him, something about how he spoke and carried himself, that plucked at Ra'id's suspicions. That, and the slight widening of the woman's eyes when he mentioned the Karayans. These two would bear watching.

"Blind you may be and an Astarian refugee," he finally said, "but it still doesn't explain why you're in Desert lands. Or why you're the first we've seen after all these weeks, if there's now to be a mass exodus from Astara and its surrounds."

"I can't speak for the choices of others. As for us, we're hoping to head north, skirt the Ibn Khaldun, then pass through the edge of Elvish lands and make our way to the Northlands." Again, Ara nodded in the direction of his wife. "Danae has family there."

Ra'id's gaze swung to lock with that of the woman and, for an instant, he found himself lost in her mesmerizing brown eyes. There was an intelligence and intensity there, a melting gentleness, and underlying it all, an unsettling look of entreaty that pierced clear to Ra'id's soul. But entreaty for what? For release from her bond mate? Or for help, and if so, for what kind of help?

One thing he *did* know. If she hadn't been another man's wife, Ra'id would've been the first to take this mysterious, compelling woman for his own.

Beside him, Sharifah surreptitiously sent an elbow into his side. He flushed. He must have been staring overlong.

To cover his unnerving reaction, Ra'id made a great show of scratching his jaw. "Danae isn't a Northland name. Indeed, it isn't even Gadielean."

"Her mother was a Hylean, captured in a raid by a Rune Lord," Ara offered before his wife could even find opportunity to explain. "Forgive me, m'lord. I didn't realize you were so deeply interested in our background and family history. Should I go on?"

"Nay." At the subtle note of sarcasm in the other man's voice, Ra'id clamped down on a surge of irritation. "I've heard more than enough from you." He turned to face Danae. "And what of you, my little Rasha?" he asked, using the Desert term for gazelle. "Will you allow your bond mate to do all the talking for you? Strange behavior, or so I've heard, for women of Vardenis *or* the North. Even married women."

"And should I speak when I'd only repeat what my husband has already said?" She met his piercing scrutiny unflinchingly. "I would've thought, m'lord, you'd better things to do than listen to my prattle."

"On the contrary, little Rasha. I can't think of much I'd enjoy more than the pleasure of *your* delightful company." Ra'id paused, eyed the trader who still knelt before him, then, in a lightning quick move, withdrew his dagger and made a sweeping motion with it directly at the other man's eyes.

Ara Kocharian didn't even blink. His wife, however, gasped and threw herself between her husband and Ra'id's dagger, nearly impaling herself in the process. With a horrified curse, Ra'id jerked his weapon back almost as quickly as he had extended it.

"Woman! Are you a fool?" he cried, glaring down at her as he hastily resheathed his dagger.

"And what foolish game were *you* about?" she demanded, her voice shaking as she looked up at him from her spot on the ground where she had fallen before her husband. "Ara spoke true when he told you he was blind. Did you intend to cut out his eyes just to make sure?"

"Danae." As best as he could with his hands bound before him, the trader groped blindly, trying to support his wife as she struggled back to her knees. "It's all right. Now he knows. It's over."

"Is it?" She shot Ra'id a furious glance.

"Aye, it is," Ra'id replied. Remorse filled him and he comforted himself with the knowledge that he'd had no choice but to verify this trader's claims. Once more, he drew his dagger. At the sight of it, the woman's eyes once again grew wide.

"Calm yourself, Rasha," he said, leaning toward her. "Give me your hands so I may cut your bonds."

She eyed him for an instant more, wary and fearful, then offered her hands. In two quick strokes, Ra'id freed her. Then he looked to where her husband still knelt.

"Stand, Trader," he growled. "Permit me to free you as well."

"Nay, m'lord!" Malik cried, stepping around to stand between them. "He may be blind, but he's powerfully built, and I don't believe his claims that he doesn't know how to fight. Once he's freed, there's no—"

Ra'id held up a silencing hand. "The man's also no fool. Though he might risk his own life, he won't risk his pretty little bond mate's." He shouldered Malik aside and faced the Astarian. "Will you, Kocharian?"

The trader pushed awkwardly to his feet. He nodded, a muscle jumping in his clenched jaw.

"Nay, never. You've my word on it. I'll never do anything to endanger Danae."

Though his sightless gaze was impenetrable, Ra'id heard the conviction in the man's voice and saw it in the proud lift of his chin and squaring of his shoulders. Once again, the uneasy feeling this Astarian wasn't who he claimed to be drifted through him. A plan formed in his mind.

"I beg forgiveness if our Desert hospitality has been lacking," he said. "Forthwith, I intend to make it up to the both of you. A bath, fresh clothes, and a hearty meal will be but the start of it. You'll stay with us a few days."

Ara frowned. "That's not necessary, m'lord. All we require is to fill our water bags at your spring, purchase some rations for the journey, and then be on our way. We never intended to long impose on your hospitality."

"Nonetheless, I insist. The next oasis is a good five days' travel northeast of here, and the town of Barakah is two days north. Best you rest and replenish not only your supplies, but your bodies, before moving on. Not to mention," he added with the merest hint of warning, "I'll take great offense if you refuse our hospitality."

Kocharian's lips tightened. "As you wish, but only for a day. After that, we truly must depart."

Satisfaction filled the Desert lord. At last, a slight edge of dismay darkened the man's voice. So, he didn't want to linger, did he? More the reason to keep him here even longer. Long enough, at least, to get a message to the Hakeem, requesting more information that might help identify this stranger.

"Two days," Ra'id said, countering the Astarian's proposition. "Two days is the absolute minimum I'll accept and not take offense."

Almost imperceptibly, the trader's shoulders sagged. "Then two days it'll be, m'lord. I'd never wish to offend Desert hospitality."

"Nay, that most assuredly would never be wise."

Ra'id grinned. Two days, with the aid of the messenger hawk, would be time enough and more. And indeed, after this oasis, all that awaited him was yet another troublesome warlord, with no vision for the future save for what served him and his tribe.

In truth, he thought as his glance moved once more to visually caress the beauteous Danae, *I am in no particular hurry to move on. No hurry at all.*

He supposed he should at least be thankful he had never had the misfortune of meeting Ra'id Al'Alim either in battle or in diplomatic negotiation, Vartan thought a half hour later as he sat in the other man's tent, listening to a servant fill a small, copper tub with bathwater. If he *had* ever met the man, there would've been no hope now of hiding his true identity.

Still, even that wasn't much consolation. Another two days in this camp might be all the Hakeem's son needed to figure things out. From just the brief conversation they'd already had, Vartan had quickly ascertained this Desert lord was a sharp-witted man.

It was equally evident the young jackal was already slavering over Danae. *Rasha . . .* Vartan's lip curled in a feral grimace. The cur, coveting another man's wife. Vartan thanked the foresight that had made Danae agree to appear as his bride.

Of course, if Ra'id found some excuse to kill him—the most obvious one notwithstanding—Danae would then be fair game. A gazelle . . . She'd never have a chance against that Desert predator.

"Your bath is ready, m'lord."

A girl's voice, hesitant and shy, pierced the congested fog of Vartan's thoughts. He turned in her direction.

"My thanks." He shoved to his feet. "Could you direct me to the bathing tub? Show me where the soap and towels are?"

Her little hand settled on his. "Gladly, m'lord."

The girl tugged gently and Vartan followed. He was soon standing beside the tub.

"I'll leave you now, m'lord," she said, pulling what sounded like a screen in place around him. "If you need anything, though, I'll be waiting just outside the tent."

"You've set up everything within easy reach. I'm sure I'll be fine." He heard her turn and make her away across the sand floor covered with an assortment of large carpets. "One thing more, if you please."

She halted. "Aye, m'lord?"

"Call me Ara," Vartan said. "I'm but a simple trader, not a lord."

"As you wish, m'lor—" The servant laughed. "I mean, Ara."

He didn't take long to strip off his filthy clothes and climb into the bath. The water was tepid, but in the Desert heat it felt good. Vartan scrubbed himself hard, easing his cleansing motions only over the still tender, new scars. They were all, he imagined, still an intense shade of pink. He'd be glad when they faded to white and were less conspicuous. It would be one less thing to call attention to himself, especially the two wrist wounds. There surely weren't many other men who bore such an unusual matched set.

Not too many . . . save he and Eisa. *"Whose marks he now carries . . ."* With a sudden flash of remembrance, the words of the Prophecy filled his mind. His marks . . . the marks in Eisa's side and in his wrists and ankles . . .

Vartan supposed he should be grateful Ladon hadn't also run him through the ankles, as he had his wrists and side. Still, to bear even a portion of the marks Eisa bore was frightening enough. He wasn't worthy, not of imitating Athan's Son, or of now even more closely resembling the Prophecy.

With a groan, Vartan bent over, clasped his legs, and laid his forehead on his knees. He wasn't worthy but, even more important, he didn't *want* to be worthy. The ancient Prophecy had stood unfulfilled for centuries. Let it stand a few centuries more.

He was no Guardian, no savior of Gadiel. He could barely manage to stay alive, much less protect the land. Indeed, he hovered on the brink of survival while, around him, the dangers grew. Perhaps Athan had, heretofore, led him through the maze of life-threatening horrors. Perhaps He would again. But what good could *he* possibly be to Gadiel, while he remained as helpless as a babe, at Athan's mercy and so needful of His constant care?

Choose someone else, I beg of You, Vartan thought, *if You are even considering me. I don't want this. And you can't make me accept it!*

He paused, struck suddenly by the way his words sounded. Like . . . like some petulant, defiant child. Like he had forgotten, if not totally disregarded, all the things Amma Serpuhi had taught him—and all he struggled yet to believe and live.

Shame flooded Vartan. How weak he was, how quick, at even the slightest doubt or difficulty, to forget and revert back to his old ways! He, who had always succeeded at anything he put his mind to!

The humiliating fact was, he was acting the coward, like some callow boy rather than a man. Athan had called him to the Desert to discover his destiny. He had cast his lot now with the Eternal One, and whatever happened would be His will. Trust. He *must* learn to trust, or he'd never get this right!

And if the Prophecy was part of his destiny . . . well, then he must learn to accept that, too. It wasn't about him at any rate. It was about Danae, and Zagiri, and Gadiel. It was about avenging his family, and driving Ladon and his men from the land.

From somewhere outside the tent Vartan heard Ra'id calling to one of his men. The recollection of his most immediate peril effectively swept away all other considerations. Ra'id, son of the Hakeem, the Karayans' direst enemy, and a formidable threat in his own right. Before he could find and confront his destiny, Vartan knew he first had to escape the young Desert lord.

He resumed his bath with a vengeance.

Once Ara and Danae were safely ensconced in Ra'id and Sharifah's respective tents, bathing under the close supervision of their servants, Sharifah sought out her brother. She found him at the edge of the oasis, just then sending out one of the messenger hawks. The sturdy black-and-brown bird circled lazily over the Desert that sprawled before them, then turned and headed northeast in the direction of Khaddar. They watched until the hawk finally disappeared from view.

"It goes without saying that I want you to keep a very close eye on the woman," Ra'id said, breaking the silence at last. "And, in the guise of simple feminine interest, ask her questions about her husband and their life together."

"As you will this Ara Kocharian, I presume," Sharifah replied. "In the hopes of catching one or the other of them in some contradiction."

"Aye." He sighed and scratched his jaw. "I don't trust them, or their purpose here. This trader, especially, doesn't seem to be quite the person he claims to be."

"A bit too well-spoken and civilized to be a simple trader, you mean?"

"So you've noticed that, too."

"Though it was apparent he tried to hide it, he carries himself like a nobleman. And he was too careful in his replies."

Ra'id smiled. "I knew I could count on your perceptiveness."

"This is such fun!" She grinned. "I wouldn't have missed this diplomatic journey for the world."

"It goes without saying, of course, that Malik and Farid needn't be privy to our concerns or to whatever we discover about our strange visitors."

Sharifah laughed. "It goes without saying." She turned then and set out for her tent.

ℰ ℑ

"Here, you might like something clean to wear after your bath."

In conjunction with the voice, a hand appeared over the top of the screen, holding a white linen, long-sleeved garment. The v-neck and ends of the sleeves were embroidered in looping, bright blue stitching.

Danae, finishing just then with her bath, climbed from the copper bathing tub and took the article. "Thank you. It's quite lovely."

"It's a traditional woman's dress called a *sholi*," Sharifah said. "The thin fabric and the flowing drape allow air to circulate and keep you cool in the Desert heat."

"And that's *very* much appreciated." Danae laughed and, laying the *sholi* aside, began to dry herself. "Though I find the Desert surprisingly beautiful, I didn't quite expect such intense heat."

"No one who isn't Desert bred does."

"And is that loose, long-sleeved garment the men wear over their boots and breeches also called a *sholi*?"

"Nay, and men being as they are, would be quite peeved if you called it that. Their garment is a *thobe*, which is meant for casual wear. When traveling, they add an open cloak called a *bisht* that can be trimmed with braiding and tassels. We women also cover our heads out on the Desert with a *khirya*, but the men wear a long, woven *shmaagh* held in place with a braided *agaal* that encircles the crown of the head.

"You can tell which tribe a man is from by the different colors of his *agaal*. Our tribe—which is known as the Abd Al'Alim or 'Servant of the All-Knowing'—claims the blue-and-white *agaal*. Malik Abd al Rashid's tribal name means 'Servant of the Guided,' and he wears a red-and-yellow *agaal*. And Farid Ben Wasem's tribal name means 'Son of the Beautiful One,' and their *agaal* is green and purple."

A voice rose just then from beside Sharifah. The two spoke together softly for a minute or two, then the other woman departed.

"As soon as you're dressed, would you join me for some tea and spice cakes?" Sharifah asked. "I thought you might like something to sustain you until the evening meal, which won't be served for another five hours."

"I thank you for your consideration. I *am* a bit hungry." Danae slipped the *sholi* over her head, then quickly towel-dried her hair. After finger combing it as best as she could, she stepped around the screen.

Ra'id's sister was already seated before a low, brass table set on crisscrossed, carved wooden legs. She poured tea from a small golden teapot into two crystal cups. In the middle of the table, on what looked to be a golden plate, were an enticing assortment of little cakes, some puffed and glittering with sugar, others flat and decorated with almonds and other nuts, and still others drizzled artfully with a layer of pink or tan icing.

Danae's stomach growled. She blushed.

Sharifah laughed and motioned for her to take a seat on one of the plump cushions set around the table. "You're more than a bit hungry, aren't you? When did you last eat?"

"I can't be certain, as we lost track of the time coming through the mountain, but at least a day ago." Danae took a seat opposite Sharifah. "Do you know if . . . if Ara will also be offered something to eat?"

"I'm certain he will." She slid a cup of a pale green tea across to Danae. "It's Desert custom to provide guests not only a bath, but with food and drink when they first arrive."

Danae took up the cup and drained it in a few swallows. The tea was delicately fragrant and tasted of flowers.

"This is delicious. May I have more?"

"As much as you desire. It's called jasmir tea." Sharifah filled Danae's cup, returned it to her, then also held out the plate of cakes. "Take as many cakes as you wish. Our cook always makes more than anyone can eat, and the rest soon go to waste in this heat."

That was all the encouragement Danae needed. She proceeded to polish off half the plate and drink three more cups of tea. Finally, her hunger at bay, she leaned back with a contented sigh.

"That was wonderful. Thank you so much."

212

Sharifah smiled. "It was my pleasure." She paused, eyeing Danae's now dry hair. "One of my servants, Jamilla, is very talented in grooming hair. I'd love to see what she can do with your lovely hair."

Self-consciously, Danae's hand went to her head. "I know it must look terrible. I do have a comb in my pack, though. It was a birthing day gift from—" She went pale, then swallowed hard. "From a very dear friend. And if you give me just a moment, I could go and fetch it."

"That won't be necessary." Sharifah made a dismissing motion. "Let Jamilla dress your hair. You want to look pretty, don't you, for your—"

It was Sharifah's turn to catch herself. Her face flushed hot. "I'm sorry. I momentarily forgot that Ara was blind and can never see how you look. Please forgive me."

For a fleeting instant, Danae glanced away. "Nay, he can never see how I look again. Still, I'll know, and it'll be my gift to him, representing him well, I mean."

"How did it happen? Ara's blindness, I mean."

The blond-haired woman met her gaze. "We're not sure. Likely a blow to his head."

"And did you know him before . . . before he became blind, or has he never seen how beautiful you are?"

A sad smile lifted Danae's lips. "I knew him before. He knows what I look like. I'm not beautiful, though. Not in the way you are beautiful."

"Thank you, Danae."

"Have you a husband, Sharifah? I wondered, since you sleep in a tent with only women."

"Nay, I'm not life bonded." She rolled her eyes. "Well, at least not yet. It's why we're making the grand tour of all the Desert tribes, though. My father's determined that, once and for all, I will find myself a bond mate."

"You don't sound at all excited about the prospect."

The compassionate, perceptive look in the other woman's eyes stirred a sudden sense of camaraderie in Sharifah. She opened her mouth to pour out all the frustration and distaste she had endured in the past few years, as her father paraded one repulsive suitor after another before her, then caught herself. If things had been different, Sharifah thought she and Danae might have become fast friends. But things *weren't* different. And the purpose of her conversation with the pretty Astarian woman was to discern the truth about her and her husband, not share feminine tales.

"Nay, I can't say I'm excited," she forced herself to reply, "but I'm certain all that'll change when I finally meet the right man. Like you did, I'm sure." She climbed to her feet. "Come, let's find Jamilla and have her braid your hair. Then I'll show you how to wear the *khirya*. No Desert woman is to venture outside without covering her head. As long as you remain with us, you must do the same."

"I'd be happy to honor your customs, Sharifah. Ara and I are—"

A horn sounded just then, blowing seven times in short, sharp blasts. Danae looked to Sharifah, a question in her soft brown eyes.

"It's the call to early evening prayer," Sharifah explained. "The Diya al Din follow Al'Alim's command: 'Seven times a day shall you give Me praise' and 'at night shall you arise to give Me praise.' We faithfully set aside these traditional moments of prayer eight times a day. I believe Al'Alim is called Athan in the rest of Gadiel. We've always been," she added with a smile, "Al'Alim's ever faithful people, even when most of the rest of Gadiel turned from Him and His holy decrees."

"Ara and I are also followers of Athan. Would you teach me how to say these prayers?"

214

The other woman's simple admission startled Sharifah. She had heard there were indeed a few Astarians who practiced the Faith. It was even said that a Karayan—the Usurper's only daughter—had spent time in the Goreme Valley and was now a holy woman. But such exceptional people were rare outside the Desert. Dare she believe Danae's claim?

"I'll be happy to teach you," Sharifah replied, deciding no harm was done even if Danae lied. On the morrow, Ra'id should have a message back from Khaddar. They should know the truth.

"Come," she said, offering Danae her hand. "First, let me show you how to wrap the *khirya*. Then we'll join the others for prayers."

14

Even in the midst of potential enemies, sunset prayers were a beautiful experience. *It feels so good,* Danae thought, *to worship Athan in community, to be among brothers and sisters of the Faith.* If the circumstances had been different, she might have even called the Diya al Din friends.

But they were Vartan's avowed enemies. Because of that, because her first loyalty and love were for him, she must instead be wary and guard her tongue. It would be hard, though. Already, Sharifah's kindness and pleasant manner had all but disarmed her. Indeed, Danae actually liked the woman.

Sharifah's brother, however, was a different matter. Her gaze found Ra'id across the way, where the men knelt on a separate carpet, segregated from the women. He was quite handsome, with a sun-bronzed, smoothly shaven face, a strong, sharp blade of a nose, and full, sensual lips. He wore his thick black hair in a casual style, tumbling onto his broad, intelligent forehead and down the back of his neck. His eyes were richly brown and piercingly acute, with the unmistakable look of a man neither easily fooled nor manipulated.

Danae's glance drifted back a row to where Vartan knelt, snugly ensconced between two warriors who appeared to be guarding him. Her gaze softened. He, too, looked fresh from a bath and wore a clean, white *thobe* over a pair of white breeches tucked into his boots. His long hair had been combed into some semblance of control, and surprisingly, his beard had been trimmed close to his face. She decided she liked him with the beard. It gave him a look of maturity and distinction.

Both Vartan and Ra'id were impressive men. Both bore an aura of strength and determination. Both were the sort other men would follow. And both, if ever they should join forces, would present a formidable threat to Ladon and his army.

But how to get them to set aside their centuries-old animosity for the sake of Gadiel? At present, Vartan was in far too vulnerable a position ever to reveal his identity to Ra'id. Vartan's only hope lay in approaching the Desert lord as an equal. There seemed no chance, however, of that happening anytime soon. Or, leastwise, not unless Athan intervened.

The thought comforted her. With Athan, there was always hope. When things seemed completely beyond the control of man, everything was still possible with Him. Things like the present circumstances, Danae reminded herself. Athan could bring miracles from insurmountable impossibilities.

As soon as prayers ended, most of the camp dispersed to begin preparations for supper. Danae rose and immediately headed for Vartan. She didn't get far before Ra'id waylaid her.

"The evening promises to be beautiful and mild," he said, deliberately stepping in her path. "While the supper meal's prepared, would you pay me the honor of accompanying me for a short stroll about the oasis?"

It took all of Danae's strength not to glare up at him or snap out some defiant reply. She couldn't help the angry feelings he stirred in her. Beneath the smiling lips and smooth words, Ra'id was evidently determined to keep her and Vartan apart. And she could just imagine his motive—he wished to prevent them from sharing observations and strategies, while at the same time attempt to trick them into contradicting each other.

Such a goal would not, in reality, be all that difficult to attain. Though she and Vartan had known each other for almost three years, they didn't share a history as husband and wife. They had only the meager tale they had managed to create for an occasion such as this.

That admission, along with Ra'id's unsettling interest in her, was reason enough to deny him his request. No excuse that would be acceptable to him readily came to mind, however. And some feeble protest would only heighten his suspicions. She had no recourse but to acquiesce.

"I'd be delighted to walk with you, m'lord," Danae replied, giving him her most dazzling smile. "Would you permit me first, though, to say a few words to my husband? As you might imagine, it's difficult to long be separated, especially when he cannot see where I might be."

"Fear not, Rasha." Ra'id took her by the arm and turned her in the opposite direction. "Ara knows you're in good hands. Besides, Sharifah will tell him where you've gone and meet any of his needs until we return. You have nothing at all to worry about."

Nothing to worry about, save while Ra'id was interrogating her, Sharifah would likely use *her* considerable wiles to see what she could glean from Vartan. There was nothing, though, Danae could do about it.

"As you wish, m'lord," she said, allowing herself to be led away. "In truth, there's much I'd like to ask you about the Diya al Din. Your customs fascinate me."

"Do they?" Ra'id chuckled. "Well, I must confess to a similar interest in your people."

A fleeting confusion filled her. "My people?" she asked, thinking he spoke of the Hyleans.

"Aye, the Rune Lords."

"Oh, aye." At the realization of her limited knowledge of the race of Rune Lords, Danae's brief swell of relief that he hadn't guessed her true origins fled. In its place came panic.

"My mother didn't long remain with my father in the Northlands," she said, scrambling frantically to devise some plausible excuse for her lack of knowledge, "I was but a babe when she hid us in some caravaner's wagon and we escaped. By the time the man discovered us, we were already through the Jens. He was kind to my mother, though, and they eventually married."

"But I thought your father was life-bonded to your mother. Or so your husband implied."

"Nay." Danae shook her head, hating how one lie must be laid upon another, until they became a foul taste upon her tongue—and a bitter burden on her heart. "My mother was a slave. My father was her owner, and nothing more."

"Ah, I see. I beg pardon. I didn't mean to pry into what may well be painful memories for you."

She didn't reply straightaway, instead finding fascination with the deepening shades of twilight filtering through the rafa tree fronds overhead. A warm breeze, smooth as velvet, caressed her face. The sand felt soft and yielding beneath her

219

bare feet. It was a tender, forgiving time of day and, for a brief, poignant moment, Danae wanted to cast all cares aside and savor it.

But a dangerous man walked at her side, and she must not lower her guard even for a moment. So instead, Danae looked over at him and smiled.

"No offense was taken. Ara and I most likely didn't make everything clear."

"There are a lot of things you and Ara have yet to make clear." Ra'id pulled her to a halt beside a particularly large rafa tree, its many-layered cylindrical bark bristling with what almost looked like short, stiff hairs. "I thought this might be a good time for some additional clarifications."

Danae stiffened in immediate suspicion. "And pray, m'lord, what more would you know, that we've yet to tell?"

He released her hand and, arms folded across his chest, leaned against the rafa tree. "For one thing, who *are* you, really? Ara's no more a trader than I'm some simple mouflon herder."

She could feel the blood leave her face, but tried to make her expression inscrutable. "I don't know what you speak of, m'lord. Perhaps you've confused us with someone else."

"Nay, I think not." Ra'id eyed her. "Unfortunately, I've never had the pleasure of meeting the man I suspect Ara actually to be. Fortunately, though, there are a few men who have met the man, and I have sent off a request for a more accurate description. You could help yourself, though, Rasha, by assisting me in this."

"Assisting you how?" Danae cried, for an instant losing control. "By betraying my husband?"

"If he really *is* your husband."

"And what is that supposed to mean?"

He shrugged. "Nothing, perhaps. We'll just have to wait and see what my messenger brings me, won't we?"

"If you so mistrust us," Danae offered, casting desperately about for some way to extract herself and Vartan from this rapidly worsening predicament, "then perhaps it's best Ara and I leave now. Then you can sleep well tonight, without worry of assassination or whatever other schemes you suspect we're capable of."

"Oh, I intend to sleep well tonight, little Rasha." He straightened and, reaching out, brushed aside a strand of hair the wind had carried across her face.

There was something in his eyes that sent a surge of fear through Danae. She slapped his hand away and stepped back.

Puzzlement clouded his gaze, then as if realizing how she had taken his words, he shook his head. "I didn't mean anything sordid in that. I beg pardon if my words were misconstrued. I simply meant I'll sleep well tonight because I'm placing you and Ara under guard. As of this moment, you're no longer my guests. You're my prisoners."

"But why? We've done nothing; we mean you no harm!"

"Don't you?" He gave a harsh laugh. "You come here, pretend to be people you are not, and refuse to tell me the truth. What else am I supposed to think?"

"We didn't come to hurt you. Why, we didn't even know you'd be at this oasis! All we wanted was to rest and refresh ourselves for a few days before journeying on."

"Journeying where? And why?"

Danae opened her mouth to tell him about Athan's call to the Desert, then clamped it shut. Ra'id was trying to trick her into telling him things that would endanger Vartan. She must be careful. She mustn't forget and change their agreed upon story.

"Ara already told you where we're headed."

He sent her a thunderous look. "Well, tell me again, but this time tell me the truth!"

"And would you know it if you heard it? Or will only the words *you* want to hear satisfy you?"

"And what is *that* supposed to mean?"

"What else? You see a man as your enemy because it's all you've ever believed him to be, without ever trying to know him or his heart. But then, to do that might require you to change your attitude about a lot of things, and in the doing even go against those of your own kind. To do what's right even if at great cost to yourself."

"You're speaking in riddles, woman," Ra'id muttered.

"Am I? If so, no more than *you* were a short while ago."

"Well, I tire of this game." He took her by the arm. "Time we were ending this little walk."

When he tugged on her to follow, Danae dug in her heels. "Please, Ra'id," she said, gazing up at him with imploring eyes. "Can't you just believe me when I tell you we mean you no harm? That *Ara* means you no harm, and never has? He's a good man."

He stared down at her for a long, tension-laden moment, and Danae saw the battle wage within. Then, with a ragged intake of breath, his mouth went hard.

"All that remains to be seen. In the meantime, I meant what I said. Until I can ascertain if he is or isn't who he says he is, you and Ara are now my prisoners."

His grip on her arm tightened. "Now, no more of it. And in case you were hoping to the contrary, until further notice, I'm ordering that you and Ara be kept apart."

"You're wrong in this, Ra'id," Danae cried as he began to lead her away. "You're wrong!"

"Perhaps I am," he said through gritted teeth, "but more than your fate and Ara's ride on what I do here. Far, far more."

❧ ❧

"Ra'id, come quickly!" Sharifah cried the next morning.

He glanced up from the journal he made it a habit of writing in each day and sent his sister a long-suffering look. "What is it now?"

By the looks of her, it must be something momentous. Her hair was barely tucked beneath her *khirya*—a rather wrinkled *khirya*, surprising in itself for his usually fastidious sibling—and her always sandaled feet were bare. Ra'id frowned up at her.

"I think Malik intercepted the messenger hawk. Even now, he has sent men to the tent where Ara's being held."

"By the sacred waters!" Ra'id threw down his quill pen. "I've had about all I can stomach of that man's meddling!"

He stood, threw his *bisht* on over his *thobe*, and stalked from the tent. The big trader was already outside, held before a wildly gesticulating Malik, with the ever-present Farid standing at the ready. Not far away, Danae was also being dragged from her tent.

Fury enveloped Ra'id like some wildfire. A head might indeed roll today, but it could well be other than Ara Kocharian's!

❧ ❧

"What's the meaning of this?" Ra'id all but shouted at the older man as he drew up before him. "Have you a message from my father, a message that was intended for me?"

Her heart in her throat, Danae watched Malik wheel around. There was something in the set of his mouth that

223

didn't bode well. More than just a battle over Vartan was being waged here.

"Aye, m'lord, I do indeed have a message," Malik replied. "The hawk arrived only a short time ago, and the man who retrieved the missive, not knowing whom the message was for, immediately delivered it to me. I, being equally ignorant as to the true recipient, then read the message. I beg pardon for not sending for you, but when I realized whom we now likely hold prisoner, I ceased to think rationally. All I knew was I must discover the truth. If this trader truly bears the scars Ladon gave the Karayan prince when he defeated him in battle . . . well, you know as well as I what *that* means."

"And was that before or after you killed him? This time, Malik Abd al Rashid, you go too far!"

"If you doubt my word and the message the Hakeem has sent," Malik cried, his lips pulling tight above his teeth like some Desert wolf in a feral snarl, "then see for yourself." He motioned to two men standing nearby. "Take him. Hold him," he said, indicating Vartan. "Let's see if he has scars on his wrists and right side."

In her panic, Danae managed to twist free of the man who held her and run to Ra'id. "Don't let them do this. Please, Ra'id!"

He looked down at her, his face an expressionless mask. "If Ara is truly who he says he is, then the passing humiliation of being examined will soon be over. Don't trouble yourself with such a small thing, Rasha."

Her eyes filled with tears. It was over then. Once they stripped Vartan of his *thobe*, they'd know the truth.

"Can't . . . can't you just take our word that we mean you and your people no harm?" she whispered, her hand settling on his arm. "Isn't that, in the end, what really matters?"

His gaze narrowed. "So it's true then, is it? And you've lied to me about everything."

"Nay." Danae couldn't bear the accusation now burning in his eyes. "Not about everything. Not about what really mattered."

With a savage jerk, Ra'id flung her hand away. He strode over to stand before Vartan, who calmly awaited him, each arm now held by a Desert warrior.

"Who *are* you?" he demanded.

"A fellow Gadielean above all else," Vartan replied. "Just like you. And, in times such as these, that's *indeed* all that really matters."

Ra'id withdrew his dagger. Danae screamed and flung herself at him, only to be caught and jerked back by Farid.

"Have a care, pretty one," he rasped, leaning close, "or you may well suffer the same fate."

She squirmed in his grasp, her gaze riveted on Vartan and the young Desert lord. "Ra'id, don't!" she cried. "Don't, I beg you! I'll do anything you ask! Anything, if only you don't hurt him!"

Vartan jerked his head in her direction. "Nay, Danae," he said softly. "Don't sacrifice yourself for my sake. Nothing will happen to me that isn't Athan's will. You know that."

"Enough!" Ra'id roared.

He grasped the front of Vartan's *thobe*, slipped the tip of his dagger into the fabric, and sliced it open from top to bottom. The garment fell away.

A cry went up from the people. "The marks! He bears the marks!"

Ra'id shot Danae a brief, furious look. "You were a fool to come to the Desert, Karayan," he muttered, turning back to Vartan. "It'll surely mean your death."

225

"Then it will be Athan's will," Vartan replied. "He called me here."

"And when has Al' Alim ever wasted His time on the likes of your family?"

"Athan has carried us in His heart, as much as He has all the peoples of Gadiel. It was we who were closed and blind to Him, not He to us."

Ra'id, the dagger still clenched in his fist, stared at him. Danae watched the two men face each other, one taut with fury, the other calm, waiting. She strained forward, until Farid's hands tightened cruelly into the flesh of her arms and she had to bite her lip to hold back a whimper of pain. What was Ra'id thinking? He wasn't a cruel or stupid man. Surely—

"The Hakeem long ago passed a death judgment on the Karayan male line," Malik said, stepping forward once more. "None were to be spared, and well you know it, m'lord. Finish him now. Be done with it."

"And have *you* forgotten your place, Malik Abd al Rashid," Ra'id snarled, "now to presume not only to insult my intelligence, but to order me about? My father is indeed high prince, but after him, *I* am next in authority, not you. My patience is stretched thin. Hold your tongue, I say, while you still can."

The older man colored fiercely and bowed his head. "I beg pardon, m'lord. I thought only to advise—"

"Well, you've advised! The decision as to how and when I'll execute my father's orders is now mine." He slid his dagger back into its sheath. "Bind him hand and foot," he said, motioning to Vartan, "and place him under close guard."

As his warriors tied Vartan's hands and led him away, Danae finally twisted free of Farid's now loosened grip. She ran to Ra'id, who had turned and begun to walk away.

226

"Please," she cried, reaching out to grab at his arm. "Please, Ra'id, stop and listen to me. It's not what you think. It's not!"

He drew to an abrupt halt and, eyes blazing, rounded on her. "It doesn't matter why you came here, or that you only lied to protect him from us."

At the rage emanating from him, Danae staggered backward. "He . . . he never wished harm on you or your people," she choked out through a throat gone dry. "He had hoped, instead, someday to reunite all of Gadiel."

"Aye," Ra'id said. "Unite them under the Karayans. But even that doesn't matter. What matters is he's the only thing standing in the way of the Diya al Din reclaiming the throne. And, because he stands in the way, his life is forfeit."

❧☙

"All this pacing back and forth is doing nothing but wear a path in the carpets," Sharifah observed dryly as she watched Danae's agitated walk about their tent that evening. "That and drive yourself into a hysterical frenzy."

Danae halted and wheeled around. "And what would you have me do? Ra'id refuses to talk with me; Vartan's surely to die on the morrow, and I'm helpless to do anything about it! Who wouldn't be in a hysterical frenzy?"

"Well, it won't do Vartan any good. Perhaps a bit more calm and consideration would stand him in better stead. You're not all that secure yourself right now, you know. Considering your quite evident loyalty to Vartan, and the fact you've lied to Ra'id." Sharifah smiled. "Fortunate for you that my brother doesn't see you as any threat. Fortunate for you that he has a soft spot for you in his heart."

"I *am* no threat. And neither is Vartan!" The blond woman wrapped her arms about herself and closed her eyes. "And

227

as far as trying to remain calm, I've tried, Sharifah. Tried to be calm and consider everything I could do to save Vartan." She opened her eyes, eyes now swimming with tears. "But it always comes back to Ra'id. He holds Vartan's life in his hands."

"Nay, he doesn't. If he were Hakeem, aye, perhaps that would be so. But my father's yet Hakeem, and his hatred for the Karayans is legend. Legend, and even a bit unbalanced." She sighed. "I probably shouldn't be telling you this, but Ra'id's standing with our father is, at best, tenuous. They've never viewed things with the same perspective. And surely by now you've gathered that Farid and Malik aren't with us solely as advisors?"

Danae brushed aside a stray tear that had trickled down her cheek. "They did seem rather overbearing and intrusive."

"Our father doesn't trust Ra'id. For a time now, Ra'id and I have observed that he turns to his council of advisors more and more often. And that that council poisons his mind."

"But why would they do that?"

Sharifah gave a disgusted snort. "Because they see their reign of power nearing an end. Because they see, and rightly so, that Ra'id won't so easily be manipulated."

"Well, when it comes to Vartan's fate," Danae muttered darkly, "they seem to be manipulating Ra'id pretty well."

Exasperation filled Sharifah. "Of all the possible issues to defy our father over, it most certainly isn't Karayan's fate! And, as much as I hate to see him die, don't ask me to choose him over my brother. I won't do it, Danae."

"But this isn't just a matter of Ra'id over Vartan, or of the Diya al Din against the Karayans." The blond woman closed the distance separating them and took Sharifah by both arms. "Your people, of all peoples, have always been faithful to Athan and His Son. You know the Prophecy, believe in it. And, in the knowing, how could you not realize by now that Vartan's the one named? That he's the Guardian? Even some of your people recognized the significance of Vartan's scars today. When you couple that with the meaning of his name and his blindness, with the terrible pain and loss he has suffered, and how desperate the times now are, everything—*everything*—points to him."

Sharifah could feel her anger rising, and knew it was at least in part because the same thoughts had been niggling at her ever since they had finally confirmed Vartan Karayan's true identity. Still, to admit to Danae's claims would be to cast doubt on Ra'id's decision . . .

"And if we were to acknowledge that Vartan's the Guardian," she cried, "where would that leave Ra'id? Placing his faith in a blind man without any standing, funds, or military support? A man whom Ladon has not only set a princely bounty upon, but about whom he has also warned all of Gadiel—dire consequences will befall any so foolish as to take him in, much less join forces with him!"

At Danae's horrified expression, she gave a shrill laugh. "Aye, news travels fast in the Desert. Prophecy or no, any man with a cupful of brains would be a fool to venture anywhere near Vartan Karayan."

"I didn't realize your people were so afraid of Ladon."

"We aren't afraid of Ladon! Indeed, we're not afraid of anyone, and Ladon will soon know that!"

Danae released Sharifah and stepped back. Her steady gaze, however, pierced clear through Ra'id's sister. "Aye, just as Vartan and I have suspected. Indeed, even in the short time I've been in your camp, I've gleaned enough through snatches of conversation to ascertain the true purpose of your travels.

And it isn't finding you a husband. Leastwise, that isn't the primary purpose, is it?"

Sharifah could feel the hot blood fill her cheeks. In so very many ways, Ra'id had been right to fear this pair. "You tell me, since you've apparently figured it all out."

"The Diya al Din intend to gather all the Desert tribes, then attack Ladon and his forces. Attack them and win back Astara and the throne of Gadiel—only, this time, in the Karayans' place will sit the Hakeem."

So much like a certain night before, Vartan found he couldn't sleep. *I really should, though, be getting used to living on the brink of death,* he thought with black humor, *and be slumbering away like a babe. Awaiting another dawning of my day of execution is rapidly becoming commonplace.*

But, just like the night before he had gone out to face Ladon, it wasn't so much the contemplation of his own dying that kept him awake. Rather, just as he had worried over the fate of his family, now he worried about Danae. Even if Ra'id had yet to realize Vartan hadn't so swiftly taken a second wife and that Danae was unbound to him, Vartan knew his death would unquestionably free her for the taking. Indeed, even if somehow his life *was* spared, now Danae would surely be taken from him.

Yet as Vartan considered how, one way or another, he must soon give up Danae to another man, even the merest thought stirred a bewildering muddle of emotions. Pain, anger, repugnance, and a surprisingly savage swell of stubborn refusal churned within, until he thought he might be ill from the onslaught of the acrid mix.

To give up Danae . . .

Vartan didn't know if he could so easily accept this last and most devastating of blows. Was it because he had already lost so much of his former life that he found it doubly hard to now surrender this most precious of comforts? Or did it stem from something else altogether? Something he didn't dare examine now, when he once again teetered on the precipice of life and death?

He smiled grimly. He had never imagined he'd view the loss of another human being, much less that of a woman, with such strong, if confusing, emotions. True, he had once loved Aelwyd deeply, yearning to return to her eager arms at the end of a long day, but he had also always known his wife's proper place in his life. Gadiel, Astara, his Karayan heritage, and personal honor had always held the highest places of esteem.

But Gadiel and Astara were no longer his to claim. The Karayan line was all but obliterated. And personal honor, along with the heady exhilaration of his former warrior's prowess, had vanished along with his sight. Indeed, for all practical purposes, his very manhood had died the day he had been blinded. He was worth little more than a pawn to be used, or an odious but insignificant insect to be squashed.

Yet, whenever Danae was near, Vartan always felt like a man again, a man of great significance and purpose. His blood thrummed a bit harder through his veins; his skin tingled and he came alive. Perhaps it was but her abiding faith in him, and the noble purpose she was convinced he was still meant to fulfill. Perhaps it was but the lingering memory he still carried with him of the admiration he had once seen in her eyes. Or perhaps, perhaps . . .

With a savage shake of his head, Vartan flung aside the tender hope that had insidiously entwined about his heart. He was now a weak, helpless shadow of his former self. He couldn't defend even a dung beetle battling to escape the clutches of a ravenous bird, much less another person. By the sword of Calidor, but he couldn't even help himself!

He was stripped, laid low. There was nothing left to give up save his life. His life—and Danae.

Danae . . .

Vartan's eyes burned. He blinked them several times. He must be staring unseeingly again, he thought. It had to be that. He never wept. Well, never save for that day in Voshie's hut when he had finally regained consciousness and Danae had told him about Astara and his family's fate. And then once again, when he thought Danae might die, after being struck by lightning . . .

Is this what Amma Serpuhi meant, Vartan asked himself, *when she said to gain everything you first had to give up everything? And was Danae the final symbol of the surrender of all that really mattered? Was that why it tore at him so, rending his heart, his very soul?*

Vartan shook his head, self-disgust filling him. *I've nothing left to lose, do I?* he asked, his query lifting to the throne of the All-Knowing. *I'm empty, a parched shell, drained of everything that ever made me the man I was.*

Resentment filled him, bitter and heart-searing. *What sort of Immortal One are You, to suck a man dry in order to gain his allegiance? Where is the victory, the honor, in that? And what can You ever hope to gain to further Your kingdom with followers such as I?*

Followers . . .

Vartan's thoughts flitted back to Amma Serpuhi. Aside from Danae, he had never known a more peace- and joy-filled woman. She exuded love in all its forms—for others, for the land and its creatures, for the work she did, the air she breathed, for the sun, rain, wind, for the cold as well as for the heat. She was hardly a parched shell or empty; she was full, full to overflowing.

And Danae . . . Each time he thought of her, his heart swelled with longing. She was perfect in every way, and that perfection emanated in all she did. She, too, was full to overflowing and shared that abundance with everyone she encountered.

He had tried so hard to find that same love and joy in serving Athan. Yet, though there had been fleeting moments when the effort had seemed as naught, for the most part Vartan had struggled to achieve it on sheer force of will alone. The effort to surrender, to submit, had been horrific.

Had Danae and Serpuhi paid the same price for such joy? Total and complete sacrifice of all they were and had ever been? Vartan sucked in a shuddering breath. Surely not. No one—man or woman—possessed that kind of courage, if courage it really was. More likely it was insanity, pure and simple. Even they surely had held back some small part of themselves, for themselves.

But then, what did he have to lose? For a long while now, his life had hung by the slenderest of threads, ever since that fateful morn he had ridden through Astara's huge, bronze gates to face Ladon. Why not finally surrender it all?

But I don't know how. I'm still as blind of soul as I am of sight. I haven't the words. I don't know the proper rituals. And if I bare my heart to the unknown, won't I open myself to evil as much as to good?

With a despairing groan, Vartan lowered his head until it rested against the carpet on which he kneeled. He was so lost, so afraid, so confused. It had come to this, then. He was paralyzed, exposed in all his naked vulnerability and helplessness. It was the final, the supreme shame.

Help me, he whispered, clenching his bound fists so tightly his nails scored his palms. *What, even now, have I missed? Help me see!*

You see more now, Child of Mine, a soft voice echoed in Vartan's head, *than you ever saw when you were whole. Then, your pride blinded you to My truths. Your fame and fortune were but stumbling blocks to the journey you have always been called to take. But now you begin to understand, don't you? See the mystery, the promise, the only gift that matters, hovering just beyond the pale of this world, this life.*

The journey you have always been called to take . . .

What had Danae said to him once? Something about Athan's service demanding all the strength and courage a person possessed. And that, in the end, it was the only honor and purpose in life that truly mattered.

Trust in Me, the voice came once again. *Trust and be patient. Your destiny will be revealed. When the time is right. In* My *time, not yours.*

Frustration surged through Vartan. With only the greatest effort did he manage to squelch it. Trust . . . patience. How much longer must he wait? He was literally withering away waiting.

Did you think you had surrendered everything? the voice asked with a most definite, if tender, touch of amusement. *Well, Child of Mine, think again. There is yet more to yield, more to give.*

Ah, yes. Control. My need to control my life and the world around me, Vartan thought. *I was very good at it once. People expected that of me. But no more. I already relinquished that burden. No one expects it any longer, much less thinks me capable.*

Once, that admission would've shamed if not angered him. But no more. Now, at this seemingly hopeless and desperate moment in time, it filled Vartan with a startling sense of peace—and freedom. He had surrendered his pride. He had surrendered Danae. Finally, he could attend to himself, to his own needs. Needs of his soul, so long starved and empty of something, though he knew not what.

Until this moment. A moment fraught with promise, with the glimpse of a new and far better life his heart was finally beginning to recognize, even if his head still couldn't. And Vartan knew that it was good. He had, at long last, begun the solitary portion of his journey—both a literal and figurative journey into the Desert. A journey he must make without Danae, Serpuhi, or anyone else.

A journey he had always, *always*, been called to take.

15

Danae woke to the sound of spoons clanging against the insides of pots, people walking about, and the call to sunrise prayers. This morn, however, the plaintive sound failed to fill her with peace or joy. This morn heralded the day Vartan would die.

She rolled off her little pallet and glanced around. Through the thin fabric partitioning Sharifah's sleeping area from the enclosure Danae shared with the maidservants, she could see the royal lady had already arisen and was gone. So were all the servants who had been sleeping nearby.

Horror swamped her. What if they had all gone to see Vartan's execution, and it was already over? Danae bolted upright, grabbed at the *sholi* she had worn the day before, and quickly dressed.

Not bothering with shoes or even to hide her hair beneath the requisite *khirya*, she ran from the tent. Glancing wildly around, her gaze finally settled on a crowd that had formed about a party of men and horses near the northern edge of Am Shardi. Her heart thundering in her chest, Danae headed in that direction.

Perhaps it was the frantic, forceful way she shouldered through the mass of people, or perhaps it was her lack of head covering and wild-eyed appearance, but the crowd parted before her like grain before a scythe. She pushed past to find the nightmare of yesterday replicated, with Vartan patiently standing prisoner while Ra'id listened, once again, to Malik and Farid's furious rantings.

"This is a travesty!" the gray-bearded Malik was saying, his face flushed, his arms waving as if to add emphasis to his words. "We haven't time to spare dragging this man out into the Haroun. Save us all the inconvenience, I beg you, m'lord. Just lop off his head and be done with it!"

"And I say beheading is far too merciful a fate for one such as he," Ra'id replied, meeting Malik's impassioned demands with a calm but firm refusal. "For centuries now, he and his kind have mocked the Desert and its people. It's only fitting the Desert now be the one to punish him. It's only fitting that, in his dying, he learn the true power and brutality of the Haroun—and the price that must be paid for betraying the Diya al Din."

Around Danae, a murmur of assent rose from the people. She pushed to the front of the crowd, straining to see Ra'id's face and discern his true motives. Unfortunately, the action drew Farid's attention.

With a snarl, he closed the short distance and grabbed her by the arm. "Then if it's the Haroun for Karayan," he cried, dragging Danae with him to thrust her at Ra'id's feet, "then let it be the same for his woman. Look at her! With her immodest, uncovered head, she parades herself about like some creature of loose morals. We don't want her kind among us!"

"Nay!"

For the first time since Danae had caught sight of him, Vartan seemingly came to life. He twisted in the grip of the two men who held him.

"Please, Lord Ra'id," he said. "Don't send her out into the Desert with me. She's innocent of any wrongdoing. The fault's mine. Mine alone!"

"If she's your wife,"—Ra'id's stern gaze met Danae's now uplifted one—"she's as guilty as you. And she *is* your wife, isn't she?"

"Aye, I am!" Danae was quick to reply.

"Nay, she isn't!" came Vartan's almost simultaneous one.

A grim, knowing smile on his lips, Ra'id leaned down, took Danae by the arm, and pulled her to her feet. "Now, this is quite interesting. One of you claims to be life-bonded, and the other suddenly doesn't. Whom should I believe?"

"You know as well as I that Danae's not my wife," Vartan ground out. "My wife died the day Astara fell."

"Aye, I've heard the tales." The Desert lord cocked his head, eyeing Danae speculatively. "But if she isn't your wife, why did you lie to me about it?"

"You know the reason as well as I," Vartan snarled.

"But now you no longer wish to protect her, is that it?"

"I ask that *you* take her under your protection, and be as a brother to her."

"A brother?" Ra'id laughed. "I think not. What I feel when I look at Danae is hardly brotherly."

She sent Ra'id a scathing look. "Then, to preserve my maiden's innocence, allow me to accompany Vartan into the Desert. I'd prefer to take my chances out there, than here with you."

"Indeed?" As if in feigned surprise, the Desert lord arched a dark brow. "There's but one minor problem. Neither of you has a choice in the matter." His mouth hardened and he motioned to a man holding a horse. "The day draws on and the sun won't get any cooler. Bring up the animal and help this man onto it."

"Nay!"

With a sudden jerk of her arm, Danae broke free and ran to Vartan. She threw her arms about him and pressed her face to his chest. Beneath her ear, his strong heart thudded slowly and steadily, recalling those other times she had heard it, been close to him. Surely this wasn't meant to be the last time she'd ever do so!

"Please," she whispered. "Please, Vartan, make them let me go with you. We can't be separated. What will you do alone out in the Desert? You need me."

"Aye, I need you, sweet lady." For the briefest, most heart-wrenching of moments, he laid his cheek on the top of her head, then pulled back to kiss it. "But this is one time you cannot be with me. You need to let me go. The Desert's *my* destiny, not yours. You must let me face it alone."

Let him face it alone? Even the thought of parting from Vartan ripped her heart in two. And now to let him go out alone and blind into a barren, scorching, merciless desert?

"But you'll die out there without me." The intensity of her emotions made her voice sound hoarse and strained. "And I can't bear to stay behind, not knowing, not being able to help . . ."

"Even if it's Athan's will?"

"Nay," she said, sobbing now. "Don't say that. Don't make it seem like it's Athan's will when it isn't. It isn't!"

"But it is, Danae. He has called me to the Desert, and I must find Him there. Find Him, or die in the trying."

She lifted her tear-filled gaze and saw his determination. Saw, as well, his hope.

If He so desired, Athan could save Vartan. Save him even from the dangers of the Desert. But would He? *Would* He?

"It is in Athan's hands then," she whispered.

"Aye, it is, sweet lady."

239

He smiled down at her, the light in his sightless eyes so piercingly sweet that Danae thought her heart would break. Then Ra'id's hand settled about her arm, and she was pulled away.

"Enough of the tender farewells," he muttered. "Let us be gone!"

Hands replaced Ra'id's, and Danae found herself inexorably dragged backward. This time, however, she didn't fight or protest. All she could see, all she could comprehend, was that Vartan was being taken away. Taken away to face a trial, a testing, the likes of which he quite possibly wouldn't survive.

Taken away, and she might never see him again.

Throughout the long ride that day deep into the Haroun, Ra'id heard neither anger nor complaint, nor saw even a flicker of fear in Vartan Karayan. Hands bound behind him, the Astarian calmly followed the warrior who led his horse. By the sheer strength of his legs and his quite obvious riding ability, he even kept his seat whenever his horse stumbled in an occasional hidden, sandy depression. With Vartan's features shaded from the scorching Desert sun by his long *shmaagh*, it was difficult for Ra'id to gauge his thoughts. Some of them at the very least, though, must have been of Danae.

Ra'id wanted to speak with him of the beauteous woman who had already captured his heart, to assure this man who, at the very least, was her protector, that he'd treat her honorably. Why it should matter to Ra'id what Karayan thought of his intentions came as some surprise, but he found that it did.

Perhaps he admired the man's dignity and courage. Perhaps it was for Danae's sake. Or perhaps, just perhaps, some part of him rebelled at the callous cruelty of leaving a blind man—even if he were the Diya al Din's direst enemy—alone out on the merciless Haroun Desert.

Still, there was no other recourse. It was either this or an instant death by beheading. And, though Malik had wisely refrained from accompanying them, he had sent Farid along in his place. Sent him to verify Ra'id did indeed carry out his father's orders.

The realization galled him. He had long ago wearied of the short leash his father—and even more infuriatingly, his father's advisors—kept him on. This diplomatic journey had only intensified his resentment. Intensified it to the point he felt he had only two options left—reject his royal heritage, or defy his father and incite a revolt. He had long ago given up on trying to talk to his sire.

As the day burned to noon and past, the unrelenting heat began to make Ra'id irritable, until he could barely bite back a harsh remark when Farid rode up to join him. "Aye, what is it?" he asked, shooting the man a sharp, quick glance.

"Some of us were wondering how much farther we must take this man before we execute him? Why not just kill him now, bury his body, and head back to Am Shardi? There is still time to return for the supper meal."

"And didn't I make it clear the Diya al Din would have no active part in Karayan's death? That, instead, the Haroun would kill him?"

"Aye, m'lord," Farid replied, "I heard and understood. Myself, it matters not if he dies at our hands or bakes to death on the Haroun. I but wonder how much longer we must ride to properly dispose of this man."

"And what do you imagine it would take to convince my father every effort was made to ensure Karayan's death? Hmmm, Farid?" Ra'id looked his way. "Leave him one day's journey out on the Haroun? Or perhaps a full two days' instead?"

Beneath his bronzed, leathery skin, the other man turned a sickly shade of green. A grim satisfaction filled Ra'id.

"Aye, two days should guarantee that a blind man would have no hope of survival, wouldn't you say?"

"If—if you think so, m'lord."

Ra'id nodded. "Aye, I do. Go. Inform the men who so ardently desire my decision. And Farid," he added as the other man reined his horse about, "tell them as well they have you to thank for convincing me of the wisdom of the plan."

"A-aye, m'lord." Farid lost no further time kicking his mount in its side and galloping off.

Ra'id watched him ride away, then turned back to the distant horizon. Heat waves shimmered there, distorting land and sky. Hours in this desert furnace stretched on, until they could finally make camp for the night.

He had Malik, Farid, and his father to thank for this miserable journey. A journey that, with its even more miserable outcome, in his heart of hearts sickened him to his innermost being.

After the intense heat of the past two days, the relative coolness of the small cave formed by a large jumble of rocks was a blessed relief. Vartan climbed into it with the deepest gratitude, only partially aware or caring that it meant, for him, the end of his journey. All that mattered for now was to get out of the sun. He'd worry later what to do once Ra'id and his men rode away, leaving him to fend for himself in the middle of the Desert.

Even the sandy floor of the little cave felt wonderfully cool. Vartan tore off his *shmaagh* and pressed his cheek to the ground. He had never thought gritty sand could feel the closest thing to paradise on this earth, but he almost thought he had found it. At least if he could die cool, after the inferno of the past two days, Vartan supposed there was some comfort in that.

Footsteps soon followed him into the little cave. "Here," Ra'id's voice came, surprising him. Something—a bag perhaps—landed close to Vartan's head.

"It isn't much, some food, a dagger, and a water pouch, but it's the best I can do for you."

Vartan pushed to a sitting position and felt around until he found the sack, drawing it to him. "It's more than I dared hope for. That, and my life. Thank you."

"It'll only prolong the inevitable. Still, though the rations won't last long, I'd advise not leaving this cave. It'll be a far more merciful death dying of thirst here than out on the Desert."

"Your suggestion's duly noted."

An uncomfortable silence settled between them. Finally, Ra'id cleared his throat.

"My men are waiting. I must be—"

"Danae. I beg of you. Be gentle with her, and let her go if she asks it of you."

"I'd take her to wife if I could."

"But you can't, and she'll be no man's mistress."

"I know," Ra'id said after a long moment. "I'll do my best for her."

"I can ask no more."

With that, the Desert lord dragged in a long, unsteady breath, then turned and exited the cave. Vartan listened to the low murmur of voices outside for a few minutes more before they were replaced by the jingle of bridles, the squeak of leather, and then silence. Deep, all-consuming silence.

With a sigh, he leaned back against the stone wall. A wave of resignation washed over him. He was alone, somewhere in the Haroun, with no way of knowing where he was or which way to go. Now, he truly *was* cast onto Athan's mercy.

Grabbing up the sack Ra'id had left him, he rifled through its contents. Some small packages of dried meat, slices of bread, and chunks of cheese lay on top. Next came a full leather water bag. At the bottom, just as Ra'id had said, was a small, sheathed dagger. Vartan pulled the weapon free and sank the blade into the sand beside him. If the cave's opening was large enough for a man to enter, it was also large enough for some Desert predator like a Sand Cat.

His mouth twisted grimly. The Desert was a harsh, unforgiving land. He could only hope that, if he must die out here, that he die of thirst. He didn't fancy becoming a Sand Cat's or other Desert beast's meal.

The sun beat down on the barren, bleached sands, inexorably sucking all moisture and, with it, all life away. An endless blanket of glittering death, the Desert's undulating, beckoning hills and distant, shimmering horizon were as they had always been to careless travelers—a treacherous siren's call to certain doom.

Gazing out on the Haroun, Danae wondered how she could have ever thought the arid wasteland beautiful. All she could see now was its ugliness. Nay, it was worse than ugly. It was a repulsive, ravenous monster. A monster intent on devouring the man she loved.

Nearly four days had passed since Vartan had been taken away. Ra'id and his men had yet even to return. Four days of sheer misery, waiting, watching, wondering. Unable to eat, incapable of sleep, barely keeping down more than a few swallows of water, her heart a raw, ulcerous mass thudding agonizingly in the middle of her chest.

Save for when darkness fell and she was forced to return to Sharifah's tent, tied hand and foot to prevent her escape, Danae spent every waking moment sitting out here beneath one of the rafa trees at the northernmost edge of the oasis. Sitting here, staring out onto the Haroun in the direction they had taken Vartan. Sitting here, praying when she was able and, the rest of the time, drowning in almost mindless despair.

"Help him, Athan," she muttered over and over through dry, cracked lips. "Save him, if You will, but if You won't, fill him with Your presence and peace. Don't leave Vartan out there alone. Be with him. I think I can bear almost any-thing—even losing him—if only You don't leave him to die alone."

Her thoughts flew back to that day high up on Astara's city walls, when she had watched Vartan valiantly ride out to fight Ladon. He had faced that seemingly insurmount-able challenge with the same dignity and honor with which he had accepted his death sentence out on the Haroun. This time, however, there was no one left to mourn him but her. Everything else—family, people, home—had been stolen from him. He had nothing else left to surrender.

"You've taken it all now, Eternal One," she whispered. "Ev-erything. As You have from me. What more do You wish from us? Whatever it might be, I'd offer it and gladly, if only You'd spare Vartan's life. I'd offer anything. Anything."

Once again, tears welled in her sore, burning eyes and trickled down her sun-reddened cheeks. Sobs wracked her until every muscle in her body ached. But no answer came, no solace from above. Silence encompassed her. Silence and despair.

"Danae, come away from here. Come back to my tent and eat something. You'll cry yourself to death if you keep on this way. I beg of you. Come away from here."

There was genuine concern in Sharifah's voice. A part of Danae felt compassion for the woman and the pain she must be causing her. Yet another part didn't care. Sharifah was Diya al Din, and as such was as much to blame for Vartan's torment as the rest of them. Indeed, perhaps even more to blame as the sister loyal to a brother who had carried out this atrocity.

"I've no appetite," Danae mumbled thickly. "Leave me be."

"Then come back and rest for a while. You're killing yourself!"

"I don't care."

"Well, *I* care! And so would Vartan. No matter what becomes of him, he wouldn't want for you to die!" The other woman sank to her knees beside Danae. "Don't do this to yourself. It not only dishonors Vartan, but Al'Alim as well. How can you call yourself His child and do this?"

At her accusation, something ripped open deep within Danae. Into the gaping hole surged rage.

"And how can *you* call yourself one of the Faithful and condone the murder of an innocent man?" She reared up and pivoted around to confront Sharifah, her hands tightly clenched at her sides to keep from striking out. "Where is there honor or love for Athan in that? *Where?*"

The color drained from Sharifah's face. She averted her gaze out toward the Desert. "I-I don't know. I truly don't. And I feel so . . . so ashamed."

Now that her anger had been unleashed, it was difficult to rein it back in. Danae wanted nothing more than to verbally—and physically—flail at the other woman. Let her feel just a tiny part of what *she* was going through. Let her suffer!

But even as the consideration flashed through her mind, Eisa's admonition to forgive without measure followed swiftly behind. Eisa, whose love was so strong and deep and pure that

He had chosen to die on a tree for the redemption of all, had set the example she must follow. It didn't matter what the Diya al Din had done in killing Vartan. They must stand before the throne of the Eternal One and face the consequences. All she could do was live her life in the best way left her. In the way Eisa had lived.

The anger seeped away with a sigh. "It's not your fault, Sharifah," Danae said, sagging back on her haunches. "Please forgive my lack of kindness toward you. In the doing, I *have* dishonored Athan—and Vartan."

Ra'id's sister's eyes grew moist. "You've nothing to feel guilty about. If someone had harmed one of my family, I know I couldn't be half so kind." She gave a harsh laugh. "Indeed, I'd be the first to cut out his heart. The hot Desert blood, after all, runs strong and thick in my veins."

She took Danae by both arms then, and drew her to her feet. "Will you come back to my tent now? Now that you've decided not to try and starve yourself to death?"

Though the thought of food still made Danae feel nauseous, for Sharifah's sake she gave a little nod. "Aye. I can't say as I'm any more inclined to live than I was before, but if Athan wills that I go on, then I'll try to—"

Far in the distance, a sudden flash of movement caught her eye. Danae squinted, trying to see past the endless, flickering haze. A dark blotch that hadn't been there before, then another and another, passed over the horizon, heading their way. Soon, what looked to be a small band of riders took form from the amorphous shapes.

Sharifah must have seen the expression on her face. She turned, lifted a hand to shade her eyes, and scrutinized the horizon. A smile slowly lifted her lips.

"It's Ra'id and his men," she said. "Finally, they've returned."

247

"Aye," Danae murmured, raising a swift, fervent prayer for courage. "They've returned."

Vartan managed to make the food and water last two days. After that, the only sustenance he had was prayer. Prayer and memories—of little Korien, of the good years he'd had with Aelwyd before the sickness began to consume her, of his parents, sister, and brother, of Serpuhi and that special time spent in the Goreme, and always, always, memories of Danae.

He loved her, and finally possessed the courage to face it. He had known it deep in his heart for a long while now. He had loved her as far back as Astara, just refused to admit it, clinging fast to his commitment and loyalty to Aelwyd even as his love for his wife had gradually disintegrated beneath the relentless onslaught of her madness. Yet, even in their parting at Am Shardi, Vartan had withheld the truth from Danae.

She would have enough to bear, alone now in a camp full of strangers. He didn't want her burdened with confused emotions, unrequited needs, or additional remorse. Assuming, of course, Danae felt even a tiny portion of the love he bore for her. If not, more the better that he hadn't told her. She might have then, out of pity and to spare the feelings of a condemned man, uttered falsehoods she'd long regret.

Still, in the endless hours that passed in the cave, Vartan nonetheless allowed himself to dream. There was no harm in it. His dreams would die, unspoken and unfulfilled after all, with him. They gave him comfort now, though. And, in his dreaming, he didn't feel so alone, so afraid.

He dreamed at times of Athan, too. Those dreams came to him, though, when he slept, or in that span of consciousness halfway between sleep and wakefulness. The Eternal One seemed almost tangible then, a Presence who shared the meager existence of his little cave. It was as if . . . as if but a thin veil separated the physical world Vartan still dwelled in from the world of the spirit, of the divine.

In those special times the past and the future seemed to recede, and all that remained was the present moment. A moment alive with infinite possibility, rife with unimaginable love, and saturated through and through with Athan. In those special times, so much of what Serpuhi had once said coalesced and sank deeply, drenching his soul. So much gained a truer, more profound and precious meaning.

Everything—*everything*—became more than it had once been.

"Don't be overcome by fear and turn from the path of salvation." As if she were with him now, Vartan heard Serpuhi speaking. *"The road will be difficult and narrow at the beginning. But if we remain true, never faltering in this way of life and faith, soon we shall race on the path of Athan's commands, our hearts brimming over with the irresistible rapture of love."*

Was that what had been missing all along? Vartan wondered. Love?

He had begun the journey as he always had before, determined to force Athan into his life by dint of his own effort. To find the answers and peace he so desperately craved. In the doing, though, he had tried to create a god of his own. But Athan was already there, had *always* been there, and was much, much more than any god any man could fashion. In the end, Athan had always been there for the taking, if only Vartan would stop, look, and listen.

All he could do—all he had ever been *meant* to do—he realized now, was open his heart to love. Athan would do the rest.

A tranquil stillness filled Vartan. It was all so clear now, and all so simple. As Eisa had once said, love begat trust, and trust begat even greater love. In truth, it was impossible to have one without the other.

Weariness engulfed him, and Vartan reached for it gladly. Perhaps Athan would come to him again in a dream. If a dream it had ever really been.

He didn't care anymore. The past faded from memory, the future might well never be. All that mattered was now, and that he was safe in Athan's loving embrace.

"But if we remain true . . . soon we shall race on the path of Athan's commands, our hearts brimming over with the irresistible rapture of love . . ."

16

"I left him in a small cave with food, water, and a dagger," Ra'id informed Danae and Sharifah within the privacy of his tent, a short while after his arrival back at the oasis. As he pulled off his *agaal* and *shmaagh*, then ran a hand roughly through his sweat-damp hair, his gaze found and held Danae's. "It wasn't much, but the best I could do."

"Even that, if Farid had discovered it, would've been enough to bring Father's wrath down upon you," his sister said. "You risked much, Brother, but I thank you for that."

"Aye, and I thank you as well." Danae managed a wan little smile. "At every turn, someone always seems to step forward to help Vartan. Athan's blessing is indeed upon him."

"For a time more, perhaps." Ra'id couldn't bear the look of hope shining in Danae's eyes. "He's still doomed. You must realize that. It's but a matter of time."

"Perhaps. And perhaps not."

"Well, we can't linger here in the hopes he'll return. I've nine more tribes to visit, and none of the stops will be short or sweet. I've squandered enough time already."

"Then allow me to remain behind." The blond-haired woman's eyes burned now with entreaty. "Someone needs to be here . . . when Vartan returns."

Exasperation at her unrealistic expectations filled him. "And what will you do if he doesn't return? This oasis won't sustain you indefinitely, and to venture out onto the Haroun alone, when you've no knowledge of it, is certain suicide."

"I won't be alone. Vartan *will* return!"

Ra'id looked to Sharifah. "Has she been like this since I left?"

"Danae has faith, Brother. She believes in the Prophecy and that Vartan Karayan is its fulfillment."

He eyed his sister for a long moment and saw he'd get no support from her. "None of this makes any sense! Karayan isn't going to be fulfilling any prophecy if he's dead. And nothing short of a miracle will change that now."

"It was a miracle Vartan survived Ladon," Danae cried. "It was a miracle he got this far, with everyone out to kill him, and he blind and helpless to defend himself. What is some puny desert for a man such as he, a man chosen by Athan Himself?"

Ra'id could feel his frustration rise. He'd had no heart for what he had done to Karayan. He had even less heart to kill Danae's hope. But to remain here, waiting for someone who would never return . . .

"Three days," he ground out at last. "I'll give him three days, but after that we *will* leave. And you, little Rasha, even if I have to tie you hand and foot, will leave with us." He stepped up to her and took her chin in his hand. "Agreed?"

Joy flared in her compelling brown eyes. "He'll return, Ra'id. You'll see."

***

A dank, putrid stench was Vartan's first warning of the Sand Cat's approach. Then he heard the merest brush of fur against the rock wall only feet from him on his right. There was just enough time for Vartan to grab his dagger. As his hand closed around it, the animal sprang.

Long, narrow teeth sank into the other arm Vartan threw up to protect himself. In the next instant, he slashed downward with the dagger. The blade sank into something fleshy—likely the shoulder—tearing through the beast's hide before glancing off bone.

The Sand Cat released his arm and screamed, leaping backward. Vartan crawled to his knees, the dagger ready. All his senses strained to ascertain exactly where the cat was. The animal paced the width of the cave, growling angrily. Vartan tried his best to follow the Sand Cat's movements, knowing it was but a matter of time before it again attacked.

When the strike came, the beast leaped from the left, slamming into him with a good hundred-plus pounds of weight. Man and cat toppled over, but this time the Sand Cat had the advantage. His momentum and mass forced Vartan over onto his side, the dagger and his arm twisted beneath him.

Lethally sharp teeth plunged into him again, this time into his upper arm and shoulder. He gasped in agony and rolled toward the animal, using his own bulk to try to throw the animal off balance. Claws sank into his chest and legs.

Vartan's hand was freed, though, and he slammed his fist into the side of the animal's head. With a startled snort, the Sand Cat released him and fell back. Vartan shoved away, twisting about to frantically feel for his dagger. Behind him, the stunned cat began to stir.

Blessedly, his hand glanced off something hard half-buried in the sand. He groped for it. His fingers closed around the dagger's hilt.

With a hideous snarl, the Sand Cat sprang. Vartan swung around and thrust his dagger forward. This time, it sank somewhere in the beast's upper chest. With an ear-splitting

253

shriek, the cat collapsed atop him, knocking Vartan back over. His head hit hard against the stone wall, and he lost consciousness.

Some time later, Vartan woke, or rather, the searing pains in his arm, shoulder, chest, and legs wrenched him awake. He lay there waiting for the Sand Cat to once again attack. The cave was silent.

He levered to one elbow, only to have a fierce throbbing in the back of his head join all his other injuries. He felt weak, dizzy, and a quick check of his wounds told him why. They were bleeding profusely.

With a despairing groan, Vartan rolled onto his belly and groped around until he found the Sand Cat. The animal was dead. There was some consolation in that. Though he'd most likely now bleed to death, he'd at least not be tonight's supper.

"So this is how I'll meet my end, is it?" he asked softly. "Well, I suppose it's more merciful than dying of thirst or baking out on the Desert. Still, it's not at all how I imagined I'd finally die."

He had always hoped to fall bravely in battle after winning the day for his people. He had hoped to be mourned by many and have his prowess and courage praised in countless songs and tales. *Instead . . . instead,* he thought, everything beginning to grow fuzzy, *I'll die out here alone and unlamented. When someone finally does find my bleached bones, they'll not know who or what I once had been.*

"A strange sort of destiny," Vartan muttered. "But then, You always did seem to speak in riddles, Athan. Well, no matter. Soon now, everything will be made clear, won't it? Soon I'll finally understand it all."

A freshened breeze blew down into the little cave just then. A voice, low and soothing, seemed to wing its way along with the wind. A voice calling his name.

The end must be near, Vartan thought. He was beginning to hallucinate. Still, no harm was done in crawling outside. Better to die beneath the starlit heavens, even if he couldn't see them. By the time the sun rose to scorch the sky, he'd be dead anyway.

The short journey was excruciatingly hard, his muscles barely able to pull him along. "Just . . . let me live," he whispered, "to make it . . . outside. Please . . . Athan."

And, finally, he was free of the cave. The cool night air wafted over him. He rolled over onto his back, breathing deeply. Ah, but it smelled so fresh and sweet! Let it be the last thing he remembered.

Gradually, he became aware of millions of tiny lights piercing the canopy of black that was his blindness. He blinked, puzzled. Was this the end, then? Were the lights the furthest reaches of paradise, and was he now hurtling toward it?

He stared hard, wanting to see what lay ahead. The twinkling lights began to coalesce, become closer and more intense. Vartan lifted his hand before his face and, for a fleeting instant, saw his fingers outlined by the ever growing brightness.

Suddenly, in a burst of illumination, he was caught up in a dazzling ball of light. A ball of light and, at its center, a white bird. Wings wide, it hovered there for a few seconds. Then, as it began to flap its wings, flowers appeared and floated downward. One after another they came—hundreds of perfectly formed, blue roses.

As each day passed, Danae's spirits drooped a little more. It became increasingly harder to maintain her aura of certitude regarding Vartan's return. And she found her prayers becoming more and more desperate.

Sharifah said nothing, just offered her silent support. Ra'id, all the while carrying out plans for their imminent departure, watched her with an ever intense concern. And Malik and Farid glared whenever she passed, immediately putting their heads together in heated discussion.

On the morn of the fourth day, Danae awoke to the realization there wasn't any time left. Today they'd depart Am Shardi. Today Vartan had been gone a full week. He was likely dead or dying somewhere out on the Desert, and there wasn't anything she could do about it.

The empty ache she had experienced after Vartan had first been taken away returned. Despair swamped her. She wanted to bury her head, burrow beneath her covers, and never face the world again.

But such behavior would honor neither Athan *nor* Vartan. And, though she didn't understand Athan's plan in this, it was enough that she trust in Him. Somehow, someday, the acceptance, if not the understanding, would come.

Danae rose, completed her morning ablutions, and dressed. Then, after placing the *khirya* over her hair, she left the tent. It didn't take her long to find Ra'id and Sharifah. In the coolness of dawn, they stood before a campfire, sipping steaming cups of salma as they watched the servants dismantle Ra'id's tent. Danae squared her shoulders and headed in their direction.

Sharifah was the first one to see her. She smiled.

"Oh, you're finally up. I was just about to come drag you from bed, so they could take down the tent."

"I'm sorry." Try as she might, Danae couldn't muster the enthusiasm necessary to return her smile. "I didn't sleep well last night and, when I finally did, I was exhausted."

The other woman nodded sympathetically. "I understand." She gestured to the brass pot hanging over the fire. "Would you like a cup of salma? And there's freshly baked flatbread and sweet rafa nuts, as well, to break your fast with."

"Nay, I'm not hungry." Danae forced herself to meet Ra'id's steady gaze. "You won't reconsider allowing me to remain behind here, will you?"

"Do you really think Vartan would want me to do that?"

She didn't have to think long on the answer. "Nay, he wouldn't. He'd want me to be safe and cared for."

"Aye, he would."

This seemed the best moment to broach a plan that had been forming for the last day or so. "In time, if it doesn't place too great a burden on you, I'd like to return to the Goreme Valley."

Ra'id arched a dark brow. "Indeed? And whatever for? To become one of those holy hermits?"

"Perhaps." Something about his attitude irked her. "Is there anything wrong with wishing to serve Athan in such a way?"

He laughed. "Nay, Rasha, there isn't. I just think Al'Alim has different plans for you."

"How? As a wife and a mother?"

"There's nothing wrong with serving Athan in such a way, is there?"

Danae couldn't help a twitch of her lips. Though she suspected his concern over her wish to return to the Goreme was self-serving, she also couldn't help but give him credit for turning her words against her.

"I never said there was." Unflinchingly, she once again met his gaze. "I'm just not sure anymore that such a life is for me, that's all."

"Well, we can speak again of this in—"

A cry went out from one of the warriors watering the horses at the edge of the oasis. As one, Ra'id, Sharifah, and Danae

257

turned to stare out in the direction the man was indicating. About a half mile or so away, walking steadily toward Am Shardi, was a man. Tall, broad of shoulder, he was dressed in Desert garb and appeared to be carrying something in his arms.

Danae squinted hard. The *shmaagh* shaded his face, making it difficult to ascertain his features. As he drew ever nearer, however, she could see he had a dark beard and that his clothing seemed bloodstained and torn in places. She also realized there was something very familiar about him.

Her heart leaped in her chest, then commenced a rapid pounding. "Vartan," she whispered. Lifting the lower length of her *sholi*, she set out at a run.

Ra'id called her name. A stiff, sudden breeze ripped the *khirya* from her head, but Danae didn't care. All she saw, all she knew, was Vartan had returned. Even when her feet finally touched the more yielding Desert sand, her pace barely altered. Sheer joy and exaltation fueled her limbs.

Somehow, Vartan had not only survived the Haroun, but managed to find his way back. It was truly the work of Athan, and no one, not even the Diya al Din, could deny it now.

She could see his face now, his eyes, and as his glance met hers, he smiled, let the sack he was carrying fall to the ground, and held out his arms. For an instant, Danae faltered. It was almost as if . . . as if he could see. And then it didn't matter. She was in his arms.

He pressed her close, his big body a familiar, sheltering, oh, so precious haven! She heard his heart thudding strongly and steadily beneath her ear. She tightened her hold about him and began to sob.

"Hush, sweet lady. It's all right. I'm back. I'm back."

"A-aye," Danae croaked out, "Athan be praised! You're back. But how . . . how did you ever manage to find your way? It's a miracle!"

She didn't want to ever let him go, but after a time, Vartan released her and, taking her by the arms, leaned back. "Athan did more than save my life. He restored my vision. I'm whole again, Danae. Whole!"

"You . . . you can see?" She stared up at him, scanning his eyes. His beautiful sea blue orbs stared back at her, watching her every move, every expression.

Vartan grinned. "Aye, sweet lady. I can see."

Tears welled yet again and spilled down her cheeks. "Ah, Vartan . . . Vartan . . ."

Tenderly, he wiped the tears away with the pads of his thumbs. "I know, Danae. I know." He paused to glance over her shoulder. "It appears I returned just in time. They're packing up to leave, aren't they?"

"Aye, but I convinced Ra'id to wait an additional three days after his return. And it was just enough time."

"He gave me food and water and left me in a cavelike spot. I wouldn't have made it otherwise."

"Ra'id's a good man."

"Did he treat you honorably then?"

It was her turn to grin. "Aye."

"Good. Now that I've my sight back, I'd have had to fight him if he hadn't."

She moved to the side, grabbed his hand, and pulled him forward. "Come. You might as well face Ra'id and his people and get it over with." Danae looked to where the Desert folk stood, gathered at the edge of Am Shardi, watching them. "And I'm thinking *you* had better go to them, because they're looking at *you* as if you're some apparition."

"Well," Vartan said with a chuckle as he bent to pick up his sack, "I *have* all but returned from the dead, haven't I?"

Danae squeezed his hand. "Aye, you have. And I wish you'd stop doing that. It's very hard on me, you know."

"I'm not particularly fond myself of hovering between the brink of life and death. Still, so far Athan has always pulled me through."

They started walking toward Ra'id and Sharifah. As Vartan approached, the people, clustered and behind the Desert lord and his sister, edged away until there was a good several yards of space all around. Ra'id and Sharifah, however, stood their ground, never taking their eyes off Vartan.

He drew to a halt before them. "Greetings, m'lord. I bring you a gift. A gift from Athan. It symbolizes, as well, my heart and my intentions."

Warily, Ra'id eyed the bag Vartan held. "What is it?"

Vartan set the sack on the ground, knelt before it, and opened it. He plunged his hands and arms deep into the contents, then pulled them out. Though two fell to the sand, in his hands he held fifteen or more perfectly formed blue roses. Head bowed, he offered them up to Ra'id.

Behind the Desert lord, people gasped or uttered soft cries. Ra'id's eyes widened, and he stared transfixed down at the roses. Sharifah grasped his arm, then looked from him to Danae.

"The blue rose of Gadiel," Danae thought, recalling Zagiri's words. *"Sacred . . . symbol of truth, unity, and a pure loving heart . . . carried by those who went in peace . . ."*

Her glance lifted to Ra'id's. As if stunned, as if he didn't know what to do, he continued to gaze at the roses. Danae smiled at him. Sharifah moved close, leaned over, and whispered in his ear.

"Take them. Accept them, Brother," Danae could hear her say. "It doesn't matter how he got them or why. What matters is, in all ways now, Vartan has fulfilled the Prophecy."

Like his father, Ra'id has always desired the throne of Gadiel for himself, Danae realized, watching the battle raging in the Desert lord's eyes. *Yet he also knows if he now acknowledges Vartan, he must set his own ambitions aside, likely forever.* Compassion for the man filled her. Athan asked much of all His followers.

With a shuddering breath, Ra'id at last stepped forward to meet Vartan. He put out his hands, and Vartan filled them with roses.

"In the name of the Hakeem and the Diya al Din, I accept this gift," he said, his deep voice rising to reach the ears of all gathered. "A gift that spans all differences and animosities, uniting us as citizens of a great and glorious land.

"We are no longer enemies, but brothers. It's Al'Alim's will, and let no man ever again divide us!"

"Let no man *ever* again divide us," Vartan solemnly repeated, lifting his gaze to scan the people standing behind Ra'id.

Ra'id turned, gave the roses to Sharifah, then offered Vartan his hand. "Rise, brother. It's not fitting you kneel to me."

Accepting his hand, Vartan climbed to his feet. Ra'id's quizzical glance took in his ragged appearance.

"Did picking all those roses wound you so?"

Vartan laughed. "Nay. The roses fell from the sky. It was a minor tussle with a hungry Sand Cat that ruined my garments."

"Then you must need your wounds seen to."

"Nay. Athan healed those as well, along with my sight. I'm quite strong and healthy now."

The Desert lord smiled. "You're far more than that, my friend. You're blessed by Al'Alim."

"We are all blessed, m'lord. I've but a different summons, it seems, than what others may be called to. And, worthy or not of it, I can no longer pretend ignorance or deny my destiny. Not if I am to serve the Eternal One as He so desires."

"As it must be so for any of us," Ra'id said, "no matter how difficult or bitter the service may sometimes be."

He turned, indicating that Vartan should accompany him. Immediately, Vartan fell into step beside the Desert lord, Sharifah following in their wake.

Danae watched them head off toward the center of camp. Then, swinging about, she walked to where the two remaining blue roses lay on the sand, stooped, and picked them up. Tucking the flowers into a pocket of her *sholi*, Danae rose and hurried after them.

℮ ℮

This is the single most devastating day of my life, Ra'id thought as he strode toward his tent with Vartan. Though he couldn't in good conscience have left Vartan Karayan exposed and totally helpless out on the Haroun, a part of Ra'id had also known the man's death would put an end to Karayan's disturbing presence in his life. But now, with his return—his miraculous, Al'Alim-sanctioned return—Ra'id's worst fear had come to life.

Karayan was the Guardian spoken of in the Prophecy. The Guardian all believed would be Gadiel's greatest ruler, called to save the land from its most calamitous threat. And, if the reports that kept coming in from their spies held even an ounce of accuracy, Astara and its surrounding holdings in Vardenis were now in the clutches of a brutal, even evil, man.

This could well be the beginning of the dire, desperate times the Prophecy had so long ago predicted.

Almost worse still, the Diya al Din were likely Ladon's next target. They were, after all, the nearest lands if one headed straight across the Valan Mountains. And the continued massing of troops—human and nonhuman alike—weren't needed, after all, for a realm already totally subjugated. They were being built up, instead, for the purpose of further conquest.

It was likely, as well, that Ladon knew of the intertribal feuding that had weakened the Diya al Din for centuries, making them an all but insignificant threat to any of the other Gadielean peoples, the Astarians most especially. More than anything else, the endless disputes and even occasional battles had kept the Diya al Din impoverished and mired in archaic customs and beliefs. And his father, Ra'id was forced to admit, had done little if anything to change that.

Perhaps now, though, there was at last hope. If the Diya al Din could be brought to accept Vartan Karayan as the Guardian of Gadiel, the tribes might finally unite under a common leader and for a common cause. A common cause that, Al'Alim willing, might lead to a permanent union of the Desert peoples. A union that might ultimately result in a new prosperity and advancement for all.

True, this potential leader wouldn't be Desert bred. That admission galled Ra'id deeply. Still, while his father lived, he also knew he was in no position to gain his peoples' allegiance for himself. If there was one thing that was anathema to the Diya al Din, that all the tribes agreed upon, it was their utter revulsion for the failure to render one's parents the proper respect and obeisance.

In the end, it was the only stricture that had kept Ra'id—and always would—from outright rebellion against the Hakeem and his advisors, forcing him repeatedly to bite his tongue and bide his time. That, and the fact that unless there seemed no other recourse, it went against all he deemed good and honorable to turn against his own sire. In the end, there was only one thing that would ever cause him to do so, and that was if the life-and-death welfare of the Diya al Din came into direct conflict with the will of his father.

No such issue was currently at stake, though, Ra'id comforted himself as he drew up back at the little campfire. He gestured to the cushions placed around it.

"If you will," he said, looking to Vartan, "seat yourself and take your ease. We'll soon enough be back out on the Haroun, and I suspect you may not have had much food or drink in your belly of late."

Vartan grinned. "It has been a day or two. I could use some nourishment."

As he sat, Danae set to work pouring and offering him a cup of salma, then she dashed off to procure a tur skin of fresh water. Sharifah soon had a plate of flatbread and cheese prepared.

As Vartan hungrily consumed the fare, Ra'id silently sat across from him. Ra'id's gaze, however, took in the camp, watching for signs of his people's reaction to Karayan's unexpected and most unnerving return. Most resumed their assigned duties of breaking down the tents for their departure. There were a few who, as they passed, shot Vartan a circumspect, if not fearful, look. It was Malik and Farid's angry discussion, too far away for Ra'id to hear, however, that concerned him the most.

Aside from him and Sharifah, the two men would most quickly comprehend the true implications of Vartan Karayan's return. Comprehend and find it very disturbing. More than just their prince's dominion and the people's welfare were at stake, after all.

Ra'id didn't have long to wait to discover their opinions. Just as Danae returned with a skinful of water and Vartan polished off the last of the cheese and flatbread, the Hakeem's two advisors appeared to have agreed on some sort of strategy and promptly headed their way.

"M'lord," Malik lost no time in beginning after rendering the proper bow, "though this man's return is most unusual, as is the healing of his purported blindness, in the end it changes nothing. He is still under the Hakeem's sentence of death. This time, however, Farid and I suggest it be swift and cleanly thorough. He must also be executed before all to see, so there'll be no question he's finally dead."

To their credit, Vartan and Danae said nothing, simply looked to Ra'id. The same, however, couldn't be said for him. His temper, already on a short fuse with Malik and Farid's constant meddling, exploded.

"But that's where you and I differ, Malik," he ground out, his voice low but threaded with an underlying fury. "I see the miracle in Karayan's return, while you dwell only on rules and strictures that are no longer relevant."

The older man's face reddened. "And are you implying, m'lord, that the Hakeem's orders are now to be cast aside for the likes of this—this enemy?"

"Nay, I'm saying instead," Ra'id replied, choosing his words with the greatest care, "if my father were here and had seen what we have seen, he wouldn't be so quick to seek this man's death. Since he isn't here, I'm making the decision for him."

"But, m'lord," Farid said, choosing this moment to finally join the conversation, "in decisions of such momentousness, isn't it wisest to confer with experienced advisors? It is, after all, why your father sent us along. To advise you in your inexperience."

"In my inexperience?" Ra'id climbed to his feet. *"In my inexperience?"* he repeated softly as he advanced on the man.

As Farid blanched and backed away, Malik hurriedly stepped between them. "In your gracious goodness, m'lord," he said, "forgive Farid's slip of the tongue. It's not a matter of experience or inexperience at all. Even the Hakeem wisely chooses advisors to assist him. As we are sent by him to assist you."

"And your assistance has been duly noted." Ra'id met Malik's arrogant gaze with a resolute one of his own. "In the end, though, the Hakeem is the final authority, as am *I* in his stead. And I choose not to execute Vartan Karayan, but take him as my brother and honored friend. As I suspect my father will, once he learns the truth."

"Then I must protest, and protest strongly, against your decision, m'lord," the gray-bearded man said, his voice now shaking. "I must also notify the Hakeem."

Ra'id's thoughts raced. The last thing he needed right now was, this time, for his father to hear only Malik and Farid's side of the story. The Hakeem was already ill-advised and too far away to adequately explain things to, yet if Ra'id allowed these two men to continue on this journey, they'd sooner or later find some way to get a message to his father.

There seemed only one option—short of death—to cut off their means of communication, at least until *he* wished it otherwise. Still, it would hardly be easy explaining his decision to his father once they were all back in Khaddar. Thankfully, there'd be plenty of time on the journey ahead to figure out *that* particular dilemma.

"Nay, I think not, Malik," he said at last.

The other man frowned in puzzlement. "I don't understand."

"It's simple, really. This time, your interference and subtle threats have exceeded my level of tolerance." Ra'id smiled, though the act went no further than his mouth. "Your service to me is at an end. To my deepest regret, you and Farid won't be accompanying us any farther."

17

Two hours later, amid the farewell threats and strident protests of Malik and Farid, Vartan, riding with Ra'id at the head of the caravan, departed Am Shardi and headed north. The sun soon rose to its zenith but, this day, clouds gathered, mitigating most of the Desert's usually intense heat. A breeze began to blow, cooling things even more.

Vartan chose to see it as yet another propitious sign of things to come. Leaving the two troublesome advisors behind was one as well. They had been left with supplies adequate for over a month, but no horses or water bags. Ra'id planned to send men back to fetch them, but not for a time. A time in which Vartan hoped to solidify his relationship with the young Desert lord and make significant headway in gaining the alliance of the Diya al Din.

As they rode along, a sufficient distance gradually opened between them and the rest of the group until Vartan felt comfortable broaching some difficult topics without danger of being overheard. At long last, he glanced over at Ra'id.

"There's much we need to discuss, m'lord," he said. "And, if you'll accept my suggestion, I propose we strive always to speak plainly and honestly with each other. I'd like respect and trust to be foremost between us."

Ra'id shot him an amused look. "A laudable aspiration to be sure. One, however, not so easily achieved between a Karayan and a Diya al Din."

So, must every step I take toward the fulfillment of Athan's will be so difficult? Vartan wondered, firmly quashing a swell of irritation. "Nay, not easy, but necessary," he finally replied. "If *we* fail at the outset, what more can we expect of our people? And if all of Gadiel doesn't soon join together, there's no hope—"

"I didn't say I wasn't willing," his companion cut in. "I just meant we must *both* be willing to work hard at this and swallow our pride for the sake of Gadiel. That we must always keep Al'Alim and His will before us, or our past history will surely doom us before we ever begin."

Vartan dragged in a deep, steadying breath. "Then I beg pardon for jumping to conclusions. Already, I've made an error in judgment."

"Assuredly, it won't be the last—for either of us." Ra'id chuckled. "All we can do is try."

"Aye." Vartan directed his gaze ahead. "Will you begin by telling me, then, of your father? If I'm to have any hope of convincing him to join with me, I need to know what I'm up against."

The Desert lord's lips curved in a grim smile. "You'll have many obstacles in this quest to unite Gadiel. Winning over my father will be but the first—and perhaps one of the most difficult—of them. You've already discovered one of those difficulties in Farid and Malik. The Hakeem's surrounded by nearly twenty men he calls advisors. To a man, they're all like Farid and Malik—narrow-minded, self-serving hypocrites who desperately seek to maintain the status quo and brook no dissent. Worse even, over time they've managed to gain my father's ear and confidence, to the point he now makes almost no decisions without first calling a council of these men."

"And where do you and this Council find common ground?"

Ra'id gave a harsh laugh. "We don't. Or, leastwise, the Council can and frequently does override anything I put before my father. They don't like or trust me. In retrospect, I was perhaps a bit too forthright in voicing my opinions when I first came of age. In those days I imagined, as Prince Kamal's son and heir, I possessed more influence than I truly had."

"A bitter lesson, I'm sure." Vartan glanced his way. "And how do you deal with this unfortunate situation nowadays?"

"How else?" the younger man muttered. "I play the obedient son, bite my tongue until it bleeds, and bide my time. I also try to build friendships and alliances wherever I can, as discreetly as I can. And, when that's not possible, I try at least to foster respect and hope for the future."

"When one is thwarted, seek another, better way . . ."

"I see you've been studying the sacred books. Perhaps you've another helpful saying for how to deal with a difficult parent?"

"Nothing that comes to mind, save to honor and obey him, and so be pleasing unto Athan."

Ra'id sighed. "I was afraid you'd say that. And it doesn't help your chances with the Hakeem very much, either. He wants the throne of Gadiel, knows he has no chance of it while any Karayan lives, and has commanded any and all Diya al Din who encounter you to see you dead. Already, I go against my father in letting you live." He shrugged. "So much for honoring and obeying."

"If I recall correctly, some of Athan's commands take precedence over others. I think the decree against murder is one of them."

"Aye, it is. That, along with your disturbing propensity toward fulfilling all aspects of the Prophecy, may well be our only hope with my father."

"It's a problem we'll have to face sooner or later," Vartan said, secretly pleased Ra'id had finally claimed some common ownership of the problems. "Or do you plan to take me directly to the Hakeem?"

"I haven't decided. In the meanwhile, my visit to the Abd Al'Bari tribe takes us in the direction of Khaddar. I thought, at least for a time, to continue my initial mission. It'll also be a good testing of what the reaction of my people will be toward you."

Vartan tamped down a swell of unease. Though he knew the key to winning over Prince Kamal was first to win over his people, he hadn't any idea how to accomplish that. *Once again, Eternal One,* he thought, *I must throw myself on Your mercy. Help me. Show me what must be done to fulfill Your will.*

"Any advice in regard to your people will be most appreciated," he then said, looking once more to Ra'id. "Aside from some basic instructions in Desert history and customs, I must admit to woeful ignorance."

"How much are you willing to learn?"

"Any and everything you can teach me. I think I owe you and the Diya al Din that at the very least."

The Desert lord smiled. "It's a start. The original plan for this mission, to gain support from the tribes for an attack against Ladon, was for the purpose of winning back the crown of Gadiel. Incidentally, we also hoped to acquire Astara's potential wealth and lands. Now it seems my people will be called to fight to regain what the Karayans' lost, and then return it to the Karayans."

"It would seem so," Vartan replied carefully, "but I'm not so certain it's a matter this time of Diya al Din versus Karayans, or one or the other versus any of the other peoples of Gadiel. I don't think that's Athan's plan or has ever been, for that matter. What's different, this time, is that we put aside all our personal needs and differences, and join together to follow Athan. It's the only way to defeat Ladon, and his overlord, Phaon."

"Phaon? You mean Aswad, don't you?"

Vartan grinned. "If that's the Desert term for the Evil One, aye. There's more at stake here than land and lives. Ladon wants power and glory. Aswad wants souls."

"A thorny task, that, convincing the Diya al Din—or anyone—that Aswad's intimately involved in Ladon's apparent desire to conquer Gadiel. Most, even a large number of the Faithful, don't believe evil seeks such control, or at least would attempt such an overt approach to enslave them."

"Nay, most don't, but I've seen it firsthand. And the Prophecy has warned of just such a time for centuries now."

"It may take more than your word, and what has happened to you, to convince them."

"I know." Vartan sighed. "All I can do is tell the truth and rely on Athan for the rest."

"Aye. But know that if you fail at this, you now risk more than just your life. You risk mine as well."

A mix of frustration and gratitude filled Vartan. "I'm aware of that, Ra'id. And, though the realization—and responsibility—weighs heavily on me, I can only follow where Athan leads. I can't promise success, or even a long life. The choice is yours whether you wish to join me. Yours alone."

"And *I* made my choice the moment I accepted that you were blessed and guided by Al'Alim, my friend. As long as you don't stray from the Faith, as long as you never fail to heed Al'Alim's call, I'm with you. With you, even to the giving of my life."

"Your eyes are like the deepest, richest pazot jewel. Your lips are as red and ripe as the sweetest poma fruit. And your skin . . . the softest, smoothest silk is a rough tur hide in comparison!"

A rough tur hide? Sharifah arched a slender brow at the young man kneeling before her, gazing up in ardent adoration. Well, she supposed he *was*, at the very least sincere, if extremely inexperienced in the art of courtship.

Still, of the three sons of Hammad Abd Al 'Bari, warlord of the tribe Abd Al'Bari, young Tahir was by far the most palatable of them all. But *only* palatable, and in no way a serious bond mate contender by *any* stretch of the imagination. When she chose a mate, she wanted a man, not a boy.

She glanced around at the hundreds of sun-bleached white tents emblazoned with the tribal symbol of a full moon crowned by a single star. They had been here over a week now, after a two-day journey from Am Shardi. Seven days spent in tedious and interminably slow negotiations with Hammad.

True to the Diya al Din's ingrained self-serving instincts, the Abd Al' Bari leader had bargained for every advantage he could get his grasping, greedy hands on. Convincing him to commit his warriors to a war against Ladon still remained a sticking point. In the past day or so, however, Ra'id was finally making progress.

There was at least one thing, though, for which to be grateful. Hammad had readily acknowledged Vartan and his Prophecy-fulfilling story. The tale was sure to spread to other tribes, even before they finally made their way to them. And that, if nothing else, would ease Vartan's acceptance among the Diya al Din.

"M'lady?"

Tahir's plaintive voice pierced the distraction of Sharifah's thoughts. She wrenched her attention back to him. He still knelt before her, now clasping her hand.

"Aye?" As best she could, she smiled and tried to gentle her voice.

"Will you accept my offer then? I haven't as much wealth as my two older brothers, but I could still pay the Hakeem a handsome bride price. Of my own, I've over a hundred tur, twenty-five ashtaraks, and nearly thirty-eight horses, once my five mares foal. And I'd give it all if only you would be mine."

"A handsome bride price indeed." Sharifah indicated he should stand. "And you are most charming, Tahir. But we've still eight more tribes to visit, and I'm commanded by my father to consider no offers until I've heard them all." She gave his hand a tender squeeze before releasing it. "You understand my situation, don't you?"

"Just say I have a chance, m'lady," he cried, his dark, long-lashed eyes blazing with an impassioned intensity. "It is all I need to hear to give me hope, to comfort me in my dreams!"

Sharifah supposed he had as much a chance as any of them, which, in the end, was probably no chance at all. Still, she couldn't find it in her to dash his dreams. Better that time do that instead.

"Aye, you have a chance, Tahir. You seem a good, kind man."

He sank back to his knees and, taking her hand, began to cover it with kisses. "Ah, thank you, m'lady. Thank you!"

As soon as she could extract her kiss-covered hand and make a courteous exit, Sharifah hurried away. The only consolation was that, with Tahir's proposal, she had finished entertaining offers from all of Hammad's sons. Her personal duties to her father in this mission were now complete, in regard to the Abd Al'Bari tribe at any rate. Now she could devote herself to being an extra pair of eyes and ears for Ra'id.

As she walked through the encampment, she passed her brother, Vartan, and Hammad ensconced beneath a large, red-and-white-striped awning outside Hammad's tent. Hammad's wife and daughters were just finishing serving the men salma and dainties. Sharifah's glance snagged on the girl offering Vartan a plate of cakes. The young woman was eyeing the big Astarian with unmitigated admiration. Vartan, for his part, appeared not to notice as he very politely took two of the little sweet cakes.

In the past week, Sharifah had begun to observe things about him she had never seen when he had been at Am Shardi. Perhaps his blindness had muted all the aspects she now saw. Perhaps his blindness had prevented her from considering him as a whole man. Or perhaps she had thought him before to be a common man, and now she knew him to be of the highest royalty.

Now, Vartan Karayan was worthy of her in breeding. With each passing day, he increasingly appealed to Sharifah as a man worthy to be her bond mate, lover, and father of her children. She didn't know how she had missed noting his piercingly intense, sea blue eyes. And, though beards weren't uncommon among Desert men, she found Vartan equally as handsome with one as she imagined he would be without it. He was undoubtedly well made, with broad shoulders, a height and breadth that equaled her brother's, and strong, long-fingered hands. She especially liked strong, long-fingered hands.

A union between them would be a wise political move as well. It could only help to heal the age-old divisions and strengthen the budding alliance. Vartan was a shrewd, intelligent man. A man born and bred to rule. It wouldn't be hard to convince him of the significant advantages to be had in life bonding with her.

There seemed only one real obstacle to winning the heart and hand of the most desirable man she had ever known. Danae. Sharifah knew Danae loved Vartan.

If it had been almost any other woman, Sharifah wouldn't have given her rival's feelings in the matter a moment's thought. But she liked Danae, respected her for her courage and loyalty to Vartan. She didn't want to hurt her.

The truth was, though, that Danae couldn't ever marry Vartan. He must wed a woman who would bring political and material advantage to him if he ever hoped to unite Gadiel and drive Ladon and his forces from the land. And Danae wasn't of royal, or even noble, blood. She had finally admitted to Sharifah that her father was a general in the Hylean army, but he had come up through the ranks and so was but a soldier. Danae would bring nothing of tangible value to a union with Vartan.

Sooner or later, Danae would have to face that. Sharifah was actually doing her a favor. The longer Danae went on dreaming hopeless dreams, the harder it would be for her. And it wasn't as if Vartan loved Danae in return. His affection for her was quite evident, but Sharifah had carefully watched their interactions of late. At least on Vartan's part, all she saw was a restrained fondness. He held back for a reason. And likely that reason was because all he truly felt for Danae was gratitude and a brotherly affection. Sharifah dearly hoped so.

Aye, in the end, she thought, Danae had no real claims on him. Vartan was free for the taking, and Sharifah wanted him. Wanted him more and more with each passing day.

Late that afternoon, Danae caught Vartan just as he was leaving Hammad's tent. Running up, she took his arm.

The slight smile he seemed to wear constantly of late immediately broadened into a grin. "And what might I do for you, sweet lady?"

"Only walk with me for a while," Danae answered, that familiar sense of complete content filling her once again. "We've seen so little of each other this past week and spent even less of it together. I confess I'm actually beginning to miss you."

"Are you now?" He glanced down at her as they began to stroll along. "Well, no more than I miss you. But if it isn't hours spent with Ra'id and Hammad, hammering out all of Hammad's interminable requests, then it's more hours plotting and planning with Ra'id. And then—"

"And then there is Sharifah."

"Aye." Vartan chuckled. "Then there's Sharifah. I can't believe how much she enjoys playing Crucible. Hardly a day goes by when she doesn't challenge me to yet another game. And she's quite good, too. If I beat her half the time, I feel I'm doing exceedingly well."

Danae bit her tongue rather than offer her personal opinion of why Ra'id's sister seemed to be spending more and more time with Vartan of late. It certainly wasn't because she loved the strategy game of dice and bicolored marble blocks. But anything Danae might say to shed light on Sharifah's real motives would only come across as unkind, if not jealous and spiteful. So she withheld comment. Better that her growing, but secret, conflict remain just that.

"Sharifah has a quick and agile mind," Danae chose to say instead. "And I'm happy you've finally become friends."

"Ah, my sweet little Danae." Vartan laughed as they moved past the myriad tents, out toward the edge of the high plateau overlooking one of the few rivers transecting the Haroun. "You're always the first to find the good in any situation. I don't know how I would've survived those desperate days without you."

"But you didn't need to survive without me then, and you don't need to now." She gazed up at him. "I'll never leave you. Never, until you have no further need of me."

"And when will that day ever come, sweet lady?" he asked, drawing to a halt only a few feet from the edge of the cliff. "Though we've only been friends a mere three years, in many ways, after all we've been through together, it seems like a lifetime."

Though his kindness and affection for her were evident, the only word Danae heard was "friends." Was that all, after all this time, he really felt for her? Or was he, in his own gentle way, trying to tell her that whatever she had once imagined was growing between them when he was blind must now change? That his destiny now called him to a path that could never, ever, permit him to be more than just her friend?

Well, what did you expect? Danae angrily asked herself. *What did you* think *would happen, allowing yourself to fall in love with a man so far above you? Vartan has always treated you honorably, and never promised you anything more than his friendship. It's why, in the end, though he admitted to a physical attraction, he never permitted it to go past that. He knows you better than you know yourself!*

"Athan willing, we'll never have to face that dilemma," Danae forced herself to reply. As she spoke, the sun began to sink on the western horizon, disappearing far out in the Desert. Rich hues of crimson, rose, bronze and copper spilled across the sands, drenching them in riotous color. And, as the sky inexorably edged toward shades of indigo twilight, the heavenly backdrop provided an even sharper contrast for the breathtaking sunset display.

In the long moments they stood there, watching in silent, awestruck admiration, Danae was finally able to clamp down on her bittersweet emotions, stuffing them deep into the recesses of her heart. It was enough she was with Vartan, that she was of service to him, she reminded herself over and over. Time and again he had nearly died and been taken from her. It made each and every moment a precious gift. A precious gift from Athan.

No one could—or should—hope for anything more.

Two days later, they left the Abd Al'Bari and again headed northeast, their destination yet another Desert tribe. The time Vartan didn't spend engrossed in conversation with Ra'id was monopolized by Sharifah, who seemed to possess an uncanny sense of just when to make her move. More and more, Danae felt pushed to the side, on the periphery of everything Vartan did.

Not that she lacked for company. At every opportunity, Ra'id tried to fill in the gaping hole left by Vartan's absence. As she came to know him better, Danae found she liked him very much. Still, her heart was already taken. It just seemed Vartan had no time, or interest, in her anymore.

She tried to attribute it to his increasing preoccupation with attempting to win over the Diya al Din to his cause. Tales, some fact, some likely rumor, filtered in to them wherever they went. Tales of the horrible devastation Ladon's army had wrought along Vardenis's entire coastline. Rumors he'd soon begin a march through the Valans toward the Desert. Even if but half the stories were true, Danae knew Vartan had a very short time to accomplish a massive amount of work.

It was part of the reason she resented Sharifah's selfish abuse of what little free time Vartan had. He needed to rest; he needed time to think and pray and continue to study Athan's holy words, not squander irretrievable moments entertaining Sharifah. Yet he was too kind to turn her away. Too kind and also too politically astute. It wasn't the time or place to risk antagonizing Sharifah and, through her, possibly Ra'id as well.

Danae, however, leastwise when it came to Vartan and his welfare, wasn't feeling particularly kind at all. And, about two weeks after they left Am Shardi, the fragile thread that held together her fraying patience with Ra'id's sister finally broke. Entering Sharifah's tent, she found a servant finishing the last touches to Sharifah's stunning, ebony mane of hair.

"Just weave in those crimson and green ribbons, will you, Jamilla?" she was saying. "They'll be perfect with my *sholi* and"—her expressionless gaze caught Danae's—"I want to look *especially* pretty for tonight's feast."

Hands clenched at her sides, Danae walked over and sat across from Sharifah, biding her time until Jamilla completed braiding the ribbons into her mistress's hair and departed. When they were alone at last, Danae inhaled a calming breath and began.

"I have a favor to ask of you."

"Indeed?" Sharifah didn't lift her gaze from the tray of small, exquisitely shaped perfume bottles she was searching through. "And what would that favor be?"

"Give Vartan some breathing room. All this negotiating is wearing him down. He needs time alone, time for himself. Yet whenever he is finally finished with his work with Ra'id, you immediately rush to his side, cling to him like . . . like some water sucker, and don't let him go until late each night."

"*Some water sucker?*" Ever so slowly, the other woman glanced up at her. "And has Vartan asked you to speak to me about this?"

Danae swallowed hard. "Nay. You know he wouldn't. He's too much a gentleman ever to do that."

"Or instead, perhaps he truly enjoys my company and finds it well worth the sacrifice of a bit of his sleep or time alone?" Her gaze hardened until her eyes were glittering shards of ice. "Perhaps that's really what is upsetting you. That Vartan has come to find me attractive, even desirable."

It was as if Sharifah had looked deep into her heart and seen the fear and pain dwelling there. Pride, though, wouldn't permit Danae to admit it.

"Vartan's free to find whomever he wishes attractive. All I'm asking is that you spare a little consideration for him. Is that too much to ask?"

She knew her voice had taken on an edge. Sharifah knew it as well, for she arched a slender brow. Then she smiled, a sad, knowing little smile.

"He's not for you, Danae," she said softly. "I know you love him, but there's no hope he'll ever take you to wife. If all goes as Athan wills, someday Vartan may well be King of Gadiel. He'll need a bond mate with the breeding and position not only to help him achieve that goal, but also to reign as his queen. I possess all the necessary attributes. You, unfortunately, do not."

Tears filled Danae's eyes. "You can't know that. With Athan, all things are possible."

"Aye, but there are reasons—good, strong reasons—for traditions. For royal blood to mix with other royal blood. And the people need, nay, *cherish* their traditions." Sharifah paused, eyeing her closely. "You say I'm selfish in dominating his time. Well, I say *you're* selfish in your unrealistic clinging to him, refusing to let him go, even though in your heart of hearts you know it's best. Best for him."

She reached over and took Danae's hand. "Let him go, my friend. If you truly love him, let him go."

Caught up in a smothering maelstrom of emotion, it was all Danae could do to breathe, much less deliver any sort of coherent response. *Let Vartan go?* How was that possible? Let him go so Sharifah could have him? But he was hers, had always been hers, at least in her mind ever since she had met him! It was impossible. *Impossible!*

Unsteadily, she pushed to her feet to stand there, towering over the other woman. "You've always been very clever, Sharifah. And now, you seek to turn my words, my love for Vartan, against me. But it won't work, I tell you. Vartan loves me, not you!"

"Does he?" Her perfectly formed, ruby red lips curved in a pitying smile. "Then prove it. Go, ask him. Ask him, if you dare."

18

Several times that day, Danae almost mustered the courage to go to Vartan and confront him about Sharifah. But then fear would overwhelm her. Fear that he'd finally reiterate, albeit in his usual kind, gentle way, that they could only be friends.

Caution would soon follow fear, warning her that perhaps the ever cunning Sharifah was trying to manipulate her to press the issue prematurely. Perhaps it was too soon to force Vartan to make any kind of commitment to anyone. With a horrendous war looming and a monumental task to gather an army and forge alliances still before him, thoughts of marriage were surely the farthest thing from his mind. Whether Sharifah wished it so or not, Vartan wasn't a man to be pushed into anything.

Still, Sharifah's words, accusing her of selfishly clinging to Vartan even when she knew it wasn't in his best interests, had found their mark. Always before, Danae had only wished to help Vartan in whatever way he desired. Her own needs had been secondary. Once, she had also been content to love, with no thought of anything in return. But now . . . now something had changed.

Perhaps it was simply that when Vartan had been blind, Danae had imagined no one else wanted him. Sharifah, she thought bitterly, certainly hadn't. Perhaps, when it had been essentially just the two of them, Danae had imagined they had all the time in the world, and it was just them *in* that world.

Whatever the reason, their world had spun once more on its axis, and everything had changed. If there were still a place in Vartan's life for her, she must rediscover it and claim it. But not on Sharifah's terms. On her own.

The decision comforted Danae, and she was able to go about her daily routine, a routine that now left her lonely and vaguely dissatisfied. If the truth be told, she served no real purpose in the camp and felt increasingly isolated. True, she helped with the cooking and cleaning of the dishware, shook out the myriad number of rugs that carpeted the floors of most tents, and washed and mended clothes. And there was always that laborious trek to the well three times a day to draw fresh water.

But the companionship was limited. Vartan and Ra'id were too busy. She didn't want to add to Vartan's concerns, especially with peevish complaints.

There was no one else to talk to, though. She had now all but alienated herself from Sharifah. And though the other Desert wives and daughters were kind, Danae really had nothing in common with them. Increasingly, she found she spent her free time alone, staring out into the Desert or studying the *Covenant of Athan* and praying.

The feast began at sunset that day. Vartan insisted she sit beside him, which pleased Danae to no end, especially when Ra'id took the spot on Vartan's other side, affording Sharifah no opportunity to flirt with Vartan, as was her usual wont these days. The minor victory didn't last long, however. Danae had barely played two songs for the gathering on her lyra, when a sandstorm blew in and all were forced to take to their tents.

"Come. Come," Abdul, the Ben Aban leader, cried, motioning for Ra'id, Vartan, Sharifah, and Danae to enter his tent. "It's of no import, the storm. We'll just continue the feast inside."

As Abdul's servants scurried about, bringing in the food and laying it out on several low, brass tables set before a line of twelve cushions, the chieftain took the middlemost seat. Ra'id joined him on the right, Vartan on the left. Danae wasted no time once again claiming the spot on Vartan's right. Scowling, Sharifah, who had been momentarily waylaid by Abdul's wife, was forced, once again, to sit beside her brother. The rest of the cushions were then taken by Abdul's wife and six daughters.

Gazing at the line of dark-eyed, giggling girls, Danae supposed that, this time at least, Sharifah was relieved not to have had to deal with amorous suitors. Likely to Abdul's sorrow, he could only seem to produce daughters. They were all very lovely, though, and as the meal recommenced, each one in turn entertained them with a dance or two.

In the flickering lamplight Danae soon began to relax and enjoy herself. A ferocious storm howled outside, but they were sheltered and sustained by a rich stew thick with succulent chunks of mouflon, onions, and other root vegetables dressed with a savory gravy. A variety of tur and ashtarak cheeses, fresh-baked flatbread, a garlic-herbed, boiled grain, and cups of hot, spiced salma were also temptingly offered. It certainly helped that Vartan sat beside her, brushing her arm or leg at times as he reached past her for some delicacy on one of the tables. She loved being near him, soaking up the pleasure of his presence.

"You look quite pleased with yourself this eve," he said, glancing her way before dipping a piece of flatbread into his bowl of stew, then lifting the now gravy-soaked chunk to his mouth. A dab of gravy lingered on his lips, and he licked it off and grinned.

"It's an excellent meal," Danae replied, swallowing down the sudden yearning she felt, watching him. "And it's almost better eating inside than out. More private, more intimate."

"Especially with that sandstorm whipping about outside." He glanced around. "I'm always amazed how snug the Desert tents are, even with such fierce winds. Hardly any sand blows in."

"The Diya al Din know the Desert, and have mastered it as much as any man can."

Vartan finished his stew and, as a servant passed by with an empty tray, placed his bowl on it. Immediately another servant followed, offering scented, damp towels. He took one, and wiping his hands, laid the towel on the next tray. Danae did the same.

Yet another of Abdul's daughters began to sway to the hypnotic beat of the music provided by the servants, off in one corner of the tent, who played a pair of tur-skin drums and an *intizara*, a set of long, narrow, double pipes lashed together with strips of hide. Sweets were served next. Besides the usual small iced cakes, there were sugared rafa nuts, rich, chewy, kelavi-sweetened chunks of candy, and little rafa nut–filled pies. Though Danae was already quite full, Desert hospitality demanded she at least make some attempt at sampling a few of the treats. She took a piece of candy and several sugared rafa nuts.

Eventually, all of Abdul's daughters had danced for them. Pleasantly surfeit, Danae began to feel drowsy. She leaned over, resting her head against Vartan's arm.

He glanced down at her and smiled. "Will it be necessary to carry you back to Sharifah's tent tonight, then?"

Danae looked up at him. "That sounds most pleasant. If this storm continues, though I'm certain I can walk under my own power, I might just accept your escort."

With a sound akin to an indignant snort, Sharifah climbed to her feet. "Perhaps *I* can wake Danae up." She shot the two musicians a quelling glance, and they immediately stopped playing. "Do you know the *Abra?*"

When the musicians nodded, she turned back to Abdul and the rest of the party. "Since your daughters have so graciously entertained us while we ate, with your permission, I'd now like to entertain them while they eat."

The warlord's head bobbed an eager consent. "We'd be honored, m'lady."

With that, Sharifah kicked off her soft, leather shoes and motioned for the music to begin. The drummer began a slow, rhythmic beat. A few measures later, the piper joined, adding a bright, lively melody with haunting overtones.

Sharifah smiled, shot Danae a pointed looked, then commenced to move to the music. Her lithe, curvaceous form was well suited to the dance, from the sway of her supple hips to the graceful, floating motions of her arms. It quickly became evident she was an accomplished dancer—and knew it. It also, just as quickly, became evident whom she was really dancing for.

Watching her, Danae could feel the tension begin to knot her shoulders. Her hands clenched into fists; her nails scored the flesh of her palms. And still the anger, the jealousy, grew as Sharifah sent Vartan coquettish smiles and sweeping, long-lashed gazes.

Vartan, for his part, appeared to watch her with avid admiration. He returned her frequent smiles with smiles of his own.

It soon became apparent that Danae wasn't the only one observing the unspoken communication between Sharifah and Vartan. A surreptitious look at Ra'id revealed the slight frown beginning to furrow his forehead.

But Sharifah was either so engrossed in Vartan that she didn't notice, or she didn't care. She neither ceased her pretty little dance or the disproportionate amount of time she spent swaying and dipping before him. At long last, though, the song ended. Disappointment gleamed in Sharifah's eyes and she hesitated, almost as if contemplating calling for another song. Then her brother began to clap, signaling an end to her dance.

The others joined in, Vartan a bit too enthusiastically to Danae's way of thinking. With a toss of her hair Sharifah flounced over to take a seat next to Vartan, after wedging her way between him and her brother.

"That was quite lovely," he told her, moving a bit closer to Danae to make room for Sharifah. "You've a real gift, you know."

"I was inspired by your most kind attentiveness," Sharifah said, taking his hand and giving it a quick squeeze before releasing it. "If you desire, perhaps later I'll dance for you again."

Danae didn't hear what Vartan said to her after he chuckled. She turned away, disgusted and hurt. Outside, the winds had finally died, and only occasional gusts shook the tent now. Perhaps it was time for her to leave. At the very least, she didn't think she could bear another one of Sharifah's blatant, flirtatious displays. As difficult as it was to admit, Danae didn't know how she'd react, and that disturbed her. Disturbed her greatly.

"The day has been a long one, and I didn't sleep well last night," she said, looking past Vartan to Abdul, their host. "If you'll please excuse me, I'd like to retire for the night."

The warlord's expression fell. "Your lovely presence will be sorely missed, lady. I was hoping that you, too, might honor us with a dance."

She smiled and shook her head. "I don't know how to dance, m'lord. My gifts lie in other directions."

"Aye, your gift of the lyra and your lovely voice," he said. "Perhaps you'll grace us with those particular gifts again some other night?"

"Perhaps." She rose. Vartan grabbed her hand.

"Aye?" Danae realized she was almost as angry at him as she was at Sharifah.

"Sleep well, sweet lady." Vartan gave her hand a gentle squeeze.

Before he could see the tears in her eyes, Danae pulled her hand free and turned away. Her head lowered, she stalked from the tent.

Not until she was out into the cool night air did she realize how stifling the inside of the tent had become. But then, perhaps it was just her. Anger—and even hatred—could warm more than just the emotions. And she was very angry, more angry than she had ever been in her life.

She didn't dare return to Sharifah's tent just now. If, for some reason, Sharifah returned before her fury subsided, Danae feared she might try to tear out the other woman's throat. Shame flooded her at the admission but, at this particular moment, it was truth and she must face it.

Tears filled her eyes and coursed down her cheeks. Fiercely, Danae blinked them back and staggered, half-blinded, out past the tents finally to halt beside the twisted form of an ancient thorn tree. Through the wind-torn rents in the clouds, fleeting streaks of moonlight touched the land.

As she struggled with her newly discovered, savage emotions, her weeping became gut-wracking sobs. She *hated* Sharifah. She wished her dead, rather than ever allow her to have Vartan. And that frightened Danae. She had never felt that way about anyone before.

Then out of the darkness, a hand settled on her shoulder. *Vartan!* Danae thought, a sweet, ardent joy flooding her. She whirled around.

His dark eyes burning with compassion, Ra'id stood there instead. Danae choked back a bitter cry and an even more bitter swell of disappointment. Not only was Vartan oblivious to her pain, but he was likely still back in Abdul's tent enjoying Sharifah's fawning company. Only Ra'id seemed to care.

He stepped close and tenderly wiped the tears from her cheeks. "Is it Sharifah, then?" he asked. "Sharifah and the disgraceful way she threw herself at Vartan this eve?"

For an instant, Danae considered denying the truth. Dragging Ra'id into the middle of this miserable situation wouldn't change anything. It would just make matters worse. But then, as the consideration of losing Vartan filled her, she suddenly didn't care.

"A-aye," she whispered. "Sharifah means to have Vartan as husband. She admitted it to me this very day."

"By the Blessed Waters!" He pulled her into his embrace. "I'm so sorry, Rasha. If Sharifah wasn't so desperate to find a bond mate, I know she'd never have hurt you like this. Indeed, I've never seen her pursue a man in such a manner. Never!"

"It's because she thinks he's p-perfect for her," Danae said, seeking out the comforting haven of his big, strong body. Over the past few weeks, she had come to see him as a friend, and she cherished his kindness now. "And he is, Ra'id. That's what hurts the most. That Vartan is as perfect for Sharifah as she is for him."

"And you aren't?" He chuckled softly. "If you truly think that, you're wrong, you know. Any man would be proud to take you to wife. Proud, and thankful."

She looked up at him then. "Any man but the likes of you and Vartan, you mean. I'm no asset whatsoever to men such as you, and well you know it."

A reluctant acknowledgment flashed in his eyes, before he averted his gaze. "If a man loved you," he said hoarsely, "he'd find a way. Even *I* would, Rasha, if only you loved me."

Ra'id turned back to her then, and the look smoldering in his eyes told Danae everything. Tenderness filled her and she reached up to cradle his cheek in her hand. "Oh, Ra'id. Ra'id . . ."

Then, because she wanted, for just one moment, to feel cherished, to feel desired, Danae leaned up on tiptoe and kissed him. With a low groan, Ra'id clasped the back of her head in his big hand and returned her kiss. His, however, wasn't shy and grateful. His was hungry and commanding.

He pulled her close, pressing his hard form against hers. His mouth slanted over hers, searing Danae with a fire that caught her by surprise and totally unprepared. Her hands caught in the fabric of his *thobe*, clenched it tightly. A maelstrom of confused, irrational emotions engulfed her. For an instant, Danae didn't know whether to push away or pull him close.

Then sanity returned. As much as she hungered for a man's arms around her and his lips on hers, it wasn't Ra'id she wanted. It was Vartan.

"R-Ra'id." She wrenched her mouth from his and, with all her might, shoved back. "Please. Stop."

He stared down at her in bewilderment but didn't release her. "What's wrong? Was I too rough? Did I hurt you?"

"Nay." Danae shook her head and forced a wan little smile. "It wasn't that. I just . . . I just realized this couldn't go on.

291

I wasn't thinking clearly, didn't know what I wanted. That's all."

"Well," he growled, releasing her at last, "you certainly seemed to know what you wanted a few seconds ago. And I'd say you wanted me."

Her cheeks warmed. "I wanted comfort. I won't deny that. I wanted to feel desired, to feel like a woman, if even for just a brief moment. And you've always made me feel that way, Ra'id. But . . . but it's not right. I was wrong and stupid and selfish to let you think—"

"Let me think you preferred me over Vartan?" Ra'id gave a low, harsh laugh. "I would've been sadly mistaken then, wouldn't I? No one will *ever* compare to Vartan, will they?"

Dismay filled her. "Nay, Ra'id." She reached out to him, and he immediately took a step back. "It isn't like that," she said, once again on the verge of tears. "It's just . . ."

She sighed. "I'm so upset and confused right now . . ."

This isn't helping! Danae thought. "I'm sorry. It was wrong of me to kiss you, to try to use you to comfort myself. Please forgive me. Please, Ra'id."

He eyed her for a long moment, then expelled a weary breath. "Perhaps it's as much my fault as yours. Perhaps I hoped you'd do exactly what you did." He smiled and shook his head. "Perhaps both of us weren't thinking any too clearly."

Danae smiled in relief. "I don't deserve a friend like you."

"You have one nonetheless." He offered her his hand. "Now, come back to the camp. It isn't safe on the Desert at night."

Sometimes, it isn't safe anywhere, Danae realized, taking his hand. *Especially when one lets one's heart rule one's head. When one allows the love of a man to become more important than the love of Athan and His commands.*

And that revelation, this night, was the most disturbing one of all.

The next morning, Ra'id's mood was no better than it had been the night before. He soon sought out his sister.

"Come away with me," he said, after finding her helping Abdul's wife with her weaving. "We need to talk."

Sharifah glanced up and arched a slender brow. "Indeed? And what might that talk be about, Brother?"

"Something best shared in private, that's what." He met her inquiring gaze with a stern one of his own. "Now, if you please."

Amusement lifting the corners of her mouth, Sharifah excused herself and joined him. They walked for a time until they were well clear of any curious enough to attempt to eavesdrop. That took them until they reached the old thorn tree.

Ra'id wasted no time. "Exactly what did you think to accomplish last night in your flagrant dance for Vartan?"

Sharifah's eyes widened in incredulity. "My dance was for the entertainment of all. And it was quite demure, as dances go. You offend me by saying otherwise."

He could feel his patience begin to shred. "Sister, I know you too well. Don't play that little game with me. You've settled on Vartan for your bond mate, haven't you?"

She pretended to find sudden interest in some nonexistent smudge on the sleeve of her *sholi*. "And if I have, what of it? He's worthy. Indeed, far more worthy than most of the men I've seen so far."

"Aye, he is, but that's not the issue here. Danae loves him. And who's to say he doesn't love her in return?"

"Do you think if I were convinced Vartan loved Danae, I'd be doing this?" Sharifah laughed. "I don't fancy making a fool of myself, you know. But I've seen nothing from him but a kindly affection for her. I think he realizes, as do the both of

293

us, that Danae's not a worthy mate for him. Even you have finally accepted that for yourself and have ceased your lusty looks and comments around her."

"Sometimes those in love see what they want to see, Sister. Have a care here."

"But he's perfect for me!" Excitement sparkling in her eyes, Sharifah grasped Ra'id's arm. "And think how this would help Vartan's chances, once he meets Father. Prophecy or no, Father will be difficult enough to convince of Vartan's usefulness. But if he also sees the potential of a political, as well as a life bond, between the Abd Al'Alim and the Karayans . . . well, you know as surely as I how Father's mind works. Also how the Council's mind works. In the end, it might be the only thing that'll save Vartan."

Her argument had merit. Ra'id couldn't fault his sister on that. If only Danae's heart wasn't involved . . .

"Tread lightly, Sharifah," he said at last. "And don't rely solely on your dazzling beauty. Though it's enough to win over most men, Vartan's not most men. Honesty, loyalty, and intelligence will win the day with him. Not that," he added with a grin, "he's totally immune to a beautiful woman. But you and Danae are so very different."

"He doesn't love Danae, I tell you! A woman can sense such things."

Ra'id shrugged. "Perhaps. But I also know Vartan keeps many things to himself. He's a clever man. And he may well not be ready to take *any* woman to wife just now."

"Oh, but he will be ready soon enough, Brother. Just wait and see."

"Well, you won't be able to ply your wiles much longer. Abdul is taking us to meet with his cousin on the morrow." He grinned. "Something about how his influence will ease our way."

Sharifah frowned. "How long do you plan to be gone?"

"A week, I think. Vartan and I are becoming quite good at pleading our cause. And hopefully, with Abdul along, that'll speed things up, too." Ra'id paused and cocked his head. "Of course, I hear Lufti Ben Umar has two sons of marriageable age. In all fairness, perhaps you *should* come along to assess their potential? As you have all the others so far, I mean."

"I've already made up my mind, Brother. Still . . ." A thoughtful expression gleamed in her eyes. "Aye, that's an excellent idea. Convince Danae to stay behind, and then I'll have Vartan all to myself. And if I can stir a bit of jealousy in him by flirting with Lufti's two sons, more the better."

She leaned over and gave him a quick peck on the cheek. "Thank you so much, Ra'id. I don't know what I'd do without you!"

❧

Watching them ride out the next morning, it was all Danae could do to stand there and wave, a taut smile plastered to her face. Countless times, she almost gave in to the urge to run after them, grab Vartan's leg, and beg him to take her with him. But she didn't. It was but the first, after all, of the severing of the ties that bound them. Ties she, even then, was breaking one by one.

Her heart aching, she stood there at the edge of camp, watching until they disappeared from view. Then she turned and headed back to the tent. There was much to do to prepare for the long journey back across the Haroun to the mountains.

She had already found one of Abdul's tribesmen who'd guide her. Halim, the drummer at Abdul's feast, had taken an instant liking to her lyra. Well aware it was a costly instrument, he had readily agreed to take it in payment for leading her to the mountains. From there, however, Halim informed her, she was on her own.

It was a foolhardy plan, fraught with countless dangers. But Danae didn't care. Athan would lead her. He had always done so before, and He would do so now. It was evident her time with Vartan was at an end. Vartan no longer needed her. He now had Sharifah and Ra'id, and a bright future ahead of him. It was time to let him go, or forfeit her very soul.

From the events of the past several days, it had become increasingly evident she had allowed Vartan gradually to gain precedence over Athan in her heart. She had permitted anger, jealousy, and even hatred to take hold. And, as hard as it was to admit, it was neither Vartan's nor Sharifah's fault. It was hers. Hers alone.

Things would be better for all if she left. Vartan could choose Sharifah or any other woman he desired, and she'd not be around to see it. She'd not be around to watch her heart shrivel and die, destroyed from the inside out.

"Tell me if I'm wrong to do this," she prayed softly as she walked back to camp. "If not, I'm leaving, Eternal One. Guide me, if You will, to where You next wish me to be. And, most of all, help me find the strength to go on without Vartan."

19

A week later, they were but two miles from Abdul's camp and nearly at the end of their return journey, when the messenger reached them. After only a brusquely formal bow, the man presented Ra'id with the missive from his father. Protocol required the immediate opening and reading of any communication from the Hakeem, and Ra'id did so.

"What is it, Brother?" Sharifah asked, noting his sudden scowl.

"Nothing that I didn't expect," he said, glancing from Sharifah to Vartan. "Apparently Malik and Farid found some way to contact my father. He commands us to ride for Khaddar posthaste."

"It's for the best," Vartan replied. "Time grows short. We need to call up the Desert tribes and begin forming them into a cohesive army. And we can't do that without the Hakeem's leave."

Ra'id nodded. "Best, then, that we get back to camp. Considering the time of the day, the soonest we can depart for Khaddar will be the morrow."

As one the party set out and, a half hour later, entered the Ben Aban camp. Servants ran out to take their horses. Others

297

rushed over to offer cooling drinks. As Vartan gulped down the contents of his cup, his gaze scanned the encampment.

"Strange," he muttered, finally handing his empty cup to one of the servants, "that Danae hasn't come to greet us."

"Perhaps she's resting in my tent. I'll go and fetch her," Sharifah said, tamping down an unpleasant sense of foreboding. Danae's absence was indeed most strange. Any other time, she would've been the first one to greet them.

Vartan shot her a look of gratitude. "Would you? I confess I'll not breathe easier until I see her sweet, smiling face."

Clamping down on a surge of frustration, Sharifah headed for her tent. Vartan didn't have to act so worried, she thought. It wasn't as if Danae could come to any harm among these people. And it wasn't as if they had been gone that long, either. If she didn't know better, she'd almost imagine he was besotted, pining after his beloved.

By the time she reached her tent and stepped inside, her temper was already on the rise. When she found no sign of Danae, it exploded.

"Where's that confounded Astarian woman?" she all but hissed at the first servant unfortunate enough to happen by. "I have better things to do than waste my time ferreting out her latest hiding place!"

"B-but m'lady," little Nawar stammered, shrinking back from her mistress's fury, "hasn't anyone yet told you? She's gone. She left with Halim, the drummer, just two days after you and the others departed."

"She left? To where? And why?"

Even as she voiced the questions, an inkling of Danae's reasons crept into the back of Sharifah's mind. With it came a feeling of nausea. Ra'id would blame her, and Vartan . . . Vartan might never forgive her. Ah, curse Danae! She wasn't supposed to run off. She was just supposed to relinquish any claim she might've had on Vartan's heart. Just honorably step aside, not play such an underhanded, conniving trick.

"I don't know much, save what Halim's wife told me," the serving girl replied. "Danae didn't leave any note or message. She just agreed to give Halim her lyra if he took her back to the mountains. That's as far as he said he'd go, and she finally agreed to it."

Danae would only have an escort to the mountains and no farther? Sharifah's heart sank. Both Ra'id and Vartan would be livid. There was nothing to be done for it, though, but tell them the truth.

"My thanks," she said, then turned and strode from the tent.

Two irritated, anxious men awaited her.

"Where is she?" her brother was first to demand.

Vartan just watched her.

Sharifah swallowed hard. *Al'Alim help me.* "Apparently Danae has taken it into her head to run off. She hired Halim to guide her as far as the Valans. After that, who knows where she's headed? I'm told she didn't leave a message for anyone."

"Danae hadn't any money to pay Halim," Vartan said softly.

"She offered him her lyra."

The blood drained from his face. "Why?" he whispered. "Why would she do this? We were so close, and I hoped . . ." He closed his eyes and inhaled deeply, then opened them, his expression now shuttered and unreadable.

"It doesn't matter why she left," he said. "I'm going after her."

Sharifah grabbed his arm. "Vartan, that's impossible. She left five days ago. It'll take you nearly that long to reach the

299

Valans. By then, Danae will be another five days' journey into those mountains. You'll never catch up with her."

"It doesn't matter." His jaw tightened with grim resolve. "I've a pretty good idea where she's headed. And if something happens to her along the way, she'll need me."

"And what of my father's summons?" Ra'id chose that moment to interject. "Have you forgotten he demands our immediate return? Have you forgotten what's at stake here?"

His anger finally breaking the bounds of his control, Vartan wheeled around. "Nay, I haven't forgotten any of that. But you seem to have forgotten your affection for Danae. She's in grave danger out there, and well you know it. But then, abject obedience to your father matters more than anything else to you, doesn't it? Even above compassion. Even above friendship."

"Have a care, Karayan," Ra'id snarled. "*I* wasn't the one to cause Danae to leave. *I* wasn't the one to hurt her."

"And *I* was?" Vartan's gaze narrowed. "Is that what you mean, Ra'id?"

"Aye, you in your insensitive treatment of Danae, who's only mistake was to love you. And my sister, in her scheming to steal you *from* Danae." The Desert lord gave a harsh laugh. "In my mind, you and Sharifah deserve each other. In my mind, Danae's better off without the two of you. I just hate to think of her out there all alone, risking her life to accomplish that very thing."

For a long, stunned moment, Vartan stared at Ra'id. Then he turned slowly to Sharifah.

At the look of puzzled disappointment she saw burning in his eyes, all Sharifah's hopes died. She had lost him, perhaps even before she had ever had him, but there was no chance she would win his heart now.

The realization filled her with anguish. It wasn't fair. It just wasn't fair!

"All I said to her," she cried, "was that perhaps I might be a more suitable bond mate for you than she. And it's true, Vartan. You must wed someone of royal blood. I possess that, and Danae doesn't. All I spoke was the truth!"

"How could you hurt her like that?" he asked.

"I didn't see you going out of *your* way to whisper sweet words of love into her ears." In her pain, Sharifah reacted as she had always done before. She fought back. "Indeed, ever since you regained your sight, you've increasingly ignored her. What was I to think of your intentions toward her? I treat my servants better than you treat Danae!"

"Sharifah, that's enough." Her brother moved around Vartan to take her hand. "Let him be. Come away before you do even more damage than you already have. Come away."

She glared at Vartan, even as she allowed Ra'id to drag her back. "Aye, I'm at fault. I'll admit it," she said, the words spilling out uncontrollably, like floodwaters over a dam. "But even if *I* drove her away, *you* did nothing to stop it. You offered her no hope, no love. And if she'd had that, nothing I could've said would have made Danae leave you.

"But you offered her nothing. Nothing!"

Like waves upon the sand, or perhaps more like a swarming mass of dusky dung beetles, the seemingly endless ranks of black-armored foot soldiers marched up to Astara's city walls. Then turning smartly, they filed past the city. On and on they came, Hyleans and Beast Men of the Jens moving side by side with hulking Daegols. The spike-shielded animal handlers were next with their snarling menagerie: wiry, muzzled Sand Cats on stout chains; huge Gals—man haters and man eaters—with their short, thick heads and snouts, tiny ears, and dense, nearly impenetrable brown coats; and oversized, wolf-like Eyous that could outrun a horse and easily carry a rider.

In the deepening twilight, the bowmen followed. First came the Pedars wielding short, powerful, recurved bows strung with sinew, weapons well suited to their small stature and short shooting range. Clad in lightweight armor, they also bore swords and a clawlike shield. The long bowmen came next, unarmed save for their bows, quivers, and deadly hunting knives. Crossbowman followed, then pikesmen with eighteen-foot-long hooked, steel pikes. Cavalry brought up the rear, row upon row of well-armed riders on armored horses, numbering in the tens of thousands.

Far back, ground weapons and siege equipment stood at the ready: heavy timber catapults on fifteen-foot-high, wheeled frames fitted with thirty-foot-long arms and iron baskets at their ends; seventy-five-foot-tall siege towers covered in iron plates; battering rams suspended from six tall posts by heavy iron chains.

Ladon smiled. All had been thought of, all had been done, to create an invincible fighting force. Khaddar would fall in record time, and after that, it would be a simple thing to move north to annihilate the Elves of Greenwald, then batter down the gates of Friedhelm. Once inside the Dwarf kingdom, all the gold and jewels the dwarves were said to mine and hoard there would be his.

The Rune Lords were of no consequence. He'd grant the Beast Men the pleasure of hacking away at them after the rest were subdued. And the Dragonmaids . . . at present there was no way to penetrate their secret portal. Historically, though, they had never come to anyone's aid. Their threat, if they truly *were* any threat, was minimal. Besides, once he had destroyed the rest of the Gadielean peoples, if the Dragonmaids should belatedly choose to fight, they would fight alone.

Aye, in but a few days, his army would march for the Valan Mountains and the Haroun. Once through the mountains, they would make use of the rivers to transport his soldiers and siege equipment. Though rivers were few and far between in the Desert, the Bahira, the Haroun's biggest river, flowed from the foothills of the Ibn Khaldun north and east to join with the Munir River right at the outskirts of Khaddar.

Ladon smiled. Rivers that had kept the capital city well supplied with the finest silks and spices all these hundreds of years would now be used as instruments of its destruction. What was that old Gadielean saying that so fittingly described what the Bahira and Munir Rivers would soon be to Khaddar? "Athan gives, and Athan takes away—blessed be the name of Athan"?

No matter. Just as the rivers would ultimately fail the Desert capital, so would that weak, insipid Athan fail his people. Ladon, on the other hand, preferred to serve a far more powerful and ruthless overlord. Phaon had granted him all that he asked. Athan had never once answered his prayers. Only a fool would choose to serve such an uncaring, ineffectual god. And Ladon was no fool.

There was but one unfinished matter, one that must be concluded before he began the conquest of Gadiel. Word had reached him that Vartan Karayan had been seen riding now with the son of the Hakeem. That the two of them were traversing the Haroun, seeking to forge alliances with all the Desert tribes. It was past time Karayan be stopped. It was past time to send Ankine again to fetch him.

His capture should be an easy enough task, now that neither his sorceress sister nor that old woman who had taught her

303

was anywhere near Karayan. *Indeed, this very night,* Ladon thought, *I might have the arrogant fool back.*

Like some predator savoring the taste of his prey, Ladon licked his lips. The timing couldn't be more perfect. A few days and nights of torturing Vartan Karayan in the most horribly imaginative ways, until the man begged him for the solace of death, would replenish his ever-growing need to nourish himself on the fear and pain of others. And then, with the prince's broken, mutilated corpse hanging from the city walls, he'd then ride out to break the back of Gadiel.

Vartan had no appetite for supper or, for that matter, for anyone's company. Indeed, after refilling his water bag, he mounted his horse and headed back out the way they had come earlier that day, riding for a good mile or so until he reached a solitary ring of monolithic stones. Their jagged bulk spearing the sky, the huge, smoky gray rocks were a startling contrast in a sea of undulating, topaz-colored sand. Ra'id claimed they were believed by some to be sacred sentinels, sent long ago by Al'Alim to guard the Desert. But there were others, he had then added with a twitch of his lips, who were convinced the stones were the remains of lost souls and the place best be given wide berth.

Vartan didn't care which tale was true, if either actually was. He just needed to be alone. The stones would provide some shade until the sun waned, and privacy for his thoughts, which he craved even more. Not that, even out here, he truly *was* alone.

Ra'id and Sharifah's impassioned assertions echoed repeat-edly in his mind. The Desert lord had accused him of treating Danae insensitively and insisted she was better off without him. Those words were painful enough, especially coming from a man he had imagined to be his friend. But Sharifah had known far better than her brother how to wound the most deeply.

"Ever since you regained your sight, you've increasingly ignored her . . . Even if I drove her away, you did nothing to stop it. You offered her no hope, no love . . ."

Was it true? Had he come to take Danae so for granted that he had ceased to cherish her as she had always deserved? But didn't she know he loved her? Hadn't she seen it in his eyes, heard it in his voice, felt it in his touch?

Perhaps, in his determination not to be a burden to her in his blindness, he *had* become too adept at hiding his true feelings. And, ever since he regained his sight and devoted all his time and energy to helping Ra'id gain the support of the Desert tribes, he knew he spent little time with Danae. But Vartan had thought she understood, that she knew the time would come when there would again be leisure for just the two of them. Leisure to discover just how deep their affection went, and where they might wish it to lead.

Despite Sharifah's claims that he could only wed someone of noble blood, the consideration of Danae's ancestry and her fitness to reign beside him—if he truly ever again *had* a kingdom to rule—had never been a stumbling block. Any kingdom he managed to carve from the ruins of the terrible war to come would be a kingdom of new rules, new laws, where all men—and women—stood as equals under Athan. In that new kingdom, Danae would be worthy—nay, she would be *more* than worthy—to be his wife.

In that new kingdom, it would've been *he* who would come to her on bended knee and beg *her* to take him as husband.

It was yet more of his cursed pride, Vartan realized with bitter shame, that had kept him from sharing his plans with her. He was still but a penniless outlaw, with no prospects save

305

the hope now of someday avenging his family and regaining his former kingdom. He had nothing yet to offer, and he had wanted to come to her with his former power and prestige restored. He had wanted to come to her as a king. In his mind, it was the only way to honor Danae for all she had been, and still was, to him.

There was more than just pride, though, that had held him back from Danae, touching on motives even darker and more self-serving. He hadn't been blind to Sharifah's rising interest in him. True, he hadn't encouraged it, but conversely, he had done nothing, either, to discourage it. The potential political advantages—however temporary—had seemed too valuable. Vartan realized now he had simply slipped back into a role he had once performed so very, very well—the role of a clever, calculating crown prince.

"I'm not much farther along than I was before, am I, Eternal One?" he whispered. "Though my blindness finally opened my eyes to what really mattered, now, with my sight restored, I'm blind once more."

Despair filled him. At the first call of the world and its temptations, he tossed aside all he had learned and vowed to do. He was a weak, despicable man who couldn't sustain his commitment to Athan for more than a few weeks! He might as well face the truth about himself. He hadn't the heart or sufficient courage to continue on this journey of the spirit. And he was too proud to be an unfaithful, ever faltering follower.

"*There's nothing easy about a life lived in the service of Athan . . .*" In his mind, Vartan heard Serpuhi's gentle words. "*In the beginning there are a great many battles and a good deal of suffering, and only afterward comes the true joy.*"

His lips lifted in the beginnings of a smile. He remembered that day when he had first come to Serpuhi and asked her to teach him of Athan. After she cautioned him regarding a life lived in Athan's service, he accused her of trying to discourage him and turn him from the Path. To that, Serpuhi chuckled.

"Nay, not discourage, only caution and, in the cautioning, provide strength and consolation for the road ahead," she replied. *"If you're forewarned of the trials to come—trials all who seek Athan endure—you'll more easily recognize them and not let them defeat you. Remember always that the Evil One wants nothing more than for you to give up, to fail. He wants Gadiel for his own."*

Was that, then, what he was experiencing? Was this a trial, a testing of his perseverance? And was Phaon's hand somehow in it?

If so, it could only mean one thing. Phaon saw him as a growing threat. Phaon feared Vartan might indeed gain the forces to rise against his soulless minions' onslaught. But if, instead, Phaon could tempt him to give up . . .

But to refuse to give up, to continue the fight to serve Athan and obey what seemed His call to win back Gadiel, was also to ride with Ra'id on the morrow. Ride in the opposite direction of where Danae was heading. It was to turn his back on her and carry on the quest without her. And it might even be to surrender his hopes and dreams of a life with her, perhaps forever.

With a groan, Vartan leaned forward and cradled his head in his hands. "Must it be so, Eternal One?" he cried. "Is it truly Your will that I give up Danae? Say it isn't so. I beg You, don't ask it of me!"

"Vartan? Beloved?"

Out of the darkness that had crept upon him without his even noticing it, a soft, familiar voice came. Vartan jerked his head up, went rigid. It couldn't be. That voice . . . it sounded like—

"Danae?" He whirled around. She stood there, backlit by a hazy circle of light.

"Danae? Is it you?"

"Aye, of course it is, Beloved." She moved toward him until she stood but an arm's length away.

He scrambled to his feet, his heart racing. "You've come back. I knew you would. You've come back to me!"

She nodded, her pale hair shimmering in the rising moonlight. "Aye, of course I've come back."

"But why . . . why did you leave?" Vartan paused, dragged in a steadying breath. "It doesn't matter." He reached out to her, stroked a smooth cheek. "It doesn't matter. We're meant to be together. Athan wishes it so. Together . . . forever."

She captured his hand and turned her face, kissing his palm. "Aye. Together . . . forever." Her grip tightened on his hand then. "I've something to show you. Will you come with me?"

He followed her willingly. He'd go wherever she led if only she would never again leave. Yet as Danae pulled him deeper into the circle of the standing stones, some memory tugged at him. A memory of another night, and a woman who had cast a spell . . .

Up ahead, something glowed. It looked . . . looked like an enlarged, golden ring, a portal . . .

Vartan dug in his heels, jerking Danae to a halt.

She turned, smiled faintly. "What is it, Beloved? Come, it's only a short distance away now." Inexorably, she began once more to draw him forward.

He couldn't seem to stop himself and finally recognized it for what it was—a charm spell! "You're not really Danae, are you?" he asked even as his legs moved him along despite his best efforts to stop them.

"Of course I am, Beloved," she replied, modulating her voice to a low, soothing, and most compelling tone. "You called and I came. Came back to you."

Athan! The name exploded in his head. *Athan, help me!*

With a jolt that shot down his arm and into his hand, the connection between Vartan and the woman severed. She cried out and jumped back.

"Wh-what did you do?" She stared at him with horror. "And how could . . . how *could* you? You're not an *abba*, or even a possessor of dark powers. It's not possible!"

"Nay, I'm not an *abba*, Ankine," he softly said. "But I'm also not the man you last found in that cave. Since then, I've come to know and serve Athan. He healed me, after all, of more than just my blindness."

She took several additional steps back, until she stood just this side of the portal. "But you haven't the level of training to overcome me like this!"

"True enough, but Athan does, and it was He I called upon to aid me." Vartan paused, eyeing her. "As He would aid you again, if only you would ask Him."

Her gaze narrowed. "And what makes you think I want to ask anything of Athan? I'm Phaon's servant now."

He shrugged. "Zagiri told me your story, how you let your pride turn you from Athan and His Way. We're a lot alike in that respect."

"Indeed? How so?"

"Your pride turned you from Athan. My pride kept me from even knowing Him and continues to be a thorn in my side at almost every turn."

Ankine stared at him in disbelief. "You're a strange one, you are, Karayan. I come to drag you back for Ladon to torture and kill, and you stand here and talk to me about Athan and how alike you and I are."

"It's never too late to return to the person you used to be, lady." Vartan saw the suspicion flare in her eyes, but beneath that hard veneer, he also saw a flicker of sudden indecision. "You know Athan and His ways far better than I, Ankine. Don't let your pride be the end of you."

She gave a shrill laugh. "It already *is* the end of me. You don't know what I've done, what I've become. There's no hope left for me. None whatsoever."

"Why? Because Phaon, the Great Liar and Deceiver, told you so?"

"Aye, and because I know it in my heart. In all these years, never once has Athan intervened, or uttered one word to me."

"Because you're unworthy? So unworthy *He* has turned His back on *you*?"

"He has every right to. I don't deserve His love anymore."

There was a bleakness in her eyes now. The bleakness of one who had lost all hope. Vartan's heart went out to her.

"None of us, no matter if we've always been His most faithful servant, deserves Athan's love," he said. "But that's the miracle of it, Ankine! If we come to Him in our unworthiness, He'll open His arms and take us back, clothing us in His grace and love. But *never* because of any merit on our parts, for we have none. Nay, *only* because He loves us, and has loved us even before we were formed in our mother's womb."

Tears filled her eyes. For a moment, Vartan thought she might actually renounce Phaon. Then her expression hardened, and she shook her head.

"Sweet words," Ankine muttered, "but words not meant for me. Phaon may be a merciless overlord, but he has never demanded that which is most precious to me. He has never asked me to give up my pride."

"And Athan has."

"Aye."

Sadness filled him. "It's not worth it, Ankine. I, of all people, know that now."

"It's all I have!"

"Then give it away. Give it away and receive the whole world in return!"

She smiled then, but it was a smile of utter desolation. "You're a kind man, Vartan Karayan, and a better one than Ladon could ever hope to be. Because of that, I'll tell you the Hylean means to set out in two days, at the head of an army that numbers nearly a hundred thousand strong. You haven't much time left."

As she turned away, Vartan called out. "And what of you, Ankine? What will *you* do?"

"I won't return to trouble you, if that's what you're asking. Leastwise not to do Ladon's bidding."

"That's not what I meant."

Ankine gave a soft laugh. "I didn't think so. But, either way, it doesn't matter. Farewell, Vartan Karayan."

With that, she stepped through the portal. Immediately it closed and disappeared, leaving him alone once more, bathed in cool breezes and moonlight.

20

"I'm done with you, you useless piece of offal! Go. Get out of my sight!"

Through a bleary, blood-clouded haze, Ankine pushed up from the floor to a sitting position. Her head spun sickeningly, but she forced herself to look at the man towering over her.

Ladon glared down at her, his face contorted with hatred and a strange, sadistic kind of pleasure. He had taken a moment to cover his nakedness with a long strip of cloth, but offered her none to hide her own. If he had his way, she thought, he'd likely send her from the city in the same state. Fortunately, though her powers wouldn't soon heal the wounds he had inflicted this night on her body and soul, they were sufficient to clothe her—just as soon as she escaped his presence.

"As you wish, m'lord," she whispered through bruised, swollen lips. Shoving to her feet, Ankine stood there for a moment, swaying precariously before finally gaining her balance. She glanced down. Great chunks of her formerly long hair lay twisted and tangled on the floor at her feet. She raised a shaky hand to touch her head. Short, bristly clumps jabbed at her fingers.

She had once been vain enough to consider her thick, wavy mass of auburn hair her greatest glory. But no more. No more.

Her body wasn't in much better condition. Scratches and bite marks vied with rapidly purpling bruises and myriad smears of blood. Ladon had always been brutal. But tonight . . . tonight he had exceeded even that. He had become vicious, almost maniacal, until she had truly feared for her life.

Ankine swallowed hard, quashing the memories as soon as they threatened to replay what had so recently occurred. If she dared let herself think past this very instant, she might finally and completely lose her mind. *Just put one foot in front of the other,* she told herself, *turn, and walk from this room.*

She could feel him watch her as she painfully staggered toward the door. Feel his loathing, feel his intense enjoyment of what she had endured and was yet suffering. But even that didn't matter. Numbness was setting in. Ankine welcomed it. Sweet, blessed numbness, her drug, her savior.

His ice-rimmed voice halted her, however, just as her hand settled on the door handle. "I'm not done with you, you know," he said. "Though you think you prevailed in surviving this night, I've left you a little gift. A gift that'll remain with you for some months to come, until you deliver the spawn I planted in you."

Wheeling about so swiftly she lost her balance and slammed back against the door, Ankine stared at Ladon. A glimmer of a smile played about his lips.

"Aye, you carry my child," he said, the words slipping like silk off his tongue. "You see, I know you, Ankine Yerevan. After tonight, you might have put an end to your life. But that tiny ember of decency you've never been able to extinguish won't allow you to kill your unborn child, will it? And that, my tormented little sorceress, is my final, most enduring gift

313

to you for repeatedly failing me. Now you'll *have* to live and, until your dying day, see my image—and the memory of this night—in the face of our child."

Though Danae had Halim guide her past the Am Shardi oasis to the place where she and Vartan had exited the tunnel, an exhaustive search up and down the length of mountainous foothills for miles in either direction failed to locate the tunnel's opening. After a day wasted in the fruitless effort, she was forced to face the fact that the tunnel no longer existed. Though Halim was eager to send her on her way and return to his tribe, he reluctantly agreed to lead her to the next nearest passage through the Ibn Khaldun.

It was, however, another two days' journey directly north of Am Shardi at a small Desert town called Barakah. And that, unfortunately, would require another three days' worth of travel back in the direction they had just come. A total of four wasted days she could've spent getting through the Valans to the Goreme Valley, not to mention the four it had taken just to reach the oasis from Abdul's camp.

She only hoped they didn't encounter Ra'id and Vartan on the way. The grueling trek through the Desert so far had drained nearly all her strength. If they found her now, Danae thought she might shatter into thousands of tiny pieces—or lose what remained of her sanity.

With each plodding step her horse took, she had put increasingly more distance between herself and Vartan, stretching the emotional bond between them almost to its snapping point. It had taken all of her self-control to hold herself together, to not turn back, when the only thing she wanted was to be close to him again. Be near him even if, in the end, he decided to wed Sharifah. Danae was almost willing to accept even that, if only she could remain near him and gaze upon his beloved face each and every day.

But that was her anguished heart speaking. Her head told her such aspirations were madness. Her head told her that was no worthy way to serve Athan. And, in such a time when her battered, aching heart could no longer feel any love for Athan, overshadowed as it was by her love for Vartan, Danae forged onward by sheer force of will alone.

Sheer force of will which, Zagiri had once informed her, was the strongest, surest form of love. After all, she had said, when the ease and pleasure of loving Athan fled, all that was left was a white-hot fire, refined and pure. A fire that would burn, slowly and steadily, to sustain you through good times and bad.

Danae clung to that promise in the darkness of the long days and nights spent apart from Vartan, in the agonizing attempt to sever the connection she felt even now as she struggled to kill her love. Eventually, though, she realized the pain of loving him would only die with the passage of time. To attempt actively to kill it would also, in the process, kill her.

So she accepted the burden and rode on in a torpor, until the day she and Halim drew up outside the south gate of Barakah. He pointed to the road leading from its western gates toward the mountains. "Follow that path, m'lady," he said, "and it will take you into the Ibn Khaldun. After about a day's journey, you'll arrive at a juncture where the road continues west, but also branches off to the north and south. From there, journey in whichever direction you so desire."

Though she suspected Vartan might guess she would head south to the Goreme Valley, Danae had no intention of telling Halim that. "And the westerly road leads through the Valans to the coast, does it not?" she asked instead, hoping to imply that she might be planning on taking a ship from there back to Hylas.

"Aye, m'lady. Best you reorient yourself to the stars each night, though, and always take the most westerly route," Halim replied. "Remember, there are several points along the way when that road branches off in other directions. A wrong turn could set you wandering in the Valans for weeks to come." He hesitated, eyeing her. "Are you sure you don't wish to come back with me, m'lady? What you plan to do is very dangerous."

"Nay." Danae shook her head. "My mind is made."

"Then at least reconsider hiring a guide at Barakah. Someone to lead you through the mountains."

She didn't have the heart to tell him she had barely enough money—once she sold the small necklace that had been her mother's and the delicate shell comb Aelwyd had given her—to buy food for the rest of the journey, much less hire a guide. But nothing was served revealing that. The kindhearted man would only interfere and complicate matters.

"I'll give a guide some serious consideration," she said. "Unless I can buy a map somewhere in the town. That might be of great help."

"Aye, that it would." Halim hesitated once more. "If you'd like, before I leave I can help you find a suitable inn for the night, and perhaps even a reputable guide . . ."

Danae smiled. "Nay, I'll be fine. I've got to start managing on my own sooner or later, so this seems the perfect time to begin." She reached down, untied the bag holding her lyra, and handed it to him. "Take good care of this. It has been in my family for years and will serve you well if you treat it accordingly."

He looked at the misshapen bag. "Perhaps it's best you keep it, m'lady."

For a fleeting instant, Danae was tempted to jerk back the lyra. Then she shook her head. "Nay. We made a pact, and you fulfilled your part of it. Now I intend to do the same. Take it, Halim."

Reluctantly, he finally did so. "Then it's time for us to part, m'lady. Is there any message you wish to send back with me for anyone?"

Tell Vartan I love him rose to her lips, and she choked it back. Nothing was served in expressing that, she knew. Not now, when she hadn't even found the courage to leave behind any sort of explanation. What could she have said at any rate, that wouldn't have sounded peevish or jealous or simply incomprehensible?

"Nay, there's no message, Halim," Danae replied at last.

He sighed. "Then it's farewell, m'lady."

"Aye, it is."

Halim paused but an instant longer, then reined his horse around and set out, back toward the Desert. Danae watched him for a time, then signaled her horse forward. Though she had led Halim to believe she would spend the night in Barakah before riding for the mountains, a good four to five hours of daylight still remained. After resupplying in town, she meant to spend those hours putting as much distance between herself and the Desert as she could.

The farther she got from Vartan, the easier it would be to bear it. Or at least so she hoped, anyway.

The Daegol scouts found her the second day into the Ibn Khaldun. Distracted with leading her horse over a treacherous slope of scree, Danae failed to notice the four big mountain trolls until they noticed her. By then, it was too late to escape.

Huge and lumbering as they were, the Daegols could climb where no one else dared go.

Terror spread through Danae as she tried every way she could to evade them, but Daegols were much more clever than their smaller cousins, the Pedars. They soon split up, with the obvious intent of surrounding her. As they began to close in, she was forced to abandon her horse and the trail. Scrabbling up the mountainside, Danae sought frantically to reach a narrow crevice that split the huge rock and slip through it, hoping the Daegols would be too large to get through after her.

Halfway up, a noose encircled her ankle, tightened, and, with a hard tug, jerked her back down. Before she could reach the rope and free herself, the first Daegol was upon her. A huge, stinking form loomed over her, blocking out the sun, and she panicked. Screaming, kicking, striking out, Danae fought back. With a snarl, the Daegol grabbed her by the arms and lifted her into the air.

She stared, transfixed, past the visor of a crudely fashioned helmet into tiny, black eyes—eyes gleaming with a brutish, otherworldly light. Broken, rotted, but still sharp teeth filled its large mouth, and the Daegol's skin, what she could see of it, was sun-seared to the appearance of dark brown hide. The rest was covered by black, metal-plated armor, a mail hauberk, and leather gauntlets. With its elongated, misshapen face, the half-human beast looked like nothing so much as some giant feral rodent.

"What have we here?" a rough, garbled voice rose from behind the Daegol holding Danae.

Her captor shot a quick glance over his massive shoulder, then turned back to Danae. "A pretty little morsel," he replied gruffly. "Shall we split her up and eat her here, or bring her back to Ladon?"

At the sound of Ladon's name, the last of Danae's hopes plummeted. These were some of his soldiers, she realized, and Ladon was, even now, finally moving his army toward the Desert. But it was too soon. Vartan and Ra'id weren't anywhere near ready to fight him.

There was nothing she could do, though. One way or another, her life now hung by a thread.

Help me, Athan, she prayed. *Whatever my fate's to be, give me the strength to endure until the end.*

"Best we take her back to Ladon," the other Daegol said. "He might fancy her."

The beast holding her released her. Danae plummeted to the ground. Before she could even push up, the Daegol flipped her over and bound her hand and foot. Then, grabbing her by the waist, he heaved her up and over his shoulder.

Through the seemingly interminable journey back down the mountain trail, Danae alternated between nausea at the jolting ride and nearly choking at the Daegol's stench. Finally, however, as the sun began its descent toward the farthest, westernmost range, they reached the rest of the army, which had encamped on a massive plateau overlooking a narrow river gorge.

Even then, it seemed forever before her captor halted and unceremoniously deposited her on the ground. She sat there on her haunches for a time, waiting for her spinning head to steady and her lungs to clear of the foul air she had been forced to breathe for so long. At last, though, Danae lifted her gaze.

Ladon stood but ten feet away, watching her. As their glances met, instant recognition flared in his eyes. Her heart sank. Dressed in Desert clothes and with a man's *shmaagh* and *agaal* on her head, she had hoped against hope he wouldn't recognize her.

"And what fine fortune is this," he said, a smile of delight curving his mouth, "that we should once again meet? Indeed, you couldn't have arrived at a more fortuitous time."

He walked up to her, leaned down, and, grasping her beneath both arms, gently pulled her to her feet. Then, withdrawing a knife, Ladon proceeded to cut through the ropes binding her feet and hands.

"Let me go, Ladon," Danae said softly. "I'm no threat to you."

"And where would you be going, pretty one?" He cocked his head, studying her. "Home to Hylas, perhaps?"

"Perhaps." Somehow, Danae didn't think telling Ladon she was headed for the Goreme Valley would sit very well with him.

"And where were you coming from?"

No sense in lying, she thought. It was pretty obvious from the direction she had been headed where she had come from.

"The Desert."

"You were with Karayan, weren't you?" His gaze sharpened.

"Aye. You know I was."

"And where is he now?"

She didn't have to lie about that, either. "I don't know. I left him over a week ago. He could be anywhere by now."

"Why did you leave him?" Ladon reached up and stroked her cheek. "Do I dare hope you were coming to me?"

Nausea welled anew, and it took all her control not to flinch away from his touch. Even in the few months since she had last seen him, Ladon had changed. There was a subtle but fanatical look about him now, in the way he unblinkingly stared at her. His formerly handsome face seemed somehow bloated. Lines of dissipation now etched the area around his nose and mouth.

Still, it was the wintry, soulless look deep in his eyes that sent the chill through her. Thanks to Phaon's malevolent influence, Ladon was sinking deeper and deeper into a bottomless pit of evil.

Her memory of him, when they had both lived at Feodras's Court in the capital city of Orion, had been one of an insecure but eager young man, hungry for everyone's friendship and approbation. Yet even then she had seen where the rising anger and frustration at having nearly all his overtures rejected—especially toward his father—might lead. But then, in those days, there had still been a spark of something good left in Ladon. In those days, he still had hope.

She knew that the moment he had finally lost hope, he had begun the downward spiral that led him to Phaon. The question lingered in her mind, though—had he at last totally relinquished all his humanity, or was there any bit of it left? If there were, there was still a chance she could appeal to it. If there were, there was still a chance for Athan to find a way into Ladon's heart.

Danae managed a taut little smile. "My reasons for leaving Vartan are my own. And, in truth, nay, I wasn't coming to you. After all that's happened, I didn't think you'd ever wish to see me again."

"Rather," Ladon chuckled, "I'd imagine *you* didn't wish ever to see *me* again." Taking her by the arm, he began to lead her away. "Come, let's walk a ways where we can talk more privately. What I have to say isn't for the ears of others."

There wasn't much choice but to follow where he led. They walked for a time, passing through the entire camp, and the farther they went, the more Danae was struck with the sheer enormity of Ladon's army. Her despair grew. No matter how successful Vartan and Ra'id were in reuniting the Diya al Din, they surely had no chance of assembling an army even

321

close to this size. They'd need far more help than what the Desert tribes could provide, if they were ever to be a threat to Ladon.

At long last, he halted near the edge of a precipitous cliff overlooking the gorge. Far below, a narrow, tortuous river rushed past large boulders in its path, sending foaming waves and white water churning in every direction. Danae spared but one, wide-eyed look down the yawning expanse and took several steps back from the edge.

"I was very angry at you," Ladon said, coming to stand behind her and the cliff's edge. "Once I realized you had a part in taking Karayan from where I left him outside Astara's gates, I mean. I even vowed, if I should ever find you, to punish you as severely as I planned to punish Karayan. But now . . ."—he laid his hands on her shoulders and squeezed gently—"now that I finally see you again, all thought of punishment escapes me."

Ladon leaned down and, brushing her hair away, nuzzled the side of her neck. "I've never forgotten you, Danae, or lost the feelings I once bore for you. You're the most pure and good thing I've ever known in my life. When you're near me, I feel . . . I feel as if I could yet pull myself from the horrid shambles I've made of my life."

At the touch of his lips, she trembled. Once, she had almost imagined she loved him. That her love might be the answer to his pain and frustration. That she might be able to save him.

But even as he led her to believe the same, Ladon was already visiting sorcerers, buying potions to enhance his strength and warrior's prowess. Sorcerers who, for their asking price, were slowly addicting him to the potions and, at the same time, introducing him to the vast, exhilarating potential of evil. Even then, even before Danae knew anything of Athan, she saw the dangers. Saw them, and tried to turn Ladon from them.

For her efforts, she almost died when she followed him one night to a grove of trees where he had gone to meet with a sorcerer. There, in the red-gold light of flames licking eerily to the sky, Danae watched a black-hooded man hand Ladon a vial. Watched him gulp it down. And then, watched as the sorcerer conjured—or was it summoned?—a figure in the flames.

He was huge, black, and winged. He was also hideous. Danae later learned he was a Fiend, one of the lesser demons who served Phaon. She learned later, as well, this Fiend was only the first of many otherworldly beings Ladon would come to know, before he was finally ready to meet their evil overlord.

Unfortunately, the Fiend was also able to sense the presence of intruders. Before Danae could flee into the night, he leaped from the flames and caught her, grabbing hold of her right forearm. His touch sent a searing pain through her, and she screamed.

It was enough to galvanize Ladon into action. He ran to her, shoved the Fiend away, and caught her in his arms.

"Why did you come?" he cried. "Why?"

"I-I was worried about you," Danae managed to reply. "Afraid of what you were doing to yourself."

His expression hardened. "It's none of your concern. It doesn't affect what's between us."

"Doesn't affect what's between us?" She stared up at him in disbelief. "You consort with sorcerers and demons, and you think it won't change what's between us? Are you mad?"

"She cannot be allowed to leave," a deep voice rose from behind Ladon. "She has seen too much."

He shot a quick glance over his shoulder, and Danae

saw it was the faceless sorcerer who now stood behind him. The Fiend had apparently returned from whence he had come.

"Stay out of this. This is between Danae and me."

"Fool, then I leave you to deal with the consequences," the other man muttered and, in a flutter of black cloak, slipped away into the night.

The bonfire's flames now reflected in his eyes, Ladon turned back to her. "Will you betray me to the King? He'll kill me if you do."

And Feodras would, Danae well knew. The king had a particular revulsion for all things and persons who served Phaon. And it wasn't as if he bore any particular affection for his illegitimate son. Ladon, after all, was but one of many, in addition to his lawful children by his first, and now long dead, queen.

If it had been anyone other than Ladon, Danae thought she might have well gone to Feodras. But she deeply cared for Ladon, and there was still hope he might be saved . . .

"Nay, you know I won't tell the king, or anyone else for that matter," she forced herself to reply. "In exchange, you must promise me, this very night, you'll turn from this evil. I know you seek answers to how to win your father's love and your rightful place at Court. But this isn't the way, Ladon. This can only end in your destruction."

"Perhaps you're right," he said. "And perhaps I needed you coming here tonight to force me to see the truth." He paused, then nodded with grim resolve. "I'm done with dabbling where no man should ever dare go. Thank you for your courage—and love—in coming here."

They hurriedly left the grove then. For a time, Danae thought Ladon had indeed turned his back forever on the sorcery and consorting with soulless beings. Still, the experience that night changed something between them. Bit by bit, they began to grow apart. Then Hovan and Calandra had conspired to kidnap her and bring her along with them to Hylas. That was the last she had seen of Ladon until that fateful day he had challenged Vartan to battle.

She still bore, however, the mark the Fiend had made that night, glancing down now at her right forearm. A mark she would bear to her dying day, Danae supposed, not only on her arm, but on her heart in the scars her bittersweet relationship with Ladon had left. Though she now felt only compassion and concern for him, she still hoped he could be saved.

"I'll do what I can to help you," she said. "You must first, however, turn from Phaon once and for all and beg Athan's help. Only He can protect you from Phaon now."

His grip tightened on her shoulders. "That's not the kind of help I was looking for," he growled. "Rather, tell me where I can find Karayan, and everything will be over and done with right now. There'll be no need to set my army against the rest of Gadiel. You'll prevent countless deaths and the terrible destruction war always wreaks. And all that in exchange for just one man."

Danae wrenched away from his bruising hold and turned to face him. "Aye, for just one man," she cried. "But he's the one man who ultimately stands between you and your plans for Gadiel. He's the one man who, with Athan's aid, will drive Phaon and his minions from the land."

"He hasn't a chance. You saw the size of my army. One way or another, it's but a matter of time."

"Perhaps. But I mean to give him that time. I won't betray Vartan to you."

With a guttural snarl, Ladon rushed forward, grabbed her, and dragged her over to teeter on the edge of the cliff. "Think again, my pretty one," he said, his voice frosting to ice. "You can be my queen and rule at my side, or you can die now. It's your choice."

Gazing down at the expanse of nothingness just beyond her feet, terror seized her. For a long moment, Danae couldn't breathe, much less speak. To die, crushed on the rocks far below, or to betray Vartan and surrender her soul . . .

She shut her eyes, fearing the ghastly fate awaiting her either way she chose. Yet, Danae already knew what her choice must be.

"At least I still have a choice," she whispered. "And I choose Athan, and Vartan."

His enraged scream filling the air, Ladon shoved her forward. "Then die! Die, and your lover will soon join you!"

Emptiness rushed out to meet Danae as she fell, plummeting downward. *Athan!* she silently cried. *Athan, take me, hold me close, save me!*

Something big and dark loomed suddenly in the corner of her vision. She slammed into it with terrific force. Agonizing pain shot through her. Danae screamed, then everything went black.

21

Ra'id reined in his horse in the inner courtyard of Khaddar's royal palace. He turned to Vartan. "Best I meet with my father first," he said. "Sharifah will take you to a nearby waiting room and see that you have a chance to wash away at least some of the sand. Then you can refresh yourself with a cool drink."

Vartan managed a smile. "It's going to be that bad, is it?"

"Likely worse." Ra'id sighed, tossed his horse's reins to a servant, and dismounted. "It took us five days to get here. By now, I'd wager Malik and Farid have returned and are busy filling the Council and my father's head with all sorts of malicious lies."

"I'm not worried, nor should you be. The truth—Athan's truth—will prevail." Vartan climbed down from his mount.

Meeting his friend's steady gaze, Ra'id couldn't help but envy Vartan's calm assurance. But then, Vartan had yet to meet either the Hakeem or his Council. That was probably a blessing in disguise, considering he was still technically under sentence of death.

"I'll do all I can for you." Ra'id gripped Vartan's arm. "I need to warn you, though, that my success rate with my father isn't the best."

Vartan nodded. "Take heart. Before, you didn't necessarily have Athan on your side. Now you do."

The reminder heartened him. "Aye, that I do."

Ra'id turned to his sister, who had also dismounted and now stood quietly nearby. She had been unusually subdued the entire journey home. He supposed Danae's departure and Vartan's quite apparent grief—a grief that still held him in its thrall—had unsettled her.

But well it should. Sharifah had meddled where she had no business going. In her desperation to find a husband, she had hurt Danae and lost any chance she might ever have had with Vartan. Not that, he thought with a surge of compassion for his sister, she had ever *really* had any chance. It was most evident Vartan loved Danae, and would always love her.

The fact that his friend had foolishly put off telling Danae was another matter entirely. Now, however, wasn't the time to dwell on it. He had to face his father in but a few minutes more.

"Will you see to Vartan's comfort, then stay with him until either I return or he's sent for?" he asked Sharifah. "He doesn't know the palace."

She nodded. "You know I will. To do any less would be an offense against Desert hospitality."

Ra'id grinned. "I knew I could count on you."

Sharifah returned his grin with a half-hearted one of her own. "Aye, always, Brother."

There was nothing more to be said after that, so Ra'id rendered Vartan a perfunctory nod, then turned and strode away. He was soon heading down the long, colonnaded outdoor corridor that led to the hallway to the Hakeem's throne room. At this time of day, he didn't doubt he'd find his father there with his Council, presiding over various and sundry Courtly matters.

Help me, Al'Alim, he prayed as he walked along. *Guide my tongue so I may speak the right words to sway my father. But not for my sake, as I've asked for so many times before, but solely in Your service and, through You, in service to Vartan and his cause. I cannot do this on my own. I need Your help or I fear all will be lost.*

And then Ra'id reached the throne room's doors. Two armed guards flanked either side of the gilded, red rafawood doors. They came to smart attention. One then leaned over, shoved down on the crescent moon–shaped handle, and pushed the door open. Heads immediately turned in Ra'id's direction. There was barely time for a sharply inhaled breath, a squaring of shoulders and lifting of chin, before Ra'id gazed out on dozens of hostile eyes.

He lost no time striding into the cavernous room and right up to the man sitting beneath the draping, silken canopy. Curving out in a semicircle from either side of the Hakeem's huge chair were additional low-backed chairs, all filled with his advisors. Malik, glaring furiously at Ra'id, sat in the place of highest honor to the Hakeem's right. Two seats down, a sullen-faced Farid stared back at him.

Ra'id schooled his features to a stoic inscrutability and walked directly up to stand before his father. He rendered the requisite low bow, then straightened.

"As you requested, Most High and Noble One," he said, using one of his father's favorite terms of address, "I've returned, bringing the Prince of Astara with me."

"The one you were ordered several weeks ago to execute?"

So, there are to be no preliminary conversational gambits, Ra'id thought. *Well, so be it.*

"Aye, the very same one, Majesty." He met his sire's gaze with unflinching directness. "And I did obey your orders to execute him. At the time, Vartan Karayan was blind, and we

329

took him two days' ride out into the Haroun and left him there. But apparently Al'Alim had other plans for the man. He returned to us, his sight restored."

Ra'id's glance skittered off the faces of Malik and Farid. "But I assume you already know that, in addition to the other pertinent and most unsettling details of Karayan's return?"

Prince Kamal gave a snort of disgust. "Aye, I was *most* thoroughly informed. And I was also told that when you were then ordered to kill the man on the spot, you refused and proceeded to leave two of my most trusted advisors behind at Am Shardi. Men who, in my absence, you were ordered to obey as you would have me."

"And obey them I did," Ra'id replied coolly, "until they *failed* to advise me as you would have. I wasn't under the impression I was to retire my intellect and conscience just because you sent Malik and Farid along. You reared me better than that, Father."

The room went silent, not a rustle of garments or inhaled breath to be heard. The Hakeem arched a dark brow and, for a long moment, stared down at Ra'id. Then, with an imperious wave, he motioned to the men seated to either side of him.

"Go. All of you. I wish to speak with my son alone."

Malik jumped to his feet. "Majesty, I protest! Ra'id is—"

"Is what?" Prince Kamal demanded, wheeling about to face the gray-bearded man. "Isn't safe to be left alone with me? Or perhaps, instead, you just think he's too clever for me, and without your far more astute council, will convince me to do something against my best interests? Is that it, Malik?"

The older man paled. "Indeed, I meant no such thing, Majesty. In the past, though, you have always found a third, disinterested party most helpful. I but thought to offer my aid yet again."

It took all of Ra'id's considerable self-control not to offer his own opinion of Malik's claim to impartiality, but he held his tongue. Something most unusual was going on here, and he sensed it didn't require his assistance. Indeed, any interference on his part might well spoil everything.

"If and when I need your aid, Malik Abd al Rashid, I'll ask for it." Prince Kamal turned back to his son. "Come, instead, let *us* retire to more comfortable surroundings. You look as if you came to me straight from the Desert. A cool drink would stand you in good stead."

He had indeed not paused in coming to his father, save to speak for those few minutes with Vartan and Sharifah. On the contrary, he hadn't even shed his *shmaagh* or *bisht*, both of which were travel-stained and dusty. And he was long over-due for something to drink, though until this moment Ra'id had attributed his dry mouth to tension over his upcoming meeting with his father and his Council.

"A cool drink would be most appreciated, Majesty," he replied.

The Hakeem rose, walked over to his son, and, taking him by the arm, led him from the room. As they headed down the corridor to the multiple suites of rooms comprising the royal quarters, Ra'id's father glanced over at him. "You must forgive Malik. He means well, but he becomes a bit overzealous at times."

"Perhaps. He was wrong, though, when he ordered Ka-rayan killed the second time. I couldn't in good conscience obey him."

Prince Kamal halted before a door. "I am most interested in hearing your view of the strange circumstances surround-ing this Astarian. But first, let's take a short time for you to refresh yourself. Then we will talk further."

He opened the door and walked in, Ra'id following. He recognized it as one of his mother's favorite rooms. Tall, arched windows opened onto a private inner courtyard wherein burbled an intricately carved fountain decorated with a rose motif. The floors were of large blue and yellow tiles in medallion designs. In addition to the low rafawood and brass tables, the long, upholstered lounging couches were carved from the rare and costly, fragrant thuya wood. Vases of exotic flowers were set about the room, and trays of food and drink were already waiting on the tables.

Ra'id shut the door and looked to his father. "You'd already planned for us to come here, hadn't you?"

The Hakeem smiled. "Aye. As furious as Malik and Farid were with you when they arrived from Am Shardi, I knew something out of the ordinary had happened there. I but wanted to see their reaction when I told them to leave. And, since I find it increasingly more difficult to concentrate these days when my Council gets to all shouting at once, I thought it best I hear your side of the story in a more peaceful setting."

"I appreciate that, Majesty. More than I can say."

"Likely you do." His father smiled. "We haven't been on the best of terms for a long while now, after all. And I know a large part of that was my fault."

"I . . . " Ra'id's voice faded. He truly didn't know what to say. It was like a dream come true, that his father would even admit to such a thing, much less seem saddened by it. "I'm glad that time is past," he finally said. "I've always tried to do what was right, and to obey you."

Prince Kamal laughed. "Then obey me now and discard that filthy *shmaagh* and *bisht*, will you? I'm surprised anyone let you as far as my throne room, looking as you do, like some

Desert vagabond. And take some refreshment. Only then will we talk further."

Ra'id was quick to do his father's bidding. Finally, after gulping down almost four cups of the tangy, kelavi honey-sweetened poma juice and gobbling up several enticingly prepared flatbread squares topped with pale tur cheese and dried, herb-seasoned ashtarak meat, he laid back against the couch pillows with a contented sigh.

"That was indeed fortifying." Not quite certain his sire wouldn't yet revert to his old ways, Ra'id glanced warily at his father, who reclined on a couch facing his. "Thank you for your consideration."

His father didn't immediately reply, instead finding apparent fascination in rearranging the silken folds of his robe. "One of Farid's servants brought me back a blue rose." He looked up and smiled. "You see, I had spies spying all along on my spies. And be that as it may, though the rose was dried and brittle, and more purple than blue by then, I knew it for what it was. I had, after all, seen blue roses in my youth."

A faraway look darkened his eyes. "One day, a holy man close to my father's age came to Khaddar bearing blue roses. Even then, mind you, blue roses had all but disappeared from Gadiel. This Garabed urged my father and me to hold fast in our service to Al'Alim. If we did, he assured us, the time would come when the Diya al Din would rise again to their former power and wealth. Then the strangest thing happened. Garabed looked directly at me—not at my father—and said to heed the man who next came to the Desert bearing blue roses. Heed and follow him."

Prince Kamal closed his eyes. "Until now, Ra'id, not a blue rose has ever again been seen in the Desert."

Ra'id didn't say anything. *So, this is the source of Father's sudden change of heart,* he thought, his hands clenching the cloth of his *thobe. I should've known Al'Alim's hand would be in this as well.*

"Is it true then?" His father opened his eyes and turned to him. "That Karayan somehow found his way back to Am Shardi bearing blue roses?"

"Aye, it's all true. I swear it. And everyone saw Prince Vartan bring the blue roses, Father. Everyone."

"And saw that he had been blind before, and then returned with his sight?"

"He was blind. When we first met, I threatened him with a knife, and he didn't even flinch. He bore the marks of the Son, as well, on both wrists and on his right side. It was where Ladon wounded him in their battle."

"Aye, so I have heard. And then I received that blue rose . . ." He sighed. "Ever since, I have been unsettled and barely able to sleep. I have wept; I have spent hours in prayer; I have pored over the sacred books. Yet, try as I might to see things differently, I keep coming back to the conclusion that Karayan . . ." Prince Kamal swallowed hard. "I don't want to believe he is the one of the Prophecy. I don't want to accept him, knowing what it might portend."

"Even if Vartan *is* the Guardian, it doesn't mean he's also destined to rule all of Gadiel." Ra'id sat up, leaned forward. "The Prophecy doesn't speak to that."

"Nay, it doesn't, but tradition makes that man one and the same."

"Nonetheless, we can address that issue later. What matters now is raising a force sufficient to defeat Ladon and drive him and his army from the land. And we don't have much time left."

"Aye, well I know that." His father rested his forearms on his thighs and clasped his hands together. "Even now, reports place Ladon's army—an enormous army that numbers over a hundred thousand—in the Valans and headed our way." He looked up. "How goes the work gaining the allegiance of the tribes?"

"Surprisingly well, especially since the news of Vartan's miraculous return from the Haroun and reports of Ladon's growing army began to spread." Ra'id smiled bleakly. "It is amazing what the threat of war can do to stir long-buried feelings of unity and brotherhood. If only the Diya al Din could cling to such views in times of peace, there'd be no limit to what we could accomplish."

"Aye, if only . . ." Once more, the Hakeem sighed. "Well, no matter. Tell me of the Usurper's son. What sort of man is he? And can he be trusted not to turn on us, once Gadiel is again safe?"

"As hard as it was for me to do so, I haven't only come to trust him, but now call him friend." Ra'id's gaze lifted and he stared out into the inner courtyard. Sunlight caught the water flowing from the fountain, sending sparkling shards of brilliance into the air. "He's a good man, a brave man, and a man of his word. He won't betray us. He's now one of the Faithful."

"Is he now?" Prince Kamal arched a brow. "That doesn't sound like any Karayan I have ever known. Go. Bring him to me. I cannot make any lasting decisions until I meet and talk with this man."

Joy filled Ra'id. Never, in all his interactions with his father, had anything gone so quickly or easily. Indeed, they had spoken together like father and son, rather than prince and subject. It was almost past belief.

"It'll be as you ask, Majesty." He rose. "I'll fetch him posthaste." Ra'id hesitated.

"What are you waiting for, Son?" His father made a shooing motion. "Go, fetch him. Now!"

With that, Ra'id turned on his heel and hurried from the room. As his long strides carried him back down the corridor, his thoughts lifted heavenward.

Thank you, Al'Alim, he prayed. *Though Your hand's in this, even so, You surpassed my wildest expectations. Not only have You once again smoothed the way for Vartan, but You've given me back what I longed for nearly all my life. You've given me back my father.*

☙ ❧

As one servant departed with the water Vartan had used to wash his face and hands and another entered with a tray loaded with a silver flask, cups, and plates of dainties, Vartan added his dusty *bisht* to his *shmaagh* and *agaal* on the floor beside his couch. Then, with a weary sigh, he sat and reclined against the colorful cushions.

After depositing the tray, the second servant exited. As she had for the past several days Sharifah studiously avoided Vartan's gaze and instead saw to setting out the food and drink on the brass table. Finally, though, good manners wouldn't permit her to continue her little game.

"A cup of cool poma juice and, first, some of the cheese and meat sandwiches?" she asked, looking him square in the eye.

"Aye, that would be most appreciated." Immediately, Vartan sat back up. "There's no need to serve me, though, Sharifah. I can see to it myself."

As he leaned forward, she put out a hand and shook her head. "Nay. Hospitality demands the host or hostess serve, no matter the difference in social standing. Not that," she added with a stiff little smile, "I'm implying you're of lesser rank than me."

She was tense and nervous. He needed to smooth the way. Vartan lay back against the cushions.

"I never imagined you meant that."

He paused, wondering how best to broach the subject that had—for the sake of the fledgling alliance—been unofficially prohibited since the day they had returned to the Ben Aban camp. Not that he wasn't still angry at Sharifah for the meddling that had driven Danae away. He was, and struggled to reconcile it with Eisa's admonition to forgive even those who spitefully used you.

Sharifah, however, hadn't acted as she had out of spite. Vartan truly believed she had meant neither Danae nor him any harm. Indeed, he had to believe *he* was more at fault than Sharifah. He had, after all, been manipulating the situation, and *he* had known it.

"We need to talk," he said at long last. "About Danae. About my feelings on the matter."

"It's quite obvious what your feelings are," she replied, focusing all her attention on pouring him some juice. "About Danae. About what I did." She handed him the cup.

Vartan accepted it, then set it down on his side of the table. "You were right to chastise me for my neglect of Danae. It was inexcusable, not to mention selfish and cruel. I treated you unfairly, too. I wasn't blind to your advances. Indeed, I found them not only flattering, but I saw your interest in me for the political advantage it could be. So I, by my dishonest failure not to discourage you, instead encouraged you."

He exhaled a long, deep breath and looked down. "No matter what you hoped for, no matter what Danae imagined, it would've never come to this sorry end if *I* had acted honorably. If *I* had been the man Athan has always meant for me to be. For that, I beg your forgiveness and ask if there's a chance we can someday again be friends."

Sharifah eyed him impassively. "I don't know. If we can ever be friends again, I mean." She chewed on her lower lip. "It's hard, when it comes to emotions, to retrace your steps. But I can and will forgive you. I have to. Al'Alim demands it."

"In the coming days and weeks, we'll have to work closely to build and train our army. Can you do that as well?"

Her eyes widened. "Father won't permit it. No Desert woman has ever involved herself in such work, much less ridden into battle."

"Perhaps that's because we Gadieleans have never before been in such dire straits," Vartan said with a grin. "This time, though, I think we'll need every able-bodied fighter, be they male or female. Every *willing* able-bodied fighter, that is. The choice is up to you."

Her mouth lifted at one corner. "I'm willing. A Desert woman's lot has always chafed. I'll be thankful for the freedom and excitement, if nothing else. And perhaps if I'm involved in fighting to save Gadiel, my father won't be as inclined to marry me off so quickly. Indeed, I doubt many men will even find me appealing, garbed and armed and as dirty as I'll be."

"On the contrary, *I* think many warriors will find a brave warrior woman appealing." Vartan chuckled. "Especially one as beautiful as you."

She laughed and, for the first time in the past days, the sound was light and happy. "Have a care, Vartan Karayan. Your compliments might well turn my head."

"I only speak the—"

The chamber door swung open. In strode Ra'id.

Vartan rose from the couch. The moment had finally come, he thought, the tension rising anew. Either the Hakeem would see him and he'd live another day, or he wouldn't.

The Desert lord, his face inscrutable, walked up to stand before Vartan. Then a wide grin split his face.

"A miracle has occurred!" he cried, grabbing Vartan by the shoulder. "My father wants to meet you. And I think he believes in you, too, and all because of the blue roses and some strange man named Garabed, who met my father as a youth and told him to heed and follow the man who next came to the Desert bearing blue roses. And that's you, Vartan. You!"

In his excitement and exultation, Ra'id's words were coming so fast Vartan could barely keep up with him. He laid a hand over Ra'id's.

"Slow down, my friend." He frowned, puzzled. "Did I hear you correctly? Did you say the man who came to your father was named Garabed?"

"Aye." Ra'id paused, eyeing him intently. "Why? Do you know of this man?"

"Know of him?" Vartan chuckled, joy filling him. "I've *met* him. He saved us from the Pedars, then sent us into a tunnel that took us through the Ibn Khaldun to the Desert."

"But he was an older man when he visited my father and grandfather." Ra'id frowned. "Likely in his fifties, considering he was, at the time, the same age as my grandfather. He must be *very* ancient by now."

"Perhaps. I don't know what he looked like. At the time, after all, I was still blind." He shrugged. "But no matter. Danae was convinced Garabed was a holy man, and both your father's experience and ours confirm that Athan was with him."

A thoughtful look sprung into the Desert lord's eyes. "Indeed He was. I've never seen such a sudden change as I saw today in my father." He lifted his gaze and glanced to his sister. "He listened to me, Sharifah. Listened and treated me, for the first time, like a son."

Tears flooded her eyes. "Al'Alim be praised, Brother. At last. At long last."

"Come." Ra'id turned back to Vartan. "It's time we went to my father. There's much to be done, and Ladon and his army won't wait on us. Even now, he's coming through the Valans.

"Coming through the Valans," he said, his mouth going grim, "and we have barely begun to gather an army to face him."

22

Danae didn't know which hurt worse—her head or her left arm. She groaned and reached over to touch her arm, but her hand was instantly grabbed and halted.

"No, Danae," a familiar voice said. "Don't touch that. It's broken."

Her eyelids felt thick and heavy but, with a great effort, she was gradually able to open them. The blurred form of a woman, short of hair and dressed in brown, stood over her. Danae blinked several times. The image cleared.

"Z-Zagiri!" she croaked. "H-how did you get here? And where am I?"

"You're safe, my friend," Vartan's sister said. "For now, that's all that matters."

"How . . . how long have I been asleep?"

"Since yesterday, when they rescued you. Now, here. You need to drink this."

A hand slid beneath her shoulders, and she was lifted slightly from the bed. "Wh-what is it?" Danae asked.

"A nourishing drink with some herbs and other special ingredients to help your pain." Zagiri pressed a cup to Danae's lips. "Drink it all down."

The cup was made of pottery, thick and cool with a rounded edge. Danae took a sip and grimaced. "It's bitter."

"Aye, it is, but good for you nonetheless. Drink some more."

There was no dissuading Zagiri when she put her mind to something. Best just to swallow the nasty stuff and be done with it. Danae reached for the cup with her good hand and gulped it down.

"Now, may I have something else to drink?" she asked, handing the cup back to her friend. "If for no other reason than to get this awful taste out of my mouth?"

"Well, aren't you the most pleasing of patients?" Zagiri chuckled. "If I didn't know you better, I'd almost imagine my brother has worn off on you."

At the mention of Vartan, Danae's heart twisted. "Nay, not yet at any rate. But enough of my foul mood," she said, quickly changing the subject. "Where am I, and how did I get here?"

Zagiri eyed her quizzically, then laughed. "I suppose you *would* be wondering that, wouldn't you? Well, you're in Sanctuary, on the other side of the portal at Sevan House, safe with the Dragonmaids. And as to how you got here, the Dragonmaids and their dragons rescued you when you fell from the cliff."

So that's what I hit so hard when I fell, Danae thought. She had slammed into a dragon.

"I hope I didn't hurt anyone," she said. "When I fell, I mean."

"Dragons are big, tough creatures. The only thing you hurt was yourself."

"But how did they know that I needed help and where to find me? I saw no dragons, and then they were there."

"Garabed called for them to come to your aid. And as to how Garabed knew . . . well, he just does and always has."

Zagiri smiled. "Like he knew when you and Vartan were in danger, and he came to your aid. He's been sent by Athan, you know, to see to your and Vartan's protection."

There Zagiri went again, tiptoeing around the issue of why she was here without Vartan. Danae knew she was going to have to tell her sooner or later what had happened. Might just as well get it over with.

She met her friend's searching gaze. "Before you ask, he's fine. Better than fine, actually. Athan restored his sight, and Vartan's now working with the Diya al Din to gather an army. Or he was when last I saw him."

"He can see again?" His sister's eyes turned bright and moist.

"Aye."

"Oh, thank You, Athan." Zagiri closed her eyes and clasped her hands before her. "Thank You!" Then, as if she suddenly recalled the rest of Danae's explanation, she pulled a stool over to the bed and sat. "But you are no longer together. Care to tell me why?"

Danae bit her lip and looked away. Would it ever get any easier?

"Vartan didn't need me anymore. And he'll likely soon wed Sharifah, the Hakeem's daughter. I decided my continued presence would just be a hindrance, so I left."

"That doesn't sound like my brother," her friend replied, her gaze filled with compassion and a woman's understanding. "That he'd so easily and quickly fall in love with another woman—when I know he loves you."

"He doesn't love me, Zagiri." She gave a sharp little laugh, sensing that the other woman guessed there were deeper issues involved than just Vartan's need of her, or lack thereof. "After all this time, Vartan has never said one word about love or commitment or a life together. He knows as well as I that I'm not worthy of him, and now, of all times, he needs to wed wisely and well."

"And this Sharifah *is* the right woman for him?"

"Aye." Danae nodded vehemently. "She's of noble blood, and a marriage between them would only strengthen the ties between Vartan and the Diya al Din. Ties he desperately needs if he's ever to have a chance to defeat Ladon."

"Vartan has always been a very resourceful man." Zagiri leaned forward. "He could find another way if he wished."

This conversation was beginning to head back into a circle, and Danae was already past weary of discussing yet again what she had so long revisited in her heart and mind. "Evidently Vartan didn't care to find another way. And I knew if I stayed around him much longer, I was sure to make a fool of myself. So I left. It's over and done."

Her friend finally got the less than subtle hint. She leaned back.

"And where were you planning on going, alone as you were through the mountains?"

"I don't know." Danae shrugged. "I thought to revisit the Goreme Valley and spend some time with Serpuhi. If I can't figure out what to do with my life in the peace and silence of that valley, well, then I never will." She yawned hugely. "Whatever did you put in that drink anyway? I can hardly keep my eyes open."

"Oh, nothing much really. Just something for the pain, something to hasten your healing, and something for sleep. Sleep is, after all, one of the best remedies for what ails you."

"Aye, it is indeed," Danae muttered, her eyelids sliding shut almost as if they had a mind of their own. "Still, I don't want to impose on the Dragonmaids' hospitality. They surely don't appreciate uninvited guests."

"And weren't *you* the one who expressed an interest in meeting them and their dragons one day? This is your golden opportunity."

Zagiri stood and, bending down, pulled the coverlet up and tucked it beneath Danae's chin. For the briefest moment, Danae's eyes flickered open, then slammed shut again.

"Maybe just for another day or two then," she said, her tongue suddenly awkward and unwieldy. "If they don't mind . . ."

Though her left arm ached and her head still throbbed whenever she turned it too quickly, by the next day Danae was already walking a bit around her little room. Her appetite had also returned in full force. Zagiri, however, cautioned prudence and insisted she take a long morning and afternoon nap, then retire early that night. A couple doses more of that repulsive concoction were added for good measure.

By the following morning, Danae was ready to leave the increasingly dull confines of her room and explore her new surroundings. Yet, once again, Zagiri asked her to remain inside.

"There's someone you must meet first," she said. "You can't wander around here without proper permission and direction, you know."

"So I'm gathering that giver of permission and direction isn't you?" Danae sighed and eyed the stool, wondering if it was tall enough, if she stood on it, to afford her any view through the room's high only window. "They're rather secretive, the Dragonmaids."

"On rare occasions, they've been known to take in some injured or dying outsider they've found in the mountains. This is the room they use to attend to their patients. But, just as soon as it's safe to send the stranger on his or her way, they do so. Theirs is a hidden, ascetic life lived in service to

Athan, and they mean to keep it that way, untainted by the outside world. They also," she added with a wry smile, "don't need any outsider learning anything about them that might ultimately threaten their safety or their way of life."

"But you know I'd never do either." Dismay filled Danae. "Can't you tell them that? That I'm ever so grateful and honored they would even help me, much less take me in?"

"And *we* are equally honored by your presence, Child of Athan," an unfamiliar feminine voice interjected just then.

Danae whirled around and, for her effort, nearly lost her balance. Frantically, she grabbed for the bedpost to steady herself, blushing in embarrassment at her awkward display.

"M'lady." Zagiri bowed, then straightened. She turned to Danae, giving her a nod of her head and a pointed look.

Danae took the hint and bowed. "M'lady," she said, then slowly lifted her head.

A woman stood dressed in a long, white robe topped by an equally long, wide band of black cloth that hung from her shoulders. The band fell to her feet both in front and back. She also wore a simple black veil held in place by a circlet of interwoven gold wire, and what could be seen of her brown hair beneath it was streaked with gray. She was tall and carried herself with an air of authority, but the gentle light in her blue eyes bespoke of a compassionate nature nonetheless. She also, Danae realized, reminded her of someone, though at this particular moment she couldn't recall whom.

"I am Lysanor, Queen of the Dragonmaids," said the woman with a smile. "And I have waited with much impatience to meet you, my child. It isn't often, after all, that Athan's august messenger comes to me and asks for my assistance. You must be especially beloved by Athan."

346

Danae couldn't help but blush again. "I didn't know that Garabed was one of Athan's messengers. I thought he was but a holy man."

Lysanor laughed softly. "Oh, he is certainly holy. He just isn't quite like the rest of us. You are blessed to have him as your special protector."

Danae wanted to protest that she wasn't worthy and that it was all some big misunderstanding, but didn't. To do so would discredit what all of them had done for her. And besides, she didn't know what might truly be at work here.

"Aye, Athan has blessed and protected me," Danae said, meeting the Dragonmaid Queen's astute gaze. "But not because of any special worthiness on my part. Far from it. He watches over me because He loves me, and all I can do in return is love and try always to serve Him."

"As must we all. Still, it seems Athan has some special task for you in mind. Have you as yet been enlightened as to what that duty might be?"

Her question took Danae aback and, for a long moment, she couldn't speak. Athan still had some special task for her?

"I don't know, m'lady," she finally replied. "Once, I thought my purpose was to serve Him by serving Vartan Karayan, but that calling is no more. Vartan no longer needs me, and to remain with him was to"—she inhaled a shuddering breath, deciding she might as well tell everything, even the ugly secret about her shameful response to Sharifah—"was to threaten my relationship with Athan. And even for Vartan, I couldn't do that. So I had to leave him."

"Danae," Zagiri breathed in dismay, "you didn't tell me that. What did Vartan do to you?"

Remorse filling her, she turned to her friend. "It wasn't Vartan. He never failed to treat me honorably. It was me, Zagiri, and the feelings I had for him. Feelings that led to jealousy, anger, and even hatred for Sharifah. If I'd stayed, I soon would've shamed myself and dishonored Athan, so I fled. Perhaps I was wrong to do it, but I didn't know what else to do, so I fled!"

Tears flooded Danae's eyes and spilled down her cheeks. "I miss him so! Not a moment goes by when I don't want to return to him. I even dream of Vartan in my sleep! Yet, in my heart of hearts, it didn't seem as if Athan wanted me there anymore. What else *could* I do but leave?"

"Oh, sweet friend!" Zagiri rushed to her side and put her arms around her. "If it was Athan's will, of course you had to leave Vartan. I just thought . . . hoped . . ." She stopped and took a deep breath. "Well, it doesn't matter. You're here now, and perhaps this is where Athan meant for you to come. Perhaps *you* were the one I was to prepare the way for."

Danae stared at her through her tears. *Prepare the way . . . Athan told me I must . . . go to Sevan House and prepare the way . . .*

It all made sense now, Athan's strange request to Zagiri, Danae realized, a fierce exultation filling her. Then *both* she and Zagiri had been destined for Sevan House and the Dragonmaids' secret place. But why?

She looked to where the Dragonmaid Queen stood. "I don't know why Athan has called me here, but it appears He wants me to stay. I don't know what purpose I'm meant to serve, but until His will is made clear, I'll do whatever you wish to earn my way. And I'm a hard worker." She smiled at her friend. "Just ask Zagiri."

Lysanor didn't immediately respond. "It is all very strange, your coming here, especially considering from what and from whom you recently came," she finally replied, a tiny frown forming between her brows. "Still, none of that is your fault. Until Athan directs us otherwise, you are welcome to abide with us."

348

She glanced around the room. "I imagine these four walls are beginning to close in on you. Have you sufficient strength for a short walk?"

"Most certainly!" Danae grinned. "I'd love to see this place, and especially the dragons. I must confess to an enduring fascination with them."

Zagiri nodded. "I can vouch for that, m'lady. Danae has spoken several times of her desire to meet Dragonmaids and dragons alike."

"Then her wish will finally be fulfilled." Lysanor walked over and held out her hand. "Come then, Child. The dragons await."

Danae grasped her hand and, with every step they took through the small, simple dwelling to reach the outside, her heart beat ever faster. *What will these mythical creatures look like in close quarters?* she wondered. *Will they be ugly, fearsome beasts? Will they snarl and spit fire at me?* She had no way of knowing. In all her years in Gadiel, she had only seen them a time or two, flying far overhead.

It was bright and warm outside. After the shadowy coolness of the thick-walled house, the sudden light blinded her. The sun's heat, however, was a welcome boost to her spirits and her sore arm. The blood seemed to flow more effortlessly through her veins, and a burst of energy invigorated her.

She glanced around with avid interest. Surrounded on three sides by steep mountainous walls, a vast, grassy plain eased slowly down to a narrow, blue-green alpine lake. The base of the walls was dotted with countless cavelike openings. Four long, three-story buildings of familiar tan-mottled agarat stone formed a large square that Danae suspected was the Dragonmaids' living quarters. A short distance away stood a triple-spired building that was obviously a place of worship.

Several groves of trees stood in shady clumps around the buildings, before blending into a small forest extending almost to the back of the valley. Yet Danae also saw fields of grain, and ashtaraks and mouflon grazing in several large pastures. There were orchards, as well, of fruiting poma, pirit, and mala trees.

"You seem a very self-sufficient people," she said as they walked along.

"It was one of Blessed Metsamor's decrees," Lysanor replied, "that we not depend on others for support. And that, although our vocation is to devote our lives primarily to the singing of Athan's praises, we also work by the labor of our hands."

"What a wonderful calling—to sing Athan's praises all one's life."

"It is what first attracted the dragons to us long ago. They, too, love music and love to sing. Not that they sing in words, mind you," the older woman was quick to add. "But their voices, some bass, some baritone, some soprano, humming and crooning along in perfect harmony, add to the beauty of our praises. It is quite wonderful to hear."

"So that's how the Dragonmaids and dragons came together," Danae said. "I had always wondered how that came about, knowing that the dragons at one time lived in the outside world."

"As did the Dragonmaids. Our origins were the holy women of Sevan House. But when the persecution of the Faithful drove them into Sanctuary, thanks to Blessed Metsamor the dragons were already there, almost as if they had been waiting for the women. The music of the holy praises was but the first thing that drew the dragons to the women. Then, dragons and women alike began to help each other, and, over the course of many centuries, a special relationship grew that eventually transcended the physical realm. Both found love and acceptance and safety in the other."

"What a beautiful story. I greatly look forward to—" Danae stopped short as a faint sound caught her ears. It was low, mournful, and sounded . . . sounded almost as if someone were weeping.

Lysanor halted. "What troubles you, Danae?"

She frowned, puzzled. "I don't know. For a few seconds, I thought I heard someone crying." She shook her head. "Likely it was my imagination."

"Aye," the Dragonmaid Queen said, staring at her for a fleeting instant before resuming her forward progress, "likely it was."

Several young women passed by just then. They were garbed in short, white hooded robes, coming just to mid-thigh. Below the robes they wore black breeches and knee-high black leather boots.

"Those are some of our riders," Lysanor explained. "They have recently returned from a training flight."

A thrill coursed through Danae. "A training flight? I didn't know you trained your dragons." She laughed a bit self-consciously. "But then, there's very little I really *do* know about the Dragonmaids or the dragons."

"The training is primarily for the young ones—we call them dragonets. By age four, they have reached nearly their mature size and are strong enough for extended flight. It usually takes a good year of training before they are considered skilled enough to safely take outside the portal."

"You train them in the skies overhead then?"

"Aye. There are many maneuvers and wing formations to practice, and increasingly strenuous strengthening drills to keep the dragonets challenged for the first year. After that, for another year or two the dragonets fly in the vicinity of Mount Talin before they graduate to full dragon status. Frequently their riders are novices as well, which lengthens the training

351

process. However, if a novice rider is placed with an older, experienced dragon, the process can be greatly expedited."

"How exciting. Is it ever possible to watch them train? From down here, I—"

Once again the weeping came, this time stronger, as if it were closer by. Again, Danae halted and glanced around.

"What is it, Child?"

"The weeping." She looked to the Dragonmaid Queen. "I'm not imagining it this time. It's much louder now."

"And where would you say it is coming from?"

Danae looked around, listening. It wasn't coming from any of the buildings they had just passed, and there weren't any other women close enough to be crying that loudly . . . Her gaze settled on a long line of caves about fifty yards away.

She cocked her head. "I think the weeping's coming from over there." Danae pointed toward the caves.

"Indeed?" Lysanor looked at her with guarded interest now. "Then let's investigate, shall we?"

"Of course. Whoever it is, she sounds as if she's in terrible distress."

Her concern growing the nearer they came, Danae hurried behind the older woman until they drew up at the caves.

"Which cave?" Lysanor then asked. "I don't hear anything."

Danae thought it exceedingly strange the queen couldn't hear the heartrending sobs. They were so loud now they almost reverberated in her head. But perhaps Lysanor was hard of hearing. It seemed improbable in a woman of her age, but it was the only plausible explanation.

"There." Danae indicated an opening three caves down from where they were standing. "I think the weeping's coming from that one."

"Would you go in and see what you can do, while I fetch some help? Perhaps she is injured, or ill."

Danae hesitated. "I don't know what I could do. I'm a stranger. I might even frighten her."

"Nay, you won't do that. You have a kind heart. She will know that straightaway." Lysanor laid a hand on her arm. "Will you do it for her sake? She is so alone and confused."

Danae couldn't shake the feeling that everything wasn't quite what it seemed. Still, if there were any way she could help someone in need . . .

"Aye, I'll go and stay with her until you and the others return. It's the least I can do."

The Dragonmaid Queen smiled. "Good. I won't be long. I promise."

Lysanor headed back in the direction they had come. Danae hesitated again, as the sobs echoed loudly now in her head. Then, with a resolute set of her shoulders, she set out for the third cave.

It had a good-sized opening, at least fifteen feet high and nearly that wide. It was dark inside, though a dim light glowed far ahead. As Danae walked carefully along, keeping a hand on one wall, she slowly realized that a tunnel led off from the back of the first cave. A very wide and high tunnel.

The weeping was definitely coming from somewhere beyond the tunnel. Danae swallowed hard. The poor woman might well have stumbled in the dim light and hurt herself. And, as far back as she was inside the mountain, they would definitely need help getting her out.

The light began to grow brighter. Up ahead, Danae could see an enormous opening into what looked like yet another cave. Surely this was where the unfortunate woman wept.

"Hello?" she called. "I'm coming. Don't be afraid."

A low moan emanated from somewhere in the back of the cave. Danae quickened her pace, always keeping her hand on the surprisingly smooth tunnel wall. And then she entered yet another, even larger cave.

High-ceilinged, lit from within by sparkling, luminescent stones embedded in the walls, it was a beautiful, shimmering sanctuary. The floor, however, was surprisingly of sand. Warmth radiated from it. And the air, even so deep now within the mountain, smelled fresh and clean.

But where was the poor woman? She looked around, searching for her. Something moved in a darkened, far corner.

"Is that you?" Danae called, stepping out toward her. "If so, let me see you."

The weeping ceased. "Wh-what are you called?" a voice came in her head.

"Danae," she answered slowly. *How strange,* she thought, *that I seem to hear her in my head rather than with my ears.* "I'm a friend. Queen Lysanor sent me. What's your name?"

There was more movement from the far corner, and a rasping sound as if something hard was being scraped across the sand. A long nose with flared nostrils appeared first from the shadows, then a horned and crested head peered out with huge, heavy lidded eyes. The crystalline light glinted off thick scales, sending coruscating beams of brilliance everywhere. Yet, even with the distracting, flashing display, Danae could see this was a very large, mature golden dragon.

"My name's Celandine, and I'm so glad you found me," a low, mellifluous voice sounded in Danae's head.

This can't be happening, she thought. *I'm talking to a dragon.*

"Aye, you are," Celandine's voice came once more. "But not just any dragon, mind you. Only a very special friend can hear me in her mind. And that means I'm now *your* dragon, and we're fated to be forever friends."

354

23

Four weeks later, Ladon looked out on the ruin that was now Barakah and ground his teeth in frustration. His army lay encamped along the base of the Ibn Khaldun for miles in either direction, hugging as close to the afternoon-shaded base as the soldiers could manage. Some had pitched their tents down both sides of the Bahira River, taking shelter in the sparse growth of trees growing along the banks. Still, the heat was sweltering this close to the edge of the Haroun Desert, and men and Beast Men alike were already beginning to grumble.

It seemed everything that could go wrong had gone wrong. Unseasonably violent storms had struck halfway through the Valans, pelting them for five days running with heavy rain and even hail. After the second day, it had become too perilous to move the army, and they had made camp on the first reasonably level spot. Unfortunately, that decision came too late for the three companies of men responsible for the loads of lumber being carted along one particularly narrow mountain road.

A landslide had wiped out nearly five hundred men. Not that the loss of a few human lives was of any concern with an army this large. But most of the lumber designated for building barges to float the siege equipment and army down the Bahira River to Khaddar, had been lost as well. And *that* had put a definite halt to Ladon's painstakingly detailed plans.

Once the rains had finally stopped and another few days were added to allow the terrain to dry a bit for safe travel, the army had moved on. Ladon had to send almost a thousand men back through the Valans to find the closest stand of trees, though. As luck would have it, the next closest trees grew in the distant coastal range, and the trek back with new lumber had been hampered yet again by storms and subsequently slow travel.

And it wasn't as if this side of the mountains was a particularly fertile region. With each passing day, Ladon had to send his men out farther and farther into the Desert to pillage the few little towns that lay between them and the capital city for additional food and supplies. If they didn't get the barges built soon, they might as well forget the siege equipment and just march straight to Khaddar.

Thankfully, though, the barges would be finished in another few days. It would take a few days more to load the siege equipment and fasten it down, then they could finally move out. *Less than another week at the worst,* Ladon thought, *and we'll finally commence the final leg of the journey.* Odds were, before this new month was out, Khaddar would fall and the Diya al Din would be defeated.

He smiled grimly. It had taken three long years to subjugate Astara. Even including the trek through the Valans, the Desert would be his in under two months. And he'd wager the Dwarves and Elves would take even less time to subdue. If the Elves provided any resistance whatsoever, he'd just set fire to the entire Greenwald. And if the Dwarves got stubborn, he'd wall them up inside their vast caves until they starved to death.

Aye, this conquest was indeed proving easier and easier. He could almost taste the final victory, see himself being crowned King of Gadiel. Finally he would gain the respect and awe to which he had always been entitled. Very little, actually, had been all that difficult. He supposed he had Phaon to thank for that.

If only he could've convinced Danae to see things his way. Once, she had been so sweet and malleable, so eager to please, so loving. He had imagined her the perfect woman for him. But even before she had come to Gadiel, she had developed an overblown sense of conscience. And contact with some of these Athan-crazed Gadieleans had made it even worse.

If only Phaon could've gotten to her sooner . . .

The look on her face as he pushed her from the cliff haunted him still. It was a look of terror, entreaty, and disbelief. Yet that final expression of sorrowing pity had been the one that twisted his gut even now.

What irony that she, who was about to fall to her death, felt pity for him, who would soon be the conqueror of all Gadiel. It was enough to make him laugh.

But each time Ladon tried, he found he couldn't. Like some fish bone, the triumphant sounds caught in his throat. To his shame, he couldn't even bear to watch her fall and be crushed on the rocks below, couldn't savor the utter sweetness of the experience. On the contrary, just as soon as he had released Danae, Ladon had turned and walked away.

There were some things too unpalatable even for him to feed upon.

With Ra'id beside him, Vartan watched the motley army of Desert men and women practice cavalry charges across the large parade grounds on the north side of Khaddar's outer defenses. Though most were excellent riders, they couldn't seem to keep their ranks closed at a full run, and soon ended up entangling with the ranks behind them until it all became a huge, confused melee.

He shifted his gaze to the archery ranges. Though she would've vastly preferred a cavalry position, Sharifah—at both her father's and Ra'id's insistence—had been assigned to the far safer role of archer. Not that *any* duty would ultimately be safe, Vartan mused dourly, once Khaddar was overrun.

At least the bowmen hit the targets most of the time. Problem was, there were just not enough bows. No one in the long lines was getting sufficient practice time.

More bows and arrows were being fashioned as quickly as possible, but wood was scarce and it took time to find or buy it. But then, they were dismally short of *all* sorts of weapons and armor. In the past, the Diya al Din hadn't needed any armor for their swift, unexpected raids on their Desert neighbors. But this time swift, unexpected raids wouldn't work. The Desert warriors would wear down long before Ladon's better trained and more heavily armed men did.

"Ladon's barges are nearly ready," Ra'id muttered from beside Vartan. "My spies tell me they'll set off down the Bahira in another few days. Even if we had a sufficient number of soldiers, we're not ready. Not nearly ready."

"The Dwarves know how to fight, and they've the armor and weapons," Vartan said. "And the Elves are the best bowmen in Gadiel."

"Our couriers left five days ago. They should be just reaching the Dwarves' capital city, and probably on their way back from meeting with the Elf High Prince. And as far as the Rune Lords go, well, we won't hear anything for another two weeks, even with the use of a messenger hawk for the return reply." Ra'id shook his head. "If a miracle occurred and they decided to march posthaste, the odds are the Northland army still wouldn't reach us in time."

"They would if we held off Ladon for a couple of months. *If* the Rune Lords would even come."

Vartan withheld his true assessment of the situation, a situation which was dismal indeed. The Rune Lords had never, or at least in the recent history of the past five hundred years, left their frozen lands. In actuality, they rarely received Gadielean emissaries of any kind in a cordial manner. As to the Elves, Vartan's former father-in-law, Myrddin Ap Garnoc, hated him so deeply that he might even sacrifice the Diya al Din, refusing to come to their aid, just to get back at Vartan. The Dwarves were the only real possibility, and they weren't particularly fond of any of the rest of Gadiel's peoples.

"The Dragonmaids are the only ones who could arrive in time," Ra'id said, a thoughtful expression on his face. "Can you imagine what havoc they could wreak with those huge, fire-breathing dragons of theirs? One dragon would be the match of what? Five hundred or more men?"

Vartan chuckled. "That sounds a tad optimistic. Still, who knows what military value the dragons might hold? As far as I can tell, they've never been used in battle."

"It doesn't matter anyway. Holed up in that secret hideaway of theirs, the Dragonmaids will likely be the last ones to discover what's happening out here. And when they do, it'll be too late."

"Aye, it might well be." Vartan leaned on the outer wall and frowned. "Still, if only there was some way of getting a message to them. But no one knows where that portal is."

"Perhaps if we sent someone to Sevan House. He or she— actually, the chances would be much better if we sent a woman than a man—could hide and perhaps intercept a Dragonmaid and her dragon at just the right time, when they leave the portal."

"Perhaps." Vartan expelled a weary breath. "Let me think on that. We're trying all the other peoples. Nothing's lost trying the Dragonmaids, too."

"Nay, nothing's lost. Not in our situation." The Desert lord made a sound of disgust. "Look at the cavalry. Have you ever seen a more disorganized charge? I can't bear to watch any more. I'm going down to that parade field to see what I can do."

"Aye, do that, would you?" Vartan murmured, his thoughts already somewhere else.

From a distant place, he heard his friend stride away, his boots clicking on the glittering white agarat stone walkway. Vartan was already totally focused on the problem at hand. Though the subject of the Dragonmaids hadn't come up in the initial plans, Vartan knew he dared leave no possibility untried. Ra'id's suggestion to plant a spy near Sevan House, however, was likely doomed to failure. They needed, instead, someone who might know where the portal was and not only could enter it, but possessed sufficient influence with the Dragonmaids.

But whom would those women respect, listen to?

There was only one possibility: Amma Serpuhi.

A longing to go to her himself filled Vartan. At a time like this, when things looked so dire and desperate, he hungered for her wisdom and assurance that, in spite of everything, they, as Athan's faithful servants, would prevail. He longed, as well, for the peace of the Goreme, for just a brief respite from the worry and strain. Yet, almost more than anything else, Vartan hoped to find Danae there.

He didn't let himself think too much about her these days. He didn't dare, fearing the strength- and mind-sapping despair thoughts of her would stir. These days, he needed to devote all his faculties to the enormous task of preparing for war.

He couldn't be the one to go to Serpuhi. Not now. There was too much to be done here, and his presence was mandatory. He was a leader once more. A leader whose heart was beckoning elsewhere, while his head knew just as clearly where his true calling lay. His first duty was to Athan and Gadiel. His *heart's* calling must wait a time . . . and perhaps forever.

The rays of the sun, setting behind the Valans, stroked the land with red-gold light. Down below, Vartan watched Ra'id gallop from the city gates on his ebony steed, headed for the parade field. He sighed and shook his head. Though an hour of light might yet remain, there wasn't much more the Desert lord could do this day to improve the cavalry charges. There wasn't much *he* could do about sending out a courier to Amma Serpuhi either.

But the morrow was another day. In the meanwhile, he'd write Serpuhi a letter and choose the proper person to deliver it. His day was far from over. He had a long, long night ahead of him.

She had never realized hatred could burn so deeply or so totally fill one's life, permeating everything one thought and did. She had never known, because she had never hated someone as she hated Ladon. Indeed, more than five weeks since she had been banished forever from his presence, he filled her thoughts like he never had when she had been frequently summoned to attend him.

But then, before, Ankine hadn't carried his child within her, reminding her each and every day of what he had done—and why. And, as if the knowledge of what was yet to come wasn't punishment enough, the morning sickness and utter weariness were. There were days of late when sweaty and spent from gut-clenching bouts of vomiting, she couldn't drag herself from bed until well into the afternoon. And then there were other days when the despair grabbed her by the throat, all but strangling her.

Ankine wanted nothing more than to die. She hadn't realized until now what even the tiniest glimmer of hope could do to keep one going. But now she knew, for all hope was gone.

Yet still, Ladon had spoken truly. Though she hated herself almost as much as she hated him, she couldn't bring herself to hate—or kill—an innocent child. Even a child that was half his. Though the babe would never, ever, know its father— she would make certain of that—it would have a mother. It wouldn't be raised by strangers, as she had been, even if those strangers *had* been kind and loving.

Doubts nagged at her, though. What could she possibly offer this child? She was damaged beyond repair, a discarded piece of used goods, cast out onto the dung heap of life. Unfaithful friend, thief, betrayer of all that was fine and good, and now a husbandless mother. Even Athan had turned His face from her.

"It's never too late to return to the person you used to be . . ."

With a furious shake of her head, Ankine flung the memory of Vartan Karayan's words aside. He didn't understand. How could he? He was a man of honor and had almost died to uphold it. He hadn't ever fallen into immorality or broken vows, or done wicked things.

"None of us, no matter if we've always been His most faithful servant or not, deserves Athan's love . . . He loves us, and has loved us even before we were formed in our mother's womb . . ."

Listening to the prince that night out there on the Desert, she had almost believed him. She had wanted to. There was something in his eyes and his words that touched her. Touched her almost as if . . . as if she saw Athan—or Eisa—gazing at her, speaking to her, through him.

Saw and remembered how it once was for her. In the Goreme, warm and safe and sure in Athan's love.

But she had hurt so many people since then, broken so many of Athan's sacred commands. Ankine wasn't even certain she knew how to turn back, to change. And her pride was yet a mighty, unwieldy stumbling block. Even Ladon couldn't beat or shame it out of her. On the contrary, she clung to it more fiercely now than she ever had. It was all she had left.

"We're a lot alike in that respect . . ."

The vestiges of a smile tugged at her mouth. Aye, she could well imagine Vartan Karayan had once been proud. He was Crown Prince of Astara and, in many ways, the ruler in all but name. He was handsome, clever, and by all accounts, the greatest warrior Astara had ever seen. He had a lot to be proud of.

There had been more in his words, though, than just an admission of his own prideful failings. There was an unspoken understanding of the pain it caused and the effort it took to overcome it. And there was acceptance. Absolute, nonjudgmental, loving acceptance.

Had he been offering sanctuary as well as assurance of Athan's love? It had seemed so. Yet perhaps it wasn't the best time now—or the wisest thing—to go to him, cast her lot with his. Odds were he, and whatever army he might be able to raise, would soon be slaughtered by Ladon's far larger one. Perhaps it was best just to stay here, hidden away in her little hut in this out-of-the-way forest, and let things happen as they would.

Still, if there were some way she could aid the prince in his war against Ladon . . . Besides her ring and its powers, she could read and interpret most ancient scripts. She could compel others to obey her. Any of those abilities might be of use to Vartan Karayan.

Aye, Ankine thought, she still had special talents, talents that could be utilized against Ladon. And she had nothing to lose. Either Vartan would take her in, or he wouldn't. If he did, she would offer him all the loyalty and devotion she once had given Phaon.

She indeed had nothing to lose. And revenge against Ladon would be sweet. So very, very sweet.

c℘ ℘っ

With a weary sigh, Vartan rolled up the letter to Serpuhi, sealed it with wax, and slid it into a stiff, leather cylinder for protection. He sealed the lid with additional wax and affixed the royal seal of Khaddar to it with the signet ring Prince Kamal had given him. Then he laid it aside and leaned back in his chair.

All was now in readiness. The messenger had been chosen and would ride out toward the Valans at first light, taking a more northerly route to avoid Ladon's army. Once well into the Ibn Khaldun, however, she would turn south and head for the Goreme Valley. The detour would add several days to the journey, but was necessary. Any hope of reaching the Dragonmaids of Mount Talin would be lost if their messenger were captured by Ladon's army.

Perhaps he shouldn't have, but he had included a brief paragraph at the end of the letter, inquiring about Danae and asking Serpuhi to convey his love to her. It was far less than Vartan really wanted to say, but this wasn't the time, or the proper medium to say all he truly felt. For now, it was the best he could do. Later, when and if they finally reunited, he would pour out his heart to her.

He looked to his bed. It was past time he take his rest. The morrow would, as had all the days of late, be long and arduous. After the heat of the day, however, the room was stuffy and warm, and he wasn't exhausted enough as yet to ignore it. A walk outside in the cooler night air might help, though.

Vartan rose, left the room, and was soon striding down one of the long palace corridors. So much had changed in his life of late. From the first meeting with the Hakeem, he had been warmly welcomed and well treated, dressed in finely woven robes, dined on the most exotic of delicacies, and housed in the best of the guest rooms. His every need was seen to by servants. He couldn't have asked for more if he had been back in Astara, reigning now as its king.

It was a life so very familiar yet, at the same time, now felt surprisingly ill-fitting. Or perhaps, Vartan mused as he walked along, not precisely ill-fitting, for he well knew this kind of life and was trained for it, but lacking. Only Athan could truly satisfy him now. Athan, and the presence of the woman he loved.

Still, he had so much more now than he ever had before, Vartan admitted as he passed through an open doorway onto a long, high balcony overlooking the city. He had the knowledge and love of Athan. Everything he did and hoped for had a deeper, more spiritual purpose. He strove now not just for the present moment for Gadiel and its peoples, but for its future.

Hereafter, whatever came of his efforts, they were special and blessed because he made them for Athan, not just for himself. In this time of danger and dire consequences, there was yet some comfort and peace to be found in that.

The night breeze was pleasant, cooling his skin through his lightweight, sweat-dampened *thobe*. Vartan walked to the balcony railing, leaned on it, and closed his eyes, savoring the gentle wind's caress. Below, out on the Desert, the twelve tribes' campfires burned, reminding him of a night not all that long ago, a night he had imagined was the last one of his life.

He might well experience that sort of night again. Ladon would definitely see to that, if he could. But this time, there would be no Danae to comfort him, or understand. This time, if it came to that, he'd go it—

A sense he was no longer alone filled him. Vartan straightened and turned. There, not more then five feet away, stood Ankine. Behind her glowed the dim outline of her portal.

"You're getting to be a regular visitor," he said with a crooked smile. "On another errand for Ladon, are you?"

Her eyes glittered, hard and frosty, in the moonlight. "I'll never serve him or Phaon again," she muttered. "I come tonight of my own accord."

"Then I welcome you, lady, and ask how I may serve you."

Ankine's lovely mouth quirked. "Rather, it's I who offer you *my* services, if you'll have them. In return, I ask only for your protection. My needs are few, though I suppose it's only fair to warn you that I'm with child. In time, there'll be two mouths to feed instead of one."

Vartan studied her. In charity, he knew he should take her in. But dare he trust her? She had made no mention of Athan, or told him the reason she had left Ladon. Or had she?

"Your child. Is Ladon perhaps its father?"

She glanced away for a moment, then met his gaze. "Aye, but you needn't worry he'll ever come for me or his child. The conception was my punishment for failing him."

He didn't need to ask how she had failed Ladon. He already knew.

"But why do you now come to me?" Vartan asked. "Considering the current state of things, my protection might not last very long."

"Perhaps not." Ankine smiled thinly. "Still, I'd rather end my days striving to destroy Ladon than hiding away and waiting things out. It may come too late, but I'd like to try and make retribution for some of the harm I've done."

"And what of Athan? Does He enter into this anywhere?"

Her smile faded. "I don't know. Your words, the last time we met, gave me hope . . ." She shook her head. "But I've done so much that's evil, hurt so many people . . ."

Aye, he thought, people like Serpuhi in particular. A sudden inspiration came to him. Ankine could never truly accept Athan's forgiveness until she forgave herself. And she would never forgive herself until she asked and received Serpuhi's forgiveness.

"If you will, I need you to do something for me."

Her eyes widened, and Vartan saw hope flare.

"Anything. I'll do anything as long as it isn't evil. Whether I ever find my way back to Athan or not, I'll not do anything wicked ever again."

"Is the use of that portal in itself evil?"

She looked puzzled, but shook her head. "Nay. Indeed, before I stole the portal ring, it was always used for good."

"Then I want you to use it to take a letter to someone. It's of vital importance that it reach this person as soon as possible. Will you do it?"

"Aye. Of course I will, and gladly. Where do you wish for me to deliver the letter, and to whom?"

"It needs to go to the Goreme Valley," Vartan said, steeling himself to the look of horror that exploded in Ankine's eyes. "It needs to be delivered to Amma Serpuhi."

She stood there overlooking the Goreme, her heart thundering in her breast. Memories swamped her, drowning her in a floodtide of longing and regret. But the bitterest, most painful realization was that she could no longer enter. She was no longer, and would never again, be pure.

More than anything she had ever wanted, Ankine wanted to turn and walk away before Serpuhi knew she was here. Vartan would have no way of knowing if her mission was successful or not. She could tell him she had delivered the letter and then left. That Serpuhi had refused to speak with or forgive her.

He would have to believe that. *She* believed that was what would happen. But she had also told him she would never do anything wicked again. Even if Serpuhi chose to ignore her summons, Ankine knew she had to try. Whatever Vartan ultimately believed, she would at least have told the truth.

Closing her eyes, Ankine sucked in a deep breath, then mentally sought out Serpuhi. She knew she had found her when a soft, gentle presence seeped into her mind. Happiness filled her. If even for a brief moment more in her life, she would touch and savor the goodness of her foster mother.

Not for my sake, Amma, do I call to you, she silently said. *It's for Vartan. Will you come, meet me at the entrance to the Goreme?*

Aye, Child, her old mentor replied. *I'll come.*

Each minute that passed, as Ankine awaited Serpuhi's arrival, was more excruciating than the last. She deserved whatever Serpuhi would say. She had more than earned the anger, the disgust, the rejection she would surely see in Serpuhi's eyes. She just didn't know if she could survive the pain and shame.

And then the old *amma* was there, hurrying up the steep path leading out of the Goreme, eagerness and joy in her eyes. For a confused instant, Ankine almost turned to see who behind her caused Serpuhi such excitement. But she knew no one was there.

And then Serpuhi held out her arms. "Oh, my Child," she cried. "Come to me. Come!"

Tears flooded Ankine's eyes. She stumbled forward, almost falling into the old woman's arms.

"*Amma* . . . mother," she sobbed. "Forgive me. Oh, forgive me!"

"Aye, Child. Aye," Serpuhi crooned, holding her close. "I long ago gave that over to Athan. Long, long ago."

Cradled in strong, loving arms, Ankine wept for a long while. Finally, though, her tears ceased. She looked up and, as she had when she had looked into Vartan's eyes that night, saw Athan mirrored there. Ankine smiled.

"He has forgiven me as well, hasn't He?" she asked in wonderment.

"Aye, He has. Long, long ago."

24

"I think you're ready to fly solo today," Olwyn said as she and Danae headed to the open practice area to join their dragons. "When it comes to maneuvers, you're a surprisingly quick study. Almost as quick as you are in your spiritual studies, or so I've been told. And, for only practicing flight for a month, you and your dragon already have such a strong, instinctive rapport . . ."

The older Dragonmaid shook her head in amazement. "Still, you mustn't fall prey to overconfidence or ask your dragon to do more than you're ready for. She'll do anything to please you, even if it's foolish or dangerous. Absolutely anything."

"So the rider, for the sake of both, must always exercise sound judgment and extreme caution, is that it?" Danae asked.

Her teacher nodded. "Aye. Always, and in every circumstance, be it routine or in time of battle."

Danae frowned in puzzlement. "Battle? And when have the Dragonmaids ever gone to battle?"

"They haven't. Still, we train in case the day ever comes . . ."

"Comes for what?"

"Comes when we have to defend Sanctuary." Olwyn shot her a grim look. "Phaon has tried before to breach our portal. He'll surely try again someday."

"I didn't realize . . ." A sudden thought struck Danae. "And what of the rest of Gadiel? Would you ever fly the dragons to defend it from Phaon and his minions?"

"That would be up to Lysanor. If you want my opinion, though, nay, we'd never risk the dragons for the sake of Gadiel. It was the citizens of Gadiel, after all, who tried all those hundreds of years ago to hunt down and kill all the dragons. They saw a threat where there never was one—the dragons have always been peaceful, solitary creatures—but because they didn't understand them, they feared and sought to destroy them. As they tried to do to the Faithful, 'they' being especially the Astarians."

She gave a snort of disdain. "It's why we've never involved ourselves in the ever-changing politics of the outside. They've all proven over and over that none of them can be trusted."

"But things are different now," Danae began. "Times—and leaders—have changed—"

"Well, all that doesn't really concern us now, does it?" Olwyn drew up before Celandine and her own dragon, who until their arrival had been dozing together in the warm sun. The big female was a deep, striking bronze that complimented Celandine's rich gold.

Up until today, Danae had only flown with Olwyn on Celandine, initially in the second seat behind her instructor. After experiencing that first flight, she went up again and again in the second seat to learn by heart all the standard maneuvers: right and left turns, and right and left climbs, and dives. That accomplished, she moved into the primary seat, with Olwyn along only to advise and fine tune. From here on out, though, she thought with a shiver of excitement, she'd be riding Celandine alone, with Olwyn flying nearby on her own dragon.

It had been just a month ago that she had bonded with Celandine, there in that deep, second cave. That very eve, Lysanor asked her if she wished to begin training to become a Dragonmaid. Still in a joyous haze from the intensity of her recent bonding, and feeling as if she had found her life's true calling, Danae immediately agreed and donned the simple black tunic, boots, and breeches of a Dragonmaid candidate. She would remain a candidate, she was informed, for six months. Then, if deemed worthy to continue, she would next progress to Dragonmaid novice for another two years before making solemn, lifelong vows.

Not that there was any worry of her fitness, Celandine had smugly informed her. A dragon knew straight off who was worthy and who wasn't. Celandine wouldn't have bonded with her otherwise.

Still, Danae couldn't believe the whirlwind of activity and learning that had commenced since then. She couldn't believe her rapid progress, either. Though an experienced dragon was an invaluable aid to a novice rider, Danae knew she had moved through the initial Dragonmaid training far faster than most. It was almost as if she had always been meant to be a Dragonmaid, as if some nameless Dragonmaid ancestors had passed along the talents that seemed to come now with such ease.

Celandine's soft, melodious voice pierced Danae's thoughts. *Are you glad finally to be riding me all alone?*

Danae smiled as her dragon finally lifted her head and blinked her large, luminous green eyes. *You know I am. It'll just be you and me now, alone, high up on those air currents. I just want to do well, and not disappoint either you or Olwyn.*

You'll do fine, came her dragon's gentle assurance. *We won't let each other down. Not ever.*

There was an undertone of pensive hopefulness in Celandine's voice. Compassion for the still sorrowful dragon filled Danae. Celandine's former Dragonmaid rider had died but a week before Danae arrived in Sanctuary, falling to her death while flying observation over Ladon's army. A horrendous rainstorm had blown in, sending vicious bursts of sudden wind hurling through the mountains. One such hard gust had unexpectedly slammed Celandine against a high mountainside, unseating her rider. Momentarily stunned, the dragon hadn't reacted swiftly enough to dive after her rider, and the woman had broken her back striking a jagged outcropping of rock before Celandine could reach her.

It was all the grief-stricken dragon could do to carry her rider, tenderly clasped in her huge foreclaws, back to Sanctuary before collapsing. After the burial rituals were complete, she had crawled into her inner cave and refused to come out, until Danae had found her several days later. One of the first things Olwyn had told Danae, once she had been assigned as her instructor, was that her arrival had surely saved the dragon's life. Bonds between dragon and Dragonmaid, after all, weren't only for life. If one died before the other, the ensuing shock of that bond severance often killed the survivor as well. In very rare cases, that tragedy could be averted by the timely arrival of a second bonding candidate, who must so closely match the bereft one in mind and heart that a new bond could be formed. Such had been the case with Danae and Celandine.

Such a revelation wasn't one of the more comforting aspects of her initial education, but Lysanor demanded Danae hear it before accepting Celandine's offer of a bond. Not that the dragon would be dying of old age anytime soon. Celandine was only fifty years old, and female dragons had been known to live up to five hundred years, while the males could survive even longer.

Luckily for the dragons, life in Sanctuary extended the Dragonmaids' life span equally as long, unless they died by accident or from some devastating injury. Anything else could usually be handled by the strange, bitter concoction Danae had had to drink when she had first arrived. It was an amazing and, for Danae, bone-healing mixture whose primary ingredient, she later learned, was an oil secreted by young dragonets which had miraculous healing properties.

There are so many wondrous things yet to be learned, Danae thought as she used Celandine's huge foreleg and a knotted climbing strap that hung from the riding saddle to clamber up onto the dragon's back. Once she was snugly ensconced in the sculpted front of the two-person saddle, Danae pulled up the hood of her candidate's black tunic and slid the leather flying goggles over it, effectively anchoring the hood in place.

The black tunic and hood, as well as the breeches worn for flying, were made of a tightly woven mouflon cloth that kept out the cold air one frequently encountered when high aloft. On the days when there were no flights either for training or observation, Dragonmaid riders wore much the same garb as Lysanor and the nonriders, save instead of a black veil, their white robes were fitted with hoods. Hair was either kept short or was braided and wrapped in a tight bun at the nape of the neck.

In addition to the white hooded tunic, boots, and breeches of vowed Dragonmaid riders, Flight and Wing leaders also bore colorful braided bands encircling their right sleeves. Blue and red denoted leaders of the smaller, fifteen-dragon Flights. First Flight Leader wore an additional blue and red crest sewn on the center of the circular braid. Second Flight Leader, who assumed command of the flight if anything should happen to the First Flight Leader, wore the plain blue and red circular braid.

Wing leaders, who commanded four Flights, were designated by blue and yellow braids. There were ten Wings total, made up of four Flights each, so conceivably up to six hundred dragons and riders could be flying in formation at one time. Lysanor was both Dragonmaid Queen and Wing Commander, and she or her designee wore the blue and yellow braid topped with a red and blue crest.

Surprisingly, only female dragons flew in the Flights and Wings. Larger and stronger than their male counterparts, females possessed sufficient stamina to sustain the occasionally extended time in the air. They were also the only ones capable of breathing fire. Males, for that reason, were relegated to short training flights within the confines of Sanctuary with maturing dragonets and novice Dragonmaid riders, and, of course, the quinquennial mating flights.

Are you ready? Celandine's voice came just then.

Excitement thrummed through Danae. *Aye.* As she had been taught, she used her legs to signal takeoff consent.

With a swift crouch, Celandine used her strong hind legs to fling herself aloft. Danae experienced a hard, upward jolt, then a rapid beat of huge, leathery wings. The ground fell from beneath her, and wind rushed over her face. Exhilaration filled her. They were flying!

It didn't take Celandine long to find a thermal air current and begin a slow, leisurely glide in the skies above Sanctuary. For a time, Danae just savored the exquisite sensation of flight, of being one with a massive beast as they soared high overhead.

Somehow, the sky looked bluer, the clouds whiter up here, the grass a velvety green, the alpine waters of Lake Kundry an even deeper, more intense turquoise blue. Sunlight glinted off Celandine's golden scales, sending sparkling bursts of brilliance everywhere.

Happiness flooded Danae. This felt so right, so good. She was so blessed to have come to this place, to have found Celandine.

A low, melodious humming insinuated itself into her mind. It was Celandine, Danae realized, mirroring her own joy and sense of satisfaction. She smiled. To be understood before one said a single word, to be accepted and loved without conditions, surely this was but a foretaste of Paradise and the full revelation of Athan that was to come. Yet, in her special friendship with Celandine, she was privileged to experience a glimpse, however nominal it might be, now in this life. She would always, always, be grateful to Athan for this singular and most unexpected gift.

Olwyn's signaling you, the dragon said. *I think she wants to begin the training maneuvers.*

Danae glanced to her right. The other rider was indeed indicating Danae should move into the structured ritual of turns, climbs, and dives. She nodded her agreement. Then, with a nudge of her right knee, she sent Celandine swerving off to the left.

☙ ❧

An hour later, Olwyn indicated the training flight was over. Reluctantly, Danae complied. Even after upward of twenty flights in the past month, she experienced the same excitement and soaring sense of freedom each time, and always found the flights far too short for her tastes. Celandine, however, was still recovering from the terrible emotional and physical toll of losing her first rider, and needed careful conditioning to bring her back to full flying stamina.

Danae and Olwyn spent an hour on the ground washing down their dragons, feeding them a measured amount of grain, berries, and small aquatic animals to keep them in flying trim, and cleaning and oiling the saddles. Then they returned their equipment and feed tubs to the storeroom and headed back to the refectory for a cool drink and a snack. They had barely sat down, however, when one of the young kitchen apprentices dashed in and, in her excitement, broke the customary silence observed in the refectory.

"The *Amma*'s here!" the thirteen-year-old cried. "Lady Lysanor's heading down to the portal even now to welcome her!"

Danae looked to Olwyn. The older Dragonmaid grabbed the girl as she rushed by.

"Which *amma*?"

"Why, Amma Serpuhi, of course." Blue eyes in a freckled face gazed back at her with an expression of incredulity.

Olwyn released her and, turning to Danae, rolled her eyes. "Who else, of course?"

"Serpuhi's a dear friend of mine." Danae pushed back her chair and rose. "By your leave, I'd like to go and greet her."

"Suit yourself. Likely you won't get within ten feet of her, though. Everyone's a dear friend of hers."

Danae grinned. "That's fine, too. I'll be content just to catch a glimpse of her for now."

She left Olwyn pouring a glass of chilled poma juice and popping chunks of mala fruit into her mouth. It didn't take long to figure out where Serpuhi was. The ever growing crowd of Dragonmaids near the portal entry was a more than adequate indicator.

As Danae drew up at the back of the crowd, Zagiri caught sight of her. She waved to Danae, indicating she should join her. That was easier requested than done. Zagiri was standing at the front of the crowd, directly behind the Dragonmaid Queen near the portal. Thankfully, no one seemed to mind as Danae moved toward Zagiri.

Finally, Danae reached her friend. "Isn't it wonderful to see Serpuhi again?" she asked. "I can't wait to greet her."

"Well, that might be a time in coming," Vartan's sister replied with a wry smile. "I'm afraid her visit isn't for social reasons."

Danae looked to where Lysanor stood a short distance apart from them, talking to Serpuhi. Both women's expressions were serious. Fear stabbed through Danae. For some inexplicable reason, she knew their discussion had to do with Vartan.

At that moment, Serpuhi lifted her gaze and scanned the crowd. Their glances met. The old *amma* smiled, then looked back to Lysanor and said a few more words. The Dragonmaid Queen glanced over her shoulder, searching now until her own gaze alighted on Danae and Zagiri.

She frowned, but immediately motioned them to come forward. The two women looked at each other, then hurried over.

Both bowed before Lysanor and Serpuhi. Though the Dragonmaid Queen said nothing, their old friend laughed and, taking them by the hand, pulled them forward into the embrace of her arms.

"Ah, but it has been so long since last I saw you," Serpuhi said. "I know it's just a bit over two months, but it seems like a year." She leaned back and eyed them closely. "Well, neither of you seems too worse for the wear. And now both of you are with the Dragonmaids, and Danae looks like she's training to be a rider."

Until this moment, Danae hadn't realized how much she had missed Serpuhi, a woman who had become almost like a mother to her. She nodded, grinning all the while.

"Aye, I started the training a month ago, and I have my own dragon—I love it, Serpuhi. I love it!"

Something flickered in the old woman's eyes, some memory or consideration perhaps, then it was gone. Serpuhi released them and stepped back. She looked to Lysanor, who stood beside her.

"I would like Danae and Zagiri to be present when we speak of my reason for coming here. It concerns them, as well."

The Dragonmaid Queen arched a dark brow. "Indeed? And would you require an immediate meeting, or would you care first to have something to eat and drink, then rest for a while?"

"I would prefer to meet now. Time is of the essence." Amma Serpuhi looked around. "Somewhere private, if you please."

"As you wish." Lysanor indicated the building of worship. "There is a room beneath the high altar that would suit. Come along, then."

The crowd parted before them. A feeling of unease pricked at Danae as they walked along, but she doggedly sought to calm the frantic beat of her heart and rising sense of fear. *Just let Vartan be alive and well,* she prayed. *I ask for nothing else, Eternal One. Nothing, at least, for myself.*

It didn't take Serpuhi long to address the issue at hand. As soon as they were all seated around a long turkawood table, she began. "Even as we speak, Ladon is preparing to send his army down the Bahira to Khaddar. The Diya al Din are outnumbered over five to one. They need help."

Danae leaned forward, hiding her sudden eagerness with difficulty. "Is Vartan with them, leading them?"

Serpuhi riveted her gaze on her. "Aye, Child. He leads them."

"And what is it to us," Lysanor asked frostily, "if Vartan Karayan leads them or not? What does this war matter to the Dragonmaids, any more than all the rest have over the centuries? You well know our policy, Serpuhi, when it comes to involving ourselves in the affairs of the outside—which, of course, is not at all."

"It matters, Esteemed Lady," the old *amma* replied, turning back to the Dragonmaid Queen, "because this war is not like all the wars of the past. This war pits Phaon and his minions against us all. This war is for Gadiel's heart and soul."

Lysanor sighed. "With all due respect, Serpuhi, aren't you exaggerating a bit? Ladon is a Hylean with aspirations of grandeur, to be sure. He covets a kingdom of his own as proof he is worthy of the royal blood that runs in his veins, however illegitimate it may be. But a foreigner attempting to seize the lands of another country is hardly unusual. It happens all the time. And what does Phaon have to do with it? For the most part, Gadiel has long been a godless country. Phaon doesn't need to fight a war to win it. He can have Gadiel anytime he wants it."

"Even a small group of the Faithful can hold Gadiel against Phaon, and well you know it, Lysanor." Something akin to anger sparkled in Serpuhi's eyes. "But only if they stand together. Only if they follow the Guardian."

"Aye, and when the Guardian comes, I'll be the first to follow him. But it isn't Vartan Karayan. It can't be."

Danae had held her tongue for as long as she could. "And why do you say that, m'lady?" she asked softly. "Why *can't* it be Vartan?"

"Aye," Zagiri added her own demand, "why can't it be my brother?"

The Dragonmaid Queen looked to Serpuhi and, for a long moment, their gazes locked. Understanding arced between them. The old *amma's* eyes darkened with compassion.

"Tell them, Lysanor," Serpuhi said. "It's past time you lance that festering wound."

After a time spent staring down at her hands, the other woman began. "I wasn't always called Lysanor," she said as her troubled glance met Danae's. "That was the name I chose when I took my life vows as a Dragonmaid. You will also have such a choice the day you take your vows. I was born Arwydd Ap Garnoc. I am the eldest daughter of Myrddin, High King of the Elves of Greenwald." As she spoke, she slid the veil off her head, revealing her delicately elongated Elvish ears. "I have three brothers, and Aelwyd was my only sister."

Beside her, Danae heard Zagiri gasp. Her own gut clenched as she grasped the significance of Lysanor's revelation. Now she finally knew why, when she had first met the woman, she had sensed something familiar about her. She had seen Aelwyd's resemblance in Queen Lysanor and had not realized it.

"I served Aelwyd for the last three years of her life," Danae said. "She was my friend."

"Aye, though I never spoke of it to you, I soon learned of your connection with my sister. And, because you did know Aelwyd, you must also know how terribly she must have suffered in the end." A bleak, haunted look filled the Dragonmaid Queen's eyes. "My sweet, beautiful little sister . . ."

Zagiri made an anguished sound.

"Vartan loved her, m'lady." As Danae spoke, she reached over and took Zagiri's hand, squeezing it. "Loved her to the end."

"Nay." With a savageness that was startling, Lysanor shook her head. "It wasn't love that took her from us. It was selfishness and pride. Our father warned him what would happen, but Vartan didn't care. He wanted Aelwyd, and that was all that mattered. It's all that has ever mattered to him—getting what he wants!"

"That's not true! Vartan's good, honorable—"

"He has changed, Lysanor," Serpuhi chose that moment to interrupt, sending Danae a steady, quelling look. "He has gone through myriad trials and testings. He has been brought low, suffered greatly, and come to renounce his former life and turn to the Path of the Faithful. And Athan has blessed him, named him Guardian of Gadiel."

"It's not possible!" Lysanor cried in anguish. "How can you know this with such certainty? How!"

"I know this because I was his teacher," was Serpuhi's simple reply. "I saw into his soul, and found it worthy."

Tears flooded the Dragonmaid Queen's eyes, and, deep within them, Danae saw the battle being waged. Unresolved grief and a thirst for justice warred mightily with the realization that Serpuhi truly believed what she was claiming, warred with the deep respect and love she so evidently bore for the older woman. Lysanor, for all her exalted status and ideals, Danae realized, was also a flesh-and-blood woman like the rest of them. A flesh-and-blood woman who struggled still with forgiveness and loss.

And then something slid down over her eyes, something dark and heavy, shuttering their expression. Lysanor's mouth went taut with determination.

"More than just my desires are caught up in this," she said. "Even if my decision *were* based solely on my conviction that Vartan Karayan is a changed man, a man worthy of allegiance and support, it must also be made with the welfare of the Dragonmaïds and dragons in mind. And tradition holds that we don't involve ourselves in the petty squabbling and self-serving gambits of those outside Sanctuary. It has served us well for centuries. I can't—and won't—break with tradition now."

Listening to Lysanor all but pronounce Vartan's and the Diya al Din's death sentence, something within Danae snapped. She leaped to her feet. Leaning forward, she placed both hands flat on the table top and glared at the Dragonmaid Queen.

"And I say you're letting your hatred for Vartan cloud your judgment, m'lady!" Despite her best efforts to contain it, Danae's voice vibrated with emotion. "You're protecting nothing—absolutely nothing—in hiding behind a false screen of tradition. Phaon might spare you and Sanctuary for a time more, while he sets Ladon against the rest of Gadiel, but sooner or later he'll come for you. Tradition won't save you then. Not when you're all alone and there's no one left to ride to *your* aid."

The Dragonmaid Queen's face reddened. "We will never be alone. We will always have Athan. Always."

"Aye, but will He hear you when you call? Or will He instead cast you off forever because, in forsaking your brothers and sisters, you just as surely forsook Him?"

"How dare you speak to me thusly?" Her face gone white, Lysanor shoved unsteadily to her feet. "You, who have so recently asked leave to remain with us, become one of us. Leave me now, before I banish you forever!"

At her words, a sharp pain lanced through Danae. A voice whispered in her mind, desperate, pleading. *Don't, dear friend,* she heard Celandine cry. *Don't leave me! Please . . .*

Danae's heart twisted. An iron band seemed to constrict her chest. A vivid image of Celandine writhing in agony, dying, filled her mind. Gentle, adoring Celandine . . .

All the fight and righteous anger drained from her in one debilitating rush. How could she leave Celandine? She loved her.

Danae lowered her head, expelled an anguished breath. "I beg forgiveness, m'lady. I had no right—"

"You had *every* right, Child," Serpuhi cut her off, her usual soft voice now stern and bluntly forthright. "And you only spoke the truth."

Danae lifted her head and sent her old friend an astonished look.

"But, truth that it was," Serpuhi added, "your presence—and that of Zagiri as well—is no longer required. This is now a matter between Lysanor and me. Leave us, if you will."

After that, there was nothing more to be said. Danae bowed first to Lysanor, then to Serpuhi. Then, Zagiri at her side, she walked from the room.

25

Three days after she had departed Khaddar to go to Serpuhi, Ankine stepped back through the portal in a secluded spot in the palace gardens. For the time being at least, Vartan had requested she use the ring as discreetly as possible so as not to unsettle the city residents, and she had done so. Her assessment that the Diya al Din would ever accept her or her powers, however, was far less hopeful than Vartan's.

Still, there's no point dwelling on future possibilities, Ankine thought as she set out to find Vartan. Living each day as it came was challenge enough. Challenge *and* gift, now that she was once more safe and secure in Athan's love.

She finally found him in the library, poring over a huge map of Gadiel with Ra'id. Though Vartan's face brightened when she was announced and strode into the room, suspicion and hostility immediately glittered in Ra'id's eyes. She steeled herself against the barely contained animosity emanating from him, and walked around him to stand on Vartan's other side.

"Welcome back, Ankine," Vartan said, turning to her. "Was your trip to the Goreme profitable?"

"Aye, for me, it most certainly was." She smiled. "Serpuhi and I are reconciled. And Serpuhi was most happy to convey your message to the Dragonmaids." Ankine's smile faded. "Unfortunately, their queen was unwilling to ally with you. According to Serpuhi, Queen Lysanor's your late wife's sister. She also said you'd understand."

A bleak expression flattened Vartan's gaze. "Aye, I understand. It explains a lot." He went silent for a long moment. "Did Serpuhi have anything to say about the rest of my letter to her?" he asked at last. "About Danae, I mean?"

"Only that Danae is not in the Goreme."

More than anything, Ankine wanted to tell him where Danae actually was, but Serpuhi had asked her not to. It had been Danae's express wish that Vartan not know she was with the Dragonmaids. Her former life was over and done, she had told Serpuhi. She was now committed to the Dragonmaids and her dragon. Nothing was served looking back. Nothing was served for her, or for Vartan.

On his other side, Ankine heard Ra'id softly curse.

"What if Ladon has her?" he asked, shooting Vartan a furious look. "By the Blessed Waters, if Ladon has Danae, I'll never forgive you!"

"Well, join the line then," Vartan muttered, his own voice going taut with anger. "I thought it was bad enough that the Elves hate me, but now to discover I'm equally loathed by the Dragonmaids . . ." He paused, drew in a deep breath, then shook his head. "There are times when I think Athan made a grave mistake in choosing me to lead Gadiel against Ladon. Or else, *I've* made a grave mistake in imagining that He *did* choose me."

"So, you've heard back from the Elves, have you?" Ankine asked.

"Aye, and the Dwarves as well. Both have also refused our call for aid."

Concern for him filled her. "What will you do?"

"We were just discussing our options when you arrived." Vartan made a motion toward the map. "Trying to devise all sorts of delaying actions to keep Ladon from Khaddar until the Rune Lords arrive. If they do."

"This talk of war is nothing, I'm sure, that would interest her," Ra'id said, his teeth gritted. He leaned out past Vartan and leveled a frosty gaze on her. "If you've said all you've come to say, please leave us now."

Heat warmed Ankine's cheeks. She knew she had well earned the Desert lord's and his people's distrust, but it still hurt. There wasn't much she could do, though, but bear it meekly and in silence.

"By your leave, m'lord," she said, looking to Vartan, "if you've no further need of me . . ."

A compassionate understanding burned in his eyes. "Our past failings come back time and again to torment us, don't they? Somehow, though, we must find the courage to fight on. Athan, after all, gives us difficulties to make us strong."

She smiled up at him. "Then He intends to make us both very strong, doesn't He?"

"Aye. We'll need it for the hard times ahead, I'm afraid."

Gladness filled her. Even in the darkest days, Athan had been there for her, guiding her to yet another chance at salvation. And only Athan would choose a man she had tried mightily to lead to destruction as His instrument. Who would've guessed, that first time she had encountered him in that cave in the Valans, that Vartan Karayan would be such a gift to her?

"I'll take my leave then, m'lord." With that, Ankine bowed, turned, and walked from the room.

Vartan waited until Ankine had shut the door behind her, then turned back to Ra'id. "When it comes to the fabled

Desert hospitality, yours was sorely lacking with Ankine, my friend."

"Was it now?" Ra'id gave a snort of disgust. "Well, times are dire, and I don't care for one of Ladon's sorceresses so close or being asked to convey messages for us. How can you be certain exactly where she went on that little trip of hers? Perhaps the woman never delivered that message to Serpuhi at all, or perhaps, even worse, she visited Ladon to give him a full report on the dismal state of our situation. Did that possibility ever cross your mind?"

He had suspected this was at least part of Ra'id's hostility toward Ankine. Mistrust. And Vartan couldn't blame him. Ra'id didn't know her. Indeed, *he* hardly knew the woman himself. But there was still something about her . . . something he had seen in her eyes, heard in her voice and words, that filled him with confidence in her. But how to convince Ra'id of something even *he* had difficulty articulating. He didn't know why, but he just *knew*.

"Nay, the possibility didn't cross my mind," Vartan replied, "because I trust Ankine. And we need her abilities to use that ring to open portals."

"As if it did us any good this time!"

"We can't force anyone to join us if they don't want to, Ra'id."

"Easy for you to say." The Desert lord stared down at the map spread on the table before them. "Your city's gone, as are your family, and your people are defeated and scattered. I've yet to face that, but face it I will soon enough. And no one, absolutely no one, seems willing to come to our aid."

"No one was willing to come to *our* aid, either," Vartan said softly. "So we fought on alone, did the best we could. And, because we fought alone, we were defeated. Now it's the Diya al Din's turn and, if no one joins you, eventually it'll be their turn, until finally Ladon will have all of Gadiel."

Ra'id shot him a narrowed glance. "Did you know that my father received a secret courier from Ladon a few days ago, promising he'd spare us if we immediately surrendered and turned you over to him?"

Vartan went very still. "And will you? Surrender and turn me over to him?"

The younger man laughed, the sound raw, harsh. "If I thought it would be the end of it, aye, I'd be tempted to consider his offer. But it won't. No servant of Phaon can be trusted. Ladon would just kill you, then resume where he left off with us. I know that, and so does my father."

"So much for friendship," Vartan growled, a confused mix of anger and hurt roiling within. "So much for doing what's right in Athan's service."

"I said I'd be *tempted*, not that I'd do it," Ra'id snapped back. "You requested we always be honest with each other, and I was being honest. And don't play righteous with me. Not when you continue to ignore my concerns over this sorceress. Not when you enlisted her aid, took her in, without even once consulting with me. So much for this being a joint alliance on our parts!"

Vartan opened his mouth to snarl back some equally angry comment, then clamped it shut. Ra'id was right. He *hadn't* consulted first with him before enlisting Ankine's aid and sending her off to Serpuhi.

"You're right," he said. "I didn't talk with you first. Time was of the essence and perhaps, as well, I knew you'd be against it."

"And what else will you decide to shut me out of? Until, in time, you take over everything and, like all the Karayans before you, shove the Diya al Din aside in your insatiable quest for total power?" He turned to face Vartan. "But perhaps that has been your plan all along. To use us and—when we're no longer of any value—cast us aside."

Listening to the Desert lord, Vartan saw how easily the trust and mutual support could slip away if they both didn't strive always to treat each other with fairness and respect. He silently cursed his impulsive act of sending out Ankine without first talking with Ra'id. Once again, he fell so easily back into past actions that had served him well. Until this moment, Vartan hadn't realized how much he disliked sharing power with anyone.

"I humbly beg your pardon, Ra'id," he said, his face burning with shame and the effort it took to apologize. "You're right. In my pride, I thought I knew better than you what needed to be done. And I made a decision I shouldn't have made without first discussing it with you. You deserved better, and for that I'm deeply sorry."

"You'll do it again, and you know it! I'm no fool. I see now how it is to be with us."

"Nay, this isn't how it's to be with us." Vartan paused, dragged in a deep breath. "I made a mistake, Ra'id. I'm asking for your understanding—and forgiveness."

The younger man didn't say anything, and Vartan could see a battle waging in him. Finally, though, Ra'id sighed.

"Fine. You're forgiven. But if ever I get the feeling you're using me, Vartan—well, I don't know how much forgiveness I have to spare."

"If ever you feel what I'm doing might endanger the Diya al Din, then you've every right to confront me about it. About Ankine, however," he was quick to say when he saw a resolute look come into Ra'id's eyes, "if you can't trust her as yet, can you trust my judgment of her? No matter what she became or did, I truly believe she has repented and again wants to serve Athan. And, as Athan's followers, we *are* expected to offer forgiveness, aren't we?"

"Aye, you know we are." The Desert lord shook his head and turned back to stare down at the map. "But it isn't just about me and my concerns. People are beginning to talk. They wonder if she hasn't bespelled you."

"And do *you* think she has bespelled me?" Vartan couldn't help a grin. "Tell me true now."

Ra'id scowled. "You don't seem much changed. You're still the stubborn, overbearing lout you've always been."

Vartan laughed. "Well, that's a relief to know." He gestured to the map. "Now, perhaps it's time we were getting back to the subject of our discussion. Ladon has had a few setbacks in the past days, but he's surely on the verge of setting sail down the Bahira. And we've got to find a way to stop him."

"Well, I've a few ideas," Ra'id said, resting his forearms on the edge of the table. "There's this narrow bend in the Bahira, about thirty miles upstream. If we can find a way to slow, if not stop, the barges for a time there, we have a chance of sinking some of them. Some that, hopefully, carry siege equipment . . ."

⟡ ⟡

"I think it's time we try a longer flight outside Sanctuary," Olwyn said two days later as they carried their flight saddles from the storeroom. "I need to teach you the finer points of terrain recognition, for whenever you're in unfamiliar territory. And,"—she paused to shoot Danae an impish grin—"some preliminary lessons, as well, in flaming technique."

"Flaming technique?" Danae's heart skipped a beat, then began a wild hammering. "But the dragon's the one who breathes the fire. What do I have to do with it?"

"Well, for one," Olwyn replied, setting out toward the open field where both their dragons awaited them, "your dragon never flames except by your leave. And, for another, you need to learn the area covered by your dragon's fire, so as not to burn any of your fellow flight members or harm innocent bystanders. And if you don't know the amount of room needed to maneuver when your dragon's flaming, you could even singe yourself and/or your dragon if you turn her too close to her flames, or to the flames of another flight member's dragon."

Danae sucked in a startled breath. "Oh, my. This is more complicated—and dangerous—than I imagined."

"Aye, but isn't everything about dragon riding?" Her friend graced her with an amused glance. "It takes more than a dragon bonding to be a competent Dragonmaid rider. Hence why we spend so much time training new dragons and riders."

"I'm glad you do." Danae halted as they reached the dragons. "It's all so very fascinating and wonderful, though. And I don't think I'll ever tire of riding Celandine. Not ever."

I find as much pleasure in taking you into the sky, Celandine's soft, melodious voice insinuated itself into her head. *Every day with you is a fresh, joyous experience.*

Danae smiled. Being with Celandine was like finding her other half. Without any effort, they understood, loved, and accepted each other. There wasn't anything they couldn't say or think in which the other found offense. Celandine loved her just that much.

Are you up to a long flight today? she asked the huge beast.

Aye. Where are we headed?

The dragon's question gave Danae pause. *I don't know. Let me check with Olwyn.*

"Where exactly are we going?" She looked to the other woman, who was even then readying herself to cinch the girth of the saddle her dragon had taken in its teeth and gently flung up onto its back.

Olwyn shrugged. "Pick a spot within a two-hundred-mile range. We can practice flaming through the mountains along the way, where there's little to burn up, then work on terrain recognition once we get into more unexplored regions."

According to Serpuhi, Vartan was in Khaddar, or somewhere in its near vicinity. Even though she had no inclination to meet with him—and he certainly would never recognize her from so far aloft and in her riding gear—somehow the thought of being near him, if only for a short time, tugged at her.

"We've yet to fly over the Desert," she replied, steadily meeting Olwyn's gaze. "I'd think, with all that sand, terrain recognition would be a real challenge. Let's fly to Khaddar and back."

"You don't take the easy way for anything, do you?" Olwyn finished tightening the cinch, then looked pointedly at the saddle Danae still held in her hand. "Flying to Khaddar, though, actually isn't that hard. You find the Bahira River, then follow it downstream until you reach the city."

"Well, in that case, let's pick something that's more of a challenge," Danae said half-jokingly as she handed her saddle to Celandine. "Out over the Great Sea, perhaps?"

The dragon opened its mouth and delicately took the leather contraption in her teeth. Then, with a backward flip of her head, she tossed the saddle onto her back. With a few shrugs of her massive shoulders, she settled it into exactly the right spot.

"Nay, I think the Desert's fine." Olwyn stepped onto her dragon's big foreleg and pulled herself up. "After all, we have yet to practice rescues over water."

"And why would I need to know that?"

393

Olwyn smiled. "Why else? In case you ever fell off your dragon, of course."

❧ ☙

With what seemed like half of Ladon's army in furious pursuit, Vartan, along with Ra'id, led their small force of cavalry and mounted archers racing back toward Khaddar. Fortunately, the Desert-bred horses were far more sure-footed and possessed of endless stamina, and the rocky terrain on either side of the river lent itself to their particular abilities. They soon left their more heavily armored and cumbersome pursuers far behind.

In some ways the day had gone well. The stout ropes they had managed to string across the river at Whitewater Bend had done their job. Not only had many of the occupants of the first few barges been knocked into the water, but the little resistance force had even managed to topple two siege towers and one catapult. Unfortunately, the majority of the siege equipment was positioned much farther back in the floating armada. The Daegols' massive war axes also eventually hacked through the ropes; barge upon barge of archers returned fire, and Ladon's soldiers soon poled their way to either side of the river, where they disembarked. All told, the guerilla attack had resulted in far too little gain.

But then, Vartan consoled himself, that *was* the purpose of tactical harassment and sabotage. Hit swift and hard from cover, then, when the opposing force finally reorganized and battled back strongly enough, retreat to fight another day.

If only they'd had sufficient time to maximize the effect of their guerilla warfare before Ladon reached Khaddar. But they hadn't the luxury of time. At Barakah, Ladon and his massive army had been out in the open. Sneak attacks wouldn't have worked. Khaddar was better situated as a base for such attacks, but now it was too late. At the rate the river was carrying Ladon's army, they would be at the capital city in another two days.

There were other difficulties, as well. It had taken a considerable amount of time to organize and train up the myriad Desert tribes into even a halfway workable army—and still there were far too few of them to make more than a minor dent in Ladon's overall fighting strength. A full frontal assault anywhere along the river right now would severely weaken the much smaller Diya al Din army. Besides, Ladon could land his hundreds of soldier-filled barges far too easily. After the surprise of the ropes across the bend, Vartan suspected his crafty opponent would unload a goodly number of men from here on out to march along the river and guard the barges.

There was little advantage to be gained in further harassment, especially considering the relative lack of cover along most of the river downstream. The Desert defenders were little more than flies biting at the thick hide of a massive, forest Elaphas, drawing but a bit of blood and irritation as he slogged steadily onward. They were also flies that were, with each passing day, in ever increasing danger of being brutally squashed.

"We surprised Ladon and bloodied some of our youngsters," Ra'id said when they finally put enough distance between themselves and Ladon's army to slow their horses. "Aside from that, though, we accomplished little."

Vartan shot him a wry glance. "And did you seriously expect to accomplish much more than that? Still, it was a victory for us and, right now, Khaddar needs that. If ever they lose hope, it is the end of them."

"Well, then let's keep up the hope, until Athan deems fit to send us some help or, better still, just opens up a big hole that swallows Ladon and all of his army into its depths." Ra'id sighed and shook his head. "One way or another, Vartan, that's what it's going to take to win this one."

Vartan swung his gaze back to the Desert before him. "Aye, that's indeed what it'll take," he replied, keeping his expression and tone positive even as he struggled with his own rising despair. "Thankfully for us, Athan's capable of all that, and more."

☙ ❧

As they glided on a thermal current over the Desert, Danae saw fierce activity occurring below near the river. Then, the frantic scurrying and circling about seemed to end as a group of riders broke away and headed northward.

Can you drop down a bit? she asked Celandine. *I'd like to see what's going on down there.*

If you wish, her dragon replied. *I can tell you, though, that it's two armies fighting. The one leaving, however, seems grossly outnumbered by the other coming out of the river.*

Still, if you would . . .

Celandine immediately complied, diving gracefully downward in ever-widening circles until Danae could finally make out the dress of the riders racing across the Desert. They were Diya al Din, and the two leaders wore blue and white *agaals* over their *shmaaghs*.

She'd wager one of them was Ra'id, and the other . . . well, he was big enough to be Vartan. A dull pain throbbed deep in her heart. A yearning to go to him filled her. Then, with a superhuman effort, Danae squashed it.

Climb back to Olwyn, if you will, she instructed Celandine. *I've seen all I need to see.*

Not interested in the monstrous army behind us then?

Nay. Danae's reply was clipped. *I'm well aware of who and what* they *are.*

The golden dragon instantly obeyed, and they were soon back in level flight alongside Olwyn. *She says that wasn't part of the training,* Celandine repeated what had apparently come to her from Olwyn through her dragon. *She says, don't ever do that again without permission from a senior rider.*

Danae bit back a surge of irritation. It was Olwyn's right as her instructor to chastise her whenever needed, and if this was against the rules for new riders, then she was indeed at fault. Still, in that moment when she had wondered who the horsemen racing away were, Danae hadn't stopped to consider rules, safety, or permission. When she considered the possibility that one of them might be Vartan, Danae had gone because she just *had* to find out.

Tell her I'm sorry, and that it won't happen again, Danae replied. *I just thought I recognized . . . recognized some old friends.*

There was silence for the few minutes it must have taken for Celandine to convey her message, have Olywyn's dragon speak with her rider, and then relay Olwyn's answer back the opposite way.

She says it's time we were returning to Sanctuary.

Celandine's voice washed over Danae like a soothing balm, restoring her earlier peace of mind. Danae glanced over her shoulder for one last glimpse at the retreating riders, but they had already disappeared over a large sand dune.

Aye, it's time, she said. Then, with a few nudges from her legs, Danae signaled the dragon to turn and head toward home.

26

Two days later at dawn, Danae awoke from a sound sleep, gasping for breath, her heart racing, her body bathed in sweat. For several minutes she sat upright in bed with her head on her knees, clutching her legs for support as she fought to regain control of herself. Then, as she lifted her head to gaze out the small, stone-cut window opposite her, the first rays of the sun slanted inside.

Crimson flooded her room, drenching the walls and floor until it seemed to be dripping in blood. And then Danae knew what had woken her. Ladon had attacked Khaddar.

Perhaps it was the realization of the impending battle that had permeated her conscious and unconscious moments in the past days, until it had finally assumed such graphic expression in her dreams. Whatever it was, Danae found herself flying over the midst of horrific fighting, with swords thrusting and axes slashing until blood flowed like rivers and gore splattered everywhere. And then Celandine had gone down. In the deepening twilight, Daegols and Pedars had set upon her, dragging Danae from her dying dragon's back, pulling and tearing at Danae until she screamed in agony—just before she was ripped apart.

It was then she had woken, the stench of battle, the smell of death, so fresh and real she had almost, for the first wakeful instant, imagined she was still there. But she wasn't.

After a time her terror receded. Relief flooded her. The relief, however, was soon replaced by a rising awareness of what Vartan and the Diya al Din were experiencing—and guilt for her own safe and sure existence. Nearby, the bells tolled the call for dawn prayers. Sounds of others rising to dress and hurry to the chapel emanated from the rooms around her. Danae pushed from her bed. It was the start of yet another beautiful, blessed day in Sanctuary.

She washed, slipped on the candidate's black, hooded robe and sandals, and quickly combed and braided her hair. Leaving her room just in time to join the other Dragonmaids heading to prayers, Danae fell into the silent line of black-and-white-clad bodies.

This morn, however, prayers failed to inspire in her a peaceful, loving attitude for the day to come. It seemed like the ancient words were all about war—of girding oneself for battle, of the Eternal One putting to death and giving life, of donning the armor of Athan and Him being the rock, fortress, and stronghold of one's life. Combined with the still-vivid memories of her nightmare, Danae found herself continually distracted and unsettled.

As was the custom, Lysanor awaited each Dragonmaid when she departed the chapel, greeting each in descending seniority with a brush of lips on her cheek. And so it happened that Danae, as the newest candidate, was the last to leave. One look at Danae's troubled expression and Lysanor halted her before she could slip by.

"What is it, Child?" she asked, concern in her eyes. "What distresses you so?"

Lysanor won't be pleased to hear what I have to say, Danae thought, and almost considered not telling her. But then something deep within her rebelled. People outside Sanctuary were fighting and dying for the Dragonmaids' sake, as well as for their own. It was past time Lysanor not only faced it, but responded.

"I awoke this morn to a vision of men fighting and dying, m'lady," she replied. "Ladon has begun the attack on Khaddar."

The Dragonmaid Queen frowned. "It is no concern of—"

"Aye, it *is* our concern," Danae said, interrupting her with a vehemence surprising even to her. She glanced around. "I beg a private moment with you, m'lady."

Lysanor rolled her eyes. "Really, Danae. I have many duties demanding my attention this morn. Can't it wait?"

"Nay, it cannot. This issue's causing me severe spiritual distress."

She knew the queen couldn't deny such an entreaty. As Danae expected, Lysanor's lips drew into a tight line, but she finally nodded her curt acquiescence.

"Come, then. Follow me."

Lysanor turned on her heel and stalked down the corridor, her stride so long and swift Danae was almost forced to run after her. Fortunately, they didn't have far to go before halting once more, this time before the Dragonmaid Queen's office. The older woman shoved open the door and motioned Danae inside.

The room was large, also functioning as a library for the ancient tomes too delicate for common use. Four tall, deep bookcases were filled with parchment scrolls tied with bits of ribbon, and large, leather-bound and hand-tooled books. Aside from those treasures, the room held only a well-worn desk and two chairs. As Lysanor walked around the desk to take the chair behind it, Danae halted at the other one.

"Sit," the Queen said. "Nothing is served with observing the usual formalities. Sit and tell me what you wish to say, so I can then get on with my day."

Lysanor had already discounted her and her concerns, Danae thought. Anger flared.

"The fate of an entire people," she said as she took the chair across from Lysanor, "is hardly a thing to be taken lightly, or cast aside for the routine duties of one's day."

The older woman arched a dark brow. "And since when is it a candidate's place to lecture her seniors?" She rested back in her chair. "I can't say your behavior of late has pleased me. I assumed, when you asked to be accepted for training, that you would put the influence of that unfortunate man behind you. But now . . . now I wonder if you ever will."

"Vartan's influence—or lack of it—has nothing to do with this, m'lady." Danae leaned forward and, forgetting the usual rules between Dragonmaid and queen, laid her forearms on the edge of the desk. "It's wrong to turn our backs on the Diya al Din, just as it was wrong when the rest of Gadiel turned their backs on Astara. And it has to stop before we're all destroyed."

"You are a very emotional child, you know." Lysanor sighed and shook her head. "Have you always been this way, or has Karayan just corrupted you, as he did my sister?"

"If you mean, is Vartan worthy of both *my* and Aelwyd's love, aye, he is. And he is equally worthy of all our loyalty. He's the Guardian, m'lady. In him lies our only hope."

Eyes blazing, Lysanor leaped to her feet. "How dare you! How dare you place a man over Athan? *Athan* is our only hope, not Vartan Karayan!"

Danae looked up at her. "I never meant Vartan's more important than Athan. I only meant Athan has called Vartan to save Gadiel *in His name*. You just refuse to see the truth because you're still so caught up in the throes of your pain and bitterness toward him. And you need to let it go, m'lady. You need to open your heart to forgiveness."

"Like you have forgiven him for betraying you? For using you, then when he had no further need of you, casting you aside for another woman?"

The words stung, coming as they did from a woman whom Danae had come to respect and love. They didn't hurt like they had before, though. The realization surprised her, but on closer inspection, she knew the reason why.

"I know Vartan," she said. "I've been with him, in one capacity or another, for over three years now. He didn't betray me. He never made any promises. And I stayed with him as long as I did because aye, he needed me, but also because I believed Athan wished it so. I'd be with Vartan today if I thought it was Athan's will. But I don't. Indeed, until now, I'd begun to believe Athan called me to be a Dragonmaid."

"But not anymore, is that it?" Lysanor glared down at her. "Just as soon as your lover seemingly needs you again, you gladly throw everything—and everyone—else aside to run back to him. Have you no honor? No pride?"

"It's because I *have* pride and honor that I'll not turn from those who need me!" Danae cried. "Where is *your* honor? Where is *your* conscience? Where is love for Athan and His children in all this?"

"I don't have to explain my reasons to you!" The Dragonmaid Queen turned and headed to the room's only window, then, halfway there, halted and glanced back at her. "Do you really intend to leave us, then? Is that what all this is leading up to?"

Leave Sanctuary? Danae knew if she did leave, she would never be permitted to return. The thought filled her with pain. She loved Sanctuary. Loved the life, the warm friendships she had so quickly and easily formed with many of the Dragonmaids. Save for the brief time she had been with Vartan in his blindness, she had never felt so useful, so needed, so fulfilled. And then there was Celandine . . .

The last thing Danae wanted was to leave Sanctuary, to lose this beautiful, precious life. And for what? To return to a harsh, dangerous, and frequently ugly world outside?

"Nay." She shook her head. "I don't want to leave Sanctuary or the Dragonmaids. I love it here. I feel complete, fulfilled here."

"And we love you, Child, and want you to be with us." Warmth and affection emanated from the Dragonmaid Queen now. She turned and walked back to stand before her desk. "What would you do outside? You are only one person, and you are certainly no warrior. Not my sweet, gentle little Danae. What possible difference could you make to turn the tide of battle? The most likely thing that would happen is you would be recaptured by Ladon, and you don't want that, do you?"

Even the mention of Ladon filled Danae with horror. She didn't think she could bear to look into his soulless eyes ever again. It was like peering into a bottomless pit. She feared if she stared too long, she would lose her balance and fall, never to come out again.

He had always had that empty, hungry look about him, Danae realized now. As if . . . as if his need for love and acceptance was slowly eating him alive. Ladon would never, though, find the acceptance he so dearly craved. He would never be found worthy.

They were alike in that, Danae realized. Neither had ever felt worthy of the person who mattered most to them in life. For Ladon, it had been his father, King Feodras. And for Danae, it had also been her own father and then, later, Vartan. Perhaps, that was what had drawn her and Ladon to each other all those years ago. Instinctively, they had sought out kindred spirits.

There, though, the similarity ended. Ladon had been willing to do anything—absolutely anything—to procure acceptance and respect. He had even been willing to turn to evil. She, on the other hand, had endeavored to win approval and love by denying her own needs for the needs of others. Good little Danae . . .

Lysanor was right. What possible difference could she make if she left Sanctuary? She wasn't a warrior, indeed, she wasn't even all that brave. And Ladon and his army stood between her and Vartan. How ever did she expect to get to him?

"Celandine could take me past Ladon and his army," she said at last. "*She* could get me to Vartan."

Her eyes wide, Lysanor reared back. "You can't do that! It is unheard of. No Dragonmaid has ever permanently left Sanctuary and taken her dragon with her!"

"But if a dragon and Dragonmaid are bonded, why isn't it possible?" Danae cocked her head in consideration. "Isn't the dragon's first loyalty to her rider, above even her loyalty to Sanctuary or to you, m'lady? And, besides, if I left Celandine behind, it'd surely be the death of her."

"It could well be the death of you, too," the other woman snarled. "The bond is equally as strong in you as it is in her."

Danae hadn't given that much thought. What if severing the bond was indeed fatal to her? Yet it might be equally fatal to hide here in Sanctuary and live with the knowledge of her selfish cowardice for the rest of her life.

"It's a chance I'm willing to take, m'lady," Danae replied, lifting her chin and meeting the queen's icy gaze. "Better to die trying to follow Athan's call to risk my life for the sake of others, out of *love* for others, than to live as a coward. Indeed, what else *is* there for us who claim to follow Athan? Even His own Son, Eisa—though He, too, was afraid and had His doubts—never swerved from the call His Father placed on Him. His love for us was just that strong, that deep, that faithful."

Danae smiled. "How can I do any less? Indeed, how can *any* of us do any less?"

"I forbid you to leave." As if the action would put a final and most definite end to the discussion, Lysanor walked around the desk and headed for the door. "And I forbid you, as well, ever to speak to me about this ridiculous, hopeless idea of yours. Go back to your studies, Child. Go back to your rider's training. You are safe and loved here, and that's all that matters."

That's all that matters . . .

Not very long ago, Danae had believed that herself. She had found everything she had ever been seeking here. Surely Athan had called her to this place, this life, in service to Him. But now she knew it had only been part—a *very* small part—of the call.

Aye, she was meant to be a Dragonmaid, but for a purpose that transcended Sanctuary and a safe, simple life. She had been called to be a Dragonmaid in order to prepare her to stand and fight in Athan's cause. That cause, however, now lay outside, in the world, in service to Gadiel. Outside, because that was where the true trial and testing for her lay. To flee them was to turn her back on Athan and His will for her. To turn her back on all that *really* mattered—her trust in Him and His love.

A fierce, exultant joy flooded Danae. At last . . . At last she had discovered the heart of her calling. It had always been to serve Gadiel—first in saving Vartan's life and standing by him until he was strong and whole again, until he finally discovered and accepted his own call—and now, when she saw what she must next do. Yet the greatest source of satisfaction lay in the realization that she was worthy of the calling. Worthy, because Athan found her so.

"Nay, m'lady," Danae whispered. "I cannot obey you in this. I grieve for your loss of your sister. I loved Aelwyd as well. And I know forgiveness is a hard thing. But I also cannot stand by and allow your pain-twisted heart to keep me from what *I* must do. From what is right. Just as you must someday face Athan and the consequences of your decision, so must I. And I refuse to face Him with a heart full of regrets, a life filled with failings."

Danae drew in a ragged breath. "Nay, I won't—I can't—obey you in this."

Her body rigid, her back ramrod straight, the Dragonmaid Queen stood facing the door for a long, tension-laden moment. Finally, with a deep sigh, all the energy—and anger—within her seemed to disappear.

"I need to spend a time in prayer," she said softly. "Will you wait on me?"

"Aye, I'll wait," Danae replied, hope, for the first time, slipping its tendrils about her heart. "But don't tarry overlong, I pray. Time's of the essence. And no decision's just as much a decision as any you'd willingly make."

❧ ☙

Despite the overwhelming odds and the crushing power of the catapults and battering rams, it took until well into the night before Ladon's army managed to break through nearly simultaneously at Khaddar's eastern and western city gates. Until then, Vartan had been able to keep the Diya al Din army spread out well enough along the outer walls to successfully repel the endless ladder and siege tower assaults. *Barely* successfully, but at least they had managed to hold back the swarming mass of Daegols and their more human counterparts.

As the sun had set behind the distant Ibn Khaldun mountains, however, the darkness-loving Pedars finally ventured out from their leather-covered wagons. Their additional force, which numbered in the tens of thousands, was the final strain on the already overtaxed but valiantly fighting Desert army. Khaddar was under attack from too many places at once. The only remaining choice was whether to direct the defense against the thousands of ladders swooping down everywhere onto the walls and from the siege towers' bridges, or at the men directing the battering rams and catapults.

Vartan had chosen the most pressing problem. If they were overwhelmed at the walls, the gates would soon fall at any rate—from inside. He could only hope the gates would hold long enough to throw back the wall attack.

Alongside the Desert warriors, Vartan had fought for what seemed like hours, slashing and hacking at one black-armored soldier after another as they scurried up the ladders and over the walls. His muscles ached from the effort it took to wield his sword, and after a time he couldn't even feel his arms. Blood began to coat the parapet walk and crenellated battlements, until his boots slipped and he could barely keep his footing.

And then it didn't matter anymore. With a sickening shriek of splintering wood, the battering rams drove through the gates. In but a matter of minutes, Ladon's army would be pouring inside.

"Pull back!" Vartan roared. "Pull back!"

Signal flags waved wildly as men heard Vartan's order and sent messages flying down along the parapet walk in both directions. There was no need to explain further. Everyone knew the inner walls were the only place left to go.

As men scrambled down the steps leading to the four inner gates, Vartan, one hand gripping his sword, the other clenching the top of one stone battlement, stared out on a night lit by thousands of torches and bonfires. In the dim light he watched soldiers and cavalry, so thick with bodies of both man and beast he could barely make out individual forms, surge forward, their triumphant voices blending in a huge, deafening roar. Drums beat a steady, rhythmic beat until the sound reverberated off Khaddar's walls. Trumpets blared, their raucous, high-pitched bursts only adding to the fearsome cacophony.

A day, he thought. It had taken but one full day to break through their outer defenses. As well built as Khaddar was, it had never been Astara's equal. And Astara had never seen the size of the force that had now become Ladon's army.

Still, the relative ease the enemy troops had had in breaching the city's main defenses rankled Vartan. Indeed, it was a severe blow to his pride. The Diya al Din had heard of his impressive defense of Astara, a defense that had lasted three long years. They had looked to him as the man capable of achieving the same results for their city. But no more. This night, they would know him for the charlatan and failure he was.

A hand gripped his shoulder. "Come on," Ra'id said, his face as smudged with dirt, his armor as bloodied, as Vartan's surely was. "Ladon's army's about to break through the gates. You don't want to be caught out here to face them alone."

Vartan was half-tempted to tell his friend the end result would be the same. They'd not hold the inner keep even through the next day. But Ra'id and the Diya al Din deserved better than that. They deserved his continued presence and active involvement until the very end. They deserved, as well, the faith—and hope—in Athan that had brought him here in the first place.

Vartan managed a lopsided grin. "Might be what Athan planned all along. Just let the Guardian destroy Ladon and his army single-handedly."

Ra'id gave a disdainful snort. "Getting a bit overly impressed with yourself, are you?" Once more he tugged on Vartan's arm. "Let's save all that bravado for the morrow. It'll take them most of the night to get those siege towers and battering rams up the city's streets to the inner keep's gates. If we're lucky, we might even have a chance for a few hours' sleep."

"Aye, sleep," Vartan said with a weary chuckle, as he finally followed his friend. "And would any food and drink be in the offing as well?"

"Why not?" The Desert lord's mouth twisted grimly. "No sense leaving behind anything for Ladon and his men."

As it had always been before another day of battle, Vartan didn't soon take his rest. Instead, after washing away the majority of the day's grime and gore and consuming a light meal of roasted mouflon and vegetables, he excused himself from the somber gathering in Prince Kamal's private quarters and went outside to stand on the balcony. Rather than staring out yet again onto the disconcerting scene of enemy campfires, this time Vartan lifted his gaze to the stars.

At first, his thoughts involved battle strategies and how best to maximize the men around the much smaller keep. They had already reinforced the two gates with huge, thick poles. The pots of oil to pour down on the attackers were simmering on hundreds of fires around the bases of the wall. Swords, pikes, and axes had been cleaned and sharpened. The bowmen were well supplied with arrows. All were well fed, their wounds cared for, and they should manage at least a few hours' sleep before the fighting began anew.

There seemed nothing else left to be done, neither in preparation nor in additional planning. The strategy was simple. Hold back the enemy from pouring over the walls or battering through the gates. Simple . . . and ultimately futile.

Where did I go wrong? Vartan asked, lifting his thoughts heavenward. *Where did I misunderstand or fail You, Eternal One? Was I wrong in believing You chose me to lead these people, to save Gadiel? If I was, it is not right the Diya al Din pay the price for my vainglory and foolishness. Spare them, I pray, and punish me instead. Spare them, Eternal One, please.*

"M'lord?"

Vartan whirled around. Ankine, dressed in a deep emerald green gown, stood behind him. Short, auburn curls cupped her delicately shaped face.

He sighed and forced a smile. "Aye, lady? What is it you wish?"

She walked up until she stood a few feet away from him along the balcony. For a time, Ankine gazed out onto the starlit night. Then she turned, and squarely met his questioning gaze.

"It'll not go well for us on the morrow, will it?"

"Likely not."

"Have you given any consideration to what you'll do? When the end comes?"

It was a strange question. He shrugged. "Die, I suppose, alongside Ra'id and the others. What else *is* there to do?"

"Perhaps Athan doesn't intend for you to die. Perhaps He means for you to live to fight another day."

She was working her way around to something. Vartan's patience, however, was worn about as thin as his strength.

"Spit it out, Ankine," he growled. "What are you suggesting?"

"Surely my coming to you in these last days was Athan's will. Not just for my sake, but for yours as well. Perhaps it was also why, when I offered to return Metsamor's ring to Serpuhi, she refused, saying it had always been meant to serve the Faithful, and what better time and person to use it for but you?"

Vartan frowned. "I don't see how the portal ring could be of much use now. It can't transport all Khaddar's citizens through it, can it? Or, better still, send Ladon's entire army into some bottomless abyss?"

"Nay." Ankine smiled sadly. "It can only take a few. And I can only wield it for a short while before my strength fades and I must rest before using it again. I was thinking, instead, of sending you through it to a safe place. So you could escape Ladon; live to fight another day."

"And do you tempt me, lady? Tempt me to betray those Athan has entrusted to my care? Tempt me to desert them in their hour of need and run away?"

Ankine gave a horrified gasp. "Oh, nay, m'lord. Never. Never!"

He gazed down at her and saw no guile or treachery in her offer, but only a sincere intent. For a brief instant, Vartan allowed himself to consider that perhaps it was indeed Athan's plan. Though Ladon might win on the morrow and annihilate the Diya al Din, as long as the Guardian lived there was still hope the Prophecy might yet be fulfilled.

"The choice isn't yours, m'lord," Ankine softly said, as if looking into his mind. "It's Athan's. It has always been His."

411

"If it *is* His choice, lady." He shook his head. "I've been pondering this for a time now. Athan's will, I mean. What if Athan's plans for the Guardian have always been different than what we all assumed them to be? What if the Guardian was never meant to be a warrior king? What if he was meant, instead, to be something else, *do* something else?"

"But what else might that be?"

"I don't know, Ankine." He closed his eyes, threw back his head, and sighed. "I wish I knew. Oh, how I wish I knew!"

"Sometimes, it isn't the knowing that's important. It is the acceptance . . . and the surrender."

Vartan opened his eyes and jerked around to stare at her. In that moment she had uttered those words, he had heard not only Ankine's voice, but Serpuhi's, and through her, Athan's.

So, this is how it's to be, then? he thought, turning to the One who was fast becoming his closest friend and confidante. *You now demand even my efforts to serve You as I imagined You desired. Have I been at it again—trying to mold and control even Your will into the image I thought it should be? Forgive me for that, Eternal One. I meant well. Perhaps in my eagerness to be a man of action in Your cause, I was too hasty and, once again, too prideful.*

But then, I've fought You every step of the way, haven't I? First by rejecting Your overtures of friendship and love, then by my denial that I was the Guardian. And I fight You still, in the refusal of my true call. Even now, when I tell myself I've yielded everything to You, my pride still creeps in to try to shape Your will into something I'll find acceptable. But not what You desire. Not what will most surely form me into the man You've always meant for me to be.

"You must become like clay in His hands," Ankine intoned the words of chapter 34, verse 19, of the *Covenant of Athan*.

"Only then can you serve. Only then can you fulfill your true destiny . . ."

"Even if it's to die in the doing?"

"Aye, or even in living to fight another day."

"Back to that again, are we?" He chuckled. "Somehow, though, I don't think He'd ask me to do something that dishonorable."

"Perhaps. But consider carefully if that isn't just your pride speaking. And can it ever be more important than Athan's will?"

Vartan laughed. "We understand each other all too well, don't we? About how insidious pride can be, clothing itself sometimes even in seemingly altruistic guises."

She smiled. "Aye, m'lord, we do."

"Still, I deeply appreciate your offer," he said, sobering. "*And* your loyalty to me. I'll give your proposition much thought and prayer. So as not to let pride taint what must be."

"It's all anyone can do." She turned to go.

"Wait, Ankine."

She halted, looked back at him. "Aye, m'lord?"

"Even if I don't feel it's Athan's will that I escape through the portal, if things turn bad . . . if it appears you'll be captured or killed, use the ring yourself. Take it back to Serpuhi until she deems fit for it to be used again. One way or another, Blessed Metsamor's ring mustn't fall into Ladon's hands."

Ankine nodded. "It'll be as you ask, m'lord. If things turn bad . . ." With that, she departed.

Vartan waited until he could no longer hear the sound of her footsteps on the stone floors, then resumed his study of the night sky. Despite Ankine's kind offer, he knew he belonged here. Beyond a shadow of a doubt, that one thing was certain. If he truly *was* the Guardian, warrior or no, he was Guardian of all. Besides, he owed the Diya al Din a special regard. They had been the first to place their trust in him, follow him.

He had been right about Ankine, though. She was indeed a brave, honorable woman. If it was the last thing she did, she wouldn't let Ladon gain possession of that precious ring.

The realization filled Vartan with a soul-deep satisfaction. No matter how the morrow went, at least someone would survive to tell the tale of the Battle of Khaddar. At least there was hope their sacrifice might stir the other peoples of Gadiel to action.

It was the only hope that remained in this bleak, bitter night. Yet again, Vartan feared he had failed Athan, that his pride had closed his eyes once more, and it was now too late. There was nothing to be done, though, about opportunities missed. All that remained was to beg forgiveness and struggle on. To offer up, yet again, his pride on the altar of remorse and surrender.

Perhaps, just perhaps, something good for Gadiel could still come of that.

One thing was certain. Unless Athan plucked him bodily from the midst of his comrades in arms, Vartan was certain he would die on the morrow. His pride might well be the end of him, but he wouldn't leave the people who had become his friends and new family any other way.

27

Like swarms of ravenous insects, the enemy soldiers spilled up and over the walls. Time and again, the Desert warriors beat them off, shoving ladders full of grotesquely armored and visaged beings backward to teeter precariously upright before toppling over, carrying their screaming occupants with them. The ones who made it to the battlements were slaughtered as they scrambled over the walls, then pushed into the following man. Archers rained arrow after arrow down on the enemy troops operating the catapults and battering rams. Buckets of boiling oil were poured over the walls, sending mortally scalded soldiers staggering away, shrieking in agony. Yet still their attackers came, in surging, relentless, heartbreakingly endless waves.

As the day wore on, the Desert sun burned hot and bright in a cloudless sky. There was no shade on the battlements, high up above the city streets. The glare was blinding; the superheated stones were scorching to the touch. Vartan was forced to call out some of the older children and elderly from the safety of the palace to carry water up to the soldiers. Yet even the water provided only temporary relief. Many collapsed from the combined exertion of nonstop battle and the blistering heat.

So far the gates were holding, but Vartan knew their breach was but a matter of time. Despair nibbled at the edge of his confidence. What was he hoping to accomplish, anyway? Buy time? For what? No one was on the way, coming to their aid. What possible purpose was served in prolonging everyone's agony?

Yet, as horrific as the next few hours might be—as heart and body and mind were stretched up to and past their breaking point, until one thought even death was a far more merciful fate than continuing to live—he knew it could be no other way. Surrender was unimaginable, and honor could bear no less.

In late afternoon, the gates began to weaken. Vartan had little time to spare them much thought. They had done all they could to strengthen the city portals. He had other things to concern him, like shoving ladders from the walls—when he wasn't engaged in hand-to-hand combat.

He fought in a kind of haze now, his sword parries and thrusts taking on a rhythmic, almost mechanical effort. Sweat poured down his face. His muscles quivered with exhaustion and—he suspected—the early stages of dehydration.

And still the soldiers poured over the walls. Men fighting along the battlements began to fall more frequently now, either pierced by arrows sent from archers on the siege towers, or in some misstep that opened them to a killing sword thrust or slash of a war ax. Then, down at the smaller of the two gates, the battering ram finally broke through.

Athan, help us! Vartan silently cried. *If You mean to help us, help us now. Now, before it's too late!*

High above, an unearthly cry filled the air. For an instant, he thought it must be yet another weapon of Ladon's just now brought into use. But then, as Vartan lifted his gaze heavenward, he saw the answer to his prayers.

Hundreds of dragons, reds, greens, bronzes, browns, blacks, golds, silvers, and blues, glided overhead in several layers of long, straight lines. On their backs rode white-hooded riders. An instant later, the first and lowest flying group dove, split, and the dragons belched fire.

Concentrating their efforts on the army still waiting outside the city to march in through the walls, the dragons strafed them with flaming breath. Long, lethal claws extended as they neared the ground, cutting long swathes through the now milling, terrified soldiers. The once orderly formations broke and ran, some for the gaping city gates, the rest toward the river.

Instantly, the Dragonmaids divided into groups. Some pursued the troops fleeing Khaddar. Others continued to attack the soldiers now frantically shoving their way into the city. With amazing precision, they overflew Khaddar, shooting flame up and down the streets.

Each time, however, that a dragon neared the inner keep, it would extinguish its flames, pause in midair to grasp a siege tower or catapult, then turn and carry it a short distance before dropping it to shatter atop yet more fleeing soldiers. In just a short time, the walls of the inner keep were amazingly bare of enemy soldiers.

A cheer, weak and wobbly at first, rose from the Desert warriors, gaining in strength as the dragon-wrought carnage continued. The Diya al Din made short work of the remaining enemy still on the battlements, then looked to Vartan.

"To horse!" he cried. "To horse! Let's drive them back across the Desert. Let's drive them into the mountains from whence they came!"

They answered him with an exultant shout, then scrambled for the stairs and the inner courtyard where the horses were tethered. Ra'id soon joined Vartan.

"How did you manage that feat?" he asked, casting a quick glance upward. "I thought the Dragonmaids had flatly refused us."

"So did I." Vartan grinned as he strode along toward the stairs. "Seems Athan had other ideas, though."

"Aye, so it seems, and not a moment too soon, either!"

By the time they arrived at the inner courtyard, their mounts—along with most of the cavalry—were waiting for them. As they swung up onto their horses, another cheer rose. Banners of the twelve tribes flapped in a sudden, stiff breeze. The sun slipped behind newly formed clouds. And, outside, the dragons roared and spewed fire.

"Ladon's army sounds as if they're having a hard time of it," Vartan shouted, standing tall in his stirrups. "Let's see if we can make things even worse!"

With that, he signaled his mount to move to the head of the army. The courtyard's wide doors opened, and Vartan led his men—*his people*—forward.

⟳ ⟲

Two hours later, the battle was all but over. What remained of Ladon's army had fled back to and across the confluence of the Bahira and Munir rivers. The rest were scattered about in lifeless, smoldering clumps on the plains surrounding the city. The Flights of dragons that weren't still pursuing the enemy stragglers circled overhead, seeking out their own wounded. A Wing of Dragonmaid riders, however, soon landed on the parade grounds outside Khaddar. It was there Vartan and Ra'id headed with a group of their own men.

Only one Dragonmaid climbed down from her dragon as Vartan and Ra'id dismounted and walked toward the huge beasts. Dressed in the white, hooded tunic, black boots, and breeches like the rest, the only thing that distinguished her was the presence of blue and yellow braids, topped by a large blue and red crest, encircling her right sleeve. She shoved up her flight goggles as they approached. A pair of sparkling green eyes stared back at them from a soot-smudged face.

Vartan halted and rendered her a courteous bow. "My name's Vartan Karayan, and this"—he half-turned to indicate Ra'id—"is the Hakeem's son, Ra'id Abd Al'Alim. We're the leaders—"

"I know who you are," the woman said with a laugh. "We're not as isolated as some might imagine. My name's Olwyn. I'm Captain of our First Wing and, in Queen Lysanor's absence, Commmander of all the Dragon Wings."

"Welcome, Olwyn. You've our deepest gratitude for your most timely arrival and assistance." Vartan grinned. "Indeed, I daresay we wouldn't have survived much longer *without* your help."

At his side, Ra'id gave a disgusted snort. "I don't know about you, but I was just beginning to enjoy myself. Wouldn't have long survived. Hah!"

The Dragonmaid turned an amused gaze on Ra'id. "Then I'm grateful you at least saved us a few of those nasty Daegols and other beasts to practice on. It's not often we get a chance at such realistic battle drills, after all."

Vartan was tempted to comment that he had always understood the Dragonmaids had, until today, never gone to battle, but he decided to let the observation pass. All that really mattered was that they had come and the battle was over.

"There's sure to be a feast this night," he said instead. "We'd be honored—wouldn't we, Ra'id?—if you and your dragons and Dragonmaids would join us. Also, let us offer the services of our healers to aid your own wounded, be they maid or dragon alike."

"Aye, most certainly," Ra'id was quick to add. "Nothing's too good for our new friends and allies."

"Your offer's most kind," the Dragonmaid leader replied. "However—"

She stopped short and cocked her head, standing in silent concentration for several minutes.

Vartan and Ra'id exchanged quizzical glances.

Frowning, Olwyn finally expelled a deep breath. "It appears one of our dragons is down and wounded, as is her rider. Unfortunately, this particular dragon seems unwilling to let anyone near her."

"Even another Dragonmaid?" Vartan asked.

"Aye, in this case, apparently so. The dragon and rider are newly bonded, the dragon having only recently lost her first rider. It sounds as if she has gone into some sort of protective rage."

"Can't her rider reason with her?"

Olwyn shook her head. "Nay. She's so badly wounded that she's unconscious. And we need to get to her before she bleeds to death."

Though he knew little of the Dragonmaids and even less about their dragons, Vartan felt compelled to offer his aid. "Why don't we venture toward this dragon and her rider? Perhaps once we survey the situation, we can fashion some plan to solve this problem."

She eyed him for a long moment, then nodded. "You're welcome to come along. However, the final decision as to how to proceed must be mine."

Vartan looked to Ra'id, who quickly gave his own assent. "Of course," the Desert lord said. "What do we know of dragons, anyway?"

The scene that greeted them out where the river plain finally met Desert, however, hardly reassured Vartan that the

Dragonmaids had the situation under any better control. A rather large, golden dragon, several arrows protruding from her hide, lay curled up, and the limp, white-clad form of a woman sprawled on her back. Two arrows pierced the Dragonmaid's body as well, one in her right thigh, the other high up in the back of her right shoulder.

Two Dragonmaids stood about fifty feet from the pair and, each time they took a step forward, the golden dragon bared her teeth. Vartan also noted several charred bushes about ten feet in front of the Dragonmaids. This was indeed a ticklish situation.

Olwyn, who had flown ahead on her dragon, was already signaling the two brave Dragonmaids over. Vartan and Ra'id just managed to dismount and join the Wing Commander as the Dragonmaids halted before her.

"No success yet?" Olwyn asked.

The taller of the two women shook her head. "She's in so much pain, I don't think she even knows friend from foe anymore. And she has nearly flamed us three times so far."

"Let's see if my dragon can get through to her," Olwyn said. She paused for a few seconds and looked directly at her own dragon.

By now, Vartan had pieced together that the Dragonmaids and their dragons communicated by some form of thought transference. Myriad questions rose to his lips about this amazing ability, but as the seconds passed and Olwyn's expression turned more and more serious, he decided to save them for a more appropriate time.

Finally, she turned to him. "My dragon can't reason with her, either. And I fear the worse the dragon's rider's condition becomes, the more irrational and dangerous her dragon will be."

"Then there seems no other choice," Ra'id interjected gruffly. "You must kill the dragon to save the rider."

The Dragonmaid leader shot him a furious glance. "How like you men of the Desert, to leap so quickly to the easiest, most brutal solution."

He glared back at her. "And have you a better one? Or would you prefer to let them both slowly die out there?"

"You don't understand how it is between dragon and rider," she snapped back. "Severing their bond in such a sudden, violent manner could also kill the rider, especially as weak as she now is."

"But what other choices are there?" Vartan chose that moment to intervene before the situation worsened further. "If there's anything I can do—anything to help—please tell me. It's the very least we can do after all you and your Dragonmaids have done for us."

Fleetingly, Olwyn looked away, then slammed her gaze back into his. "There *is* one possibility. Someone who has an equally strong bond with the rider might be able to get through to the dragon. The dragon might sense the bond and realize she could trust that person."

"But who would that be?" Even as he asked, Vartan had the feeling Olwyn had someone very specific in mind. "If it's not one of your Dragonmaids, and it's someone I can fetch for you—"

"It's you, Vartan Karayan," the woman said. "Only your bond is potentially as great as the dragon's."

As he tried to sift through what she was saying, Ra'id softly cursed beside him.

"It's Danae, isn't it?" the Desert lord demanded hoarsely. "Isn't it?"

Vartan locked glances with her and, in Olwyn's green depths, saw the answer. "But how? How did Danae manage to find the Dragonmaids? And how do you know about us?"

"Does it matter?" she asked. "Suffice it to say, I was her instructor, and we talked of many things besides riding dragons. Now, will you go to her dragon or not?"

He lifted his gaze and looked to where the dragon lay, snarling now with fangs glinting lethally in the sun, long, curved claws at the ready. For just an instant he stared at the golden beast, before his glance moved to the slender, motionless form of the woman slumped on its back.

Danae . . .

"Tell me what I must do to convince the dragon that I mean Danae—and it—no harm," he said at last.

"Nay!" Ra'id's hand settled on Vartan's shoulder. "Are you mad? That dragon's crazed with pain and fear. And I haven't heard they particularly like men even when they *are* in a good mood."

Frustration filled Vartan. "And what would you have me do? It's Danae, Ra'id."

"I know it's Danae!" The Desert lord chewed on his lip. "After all that has been accomplished here this day, we can't risk you. I love Danae, too. Let me go in your place."

Vartan stared deep into his friend's eyes. Ra'id did indeed love Danae, as a man loves a woman. Jealousy skittered through him, and then was gone. If he had lost his chance with her, so be it. Likely she deserved better than him at any rate.

"It isn't who loves her more or is most worthy of her," he said. "It's who the dragon will recognize has the deepest bond. And, whether I deserve her anymore or not, I *can* lay claim to that."

"But you're the Guardian! Times are still precarious. What will we do if we lose you?"

"And what sort of Guardian would I be, if I turn from those in need?" Vartan pried Ra'id's hand free. "It's not just Danae

423

who's hurt and in danger. It's also her dragon, a dragon that is as much our friend and ally now as is her rider. And if, as the Guardian, I can't engender trust, then what good am I to Gadiel?"

"This isn't the time or the place, Vartan," Ra'id ground out. "This is an animal. An animal!"

"Aye, she's an animal, but a very special animal created by Athan and, I'd imagine, very precious in His eyes." He smiled, a sudden, piercingly sweet surety filling him. "Someone must make the first overture. Someone must be willing to do things differently, or we'll never heal this land."

"But an animal, Vartan . . ."

With a chuckle, he turned to Olwyn. "Any suggestions as to how to approach this dragon?"

A curious light gleamed in her eyes. "For one thing, I'd suggest shedding your weapons and hauberk. Best to look as nonthreatening as you can. And, for another, gauge your actions to her response. If she begins to act anxious, drop your gaze and stop whatever you're doing. And when you speak, keep your voice low and soothing. As for the rest"—she shrugged—"you'll have to decide what to say to convince her you're Danae's friend. Dragons do, you know, understand human speech."

"That's a most useful piece of information," Vartan said as he unbuckled his sword belt and handed his sword to Ra'id. Next, he removed his *bisht*, *thobe*, and chain mail hauberk. Clad now in just a loose, linen shirt, hose, and boots, Vartan paused only a moment more.

"Keep me in your prayers." His glance moved first to Ra'id, then to Olwyn, who nodded. Turning on his heel, he set off with a strong, sure stride.

When he reached the spot where the two Dragonmaids had halted, the golden dragon lifted her head and gave Vartan an icy stare. He stopped, spread his arms wide in a gesture of peace.

"My name's Vartan," he said, keeping his voice low. "If Danae's conscious, ask her if she knows me. She'll tell you we're friends, and have been for over three years now. She saved my life. I don't mean either of you any harm."

When the dragon continued to eye him, he took a few more steps forward. A snarl emanated from deep in her throat, and a few tendrils of smoke wafted from her nostrils. Vartan drew to a halt once more.

"She's hurt, dragon. You can't help her. I can. Let me come nearer. Please."

He dared a few more steps forward. With a sibilant hiss, the dragon shoved to a sitting position. Fangs bared, eyes gleaming, she towered over him. He knew she would give him no more warnings.

Vartan inhaled raggedly. "Do you mean to kill me, then? You'll have to, you know. I love Danae, and I won't desert her in her hour of need. I've caused her enough pain. I won't stand by and let her die as well."

Once again, he began walking forward. With a deafening screech, the dragon reared up on her hind legs. Fire spewed from her nostrils, igniting his shirt. He tore at the flaming garment, managing to rip most of it from him before it burned him. As he did, behind him he heard Ra'id's angry shout and cries of concern.

"You weren't sure if I had a weapon or two hidden under my shirt, were you?" Despite his pounding heart, he managed a crooked grin. "Well, as you can now see for yourself, I'm totally unarmed. I don't mean you any harm, dragon. I know how important you are to Danae. I know she loves you."

He was only twenty feet away now. Close enough to see the sweet curve of Danae's cheek, her small, delicate hands, the sinuous shape of her leg beneath her breeches and boots. To hold her one more time in his arms . . . Oh, how he ached to do that!

"Kill me if you must, dragon," he said, holding his now bare arms out and beginning to walk forward. "If she lives, though, she'll know what you did. Just as she would've known if I'd killed you. The question is, are you willing to risk losing her love over the likes of me?"

Furious, bejeweled eyes glared down at him. Hideous sounds rose from deep within the dragon's chest. Yet in that final instant when Vartan was certain it was his last on this earth, the golden beast groaned and sank back to the sand.

Relief swamped him. For a dizzying second, the world spun. Then, with a deep lungful of air, he cleared his head.

He stood beside the dragon and stared up at Danae, slumped over high above him. A long piece of braided leather, apparently used for climbing up onto the dragon's back, hung down from the saddle. The end dangled about ten feet from the ground. There was only one way to reach it.

"I beg your pardon, dragon," he said, "but I'm going to have to step up on your foreleg to get hold of that climbing rope. Unless you have a better idea?"

Something akin to exasperation rumbled in the dragon's chest. Then the beast twisted back, opened her mouth, and before Vartan could do more than utter a startled yelp, she gently took him in her teeth and lifted him into the air. The next thing he knew, she had unceremoniously placed him on her back, directly behind Danae.

It took a second or two to catch his breath. Then Vartan scooted forward, took hold of the arrow in Danae's shoulder, and tugged it free. Next, he did the same for the one in her thigh. Both sites began to bleed even more profusely than before. Using what remained of his shirt, he tore it into pieces and bound the wounds as best he could. Then, Vartan carefully turned Danae around and lifted her onto his shoulder.

"A little help getting down would be appreciated, dragon."

The golden dragon turned her head once more and carefully placed her huge jaws about them both. As they touched ground once more, Danae moaned. Vartan pulled her off his shoulder and cradled her in his arms.

"Hush, sweet lady," he murmured. "You're safe now."

"V-Vartan?" Danae rubbed at the goggles covering her eyes. "I-I can't see. Is it . . . is it really you?"

With an infinitely tender touch, he pushed the goggles back and off her head. Soft brown eyes stared up at him. Confusion dulled their brilliance but, gradually, they cleared and recognition flared.

"It *is* you," she whispered. "Athan be praised . . ."

"Aye, Athan be praised." His throat went tight as he watched her sink back into oblivion. "Athan be praised."

28

"The healer said Danae's well enough to receive visitors now. I've already sent a messenger off to Vartan, who is currently out on the Desert working with the cavalry on some new battle tactics." Ra'id chuckled. "That was my idea, convincing him to lend his considerable expertise to the maneuvers. He was close to driving me mad with all his nervous fuming over Danae. For my own sanity, I had to find *some* way to get him out of the city for a while."

Sharifah glanced up from the arrows she was finally learning to make now that, three days later, all her postbattle cleanup duties were completed. Her brother stood towering over her, an expectant look in his eyes.

"Aye, and your point is?" she asked.

"I thought we might pay Danae a visit. You and me, I mean."

"Now?"

"Why not? You look as though you could use a break from all that work."

She looked down at the meager pile of arrows she had constructed. The shafts were straight and smooth enough, but the butt feathers that weren't already limp and drooping appeared as if something had taken random bites out of them. The head archer would likely make her replace them all.

"Now's not a good time." Sharifah fashioned a suitably regretful expression and glanced back up. "I'm finally starting to get the feel for this arrow making."

Ra'id graced what she knew was shoddy workmanship with a smile of amusement, then arched a brow. "Indeed? Then I'm most impressed by your enthusiasm for your new line of work. Otherwise, I'd suspect you were making an excuse to avoid facing Danae."

Warmth flushed her cheeks. Leave it to Ra'id to see past any and all subterfuge.

"I'm not avoiding Danae!" Sharifah shot him a furious glare. "I just . . . I just didn't wish to disturb her unnecessarily until—"

"Until she was well enough to receive visitors?" her brother smoothly interjected. "How kind of you. How thoughtful." He reached down and grasped her beneath the elbow. "Then this couldn't be a more perfect time, could it?"

She expelled an exasperated breath and laid aside the arrow she was currently mutilating. "Fine," Sharifah muttered, climbing to her feet. "Might as well get it over and done with, I suppose. What's the worst that could happen? Danae'll take one look at me and throw me out."

"Aye, that *could* happen." He grinned wickedly. "That's not the worst that could happen, though. Not in your mind at least. Having to stand there and apologize would be the worst by far."

Sharifah gave a disdainful sniff. "And if *you* imagine I'm afraid to admit when I'm wrong, you don't know me very well, brother dear. I'm an adult. I can take responsibility for my actions, *when* I think I *have* done wrong."

"And are you implying you *didn't* do anything wrong," Ra'id asked as they walked along, "when you all but drove Danae away? Is that what you're trying to tell me?"

She could feel herself beginning to get irritated with him. "It wasn't all my fault, you know. Vartan—"

"Vartan will have to deal with his failings soon enough. All you can do is address your own."

A sharp retort rose to Sharifah's lips, but she clamped down hard on it. How she hated it when Ra'id was right. And, at least in this particular instance, he was.

"Fine." She spat out the word as if it had a foul taste. "I'm woman enough to face her. You'll see."

His only reply was a rich, warm chuckle.

Danae was ensconced in a chair on the long balcony spanning several of the palace bedchambers. It was another bright, sweltering autumn day, but a generous length of awning shaded most of the balcony from the sun. At their approach the Dragonmaid healer, who had been brought from Sanctuary to attend to the wounded riders too ill to be taken home, rose and eyed them with suspicion.

"We'd like some time to visit privately with Danae," Ra'id was quick to explain. "Now that she's feeling better, I mean."

The woman gave a small, disgusted snort and immediately looked to Danae.

"Aye, I'd like that very much," she said, smiling happily at the older woman. "They're two of my dearest friends."

At her words, a shard of guilt pierced Sharifah's heart. Unexpected, shameful tears filled her eyes. She quickly averted her gaze and blinked them away. Then, as the Dragonmaid healer exited the balcony to leave them with Danae, Ra'id knelt beside the blond-haired woman.

"You look well," he said, leaning forward and taking her hand. "I don't know what Dragonmaid healers do that's different from our healers, but I can't believe how quickly you've progressed."

Danae laughed. "Did I look *that* poorly when I first came here?"

"You were on death's door. Vartan was terrified we'd lose you. You were bleeding quite badly from your wounds, you know."

She smiled. "I don't remember much of how I came here, or of that first day thereafter. But the Dragonmaids have the most horrible-tasting concoction that borders on the miraculous. It's full of all sorts of herbs and some oil produced by immature dragons. The potion can bring most anyone back from even the brink of death, as it apparently did for me."

"Sounds like we need to open some sort of trade agreement with the Dragonmaids, in order to procure that potion for the Desert peoples." He cocked his head. "Perhaps you could help us with that?"

"Perhaps. There's never an overly generous supply of dragon oil on hand, though. And, from what I've heard, it's the key ingredient."

"Well, it never hurts to ask." Ra'id laid his other hand atop hers. "It's so good to see you again. But now you're a Dragonmaid, and have your own dragon no less. However did you manage to join up with them when you left us?"

"I suppose, in a roundabout way, I've Ladon to thank for that . . ." Danae then recounted how she had been rescued by the Dragonmaids, had requested to remain with them, then had bonded with Celandine and entered dragon training.

"I think Athan's hand was in it from the start," she said, finally finishing the tale. Danae paused, then laughed. "Though I certainly didn't think so at first, I must confess."

Her glance met Sharifah's. "Will you forgive me for my anger at you? I am very sorry I treated you so unkindly."

Sharifah stared down at her, stunned. Danae was asking *her* forgiveness? She swallowed hard.

"Rather, *I* should be asking *yours*." She moved to stand beside her brother. "I never meant to make you leave. But then, at the time, I wasn't thinking very clearly. I was falling in love with Vartan, and all I knew was I wanted him." Her lips lifted in wry self-deprecation. "Not that it mattered in the end. Vartan loves you and always will. And now you two can be together like you've always wanted."

Danae's expression sobered, went sad and pensive. "Aye, like I've always wanted," she whispered, "if it weren't already too late."

Ra'id glanced over his shoulder at Sharifah, then back to Danae. "What do you mean, Rasha?" he asked, using his old term of endearment for her. "You're both alive and still love each other. And you haven't even been gone two months. That first night after the battle, we had a great feast. Olwyn attended and explained the training process to make a fully formed Dragonmaid. You've years left before you make permanent vows."

"Before Lysanor would send out dragons and Dragonmaids to your aid," Danae said, looking away, "she asked me for a sign of commitment. For some proof that my intentions were pure, that my loyalty to the Dragonmaids, to my dragon, and to Gadiel surpassed my loyalty to Vartan. And, convinced as I was that Vartan didn't love me, it seemed a simple thing to acquiesce to her request."

She turned then, meeting first Ra'id's, then Sharifah's gaze. "She said dispensations could be made in special cases. Dispensations to waive the training period required to take final vows."

As she listened to Danae's story, horror swelled in Sharifah. What had she done? *What had she done?*

"Nay," she managed to choke out. "Oh, nay, Danae. You didn't. Please, tell me you didn't!"

Tears now streaming down her cheeks, Danae looked up at her. "Aye, I did. That very night in the chapel, before all the Dragonmaids, I laid my hands in Lysanor's and made my final vows. Despite her insistence that I also take a new name to commemorate the beginning of my new life, I chose not to. My name, however, was the only thing I was able to keep.

"So you see"—she managed a smile through her tears—"all is not lost between you and Vartan. The doors of opportunity are wide open again, and there still may be a chance."

☙ ❧

Vartan rode back to Khaddar as fast as his horse would carry him. Ra'id's message that Danae was now well enough to receive visitors had reached him barely a half hour ago, and he was desperate to see her. Three long, anxious days had passed since he had rescued her and given her over to the care of her sister Dragonmaids. And then that martinet of a Dragonmaid healer, once she had arrived from Sanctuary, had refused all requests to visit, much less remain with, Danae.

But now, thanks be to Athan, he would finally be able to take her into his arms and tell her of his love. He would finally be able to do what he had so long yearned to do—ask her to be his wife. This was a glorious, blessed day!

He made the trip back to Khaddar at record speed, leaving his cavalry far behind. Ra'id must have been watching for him. The Desert lord strode over just as Vartan dismounted.

"My thanks for your message," Vartan said. "I came as soon as I received it."

433

"There's something I need to tell you." Ra'id gripped his arm. "Before you go to Danae."

"Oh, there are more than a few things I need to do before I see her." Vartan laughed. "A bath and clean clothes are but the first of them. Come, we can talk as I bathe."

"As you wish," Ra'id muttered, and fell into step beside him.

"How did she look?" Vartan asked as they strode along. "Was she still in bed, or up and about?"

"She looked quite well, if still a bit pale. And she was on the balcony in a chair. Seems the Dragonmaids have some special drink that works wonders in healing a person. Another day or two, and I daresay Danae will be up and about, walking the halls and visiting with everyone."

"Aye, that sounds just like her." He smiled. "Did she ask about me? Do you think she harbors any anger or resentment over how I treated her?"

"By the Blessed Waters!" Ra'id grabbed him by the arm and pulled him over. "I can't keep this to myself a moment longer. You've got problems, Vartan. Big problems."

He frowned, puzzled. "What do you mean? Is there something wrong with Danae you're not telling me?"

His friend hesitated, then nodded. "Aye. She has taken vows, Vartan. Though that conniving, mean-spirited queen of hers might have finally taken pity on the Diya al Din, in the doing, she made certain you wouldn't profit from it. Leastwise, not when it came to Danae. Before the queen gave her leave to send the Dragonmaids to our aid, she demanded Danae take final vows."

Vartan stood there aghast, struggling to accept the full implications of what Ra'id was telling him. Time and again, the reality of what had transpired slammed into him, and time and again he flung it away, refusing to face it. Yet inexorably the pain nonetheless seeped in, until he thought it would surely send him to his knees.

"Nay," he groaned at last. "Not now. Not after all we've gone through. It isn't fair. It just isn't fair!"

"Fair or not, it's over and done with," his friend growled, anger gleaming in his eyes. "Like it or not, now Danae can never be your—or any man's—wife."

Danae waited well into the evening for Vartan to come to her. When he didn't and darkness finally blanketed the Desert, she went out to seek him. After questioning several servants as to his whereabouts, one at last mentioned he had seen Vartan out on the western walls, walking the parapets.

Though her full strength had nearly returned, Danae wasn't certain she could make such a long trek there and back. Ultimately, she decided to await him near where she knew his quarters to be. Her wait, however, lasted almost two hours.

Tucked as she was into a shadowed overhang on a stone bench, it soon became apparent Vartan didn't see her. He passed by but, fortunately, drew up about ten feet beyond her, pausing to gaze out over the city. Danae watched him for a long moment, hungrily taking in the sight of him.

She hadn't realized how deeply, how desperately, she had missed him. Or how much she still loved him. Vows or no, Danae knew she would love him until the end of her days. Knew, as well, within the parameters of her commitment to the Dragonmaids, she would try always to aid him in whatever way she could. Her bond to Celandine notwithstanding, she also bore in her heart an indissoluble link to Vartan.

As she watched, her heart hammering beneath her breast, he sighed then turned to go. Danae leaped to her feet.

"Vartan?" She stepped from the shadows.

He froze, then slowly faced her. "Danae."

At his guarded look and flat tone, she knew either Ra'id or Sharifah had told him of her Dragonmaid vows. So he *had* been avoiding her.

"How . . . how have you been?"

Even as she uttered the question, Danae knew how trite it sounded. But there was suddenly a distance yawning between them, an awkwardness that had never been there before. She had to do something to heal that breach. She just *had* to.

Without consideration for how she would be received, or even if it was appropriate anymore, Danae strode over and wrapped her arms around him. "Never mind," she whispered. "It was a stupid question. Just hold me, Vartan. Like you used to."

For what seemed minutes but was probably only a few seconds, he stiffened. Her breath caught. What if he should push away? Then, with a low groan, Vartan clasped her tightly to him and bent his head to rest it atop hers.

"Oh, sweet lady," he softly said. "My sweet, beautiful Danae!"

She clung to him with a fierce ardor. Beneath her ear, the oft longed for sound of his strong heart thudded in familiar, comforting beats. It reminded her of another time she had spent in his arms . . . that morn at Am Shardi. She had been so happy then, when he had walked in from the Desert, his sight restored, his arms full of blue roses. She had imagined her prayers, in those long, hard days before his return, had finally been answered.

She had prayed *so* hard for him to live, to survive the Haroun's terrible testing, and he had. But she had also prayed, Danae recalled, and offered Athan *anything* if He would spare Vartan's life. Perhaps, just perhaps, this was the price Athan was now asking of her in return. Asking her to surrender Vartan one last time.

We have been through so much together, come so close so many times to losing each other, she thought. Yet now, after all the fear, and pain, and hardship, now, when they could finally reveal what was truly in their hearts, it seemed their love had never—ever—been meant to be . . .

So be it then, she thought. *He lives, and that, in the end, is what matters. Gadiel's Guardian lives.*

Suddenly, the tears came. Danae clung to Vartan, the sobs escaping in body-wracking, uncontrollable waves. And, all the while, he held her in his protective embrace, crooning deep-timbred, soothing words.

At last, spent and even a little embarrassed by her emotional response, Danae pushed back from him. "I-I'm sorry." She swiped angrily at her tears. "I don't know why I did that. I thought I'd better control of myself than that."

His beautiful mouth twisted sardonically. "Well, it's reassuring to know, even now that you've become a fierce dragon rider, that there's still a soft-hearted woman beneath it all. At least I'm familiar with the soft-hearted woman. I'm not quite sure where I stand, though, with the fierce dragon rider."

She smiled then, relief flooding her. This was the Vartan she knew and loved.

"I haven't changed *that* much, have I?"

He shrugged. "You tell me. I've never met a Dragonmaid until just a few days ago, and I know almost nothing about their customs. Ra'id informed me, though, that you've taken some sort of vows. That you're now committed for life to the Dragonmaids. And that, aside from Athan, your dragon now comes before everything—and everyone—else."

Fear clamped hard and tight about her heart. The moment she had dreaded was now upon her.

"I believed Athan called me to the Dragonmaids. After I left . . . left you, I was so lost and confused. And then the Dragonmaids rescued me, took me in, and I met my dragon . . . It all seemed so right . . ."

"It was right between us, too." Vartan grasped her by the shoulders. "I just made so many mistakes. Once again my stupid pride has kept me, until now, from telling you how I really feel. But no more. No more."

He hesitated then, as if searching for the words, and she saw something in his eyes she had never seen before. She saw uncertainty—even fear.

"Tell me," she said. "There's nothing you can't tell me, Vartan. Nothing."

"I love you, Danae," he blurted out then. "I think I was even falling in love with you in Astara. But then there was Aelwyd, and I felt so torn between you two. Felt so disloyal to her. I'd made vows, and it was dishonorable to break them, so I didn't. I couldn't."

"I know." She placed a finger to his lips to silence him. "I loved you then, too. Indeed, I loved you most of all for your honor and loyalty to Aelwyd."

He took her hand in his, pulling it down to rest over his heart. "Let me tell you everything. So you'll understand. So you'll forgive me."

"Go on then. I'll listen."

"Even after I was blinded," he said, "and nearly everything was taken from me, I still had my pride. And my pride wouldn't permit me to tell you of my love. I felt so helpless, so worthless. You deserved better. You deserved a man, and then I barely felt like one."

Even in his most dejected, hopeless times, Danae had thought Vartan more a man than any she had ever known. But what she had thought didn't matter then. What mattered was how he felt about himself.

"There were times, though," he continued after a long pause, "when I almost told you anyway. When I ached for you so badly I almost forgot my pride, almost shared my love and need for you. Perhaps if I had . . ."

Vartan glanced aside and, in the moonlight, Danae thought she saw a glimmer of tears in his eyes. Compassion filled her. *He knows,* she thought. *He knows it's too late.*

"As much as I thought I'd surrendered my pride in choosing to serve Athan," he began yet again, "pride wasn't ready to surrender me. Indeed, I realize now that, even with Athan's help, it'll be a lifelong battle. But then, when I finally regained my sight and was so full of happiness, so elated with the realization of my new calling, I think I imagined everything I did had a purer, holier motive. I think, perhaps, I even imagined I was now so strong in Athan I could do no wrong, make no mistakes. And, in that foolish assumption, bit by bit my pride crept back in."

"Perfection's a lifelong battle, and one we never achieve on this earth." She laid her other hand over his and gave it a squeeze. "And it's not the actual achievement that matters so much to Athan, but that we keep on trying, that we persevere."

He looked back to her then. "Aye, but some mistakes do so much damage, have such long-lived consequences."

"But even those can be used for good. Even those can bring us back to Athan."

"I never meant to hurt you. To make you think I didn't love you. Perhaps I just thought you'd always be there and, someday when there was time to think past all the crises and battle plans and the needs of others, there'd finally be time for us. You've always been the one person I could count on. I just thought you always would be."

She couldn't help the small flare of anger his words stirred within her. If only Vartan had offered her even the tiniest crumb of hope. If only . . .

"And I *will* always be there for you," Danae said, clamping down on her anger and pain. "Perhaps not in the manner we both once hoped, but on some other level, in other ways. As painful as it is to admit, I truly believe Athan's will was at work in this, too."

He frowned. "I don't understand. I always thought we were meant for each other."

"If I hadn't left you and been taken in by the Dragonmaids, I'd never have been in the position to convince them finally to come to your aid. And if the Dragonmaids hadn't joined you, we wouldn't be here talking about this tonight. Ladon would've taken Khaddar."

"He's not defeated, you know. We've but routed him for a time. He'll be back."

Danae smiled. "Aye, the battle for Gadiel has but begun. Still, look at all you've accomplished. You've found your way to Athan, accepted your call, and embarked on the task of uniting the land. You've truly become the Guardian."

"I still have moments when I wonder at it all. It's a tremendous responsibility, especially as I begin to discover all the ways I can fail and, in the failing, do even greater harm. Fail not only Gadiel, but Athan. And it frightens me, Danae. Frightens me like nothing ever has, and likely ever will."

Vartan chuckled. "But then, I suppose any man would be frightened, with such an almost unbearable weight laid on his shoulders."

"Yet, *because* you know this, you're better prepared to cherish what you've learned, and apply it more wisely. And you don't carry it alone," she said, lifting his hand and kissing it tenderly. "You've friends and allies now. You have me. And, most of all, you now have Athan."

"I need you as more than just a friend and ally, sweet lady. I need you as my wife."

He stared down at her with such love Danae thought her heart might break. How she wanted to admit to the same desire he so ardently voiced! But there was now more between them than the regrettable effects of pride. There were vows, commitments, and the inescapable certainty that Athan had put them on different paths, even if both paths led in the same direction, in service to Gadiel.

Still, for just a few, precious, stolen moments, what harm was there in pretending to what might have been? What harm was there in admitting to the truth?

She reached into her pocket and withdrew a scrap of linen bound loosely with a silken cord. Untying it, Danae offered one of the two dried, blue flowers to Vartan.

"Let this be a sign between us," she said. "A sign of truth, unity, and the pure love we bear for each other. A sign that you can always carry with you, to remind you that, if I could, I'd take you as husband."

Ever so carefully, Danae closed his fingers over the blue rose and crept back into the warm haven of his arms. "A sign that will never change, no matter what comes in the days and months ahead," she whispered. "Of a love that will never, *ever*, die."

Dear Reader,

I hoped you enjoyed *Giver of Roses*, book 1 in the Guardians of Gadiel fantasy series. Currently, I'm contracted for a 3 book series, with *Stone of Power*, book 2, slated for an August 2006 release. If all goes as planned, book 3 should be out in August 2007. After that, who knows? I've got a ton of ideas for additional fantasies, some stand alone and others that could easily be spin-offs or continuations of the Guardians of Gadiel series. In the end, though, reader response to Christian fantasy fiction will likely be the determining factor. So, if you liked *Giver of Roses* and/or fantasy fiction written by other Christian writers, make your interest known by telling all your friends to buy these books. Sales numbers are what make the most dramatic impression with publishers, and you can be sure they watch them very closely.

You can also check out my website at www.kathleenmorgan .com for a set of discussion questions related to *Giver of Roses* that are appropriate for book clubs (it's on my Fantasy page, under Books) as well as a listing of other Christian fantasy fiction I have read and can recommend. There, you'll also immediately note that I write not only fantasy fiction but also historical women's fiction. The enclosed excerpt in the back of this book is a sample of my latest historical women's fiction series. The first book in this series is already out, and book 2 will hit bookstores in February 2006. If you also enjoy books set in the Scottish Highlands, around mid-sixteenth century, you might like to give them a try. All my backlist for the Christian market is available. Just ask your local bookseller to order it for you.

Feel free also to contact me at my website, either to tell me what your impressions of *Giver of Roses* are or to sign up for my email readers' mailing list for notification of future books. For those of you who prefer postal mail, you can write me at Kathleen Morgan, P.O. Box 62365, Colorado Springs, CO 80962. Either way, I love hearing from my readers.

Blessings,

Kathleen Morgan

Child of the Mist

April 1564

Castle Gregor

Through a red haze of pain, Niall Campbell gazed out upon the castle's outer bailey. The early morning sun stained the sky with lavender. Save for the MacGregor sentries guarding the parapets, no one was about. He clenched and unclenched his fingers to ease the numbness in his hands, which was the only movement allowed by the tight ropes binding his limbs in a spread-eagle postion to the wooden cross posts.

Had it been but two days since his capture? It seemed an eternity. He licked his dry, cracked lips, thirst raging through him like wildfire. His battle wounds ached fiercely, yet none were severe enough to kill him before lack of water did. But then, wasn't that the MacGregor's plan—a slow, agonizing death?

With a weary sigh, Niall leaned his head against the stone wall supporting the cross posts. If only he had fallen with his men, brave lads one and all. That fate, however, had never been meant for him.

It had been a trap from the start; that was more than evident. He and his small band had no sooner ridden into the narrow draw leading to one of the MacGregor villages than the attack had begun. Once the Campbells were sourrounded on all sides, MacGregor crossbows quickly thinned their ranks. Then the hand-to-hand combat began.

Though they had fought with all the courage and ferocity of Highlanders, one by one his men fell. Eventually, the MacGregors managed to separate him from his remaining warriors, and a heavy net dropped on him from the cliff above. Pinned to the ground, his sword useless in the stout rope snare, he had turned to his dirk with desperate effect.

At the memory, a grim smiled touched Niall's lips. Before they had finally beaten him senseless, he had hamstrung more than a few MacGregors.

In the end, though, it had all been for naught. To a man, his lads were dead, and he was now a MacGregor prisoner. Not for long, though. Niall didn't delude himself as to his eventual fate. After all these years, the animosity between the clans ran deep and bitter. And he of all Campbells, clan tanist and leader of the debilitating raids in recent months, was hated most of all.

Nay, his death was a foregone conclusion. Niall could accept that with a certain equanimity. What he couldn't accept was the galling realization he had been betrayed—and by one of his own.

A foul, blackhearted traitor in their midst! But who and why? The question had tormented him all the long hours of his capture, nibbling away at his strength as inexorably as had the lack of sleep and water. A traitor, and naught he could do, neither discover who he was nor warn his clan. Naught left to do but die with the terrible knowledge unspoken, unshared.

Once again a frustrated rage grew within him. Curse the man, whoever he was! Niall twisted futilely in his bonds, accomplishing little more than abrading the bloody sores of his wrists and ankles further. The pain only fueled his anger, and he fought all the harder. Finally, his rapidly draining strength exhausted, Niall fell back, his wounds and tormenting thirst beckoning him toward a blessed oblivion.

Anne hurried across the outer bailey. The thought of her own bed, covered with its plump down comforter, had never seemed so attractive. But then, never had she felt so exhuasted.

It was early morn, and she had been up all night nursing a feverish servant, not to mention all the clansmen who still needed tending after the skirmish with the Campbells two days past. Though the victory had ultimately been MacGregors', the outnumbered raiders had sold their lives dearly.

Aye, the victory had been dearly won, but perhaps it would finally bring an end to the raids. After all, didn't they now hold prisoner the Wolf of Cruachan himself? His death, her father had assured her, would make the Campbells think twice about venturing onto MacGregor lands.

Though the man in the castle's outer courtyard had never shown MacGregors any mercy, dooming him to a slow, thirst-maddened death didn't sit well with Anne. Enemy though he was, even the thought of watching him succumb, inch by agonizing inch, made her stomach churn. It was brutally cruel and un-Christian. It was also, despite her attempts to convince her father otherwise, out of her hands.

Her steps quickened. Perhaps all the years of trying to save life made it so hard now to look at him, but in the two days since he had been tied in the bailey, she hadn't once glanced in the prisoner's direction or ventured past him unless absolutely necessary. In some way, not seeing him spared her the harsh reminder of his presence—and ultimate fate.

A low groan floated across the bailey. Reluctantly, Anne's gaze lifted toward the prisoner. His head was down, his full weight hanging from his hands. Perhaps the sound had been her imagination, but then as she turned away he moved. Anne halted, then took a hesitant step toward him. There was something familiar about him. . . .

He stirred again, attempting to lift his head, but couldn't seem to muster the strength. The slight movement, however, sent a premonitory shiver through her. She *had* seen him before, but where?

Kathleen Morgan has authored numerous novels for the general market and now focuses her writing on inspirational books. She has won many awards for her romance writing, including the 2002 Rose Award for Best Inspirational Romance. She lives in Colorado Springs, Colorado.

Other Books by Kathleen Morgan

Brides of Culdee Creek Series

Daughter of Joy
Woman of Grace
Lady of Light
Child of Promise

Culdee Creek Christmas

All Good Gifts
The Christkindl's Gift

These Highland Hills

Child of the Mist